JEAN I

(1894–1962) was born Jane Crook i[...],
the eighth of ten children. She had [...] e
age of sixteen moved with her famil[...] ,
a year later, she married mining union official Hal Devanny, with whom she
had a son and two daughters. About this time Jean Devanny became active
in the labour movement, both as a public speaker and writer, travelling
extensively throughout the country until, after the death of her youngest
daughter, the family settled in Wellington.

In 1923 her first novel was refused publication, but in 1926 her second
novel, *The Butcher Shop*, was published, only to be immediately banned in
New Zealand on the grounds of obscenity—although her assertion of a
woman's right to control her own body "irrespective of the marriage bond"
probably gave as much cause for offence as her graphic descriptions of the
brutality of much farming practice. The novel was subsequently published
in New York and Germany, and there followed three other novels – *Lenore
Divine* (1926), *Dawn Beloved* (1928) and *Riven* (1929) as well as a collection of
short stories.

In 1929 the family moved to Sydney, Australia, so that the climate might
benefit the ailing health of her eldest son, Karl. It was the start of the
Depression and, for Jean, of a lifelong struggle against economic hardship,
but she became closely involved with the social and literary life of Sydney,
particularly the various writers' organizations whose members included her
friends Katharine Susannah Prichard and Miles Franklin. In 1930 she
published her novels *Bushman Burke* and *Devil Made Saint*. She joined the
Australian Communist Party and became National Secretary of Workers'
International Relief, with whom she travelled to Berlin and Russia, as well
as within Australia, particularly in North Queensland where her
involvement in the cane-cutters' strike inspired her novel *Sugar Heaven*
(1936). By 1939, overwork, too-frequent travel and the death of Karl in 1935
had combined to take their toll of her health and she returned to Queensland
to convalesce. The following year she was expelled from the Communist
Party, on what appear to have been trumped-up sexual charges, the result of
longstanding conflict over the Party's attitudes both to intellectuals and the
writing of literature, and to feminism. Jean Devanny later rejoined the Party
– with the tacit admission that her expulsion had been unwarranted – and
remained one of its most formidable speakers, but unease on these matters
endured. After the publication of her last novel, *Cindie*, in 1949, she once
again resigned. During the last decade of her life her work focused
particularly on essays, and writings about travel, aborigines and natural
history. She died in Townsville in 1962 of leukaemia.

CINDIE

A Chronicle of the Canefields

JEAN DEVANNY

WITH A NEW INTRODUCTION BY
CAROLE FERRIER

Virago

Published by VIRAGO PRESS Limited 1986
41 William IV Street, London WC2N 4DB

First published in Great Britain by Robert Hale Limited 1949
Virago edition offset from Robert Hale 1949 edition

British Library Cataloguing in Publication Data

Devanny, Jean
    Cindie.—(Virago modern classics)
    I. Title
    823[F]   PR9639.3.D/

    ISBN 0-86068-805-4

    Printed in Great Britain by
    Anchor Brendon, Tiptree, Essex.

INTRODUCTION

Having grown up in New Zealand where she was involved in a range of political activities and wrote a number of novels focusing on the figure of the New Woman, Jean Devanny moved with her family to Sydney at the age of thirty-five. Part of the reason for this move was the heart condition of her only son, Karl, but she also intended at that stage to travel further. She suggested in an interview in the *New Zealand Herald* in 1930, soon after she arrived in Australia, that she considered "the field for writing less parochial and conservative" in Europe.

When the Devannys reached Sydney, however, the Depression was making itself severely felt and jobs were scarce. The level of political resistance was high, and they all became involved in the activities of the Communist Party. As Jean's son put it, they were "the leaders in direct struggle, so no option remained but to join them".[1] Jean Devanny had some reservations about this, both because she felt herself to be the main financial support of the family and because she already had wide experience of speaking at public meetings in New Zealand. She could see that the Communist Party would want to make full use of her abilities in a period when daily political street meetings at factories, dole centres and other places were the norm, and she was worried about a likely major diversion of energies away from her writing. However, she was soon drawn to join the Party after a march in which she and her husband were arrested and she was given four days' jail.

1 All unattributed quotations are from *Point of Departure* ed. Carole Ferrier, (St. Lucia: University of Queensland Press, 1986)

Jean did indeed become one of the Party's best-known and most effective orators through the 1930s in Australia. Many who joined at this period say that they did this as a result of hearing her speak. After an absence of several months in Germany and Russia in 1931 at a conference organized by Workers' International Relief, marital relations with her husband Hal were broken off. Later, she became involved in a close liaison with J. B. Miles, the General Secretary of the Communist Party, which lasted for some years.

Devanny first visited North Queensland, the setting of her "sugar" novels, in the mid-thirties, on one of several speaking tours she was to make for the Movement Against War and Fascism. It was during this trip that she received news that her son was ill. He had collapsed in a demonstration in Sydney, and died before she could get back. This event alienated her from that city, just as she was also beginning to be drawn by the beauty of the North Queensland landscape. When other problems in the South intensified, she was happy to be able to move to the North. Apart from short visits to the Southern states, she spent the remainder of her life in North Queensland.

Devanny had long been a champion of sexual liberation for women, and acted out this philosophy in her own relationships. The fact that she was quite frank privately on these questions, and spoke at public meetings on topics such as marriage in the Soviet Union and birth control, led to considerable hostility towards her in certain sections of the Communist Party. For many members, double standards were enshrined behind a rationale of such things, making the Party look "disreputable" in the eyes of workers.

In the early 1940s, Jean went to stay at Emuford, an isolated tin-mining settlement inland from Cairns on the Atherton Tableland. Her main motives were to find somewhere quiet to write and to gather material about the lives of the tin miners there. (Some sketches were to appear in *By Tropic Sea and Jungle* in 1944.) However, what the miners told her about their lives led her to the conclusion that they were sexist about their affairs with local women. Some of them were members of the Party, and she had begun to take on an organizing function for their branch— unable, as usual, to restrain herself from being involved in what was going on around her in the way of political activism. Joe McCarthy, the Cairns organizer, had not been pleased by this turn of events. Joe had himself fallen for Jean earlier in Cairns and, apart from the fact that he would have preferred her to work under his direction, there was probably some tension produced by the fact that Jean was having an affair with one of the tin miners. A report was forwarded to the Central Committee of the Party in Sydney containing lurid allegations about her making love on a bridge in the centre of Emuford and general "sexual immorality", including nude swimming with the men. She was expelled, but was neither officially informed of this nor allowed to defend herself. This was a shattering blow to Jean after more than ten years of working night and day for the Party. Her health suffered and she felt that she must vindicate herself. Her awareness of a number of similar cases of women members of the Communist Party being discriminated against or expelled as a result of the sexual politics then current made her more determined to fight.

After some time the Party decided to rescind her expulsion, but she never totally recovered from the shock, and continued to feel that discrimination and sexual double standards were prevalent in the Party. She was also disturbed that J. B. Miles had not asked for her own account of the Emuford events—though the illegal conditions under which the Party was operating in the early 1940s had, it must be admitted, made communication difficult, for the mails could not safely be used. Her own account of what happened, which she had attempted to forward to Sydney, was lost.

After this experience of temporary expulsion, Jean applied herself to writing throughout the 1940s, producing travel books and *Bird of Paradise*. She also wrote an autobiographical narrative designed to clear her name. Although a notice about her continuous membership had appeared in the *Worker's Weekly*, many members only read the local Party publications and assumed that she was still expelled. Even less could they be expected to be familiar with the full story of how the "expulsion" had come about. She also conceived at this time the idea of writing a series of three novels about the historical development of the Queensland sugar industry, a similar project to Katharine Susannah Prichard's West Australian Goldfields novels, *The Roaring Nineties, Golden Miles* and *Winged Seeds. Cindie* was to be the first volume in this trilogy.

Cindie combines the modes of history, reportage, realism and romance. Devanny could be seen as a pioneer of oral history in her method of assembling material for her novel; she discussed with local people the way they saw their lives and how they remembered the past. Her autobiography gives an account of a number of discussions with people in North Queensland and, in writing the novel, she combined this with research into historical sources.

From the 1860s, the Queensland sugar industry had operated on an extensive form of quasi-slavery. After December 1890 no more Melanesian islanders were allowed to enter the Colony. When the White Australia Policy was introduced in 1901, almost all Kanaka workers were to be repatriated by 1906. In 1907, there were mass deportations, bringing to an end a period in which 60,000 Kanakas had been brought to Queensland, more than a third of them by nefarious or illegal means. (Melanesians in Queensland were called Kanakas, a term which in Sandwich Islands dialect signified the general concept of "man" but which soon acquired the same derogatory overtones as the terms "nigger" and "boy".)

Devanny's novel *Cindie*, spanning as it does the period from 1896 to 1907, deals with the time in which fervent debates raged about indentured labour and the conflict of various economic and political interests in the replacement of Kanaka (and Chinese) labour with white labour. Devanny fills in details of these debates in some depth, mentioning also the widespread racism in the labour movement, exemplified in and fostered by William Lane's the *Worker*, and the *Bulletin*. Through Biddow and Cindie, she depicts attempts at an egalitarian approach which nonetheless remains paternalistic and involves the exploitation of labour. When Aboriginal workers are used to replace the falling pool of other non-white workers, Biddow and Cindie are accused by some of the other farmers of seeking to exploit a new cheap labour force. While they attempt a non-racist personal practice, the economic inequalities bound up with colonial society mean that the blackbirded Kanakas and the Aborigines dispossessed of their land have no real power by comparison with them.

In the historical context, fear of miscegenation was harnessed to facilitate both the deportation of the Kanakas and the attempted extermination of the Aborigines. The Kanaka Melatonka's fears that lead him to escape following Blanche's succumbing to him are well founded; if what had happened was discovered, he would certainly have been hung for rape.

In the case of the Chinese, a widespread racist campaign was waged to prevent their establishing themselves economically in Australia. Chinese had come to Australia from the 1850s, originally to work on the goldfields, and later moved into agriculture; they were seen by many Europeans as competition, and by many Kanakas and Aborigines as fairer employers. Racist campaigns were waged with the aim of producing their deportation too. In much of the popular press, leprosy was repeatedly connected with the Chinese, the *Boomerang* asserting in 1888 that "the Chinaman will eventually import, along with his sour, greasy carcase, some of the fearful plagues which have scourged the impure races of the East for so many centuries", and Lane's *Worker* commenting in 1895 that "if the influx of inferior races" were to continue for the next fifty years "Australia will be the most leprous country in the world". Such racist comments were commonplace in these widely read papers. A climate of fear about leprosy was aggravated by the lack of medical knowledge about how it was caught; the doctor in *Cindie* implies that it is passed on by sexual contact.

The depiction of Cindie and Blanche in the novel is a part of the complex historical construction of the figure of the "pioneer woman". Their names provide a clue to the different ways in which they can be perceived: Blanche Biddow's whiteness is stressed; Cindie Comstock by contrast is *burnt* by the sun in which she labours outdoors and comes from common—or even Communist—stock. A comparison could be made with Katharine Susannah Prichard's depiction of Mrs Watt and of Jessica on the West Australian "frontier" in her novel *Coonardoo* (1929). Despite Cindie's and Blanche's different attitudes to workers, however, they both remain exploiters, albeit in different ways. While Mrs Watt, like Cindie, may be a benevolent agent of colonization she is, nonetheless, part of that oppressive process. Also interesting is the question of how far Mrs Watt and her son

Hugh are racist; Hugh's refusal of a sexual relationship with Coonardoo, while it rejects the usual patterns of sexual exploitation of Black women by white men, can nonetheless be read, particularly now, as having some racist aspects to it, and this is also the case with the approach of Biddow and Cindie to their work relationships with non-white workers. The novels of Faith Bandler and Monica Clare offer Black perspectives on these questions.

When *Cindie* was published in 1949, the reaction of the Communist Party was highly unfavourable. They saw the novel as deviating from the Party line; Len Fox, the *Tribune* reviewer, said that he was "worried about it" and refused to review it; J. B. Miles, while sending Jean a screed of hostile comments and excerpts from Myra Willard's book, refused to discuss it personally with her. The attitudes of Fox and Miles, embodying a crudely prescriptive view of literature and showing a continuing distrust of her politics, was the last straw for Devanny. She commented on the Party's reception of her novel: "It was rejected because it featured historical truth, when what was required was a spurious *Uncle Tom's Cabin.*" At about this time she had another experience which reminded her of how little value was placed upon writers in the Party:

> A promising young speaker to whom I had lent [*Cindie*] returned it, after weeks, unread. "I didn't have time to open it," he told me, and added: "Why don't you get down to some important work, Comrade Devanny?" "Such as?" "Well, we need speakers and paper sellers, you know."

She resigned from the Party and was for the second time outside it, this time by her own choice.

Devanny was later to rejoin, remaining a formal member until her death. She increasingly devoted herself to writing, completing several drafts of her autobiography which provide much further information on how she saw events in her life, though these narratives are still constrained by problems of libel, conflicting loyalties and dilemmas about self-disclosure. Her novels, from the first published, *The Butcher Shop* (1926), had always been centrally concerned with the personal and political development of women, and often with racism; from the mid-thirties, starting with *Sugar Heaven*, there was also a shift towards an emphasis on class struggle and involvement in working-class politics and action to change society. Her novels of the late thirties and forties moved into a chronicling of the history and struggles of the people of North Queensland. She completed the sequel to *Cindie*, a novel entitled *You Can't Have Everything* that was to be the second in the trilogy, but the Party was hostile to its publication. Some of those consulted considered it too sympathetic towards the middle-class characters and it was never published.

Cindie provides a further example of the diversity of Devanny's literary production, but is also a typical work which focuses on certain concerns that are common to other of her novels. It is to be hoped that more of her writing will be republished, making possible a fuller understanding and appreciation of her work.

Carole Ferrier, Melbourne, 1986

CINDIE

PART ONE

CHAPTER I

ABOUT ELEVEN O'CLOCK ON A FINE MORNING IN AUGUST, 1896, a group of men reclined upon a patch of cleared land on the southern bank of the Masterman River, North Queensland. This narrow stream, after tumbling out of a gully cleaving the coastal range, snaked eastward through five miles of rain forest flats to flow into the Long Lagoon, that body of water separating the Great Barrier Reefs from the mainland.

Most of the men had been waiting there for some considerable time but with one exception none revealed impatience with his condition of inactivity. They yarned lazily, smoked and spat.

The exception, Randolph Biddow, did not fidget, but the agitation of his thoughts was plainly indicated by his expression. His deep-set, narrow-placed, odd eyes—one was dark brown, the other golden—were steadily directed, tensely eager, towards a bend in the river three hundred yards to seawards. Occasionally he took his pipe from his mouth and tapped its stem against his strong white teeth.

Suddenly he rose and clearly, though with a naturally soft intonation, exclaimed: "They are coming!" Followed a general upspringing of all present, a lining up on the rough log platform that functioned as a jetty.

Around the bend and up the river between the heavy walls of rain forest came a whale-boat. Three pairs of oars moved in unison, with strokes that were long and sweeping, and yet at the same time lively; each feathered oar flashed in the sun as the dark man who wielded it gave the side wrench notably peculiar to Pacific Island oarsmen.

Grouped in the bow of the boat were two women and two children, a boy and a girl. The Kanaka rowers shared the body of the boat with luggage, three white men sat in the stern. The bend in the river had scarcely been cleared when a following vessel, manned by whites and loaded with goods, came into view.

"They have brought your niggers, all right, Randolph."

5

This comment was addressed to Biddow by one of the group waiting upon the jetty.

No reply. Biddow's eyes were fastened upon that group in the bow. He could make out their faces now, the faces of his wife, Blanche, and Cindie, her maid, of his little daughter, Irene, and Randy, his son. Now the little girl pranced up, waved her hand and shouted. He removed his slouch hat from his head and waved it.

Twelve months since he had last seen them. They had grown, the young 'uns. That much was apparent while yet they were crouching down. Irene would be eight, now. Yes, eight, and Randy ten.

Now the whale-boat was gliding in to the jetty. Both children were shouting to him. Blanche was scolding them for their eager reaching out. Soon Biddow was lifting Irene out of the boat, squeezing her to him.

"Well, Randolph, I need some attention, too." Blanche's cool, rich voice stirred him out of his few moments of blissful submergence in this reunion with his child. He put Irene aside, gave a smile and shy embrace to Randy, who had scrambled out of the boat, then made to assist his wife.

Only one of his companions, old Barney Callaghan, had remained near to Biddow. The others, who had withdrawn from the jetty to allow him a measure of privacy in the reception of his family, now got busy unloading goods from the following boat, which had pulled in beside the river bank. Callaghan came forward and spoke to the children.

"Well, young 'uns! Remember me? Old Barney Callaghan."

"Of course we remember you," Irene replied. "Don't we, Randy? You came to our place in Brisbane. You brought our daddy up here. Mummy, here's Mr. Callaghan!"

"Oh, Mr. Callaghan, how do you do? I am glad to get here, I'm sure. Such a foul trip. Such a foul ship. So this is Masterman." Blanche Biddow glanced around. And as her eyes travelled over the enveloping jungle forest, blanketed with creepers and festooned with vines, forest which glittered and glinted with silver and gold as the sun found secreted jewels of moisture left by the early morning rain, the opulent beauty of her was shadowed and dimmed by apprehension.

The old man saw it. He laughed boisterously. "This is the river, Mrs. Biddow. But it's good to look at, don't you think? It's a good introduction to country that can't be bettered the length and breadth of the land."

"Yes, it's pretty, isn't it? But—let us get along, Randolph. We go somewhere, don't we?"

"Of course. It must be strange to you, Blanche, all this." Biddow, too, had noted that apprehension. "Mr. Callaghan will take you and Cindie and the children along with him." He gave a slight smile to the maid, who had hung back, standing near to, yet apart from, the six Kanakas who had dumped the luggage from the boat upon the jetty and stood beside it, waiting. "I will look after the men and goods. These are my Kanakas who have come up the coast with you."

"Oh!" Blanche, the maid and the children all turned simultaneously to stare at the dark men who had been invested by this pronouncement with new interest. The Islanders, who also had heard, and who had been keenly receptive to the change from the sub-tropical, flat, open country of south Queensland from which they had presently come, to this virgin mountainous land—swiftly opposed to the whites' blatant curiosity masks of stolid indifference.

Out of her curiosity Blanche brought a laugh, a surprising rich little chuckle. "Well, I must say they look a funny lot. But come. May we go, Mr. Callaghan? You will have my luggage along presently, won't you, Randolph? Come, Cindie."

Across the open space the little procession of women and children marched behind Callaghan towards a number of vehicles whose horses were tethered in the shade of the great forest trees. Two sulkys, he singled out from the number. Beside one of these a young island boy lounged.

Callaghan addressed the lad. "Funwala, you will drive this lady," indicating Cindie Comstock, "and the boy. We'll get along in the other trap, Mrs. Biddow. Come on, young miss. Up you go."

The two heavy-wheeled sulkys bumped out of the clearing and, taking a rough bush track, soon vanished.

Biddow had turned from the women and children to the Islanders and looked them over. Nothing to laugh at, to his eyes. Rather was he, with his wife's mirth an unpleasant echo in his ears, in some unaccountable fashion mortified. Why in God's name were these people compelled to endure the humiliation of the white man's slop-made clothes? Their working gear was not so bad. Singlet and trousers only. But these imitation fancy slops they wore now—and the straw "sailors" that three of them had perched upon the mounds of their frizzy hair—by Jupiter, it humiliated him! Made him ashamed to look at them. He snatched his pipe from the pocket into which he had dropped it before greeting his family, knocked the ashes out of the bowl upon the heel of his boot, and began to fill it as he walked over to the blacks. Six pairs of eyes came to meet his, five pairs committal of varying degrees of interest, the sixth pair neutral and, after the first glance, free roving.

The man who owned these, a native of the powerful and warlike race of Tanna, stood forward of his companions. He towered above Biddow, who was two inches short of six feet, and was built in proportion to his height. His black skin shone like satin. His physiognomy was Jewish, his nose a fierce hook. Unlike his companions, he wore singlet and trousers only, and both garments threatened to split against the pressure of his bulging muscles.

Two others of the group advertised themselves as Vauna Lava men by the fanciful, helmet-like designs into which their uncovered hair was cut and their facial tattooing. Each carried on his cheek a star cut by a sharp fishbone. Biddow was pleased to see these men, for he knew their tribe to be a friendly and docile people.

The remainder, who wore the straight-brimmed straw "sailors" above their slop suits, were nondescript to Biddow. One of them had cut the buttons off his coat and hung them on a string around his neck. By which token Biddow recognized him as the only "boy" among them freshly recruited from the islands. The others had completed their indenture term of three years in south Queensland and had been permitted to exercise their right to accept other engagements at the class of work to which by law they were restricted: agricultural labouring.

Biddow looked up at the big native gravely and spoke as

he held a match to his pipe. "You're a Tanna man. Have a good trip up?"

Black eyes came down and dwelt upon him, also gravely. "Good trip, Boss."

"Your name?"

A slight smile curved the purplish clean-cut lips. "My name? Or white man's name?"

Biddow frowned. "I said: your name?" he said sharply.

"Yes, Boss. My name Tirwana. White man call me Dick."

"Very well—Tirwana"—stiffly. "Name these other men for me."

At the sound of his true name from the lips of the white man there was a momentary flash of light from the eyes of the big native. His chin shot out. Then he straightened up and swung round on his heel. "Yes, Boss. This boy Tommy, this boy Bill, this boy Bob, this one Bill too, and this one Jacky."

"Thanks," said Biddow, dryly. "So you're the only one with a name of your own, Tirwana."

The manner of the other became withdrawn. "No, Boss. But they not my people. They can speak for self. I want to hear."

"Oh! Never mind, now. You, Bob." He addressed the man with the button necklace. "You're new to Queensland. How did you happen to be here?"

Bob took off his hat and, holding it pressed against his chest, answered timidly: "I got paper, Boss. In bag." With a swift movement he returned his hat to his head and bent to a plaited leaf bag at his feet. Rummaging for a few moments, he brought up an envelope and handed it to Biddow.

Bob, it appeared, from the information supplied by the southern Government Welfare Agent, was a "bush" boy, as distinct from the coastal boys who formed the very major number of the South Sea Islanders recruited—or impressed— for work on the sugar cane plantations of Queensland. These bush boys occupied the mountain fastnesses of their island homes and were regarded as less intelligent than the coastal tribes. In any case they were certainly less developed. For a bush boy to be recruited by the agents from Queensland meant that he would have to run the gauntlet of the feuds that raged incessantly between the coastal and mountain tribes. The boy Bob, by some means not explained to Biddow, had fallen among a group of his own island coastal men for transportation to Queensland, and as a result had fared so badly that the authorities in southern Queensland had attached him to a group of other-island tribesmen and transferred him north in response to Biddow's application for labourers.

Biddow folded the document and, with a nod to Bob, placed it in his pocket. "We'll get along," he stated generally.

By this time all but one of the vehicles, loaded with cargo from the second whale-boat, had been driven off by their owners. The boats had been tied up to the jetty and deserted, the white sailors in charge of them having insisted upon their "duty" to see safe delivery of certain potable goods at the pub that formed the hub of the nearby embryo township.

The solitary vehicle remaining was a two-horse buckboard. Biddow looked from it to the gigantic Tanna man and said hesitantly: "You, Tirwana, had better sit up in front with me. The others—you get up, you boys. Get in the trap." Seated on the driver's seat beside Tirwana, he added: "You had better hang on, Tirwana. The road's very rough. No springs in this cart."

"Yes, Boss. But this good land. Hill, bush, good land."

Biddow gave the native a clear look. "Like the island you came from, Tirwana?"

"Yes, Boss. Like it and not like it. All bush here. No palm, umbrella on top."

"Oh yes, we have palms, Tirwana. Both native and imported. You will see plenty of coconuts about, especially down at Port Denham, a dozen miles south."

A few minutes' run along the bush track and the buckboard debouched on to a large area of cleared land; cleared because the site had been chosen by a recently-elected sugar mill Directorate as most suitable for the erection of a sugar mill and township. (The Sugar Workers Guarantee Act, brought down by the Queensland Government in 1893, enabled any group of cane growers to form a company and, by mortgaging their land to the Government, obtain sufficient money for the erection of a central mill; a policy that ensured the rapid development of the sugar industry in those areas of virgin country outside the operations of the monopolistic company that determined the conditions of the planters in general throughout the mighty Queensland colony.)

As yet, besides the pub, Masterman township consisted of a few trading houses, little more than shacks, and some barrack-like dwellings which sufficed to house a number of workmen who had been temporarily imported into the district to build a two-mile tramline from the picked site of the mill, through the forest, to a point on the river close enough to its mouth to permit navigation by lighters up to three hundred tons capacity.

Biddow pulled up at a general store and, bidding Tirwana accompany him, entered it. As a result, quantities of rice, flour, treacle and various other items of an elementary dietetic nature were piled on to an already overloaded buckboard. Followed a return to the main track leading from the river, a continuing south through semi-cultivated country until, after covering about three miles in all, the vehicle turned to the right and made up a private track between orchards of young fruit trees, papaws and vegetables on the one hand, and plant cane springing between logs on the other.

Biddow swung the horses around and halted the buckboard before a slab shanty standing in the shade of a towering maple on the edge of the jungle forest. Biddow's home over the preceding twelve months, this hut. From now on, until the building of a house large enough to accommodate his family, he and they would be the guests of Barney Callaghan on the latter's neighbouring property, Palmer Estate.

"You boys will live here, Tirwana." Biddow jumped down from the buckboard's high front seat. "Pots for rice, camp-ovens for bread, tins for sugar and tea and other things—all inside the hut. Blankets, too, Tirwana, but only one bed. You will have to build your own beds. Axes and knives for cutting the timber, all the tools you will need, are here. You all settle in to-day. Make yourselves at home. I will come over early to-morrow morning and we'll get to work."

The group of dark men—one only possessed a coppery skin, the others being varying shades ranging from deep brown to Tirwana's jet black—had scrambled out of the buckboard with their bundles as Biddow talked. Now they stood still, looking around them in bewilderment.

"Where the cane, Boss?" Tirwana asked the question. "That little bit all?" He swept a massive arm in the direction of the ten acres of plant cane they had passed coming up the track. "Where the mill?"

"No mill yet, Tirwana. It's coming up the river soon. Only a little cane planted this year. You men will cut down trees for me this year. Build my house. Build houses for yourselves. You will attend to my orchards and vegetables. And make gardens for yourselves, too, when you are settled in, Tirwana. Manioc, taro, yams. I want you to be contented, Tirwana. There are plenty of Kanakas over there for company at the week-ends." He gestured towards Callaghan's property, which lay directly south. "I'll leave you now. You light a fire and cook yourselves a meal." Biddow hopped up on to the buckboard and, whipping up the horses, was soon rattling down the track towards the main road. Biddow's thoughts as he drove were a riot of intertangling suppositions and agitated speculation. Memories bitter and sweet jostled stabs of joy in the prospect of a return to family life.

Wonder at the queer lines into which his life had fallen was criss-crossed with apprehensive conjecture as to what the immediate hours and the night would bring forth. Would Blanche be kind? Was there the possibility of a new and peaceful life together being built out of this isolated venture?

A little sullenness crept into the mesh of his motile mood as his achievements of the past year obtruded themselves in all their crudity and hardship. God knew he had done well enough this time! She couldn't complain this time! Not that he could conscientiously admit that she had ever had just cause for complaint. It had suited him, his old secretarial job. He had done well enough before she had snapped him up and pestered him into engaging in business affairs for which he had less than no vocation. The mental pictures Biddow conjured up of the humiliations and shames that had derived from his failures, deepened his sullenness to a smouldering hateful resentment which in turn flared into acute nervous irritability. All he had asked of life was to be let alone! Why couldn't a man be let alone? Free to live his own life?

But the heat died out of him as his inalienable reasonableness, beyond and above all else the innermost core of the man,
bade him not be a fool. No man could live his own life. Not
once he had undertaken the responsibility of wife and children.
No man, no man, no man! The hooves of his horses clattered
the phrase at him until irritation merged into humility and
fear of his own weakness in the face of life's legitimate demands.
But with his approach to the gates of Barney Callaghan's
domain, the significance of the propinquity of his children
supervened and clarified his mood to limpidity. His eyes grew
soft at the thought of Irene, his lips curved in anticipation of
her caress.

CHAPTER II

BIDDOW FOUND HIS FAMILY AND THE CALLAGHANS PARTAKING
of a belated midday meal. At the top of the long dining-table
sat Barney, in front of him a much diminished corned beef
round, surrounded by covered dishes of vegetables. Mary, his
wife, a pale-faced, white-haired, but otherwise well-preserved
old lady, sat on his right, her place at table dictated by her
custom of dishing out the vegetables to Barney's carving of
the meats.

Blanche Biddow sat on the left of her host, with, next to her,
Consuelo, Creole wife of Barney's eldest son, Bert. He sat
next to his wife. Cindie Comstock, the maid, looking, as she
felt, not too comfortable at this sudden and unexpected elevation to the honour of a seat at the same table as her mistress,
sat opposite Bert and timidly attempted to disguise her discomfort by unnecessary attentions to her wards Irene and
Randy, who occupied seats below her. Opposite them again
were Ricardo and Esme, children of Consuelo and Bert, age
five and three respectively.

Biddows entrance caused a general stir and brought
welcoming cries from Irene. Consuelo, big with child, rose
and left the room.

"So you're here at last, Randolph, my boy," cried Barney.

"We waited as long as the old belly would let us. Grab that chair over there and push in somewhere. Connie will bring in your dinner. We put a dishful in the oven to keep it warm for you."

"Sit by me, Daddy!" cried Irene. "You shift down, Randy. Here, by me, Daddy. Daddy, Cindie's having lunch with us. Isn't that funny?"

Without a glance at Cindie, whose face had flamed and drooped over her plate, Biddow put a chair into place and seated himself. "How do you like Palmer Estate, Blanche?" he asked swiftly. "Comfortable enough, don't you think?"

Consuelo returned with a plate of meat and vegetables and placed it in front of him.

"But our place won't be anything like this for ages, Randolph, I should think." Blanche's tone was pessimistic.

"Depends upon the work put into it, my girl," Barney interposed. "Depends on the work done. Seven years ago this place was a wilderness, like Randolph's selection when he took over last year. He's done a good job, my girl, has Randolph. He's worked hard. And lived hard, too." Barney's kindly glance shuttled between husband and wife. "Different living, he's had, from the soft life in Brisbane, sitting on his behind in an office all day. He can do as good a job with his bit of country as I've done if he sticks to it."

"As you've done, did you say?" His wife rose as she lifted the meat dish. "A fat lot you'd have done if I hadn't been behind you, Barney Callaghan. Don't move, Connie. I'll bring in Toby." Mary left the room with the dish in her hand.

Barney chuckled. "And that's true enough. The Little Fella put the bone into me. Yes, it's women who count in a man's life in these places."

Blanche gave him, and then Biddow, a sharp glance. That was a dig at her. Interfering old fool. Biddow's face was red. His brows had knitted. He gave back to her sharpness a glance in which apology mingled with yearning.

Mary Callaghan returned. An Aboriginal maid carrying a tray came behind her and together they began to remove dishes and prepare the table for sweets.

Thus attended by the mistress of this place, which had her dazzled by its spaciousness and luxuriance of tropical growth,

Cindie Comstock's discomfort became acute. She gave
Blanche a strained, questioning look, and said swiftly: "Can't
I help with things?"

"Let Cindie clear away, Mrs. Callaghan," said Blanche
but without any real interest. Running through Blanche's head
was the notion that living conditions might not be so bad up
here, after all. This place was—seigneurial. Yes, something
like that.

Mary Callaghan smiled at the maid. "Not to-day, Cindie.
You must enjoy your first day with us. There will be plenty
of work for you, later, getting settled in. Now bring in the
sweets, Toby."

Barney grinned at Cindie. "I hope you've got your head
screwed on the right way, young woman. There are just about
two hundred men in this district looking for a wife and I
reckon you'll be able to take your pick of the lot. You don't
reckon on keeping her for long, I hope, Mrs. Biddow?"

Blanche looked startled at that. She stared from Cindie to
Barney. "Indeed I do! I certainly do! I couldn't manage
up here without Cindie. You are talking nonsense, surely."

All the adult Callaghan family laughed. "Nonsense, is it?"
cried Barney. "Within a radius of five miles of this table there
are dozens of planters just breaking into the sugar, and not
more than a score of them are married. And a woman, Mrs.
Biddow, as the Little Fella here can tell you, can make or
break a man in these parts. And your Cindie, Mrs. Biddow,
is a bit of a prize, if you ask me." He laughed uproariously,
leaning over the table towards the girl. "You look out, Cindie!
They'll be on to your tail like an army of tom-cats before you
can turn round."

"Cindie may not be the marrying kind," Mary Callaghan
said indulgently, to cover up the girl's confusion. "Don't
mind him, Cindie."

Said Blanche, a trifle grimly: "I should hope not, indeed."
She hastened to change the subject. "This place, Mr.
Callaghan. I don't understand your saying you have been
here only seven years. I understood, from Father——" She
glanced at him inquiringly.

"Seven years on Palmer Estate is what I meant," he told
her. "Seven years ago the Little Fella and I handed over our

selection a few miles out from Port Denham to our second son
and came up here to break in this place. I reckoned that
sooner or later the sugar would have to spread north and took
up a thousand acres on that spec. I brought up a dozen
Kanakas and a couple of white men, and inside three years I
was supplying my teams down at Port Denham with as much
garden produce as they could cart up over the Rump—that's
the road up over the coastal range—to supply the mining
fields on the Tablelands up there.

"Then I worked hard to get a mill up here so that we could
go into the sugar. Had to go into sugar or go down, in a way.
Why? Because now that the railway has been built from
Pearltown, which lies fifty miles south, up over the range to
the Tablelands, the folks up there are getting their goods up
by rail, killing my business with my teams." Barney grunted.

"Up till this year the pioneers of this Masterman area had
grown only corn, corn for the teams at the port, fruit, vegetables, rice—the high land rice—and a bit of coffee. And we
did well out of it. Damn-all well. But we big chaps in the
game—we cut our own throats, for that trade. We could have
had the railway built up over the range from Port Denham,
which would have sent this district sky-high with settlement
and prosperity; but we—a few of us—own not only the teams
that carry our produce up over the Rump, but also the lighters
that freight the goods into Port Denham from the big steamers
that have to lie out in the fairway of the Long Lagoon because
they can't get over the bar. A railway would have meant the
building of wharves and the dredging of the inlet harbour at
the Port, and that would have killed our lighter service.
Damn-all big money, our lighters made for us. And we
couldn't see past that. We opposed the little people who
wanted the railway built up from the Port, with the result that
Pearltown, with which we have no connection except by boat,
got in on us. When the railway goes right through, to all the
Tablelands settlements, our lighter service will be finished.
Most of it is, now. The big steamers now drop their cargo at
Pearltown and then proceed up the coast to Jamestown, fifty
miles to the north of Masterman, by-passing the Port. Only
small ships visit the Port and lay off the Masterman coast,
these days. That's why you had to tranship at Pearltown.

"We've got to build up on sugar, now, and use our lighters to ship it down to Port Denham. From there the big ships will take it to the refineries in the south. We've got the mill. The machinery is on its way and next year we expect to put through a crushing. There are twelve hundred acres under cane in this district. We've got good land and the best possible climate for cane growing. As I said before, it's just a question of work done."

"Oh, I don't know, Dad." Mary Callaghan spoke softly and slowly. "That sounds rather bald, and uninspiring. Don't you think so, Mrs. Biddow? The work, of course. But the spirit behind the work will determine whether the effort will be worth while. This place, Palmer Estate, is not the place it is solely because of work. It's more, I think, the aim in building it, the object."

"Oh?" Blanche was politely interested. "And what was the aim, may I ask, Mrs. Callaghan?"

"The aim was to put down permanent family roots, my child. To create a beautiful home to be handed down by Barney and me to our children. And by them to their children's children."

Rather hesitantly Biddow put in: "The hereditary principle, Mrs. Callaghan. That sort of thing seems rather—out of place—in relation to a young country like Australia."

Barney gave an exaggerated wink that took in the whole adult circle. "That's not me talking, bear in mind. That's the bustle talking that I found your mother wearing, Bert, when I swept her off her feet in Melbourne and married her. Yes, and damn-all nearly had to fight a duel with her godalmighty father for daring to so much as sit down in her presence." He chuckled. "And damned if I blame him, at that. We were pretty raw in those days, your dad and me, my girl. We had just made our big strike on the Palmer goldfields and were ripsnorting it round Melbourne, enjoying the first bit of luxury we had ever caught up with in our lives. We were in the news and got invited to a civic banquet—wasn't that what they called it, Mother?—by the Mayor, who wanted to borrow money off us. And there I met the Little Fella, my old mate here. And wasn't she a stunner, with her violin tucked under her chin!" He chuckled again.

"Now, Dad, that's enough," said Mary calmly. She rose from her chair. "Come. We shall sit on the veranda and take our coffee. You may help Mrs. Bert to get it if you like, Cindie. Ric, you may take Irene and Randy around the gardens."

"And you can give me the latest news about that old sinner, your father, my girl," Barney said to Blanche. "Tell me his latest graft, the damned old tory. It's a funny thing, what money will do to a man."

Cindie followed Consuelo along a corridor and dropped down a few steps into the kitchen. This room, a barn of a place, with the weather end of it occupied by shower bath cubicles for the use of the white members of the household, ran half the length of the house and opened on to a broad roofed-in passage-way, across which lay two small rooms. One of these was occupied by Toby, the Aborigine maid, the other by Funwala, the young Kanaka. The flooring of kitchen, passage and rooms was concrete, which was extended outside to cover half an acre of ground that functioned as a back-yard. To one side of this yard stood a slab building, containing the dining-room, sleeping and living quarters of the four white workmen employed by Callaghan. There was also attached a shower bath cubicle. At the far end of this building another hutment did duty as a dining-room for the unmarried of the two dozen Kanakas maintained by the plantation.

On the opposite side of the yard stood laundry, cookhouse and living quarters for the two field cooks, a Chinese named Lo How, and Yamada, a Japanese. Outside the cookhouse door a great ship's bell hung from scaffolding, its function being to call the near field workers up to the house for their meals.

Smooth green lawns surrounding the concrete yard disappeared into flower gardens and ornamental shrubberies. Beyond these were tiny groves of tropical fruits, scarcely less ornamental than the shrubs, and native forest trees smothered by climbers. Paths led through the lawns, gardens and shrubberies to the orchards, and beyond them again into fields of springing cane.

Looking out from the back of Palmer House one could see, in front and to the right, only lawns and shrubberies and clumps of forest, but to the left these merged into virgin forest that stretched to the foothills and climbed the range.

Within the kitchen Consuelo talked to Cindie, charming the girl with her exotic appearance and musical, richly accented speech. The natural brown of the Cuban woman's skin, only a few shades darker than the gold of Cindie's own, was now, by her condition, darkened to bluish-black beneath her large dark eyes. Her cheeks were thin, her expression weary. In the mass of her blue-black hair she wore a high Spanish comb.

To Cindie, her presence was part of the whole exciting and bewildering mesh of these outlandish conditions. She longed to ask questions. To ask the meaning of the rattle of foreign tongues that shrilled in from the back yard. Not Kanakas, she felt sure. She wanted to ask why the mistresses worked when so many servants were at hand. Toby, now. There she sat, lolling on a chair, staring at Cindie, while Consuelo made the coffee and piled the tray. At length she felt that she had to ask, to interrupt Consuelo's politely given directions.

"Why doesn't Toby get the coffee, Mrs. Callaghan?" she whispered timidly. "Is she too stupid?"

"Stupid? Toby?" Consuelo smiled at her. "I don't think so. But she pretends she is because she doesn't like work. Toby is—what you call temporary, here. Our black girl, Alice, is at the camp on the creek, having a baby. She got too friendly with a Kanaka, I think." Consuelo laughed. "Alice will be back. Alice is very clever. Very reliable. Toby, she does not bother."

Cindie took up the tray and carried it out to the veranda. Having poured the coffee and handed it round, she felt at a loss for something to do and stood about uncertainly. Blanche, deliberately it seemed to Cindie, ignored her. Feeling a fool and a little aggrieved, she at length asked: "May I go out to the children, Mrs. Biddow?"

"Yes. But don't go too far. I shall want you to help me unpack, presently."

Cindie walked across the gardens towards the children, who played and swung upon ropes in the shade of great cedars. But instead of joining them she halted midway, turned and looked back at the house. A wide, rambling structure, the front portion of it an afterthought built of unpolished boards of silky oak, the building was supported on both sides by trees whose lower spreading limbs were trimmed to accommodate themselves to the veranda. Beautiful, Cindie thought their great feathery leaves, and giving a fine shade. She must find out their name, the names of all the strange trees and shrubs set lavishly about the acres of grounds, most of them quite young looking as yet, but many bearing flowers large and lovely.

There were few conventional flower gardens, as Cindie knew such. Most plants grew big and either climbed or sprawled. That's to suit the climate, she told herself, everything in nature tended to make shade. How comfortable and fine looked the group upon the veranda, in the coolness laid upon them by those feathery trees! Veranda? With its furnishings, made of cane, it looked like an open-air parlour.

Suddenly, fancying that the eyes of the lot of them were upon her, Cindie swung about and joined the children beneath the cedars. Flowers there, too. A smother of black-eyed Susans rioted at the base of the tree trunks.

Discouraging Irene's attempt to engage her attention, Cindie wandered into the forest till she stood upon a bank of the stream that watered the property. A high bank, it was, for the raging torrent into which the stream converted in the "wet", had torn out and carried away the deep blanket of soil. The bed, ten feet down, was formed of rounded boulders over which the water burbled to fall into pools with sandy bottoms. The opposite bank vanished into immediate depths of forest almost impenetrable for the tangle of thorny creepers and climbers that massed about the trunks and clambered up to and along the limbs of the big timber trees.

A delicious scent began to rise about Cindie. She sniffed and looked around. No flowers that she could see. The scent grew more intense, drenching her flaring nostrils. Ah! at last she had it! The perfume came from a clump of great lily-like leaves rising from the gentle slope of the bank, down near the stream. Each leaf stalk was almost as tall as herself, each swaying leaf was a foot wide, two feet in length. In among the leaves were green flower buds upon thick stalks, undoubtedly the source of the rich, cloying scent, for all that they were tightly closed.

The moments of her discovery of that wild-lily stock were

to remain with Cindie Comstock and recur to her as a stimulating excitement throughout the long years of her singular and uncharted life. What happened to her then was like a conception within her, the germinating of new life. The culmination of all the bewildering and exotic phenomena of the past few days, it was of a nature to englamorize them, to enswathe them with rich promise. It seemed to suck out of her, to engulf, those aspects of this new life which had intimidated her with their strangeness, and at the same time highlight those other aspects which she had already dimly perceived might minister to her future wellbeing.

A wave of elation swept through her as she stood, sniffing up that scent. Consciously, she only got so far as to think: "I'm going to like it here. There are things to do here that I'll like."

Little wings of eager desire for action seemed to sprout from her muscles. She hurried out from the shade of the great cedars hoping that her mistress would be ready, now, for unpacking, for anything that would allow of a beginning on a day-to-day routine.

But no! The group on the veranda had made no move. The children had renounced the swings and joined Funwala, who was busily engaged about a grove of palms—strange palms, to Cindie—at the edge of the garden, near to the tall forest.

She watched the boy for some moments and then walked across to investigate the meaning of his mysterious movements. At her approach Funwala looked up and showed his teeth in a bashful grin. Cindie smiled back. "What are you doing, Funwala?" she asked. "Why are you tying those plants to the palm trees?"

His eyes went past her. She turned to follow their direction and saw that the Callaghans and Biddows were making their way across the sward towards her.

"We call them Alexandria palms," Mary Callaghan was saying, as the group came up. "A North Queensland native. Much more beautiful than the coconut, I think. We did not plant them. We simply cut away the forest growth about them. And the same with all the other native trees.

"Most of the exotics we brought back from Cuba and Jamaica. The allspice, the jacaranda, African tulips, Hawaiian peach, we brought from Cuba, the magosteens from Jamaica. Barney got the lichee nuts from a Chinaman's plantation. The custard apples, soursops, jackfruit and avacado pears, all came from the South Sea Islands, brought by the recruiters and planters at different times."

As Mary talked, the group sauntered about the gardens, pausing here and there to inspect the trees and fruits she named. Cindie, uninvited, still under the spell of her new-born spiritual ebullience, tagged along in their wake, her ears strained. Lichee nuts, carambola and Monsterio delicioso held them up for some time. The nuts and Monsterio were far from ripe but the carambola was at its most delicious state of edibility.

"It's the most delicious fruit I ever tasted!" exclaimed Blanche, after sinking her teeth into the luscious flesh. "And what a queer shape! This *is* a queer country!"

"We call that fruit five corners," said Mary. "Come, Cindie, help yourself to some fruit. They make good jam and pickles, Mrs. Biddow, as you will find out. The Chinese call them *san nim*. I suppose they came from China originally. We got our plants from the Chinese."

Out beyond the shrubberies they wandered, past a yard full of guinea fowl and turkeys, to stand in contemplation of the plantation of citrus fruits, bananas and papaws. The ground between the trees was utilized for pineapples, melons and vegetables. Mango trees, at that time of year heavily laden with brownish-red bloom, made two parallel lines to the right of the orchards. To the left, they were planted singly about a narrow clearing along the bank of the creek, a clearing reserved for the living quarters of the Kanakas. Numerous shacks made of woven bladey grass and pandanus leaves made a straight line along it, each one surrounded by its garden plot. At the far end, stables and vehicle sheds made of the same primitive materials were placed. The fields of springing cane and corn beyond and to the right were obscured by the expanse of the plantations and the density of the mangoes.

"These are the payable fruits," Barney told Blanche, "the bananas, pines and citrus fruits. We dispose of them on the Tablelands. The oranges and mandarins have not yielded as yet. I expect a good crop next year but with the growing importance of the sugar the fruit and vegetable trade will languish. The big profits are in sugar."

Blanche, however, was paying little attention to his words. And Cindie none at all. Both were engrossed by their first glimpse of Kanakas working in the fields. There were not many of them, only four, to be exact. The remainder were either chipping in the cane fields or felling timber in the forest beyond. Two black women were working in their gardens. Two naked toddlers played on the bank of the creek.

It was Cindie who made the first move towards the black women. The virgin wildness of her spirits by now had been swamped by sheer curiosity and wonder. Blanche led the rest of the party after her, as she made round the squared vegetable plots.

The native women straightened themselves up at the approach of the whites. Then the bigger and stouter of the two called to the toddlers, went to meet them as they ran towards her and bundled them into the nearest hut.

Irene cried out: "Mother! The little niggers had no clothes on! They've got no clothes on, Mummy!"

"Never mind, never mind!" Blanche replied hastily. On an afterthought she added: "They are only little niggers, you know, darling. They don't know any better. You stay beside me, Irene. You also, Randy. Mrs. Callaghan, I didn't know that Kanaka women were indentured."

"Of course you didn't know," Barney answered her bluffly. "I'd be surprised to learn that the southerners recognized our existence. Only eleven hundred miles between us but you'd think we lived on another planet. Of course we get Kanaka women. Ought to get a woman to every man, in my opinion."

"Now, Barney," Mary warned. "We only have one Kanaka woman, Mrs. Biddow. Mary, there. The smaller woman is an Aborigine married to a Kanaka. Hullo, Mary. I have brought some visitors to see you."

The black woman, upstanding and strong-looking, dressed in a cast-off dress of Mary Callaghan's, gave the group a wavering smile but she did not speak.

"Pretty good garden, Mary," Barney shouted at her.

Mary shook her head deprecatingly. "Not good, Boss." Then suddenly the mainspring of her being seemed to be loosened. The stiffness of her body dissolved into flowing, moving lines. She waved her arms pantomimically as her tongue voiced a tirade in her own island speech. It was a cascade of words, arrested as suddenly as it had begun. With its abrupt cessation the woman dropped off her like a cloak all recognizance of the presence of her visitors and stooped again to her weeding.

Barney interpreted. "She says Tommy's pig doesn't give her a chance with her garden. It roots under the wire netting and eats the manioc and yams. It has eaten up her taro down in the creek bed. She wants me to make him kill it."

"And will you?" asked Blanche.

"I'll make him build a proper sty for it. To-night."

Cindie had left the group and wandered over to the Aborigine woman who, pipe in mouth, had squatted among her vegetables to watch. With her spindle shanks, unkempt hair and skinny body, she contrasted badly with the buxom island woman. But the mildly welcoming light in her large liquid black eyes was pleasing to Cindie.

"Hullo." Cindie greeted her diffidently.

"Hullo, yourself," the woman said tersely. "You new boss over there?" She gestured north. "You new Biddow woman?"

"No. I'm not a boss. I'm the maid." Cindie drew back and spoke stiffly.

The other rose and came close to her. "Huh. You the Toby, the Alice, eh? She good boss?" She nodded her head towards Blanche.

"Yes. Yes, of course." Cindie blushed.

"Mary, she good boss." The black woman pointed her pipe towards Mary Callaghan. "She *good*. Barney good, too. He give good tucker. He like the Kanakas. He like the black man. Your boss, he good to Kanaka, you think?" A little slyness crept into her tone.

"I don't know. He—he hasn't started yet."

The black head nodded. "That right. That right." She took a few puffs at her pipe and let her eyes dwell on Blanche. They came back to Cindie in shrewd appraisal. "She flash, that one. You like her?"

"Cindie!" Blanche was calling. "Come, now. We shall go and unpack."

CHAPTER III

BIDDOW AND HIS WIFE SETTLED INTO A LARGE BEDROOM THAT opened into a fernery built upon the veranda on the right side of the house. Cindie and Irene were given a small room beside it and Randy took up sleeping quarters, in company with Bert and Ric Callaghan, on the left side veranda.

The afternoon was well advanced before Biddow was called upon to undergo the ordeal of those dreaded first moments alone with his wife. His stomach was like water within him when at length the two of them were face to face with no expectation of interruption. They looked at each other quietly, but both knew that beneath the quiet suppressed emotion rioted.

"Well, Blanche?" Biddow spoke first, but so great was the effort that his breath failed him on her name. Then, folding his arms on his chest, an unconscious move to still the wild beating of his heart, he tried again. "It's been a long time."

"Yes." Just one little word. But with it the pride of her, her erect stand, crumbled. She put up her arms to hide her face, and burst into a storm of tears. Like a flash Biddow was beside her. He was clasping her in his arms. "Love! Oh, love!" he whispered, imploring her, pressing her to him. . . .

Later, as they lay on the bed together, her head pillowed upon his shoulder, they talked companionably: of the children, the condition of Biddow's property and what its primitive condition entailed in respect of their married life.

The children would have to have a tutor. Biddow had been keeping his eyes open and thought that one of the numerous remittance men around the district would do. These fellows tutored nearly all the children of the planters. They did all right, as a rule, till their tongues got dry. Then they simply disappeared, but generally they turned up again.

"Hardly a charming prospect," commented Blanche. "In any case the children will have to run wild till our home is built. I don't like that, Randolph. This place is so—so crude. Fancy their having Cindie to eat at our table."

Biddow hastily changed the subject. "I hope to have the rough building up within a few weeks. I shall put the Kanakas on to splitting bean tree slabs to-morrow morning. Jeff Grey, my neighbour on the north side, sort of jack of all trades, has offered to direct the erection of the framework.

"Things will be pretty rough for a time, Blanche," Biddow warned. "I shan't be able to build a permanent, weatherboard place for a year or two, probably. The most I could do this year was to get ten acres under cane. Barney let me have his white workers at the week-ends to do the job."

"But Dad Hilliard will stand to you if you need more money, Randolph. You don't think a man in his position would allow me to live in a slab hut, do you?"

"It won't be a hut, Blanche. Four rooms are enough, aren't they, to make do for a while? Four rooms with wide verandas for sleeping accommodation. Anyhow, I'm not taking more of your father's money." His voice took on the aloof, extra-ordinarily quiet tone that Blanche knew by experience signified finality. "It will take years to repay him as it is."

Inwardly Blanche scoffed. Repay, indeed! She would see about that! She kept her own counsel, however.

Biddow continued more slowly. "By the third year I should be drawing a good-sized cheque, though of course a man can't be sure. Difficult to estimate the position of sugar on the markets, nowadays. The price is remarkably elastic. There's no doubt it's recovering from the ruinous price of 'ninety-four, though. This year, to our benefit, the European beet sugar crop has failed, and on top of that there's the revolution in Cuba. The disorganization there is calculated to lower the output of the Cuban planters for years. Mrs. Bert is worried about that."

"Oh yes! I dare say she would be. It will knock her people, I suppose."

"Pretty bad, it seems. It's a case of dog eat dog. Their misfortune is our gain. The heightened prices will in time lead to increased production of beet sugar in Europe, but the Queensland planters should be able to count on a few years' prosperity, at least. There's the chance of real big profits."

"And, apart from those factors, the cane grower has an advantage over all other producers. His market is at his front door. He has only to deliver his cane at the local mill and draw his money in cash. No overhead expenses for commission, storage, freight and so on. Practically no risk. Can even calculate his crop."

A silence ensued. Blanche lay still, and gradually a faint uneasiness, concern, clouded what had been Biddow's habitual scholarly expression. He moved slightly, bestowed an apprehensive glance sideways and down, but could see only a mass of black curls, a little damp from the afternoon heat, and the tiniest, most delicate of ears.

Then Blanche shuffled away from him and spoke flatly, almost tonelessly. "I suppose you know all there is to know about sugar by now, Randolph."

He swallowed a lump in his throat before replying. "I find the subject interesting, Blanche."

"Yes. Of course. You find the subject interesting."

Another silence. Then Biddow flung his body round, leant a little above her and whispered, with stammering urgency: "I'll try, this time, my girl! I'll try!" His head fell on to her breast. His words came muffled. "I've worked hard. You'll see. Ask Mr. Callaghan."

"Mr. Callaghan has already told me," she said soberly, letting her hands wander among the thick swathes of his waving black hair. The wings of her own black brows came together as she fell into a mood of worried introspection. Then suddenly she slipped from beneath him and sat up, made fists of her little hands and beat them, with measured unison, upon the bed. "Yes, you've worked hard! You've done all right! And you might have done all right all along if I had not tried to hammer a square peg into a round hole. Oh, I'm not a fool, Ranny! And Dad told me plainly enough. I've got myself into this fix. Here we are, stuck in this wilderness for the rest of our lives. And it's my fault——"

"Blanche, don't!" he interrupted her painfully. "You can't help the way you're made. Nobody can." He couldn't tell her, then, that here in this wilderness he had found life full of promise, the only fly in his ointment being his apprehension of her coming and her reaction to it.

She got up on to her knees, pressed him back upon the bed with her hands against his breast, her eyes, of the deepest brown, gleaming with storm and stress. "But you are sorry you ever met me! Aren't you? Aren't you?"

He threw up an arm and covered his eyes with it. "Don't, Blanche! I tell you I'll do all right up here."

She stilled, then with a deep sigh let her body lapse upon his and cradled his head in her arms. Rubbing her downy cheek against his dark shaven chin she got back on to the plane of more commonplace talk. "But isn't there a chance of trouble in the sugar industry, Randolph? This talk of deporting the Kanakas. Sometimes at the dinner-table, among Dad's friends, there would be a lot of talk. Some of them insisted that Dad had thrown his money away by backing you up here. They said the Kanakas would be swept out of the colony and without them the sugar would be done."

"Yes, there's a lot of talk. A lot of action, too, I believe. But I don't think it's a real issue facing us as yet. I've applied to the Government for another twelve Kanakas and Mr. Callaghan has applied for a couple of dozen Hindus. He believes that Hindus cut the cane better than Kanakas."

"But that will make eighteen Kanakas you will have, Randolph. Seems to involve a lot of money, to me."

"I'm acting on old Barney's advice. As a matter of fact, I have felt a little uneasy about it. Jeff Grey says that old Barney is not keeping up with the times. Yet—we seem to have everything our way, politically. The Premier is a sugar man. He says he intends to remove some of the burdens the sugar men carry, through the Customs, and also take off the import duties on mill supplies and bags. But"—he spoke more thoughtfully—"there are all sorts of factors arising which may complicate the general good position. I can't help thinking that the big future in sugar lies in small holdings. A lot of the old planters, the big men of the sixties and seventies, are now breaking up their large holdings into small farms and leasing them to individual farmers. They reckon that running their big properties along feudal lines, or employing a manager to do the job for them with slipshod methods, means the employment of too large a number of Kanakas. The small farmer works in the fields with his men. He manages better and gets more out of his men.

"Take Jeff Grey. He took up only two hundred acres and

so far has done all the work himself with the help of a remittance man and one coloured labourer. But of course he never
went in for vegetables at all. He came in for the cane. He
thinks, and he's no fool, that eventually, and soon at that, the
industry will be stabilized by close settlement by white farmers
and the use of new and improved implements. Maybe he is
right. I don't know. . . ."

"Oh, well. . . ." Blanche got off the bed and shook out her
voluminous petticoats. "I think I'll have a bath. Haven't
had one for a week. I can still smell that dirty little boat. . . .
I wonder what Cindie is up to. And the children." She
ran a comb through her short curls. "It's hot, isn't it? . . . I
hope Mr. Callaghan didn't put ideas into Cindie's head with
his silly talk about men, Randolph. I didn't bring her up
here to get married."

"You will have to take things as they come, Blanche."

A knock at the door. Biddow rose hastily, slipped his braces
up over his shoulders and ran his hands through his hair.

"Who is it?" called Blanche.

"It's me, Mrs. Biddow," Cindie's voice replied. "Mrs.
Callaghan wants to know if you will have your tea in your
room or come out for it."

"Oh, bring it. I'm not dressed."

When Cindie brought in the tea and cakes, Blanche, engaged in wrapping herself in a much befrilled and trailing
blue satin *négligée*, bade Biddow take the tray into the fernery.

"What are the children up to, Cindie?" she asked.

"They are having the time of their lives. But what am I to
do here, Mrs. Biddow? I'm tired of doing nothing, already."

"Well, we shall make a lot of work in the house, Cindie.
You have a talk with Mrs. Bert Callaghan. She looks as
though she needs a rest."

Out in the fernery, Blanche bent her brows above the tea-
cups. "Randolph, what do you think Mr. Callaghan meant
when he said that I had a prize in Cindie? He didn't mean
that she is good looking, did he?"

"I think he probably did." A quiet, slightly quizzical smile
touched upon Biddow's classical features and lingered.

"But she isn't—is she?"

He considered that, calling up the image of the girl before

him. Her great mass of tawny hair, like a lion's mane, her brows the shining dark of the more intimate parts of the king of beasts, the golden skin, the wide blue eyes, the straight nose, with slightly flared nostrils, the strong jaw, square white teeth. And her body was remarkably slender, to be matched with square shoulders and such powerful limbs. Not pretty. Striking.

"Yes," he said aloud. "She is good looking. Striking, I think. You will have to adjust yourself to an entirely new set of values in relation to people like Cindie, up here, Blanche. In these raw conditions we are dependent upon them. And they are jolly hard to get."

"I'd be dependent upon Cindie anywhere," replied Blanche tartly. "But I am sure she won't expect to sit at my table. She was most uncomfortable at lunch to-day. Naturally." A little disdain curled the bow of her pink upper lip.

Biddow, having drunk his tea, took a pipe from his pocket and proceeded to fill it. Having put a match to it he said briefly: "She will soon get used to the new conditions. So will you, I hope."

Blanche's eyes lifted to his, swiftly, then dropped. She crumbled a cake on her plate and thoughtfully made pellets of the crumbs.

CHAPTER IV

THE FOLLOWING MORNING BIDDOW ROSE AT DAYBREAK, TOOK breakfast in the field kitchen, and then set off in his buckboard for his selection. His mood was as clear and limpid as the morning itself. Gossamer mists were lifting from the plantation, from the garden. The leaves of the vegetation drooped with the weight of the profuse dew. Numberless birds, attracted as ever by human habitation, flashed their brilliant colours from flower to flower, from tree to tree.

As he drove out from the stables, his two light draught horses stepping freely in accord with his own eager mood, the Kanakas coming out of their huts and making up to the house shouted to each other and to him. He pulled up beside the shack occupied by Mary, her husband Tommy and their child, and shouted: "Tommy!"

Almost immediately the doorway of the shack—there was no door—was filled with the stocky body of a remarkably handsome Solomon Islander, Callaghan's head field man. His sole article of clothing was a pair of dungarees cut off above the knee. A faint reddish tinge in his skin, extending to the enormous mass of his frizzy hair, was caught by the first rays of the rising sun, giving a glowing effect that held Biddow silent, looking at him in admiration. Tommy spoke first.

"What you want, Boss?"

"I wanted to tell you that I've got six Kanakas over at my place, now, Tommy. My place, it is mostly bush as yet. May I bring them over here on Sunday?"

"They good men? They no fight?"

"Well, I don't know them yet, Tommy, but they look quiet enough."

"All right, Boss. You bring them. I look after them."

"Thanks, Tommy."

Biddow drove on. Bowling along the track to the main road he tabulated the tasks before him. One thing he regretted, in his now eager desire to have his family in a home of their own: his refusal of Barney's offer to lend him a couple of his seasoned Kanakas for the splitting of his house timber. He felt little confidence in his own bunch of "boys" in relation to such work, fresh from the south and long-settled areas as they were.

His refusal had been dictated by his sense of an embarrassing debt of gratitude to the old man for favours already rendered. But now, new-risen from the felicity of his wife's embrace, peace within him at the unexpected wholeheartedness of her submission, all other aspects of his circumstances fell into different alignment.

His Kanakas, having long ago eaten their rice, were lounging around, waiting for him. He talked with them, named Tirwana, to begin with, head man. He felt glad of the ability and experience he sensed in Tirwana, for now for the first time Biddow was facing, independently of Barney Callaghan's presence beside him and advice, the ordering of his affairs in this way of life in a big way. He could see that the Kanakas were at a loss. They were not happy in this wilderness in which it appeared they were cut off from the sociability of their own kind. And he also knew, if Callaghan's experience was worth its recounting, that unhappiness would result in bad work.

So he talked to them, telling them of the big place next door to which they could go on Sundays. He spoke of good food, of the wild pigs in the hills for the hunting, of the fishing and the garden foodstuffs they could grow around their huts.

"Good home here for you all, Tirwana," he repeated. "You tell them in island talk. I won't send them away so long as they work well and don't fight. A home here for them as long as they want one."

"They know your talk, Boss. But I tell them if you say. I tell them in Mission jabber." Forthwith Tirwana raised his voice and in pidgin, with much gesticulation, made sure that his fellows were left in no doubt as to the full gist of Biddow's words. More than anything else, the mention of wild pig broke glumness into smiles—smiles shared by Biddow when he found that Tirwana was a practised bush hand.

"Trees down south, Boss, too," he told Biddow. "Not like here, though. Here trees walk close-up. Gum-tree down south. Gums walk like men who fight. The horse, he gallops through."

So, by seven o'clock, only an hour' behind the normal beginning of the Kanaka's twelve-hour day, Biddow was able to leave Tirwana in charge of the splitting of the bean tree logs and apply himself to the digging of his root vegetables. As he worked his fork beneath the sweet potatoes—sweet "bucks", in local parlance—he figured out the extent of cleared land he could reasonably count on for planting the following year. At least fifty acres, if the further batch of Kanakas arrived on time. Ought to be here by November, which should give them at least six weeks of bushwhacking before the rains set in. Would have to build a shack for the tutor, too. But that would have to wait upon the stables and other odds and ends. Perhaps Blanche would not mind keeping the children to their books for a while.

At ten o'clock, when Barney's buggy came bouncing up the track with Mary, Biddow's family and Cindie aboard, Biddow, hot and thirsty, met them with quiet pride. In his mind, the few acres of clearing he had belted out with his own hands, hands that had previously held nothing more practical than a pen, represented something to be proud of, and subconsciously he expected Blanche to appreciate this.

But Blanche was already upset and exasperated by the heat. She was dressed in southern winter clothing, a tight, boned, pink velvet jacket with leg-of-mutton sleeves, above a blue serge skirt that swept the ground. Her buttoned boots reached almost to the calf of her leg. The weight of the plumed, wide black hat she wore, tied beneath her chin with velvet ribbons, offset the value of its shadiness.

"Isn't it hot?" were the words with which she greeted Biddow. "Randolph, I'm stifling, and this is winter."

"It's your clothes. And the scrub," he hastened to explain. "A small clearing like this in the midst of jungle forest is always terribly hot. But in a few months we shall have a great deal of it down, with only shade trees left."

"Now you can imagine the sweat Randolph put into the job of clearing the first acre in the heat of last summer, Mrs. Biddow, dear," Mary Callaghan put in.

Blanche bit her lip. "Yes," she said, forcing a laugh. "I can imagine that the men up here work hard. But the job has hardly begun, I should think. It looks as though we shall have to impose upon your hospitality for a long time, Mrs. Callaghan. Oh dear!" She wiped her face daintily. "We shall have to discard all our winter clothing. But Randolph, where are we going to live? You said you had picked out a site."

"Over there, where the Kanakas are at work. It's on a slight rise, Blanche. But you have the final say, you know. There's a small creek, a tributary of the river, a few yards to the north of it. Come up and see. I intend to leave the bush standing along the banks of the stream."

Cindie Comstock had immediately moved away from the group to wander around by herself. She watched the Kanakas at work, noted particularly the great muscular activity of Tirwana. She wondered at the Jewish cast of his features. From them she made down to the gardens, where the flower-buds of the papaws and the light green of the young banana leaves stirred her to mingled discontent and joy. She picked up Biddow's fork and tentatively drove it into the black loam. It felt good, that thrust. After a stealthy look around, she drove the fork in again, this time beneath some sweet potatoes. And when the tubers came lumpily up through the soil, some of them quite two pounds in weight, Cindie was stirred to a sudden deep concern with this fumbling in the flesh of the earth. She kept on digging, her long skirt trailing about her, sweat gathering in big drops and tumbling from her face, desisting only when she caught the soft thud of a horse coming up the track. She dropped the fork and stood, wiping her face with her handkerchief.

The horse came to a halt beside the patch of sweet potatoes and a deep voice called a morning greeting to her. There was surprise and amusement in the tone.

"Good morning," Cindie blurted out. She guessed the identity of the man. She had heard the talk of Jeff Grey's coming to help with the beginnings of the house. In her turn she was surprised at his seeming youthfulness. Surely not more than twenty-six or -seven. His build was slender, he appeared to be of average height. Cindie noted his sunburned skin and blue-eyed rugged plainness, his nose that jutted at an angle from his face, a contradiction of the dimpling cleft in the rounded but firm set chin. The most notable thing about him, though, in that period of almost universal "soup-strainer" moustaches, was the close-clipped line of blond stubble that adorned his upper lip. This distinction had the effect upon Cindie of investing him with a fleeting resemblance to Biddow, the only clean-shaven man of her acquaintance up to date.

The man's eyes were now warily solemn. "Good morning," he repeated. "I see you're a farmer already, Miss Comstock."

Cindie assumed an air of prim reproval and said stiffly: "I don't know you."

"I beg your pardon. I'm Jeff Grey. We're friendly people in these places, don't you know. Have to be. Couldn't get along, without."

Cindie glanced over to the house party. Every eye was turned in her direction. "You had better go and see *them*," she said hurriedly. "I'm only the maid."

Grey laughed and flipped his reins. "So you're only the

maid. Well, I'm willing to bet you won't be a maid long, in these parts. So long."

Cindie looked after him, suspicious of some not-quite-nice innuendo in his words but unable to place it.

That little encounter, building up her already awakened sense of new development, with its assumption of significance for her in the Masterman scheme of things, acted as a spur to the resolution, that afternoon, of an idea which had sprung from her handling of the garden fork and had grown to the proportions of practicality in the succeeding hours.

It was after the afternoon tea had been disposed of. Blanche, acting on her own discomfort, had Cindie come to her room and, with Mary Callaghan and Consuelo looking on, unpack her summer wardrobe. And there, in the companionable atmosphere evoked by the conjunction of women and clothes, Cindie brought forward her proposition. She wanted to go over to Biddow's place every day and help with the work of the gardens!

"Good gracious me!" Blanche exclaimed, looking blankly at the girl.

Mary and Consuelo laughed. "Are you used to farm work, Cindie?" Mary asked.

"No. But I want to do it."

"Well, I don't see why not. Most of our women work in the gardens."

"It's ridiculous!" Blanche found her tongue. "How can you go over there with all those men, Cindie? It's not proper."

"Mrs. Biddow!" Cindie flushed and spoke with a hint of desperation. "I think it *is* proper, up here. Mr. Biddow would be there. And as for the Kanakas—they're not *men*."

Mary looked grave at that. "They are men, all right, Cindie," she said gently. "In some ways exactly like all other men, irrespective of colour. And you must not forget that, Cindie. Our women, Cindie, never forget that the Kanakas are men. Do you understand?"

"Yes, yes, of course. In *that* way. But I meant—I meant— I wouldn't have anything to do with *them*."

Mary still looked grave. Blanche broke in: "I should think not, indeed. Whatever put such an idea into your head, Cindie? Mr. Biddow would never allow it."

"Will you ask him, Mrs. Biddow? I've got nothing to do here." Cindie sought for artificial excuses to bolster up her case. "If I got to work at the gardening, Mr. Biddow could help with the house. Besides, you know, I will have to learn to manage. Oh, I didn't mean that! I beg your pardon, Mrs. Biddow."

"You will certainly have to learn how to manage," said Blanche, shortly. "But you may learn that here. Can't she, Mrs. Callaghan?"

"If Cindie wants to work in the gardens there is really no valid reason why she should not do so, Mrs. Biddow," said Mary. "My own dear girl did a man's work when we were building up our place near Port Denham. And to-day she is none-the-less a good mother of a family for it."

"Oh, all right, Cindie. You will soon get sick of it, I'll warrant. I will speak to Mr. Biddow to-night."

CHAPTER V

THAT EVENING, BIDDOW RETURNED TO PALMER ESTATE accompanied by the district welfare agent whose job it was to administer the law in respect to the interests of the Kanakas. Combining his office with the running of a general store at the Port, this man had made his desire to talk business with Barney coincide with his obligation to examine into the conditions under which Biddow proposed to maintain his Kanakas.

The agent's business with Barney had to do with the rapid development of Masterman. The permit for a mill was bringing in its train a rush of settlers to the area, planters transferring from exhausted lands down south, miners and timber men from the Tablelands and Cape York Peninsula, a steady infiltration of Chinese. All of which signified a rapid growth of the township. The agent-merchant, hot on the scent of new business, proposed to spend money in Masterman, to erect an hotel, a large general store. But he wanted to be sure of his premises to begin with, and thus the desire to consult with Barney Callaghan.

"Go ahead," Barney told him. "In another twelve months the mill will be crushing thousands of tons of cane. Our Board has indentured a hundred or so Japanese to assist the whites in the working of it.

"But you get the store going first or I'll throw my influence against the whole scheme. One pub gives us enough trouble, let alone two. These damn-all low whites will sell the booze to the Kanakas."

Biddow left them to their palaver. He had to get off to Port Denham with a cartload of pumpkins and sweet potatoes, to catch the following day's trip up over the range by Barney's teamsters. Besides, a load of goods needed bringing for his holding, not least among them being tobacco for his Kanakas.

Midnight before he returned, dead tired. He took a shower and got quietly into bed.

Blanche wakened but, hearing his signs of weariness, lay still. She tried to go off to sleep again but, instead, a simmering unrest gradually took possession of her. An unrest compounded of angry impatience with her husband's fatigue, fear and, shortly, even horror of what this way of life, in the light of that evening's experience, might portend for her.

To say that Blanche had been bored that evening would be a gross understatement. Consuelo had retired early to bed. The agent's departure had followed, unregretted. Then had ensued a couple of hours of deadly dullness and flatness for Blanche, hours which were one long simulation of interest in topics of conversation, farm, family and national issues, which were the essence of tedium to her. At an early hour, judged by her customary standards, she had asked to be excused on the ground of fatigue.

Now, lying in the dark, she asked herself how she could possibly endure, how sustain, an interminable succession of such evenings. No plays, no dances, no congenial friends!

Her lips twisted in savage cynicism as she got around to recalling the brilliant hopes, the sweeping self-confidence, with which in the long ago she had snatched Biddow out of his "stick-in-the-mud" job as secretary to Dad Hilliard and set him on the road to "fame".

She recalled, too, her father's: "You might find you have bitten off more than you can chew, my girl. An efficient jobber, Biddow. Does as he's told. Takes direction. But no legs of his own to stand on."

And she, Blanche, had laughed and said negligently: "He is the nicest and handsomest man in Brisbane."

"Maybe. Maybe not." Oh yes, Dad Hilliard had tried to warn her! "He is certainly one of the brainiest men in Brisbane. Trouble is: he's the armchair philosopher type. A negative type. You try to force him out of his mould and you may break him."

The darkness hid the shameful blush that suffused Blanche from head to foot as a lightning review of the intervening years swept before her. She had been shamed by his shame! His shame in the eyes of her parents. Shamed worst of all by her own ignominious inability to cast loose from him nor yet to let him alone. To let him alone! She would never forget those moments when, after her most scathing and terrible attack, he had looked at her with eyes black with pain and yet in some unfathomable way remote and said quietly: "Why don't you go away from me? All I have ever asked from life was to be let alone."

It had been beyond her. It had cowed her utterly for a time. Blunted the barbs of frustration and hate and left her love for him more nearly pure than it ever had been before. And on top of her chastened mood had come the visit of the Callaghans and Barney's suggestion, inspired, Blanche very well knew, by her father, that Biddow make north.

And Blanche, still spiritually aghast before the blast of that "Why don't you go away from me?" fumbling in bewilderment at the very idea that anyone—let alone he—should prefer her room to her company, had agreed.

It is true that she had gathered no real idea of what the venture entailed, despite Barney's plain statement of facts. Her mental vision, enfevered by the shock of Biddow's blow, and his following attitude of sustained coldness, of passive resistance to her approaches, had by-passed the prospect of pioneering rigours to centre on her concept of the living conditions of "big" people like the Callaghans.

And with her there had remained a picture of Consuelo as she had looked when passing through Brisbane, homeward bound with Mary, Barney and Bert after a protracted visit the trio had undertaken to Cuba and Jamaica. Consuelo the flashing *señora*, not beautiful but exotic, alluring, exciting. Consuelo laughing as she lisped incipient English. Consuelo with her jewels, her trunks of gorgeous clothes, her mantillas, her dainty shoes. Consuelo renouncing the ordered luxury of her wealthy parents' home to accompany Bert Callaghan, dull by name and nature, to Blanche's sophisticated cognizance, into exile.

This picture of Consuelo had helped Blanche quite a lot in coming to an agreement, providing a colourful frame for a decision that arose out of stress and fear. It was evocative of dream pictures of rambling plantation homes, in which hospitality was enshrined and laughter and gaiety everlasting.

Biddow had snatched at the chance, snatched at it with an eagerness and relief so profound that, before he left Brisbane, Blanche had lapsed from a hopeful spirit of co-operation into resentful neutrality. She was defeated by Biddow's naïve pleasure in anticipation, which she could not nail down to a show of regret at leaving her, no matter how strategically she manœuvred. Their parting had been on his part almost perfunctory, on hers an ordeal of restrained angry passion which, with him gone, had burst into a furious denunciation of Biddow, his concerns, her family and life's "devilish trickery" in general. She had gone about the home of her parents, to which Biddow's repeated failures had returned her, like a termagant brooding revenge.

But a year is a long time. Long enough for the basic love between them to have triumphed over humiliations and shames and left them both receptive to the future's moulding hand.

Before half the year stipulated as essential for Biddow's preparations to receive his family had gone by, Blanche would have joined him. But Biddow had insisted on her adherence to the original programme. The hardships, the manual toil, the steaming heat of the jungle, were sweating out of him the pestilences of the past, and he felt that he must have that year to himself. Fear of Blanche's reactions to the wilderness, fear of the dutiful note in her letters, actually her prideful response to the aloof wariness of his own few scholarly screeds, made him dread the time of reunion even while he longed for the bliss of her caresses.

Blanche's first impressions of "bush life", as she termed it, had been good enough, as we have seen, to send Biddow's spirits sky-high. The metamorphosis effected in Consuelo had shocked her, it was "mortifyingly comic", she had told him, but once assimilated had been forgotten.

The Callaghan home and estate had also come up to her dreams. Given a home of her own on that same scale, with a good riding horse and a phaeton, Blanche felt she really could manufacture a passable social round, an existence near enough to her past to be livable.

The primitiveness of Biddow's selection had given her her first knock. Years, it had seemed, the expenditure of vast sums of money, surely stood between her and the beginnings of an independent "civilized" life. And on top of it had come the infinite boredom of evening in the Callaghan home, so that now she saw her immediate future as a yawning gulf of barren futility. *What* could she do with her days and nights?

Blanche fell into an unutterable depression. A mood so new to her that it, too, made her fear. It was so distinct and different from the infelicitous luxury of self-pity to which she had commonly resorted to in the past. Self-pity was a kind of strength. It was interesting, too. It carried her on from crisis to crisis, from anger to infliction of pain, to sexual abandon. Self-pity left no room for boredom.

But depression was corrosive and destructive. It weighed her down.

Suddenly she flung herself round to the man beside her and whispered urgently: "Ranny, Ranny, I hate this place! I am afraid!"

Biddow was awake and responsive to her embrace almost before the words were out of her mouth. He did not hear those words. Did not get their meaning. He felt only the clasp of her arms, the pressure of her body to his. He simply accepted her reproach as a token of wifely solicitude and desire. Had he heard them, had he heard that word "afraid" on the lips of the woman he had known only as impregnable, the repository of any and every mood except womanly fear, perhaps the basis would have been laid for a clear course of action in the future. But Biddow did not hear it. He simply yielded to her, petted her and then returned instantly to slumber.

This cured her depression like magic but left her unsatisfied and, as a result, wounded, and, before very long, critical. She dragged through the mesh of her mind incident after incident till, with the sharpened senses attendant upon restless, angry wakefulness in the night, she got around to despising herself for her outburst in respect of her own responsibility for Biddow's inefficiency. A stupid impulse! Further, she recognized the spring from which that outburst had fountained. With the self-analytical and self-critical faculty inseparable from egoism when a powerful intelligence goes with it, assisted by stabs of intuitive divining, she recognized its source as her own subtle, all-pervasive jealous conceit. She just *had* to be the pivot upon which the whole man revolved!

Cynically she permitted her apprehensions to surge around her. She was no more responsible for his actions than he was for hers. People remained as they were born. Fundamentally, temperament, the basic life force, remained more or less static. Had not she seen the steadfastness of born characteristics among her friends? Her own family? in herself? Could she delude herself into believing that her own dominant personality might alter? No! Circumstances might modify, divert, experience might dictate caution and teach suppression, but conversion—*no*. Blanche smiled savagely into the dark.

Biddow, like herself, would remain fundamentally that which he had always been. Kind men remained kind through thick and through thin and vice versa. Active men did not grow lazy. They pined if deprived of a channel of activity. Vital people remained vital, the slack remained slack. And neither could sages convert into Simple Simons nor "armchair philosophers" develop into practical men. At the same time, Blanche grudgingly conceded that no one had the right to call upon them to do so. The variety of society's needs provided unlimited scope for all sorts and conditions of men.

This last year of Biddow's experience, then, what did it add up to, apart from the revelation of an ability to sweat and endure like any Kanaka? Barney Callaghan and that young man, Grey, had stood beside him, advising and directing.

But if he had to stand on his own feet again, make his own decisions and resolve them? What then? Maybe growing sugar was simple. Maybe initiative was outside its province. Unessential.

Here, Blanche's cynical mood flared into a fury of rebellion against the whole present and future set-up. And particularly against her own persistent, demanding love for "the fellow" lying beside her. The depth of her rage can be measured by the fact that out of it she fetched a vulgarity of expression quite foreign to her hitherto fastidious tongue.

"I'll be darned if I'll put up with it!" she hissed into the dark. "I'll *make* him alter! I'll do *some*thing! There's *some*thing I'll find to do!"

CHAPTER VI

WHEN BIDDOW DRAGGED HIMSELF FROM HIS BED AT DAYBREAK and went out into the kitchen he was surprised to find Cindie there, busily engaged about the colonial oven.

"I am getting you a proper breakfast this morning, Mr. Biddow," she said swiftly, flushing up in fear of a rebuff.

"But that is not necessary." He looked displeased. "Is it my wife's orders?"

"No, oh no! But—didn't Mrs. Biddow ask you something last night, Mr. Biddow?"

"Ask me something?" He frowned. "What are you talking about?"

His coldness, and her mistress's apparent non-observance of her given word, together reduced Cindie to a condition in which she could only stand and stammer.

That released his innate friendliness. He smiled at her and said quietly: "Tell me what it is all about, Cindie."

"Mrs. Biddow said she would ask you if I might go and work in the gardens with you." Her words came with a rush.

"Oh! I came home too late for talk last night, Cindie." His eyes brightened. "But that would be a great help to me, Cindie. If you are not wanted here."

"Mrs. Biddow said it would be all right if you approved."

"That's fine. But it would be a terribly long day, Cindie. You couldn't stick out a whole day. Can you ride? But of course you can't."

"Mr. Biddow, let me have a go at the whole day. Please! I'm in the way here. The children prefer Funwala's company to mine."

"All right. Do you want to come to-day?"

"Oh yes. I put on the shortest skirt I've got. See." Far from seeing, Biddow delicately averted his eyes. "And I've cooked you a good breakfast, Mr. Biddow."

"Well, that's one thing you needn't bother about again. The field cooks are good cooks, Cindie. You eat that yourself. Lo How's feelings might be hurt if I didn't eat the breakfast he will have prepared for me."

"Does that matter?" Cindie looked surprised.

Biddow gave her a glance of displeasure and said distantly: "Be ready in twenty minutes."

The usual sunniness of August weather held. Bouncing along the track in the buckboard, Cindie was more than content to hold her tongue and assimilate the loveliness and freshness of her surroundings. The forest hummed and sang with insect life. The configuration of the country was sublime and Cindie found herself longing for a vocabulary that would do it justice. Lonegan, a great mountain that stretched for miles along the coast, was decorated with a number of knife-edged peaks linked by plateaux. The girl's lips, as perfectly chiselled as Biddow's own, but, unlike his, firm to a fault and formidable, curled with secret satisfaction at the promise she extracted from her release from domesticity into this wild and uncommensurable existence.

The sight of the Kanakas at work excited her. Biddow pulled the horses up beside the vegetable gardens and, jumping down, bade her do likewise. "If you will bag the sweet bucks for me as I dig them, Cindie, we could have pretty well the whole lot of them ready for the boat to Pearltown to-morrow."

Cindie did not want to bag potatoes. She wanted to dig in the rich black soil. But not until two hours had gone by and Biddow was fain to straighten his back occasionally did she pluck up courage enough to propose that she also take a fork.

"I would really like to, Mr. Biddow. That's easy work, you know, compared with some housework."

To her surprise he took that statement seriously. "You mean that, Cindie? Is housework really hard?"

"Of course, Mr. Biddow. Some of it, at any rate."

"All right. You will find a fork in the Kanakas' hut."

Not long before Cindie's back began to ache, her limbs to feel leaden. Biddow's glances at her became a little worried as he noted the sweat gathering and dropping, gathering and dropping, from her face and from beneath her rolled-back sleeves.

At nine o'clock he relinquished his fork. "Time for a spell, Cindie." He shouted to the Kanakas, who dropped their implements as one man and started towards their hut.

Cindie, on trembling legs, made for the grass in the shade of the trees and dropped upon it. She would dearly have loved to respond to its invitation to lie down and press her cheek into its coolness, but did not dare to so challenge decorum. She sat stiffly, mopping her brow and wondering if, after all, she had made a mistake.

When the Kanakas had boiled the billy, Biddow brought her a tin mug full of tea, milkless and sugarless, to which he added a sandwich from the store brought from Palmer Estate with them. Biddow then sank down upon the grass at some distance from her to take his rest. The Kanakas lounged near their hut.

Fifteen minutes' spell and then back to the job. "Better call it a day for digging, Cindie," Biddow told the girl. "No sense in overdoing it."

"No, no!" she cried. "I like it. It's doing something! It's real work!"

He glanced curiously at her as he replaced his pipe in his pocket, but made no comment.

By lunchtime Cindie was dazed. Her clothes stuck to her. She almost staggered as she made for the shade of the trees. Sinking down, she laid her head against a log and let the sweat dry on her face.

"You've done enough for to-day," said Biddow, authoritatively, when he brought her lunch to her.

And Cindie agreed, for at that moment she felt she might never stand upright again.

But when the time came she trailed him back to the job and began to bag the potatoes. To Biddow's objection she gave the short reply: "I feel good again, now."

But the act of bagging soon palled upon her, so, with a resolute: "I must work, too," she took up her fork. And thereafter they toiled side by side, through the worst of the afternoon's heat and into the comparative relief of its declining.

On the return journey to Palmer Estate that evening, Cindie had to cling to the seat of the buckboard to avoid being thrown out. Her body felt battered and bruised. But her mind was filled with satisfaction as a deep well with cooling waters. A lifetime of growth seemed to separate her from the day's beginning. She felt a man among men!

The sense of freedom persisted while she bathed and put on a clean frock and enabled her, for the first time, to take her place at the table in the company of her mistress consciously devoid of a sense of incongruity and submission.

Mary and Consuelo spoke admiringly of her initiative and sympathetically of her obvious fatigue. Barney joked about her fitness for the life of a farmer's wife. Blanche glanced at her from time to time, smiled a little, frowned, and kept silent. But after the meal, when Cindie rose to help Consuelo, as usual, with the coffee, and the latter checked her with: "Not to-night, Cindie. You are tired. Toby will help me to-night," Blanche, with a slight edge to her tone, commented: "Quite the heroine to-night, Cindie."

But how glad was Cindie when she woke the next morning to realize that the day was Sunday and she might rest her aching limbs in the natural course of events! The habit of years caused her to rise from her bed at an early hour but she felt no inclination to go off with Biddow when he left, later than usual, to spend the day carting the sacks of vegetables to the down-river jetty from which the farmer's produce was lightered down to Pearltown.

With her new sense of importance a guide to action, Cindie got herself breakfast in the kitchen, where the white women generally prepared their own meals, and then strolled out into the yard. She entered the field kitchen and watched the cooks preparing the late Sunday morning breakfast for the white workers and the Kanakas. Already, at that hour, Yamada was taking great slabs of bread from a brick oven built into a wall. Beside it stood an enormous colonial oven, topped with iron bars upon which stood a boiler full of rice. A frying pan was loaded with pork chops for the white workers and Funwala, who ate with these. Funwala was required to live up to the distinction of being Mary Callaghan's protégé.

Cindie noted the shelves laden with huge tins, the sacks of flour and rice. She made a mental note of everything, anticipating the time when she herself, in the Biddow household, would be more intimately connected with like arrangements.

Yamada ignored Cindie's presence, but not so Lo How. The Chinese grinned at her affably, and when she poked into a bag of rice and allowed the brown grains to trickle through her fingers, he came and stood beside her. "You likee lice?" he asked gaily.

"It grows here, doesn't it?" said Cindie.

"Yes, yes. So so. Lice on the hills." Lo How waved his arms indefinitely. "Not in swamps, like in my country. On side of hill. Damn funny." He gave Cindie a sly glance. "You work on farm yesterday. You grow lice, Missie?"

"You mind your own business." Cindie spoke with asperity, but as she turned and looked full into the Celestial's broad ugly face she was unable to refrain from emulating his grin. "Do you do the cooking and Yamada the baking?" she asked him.

"Oh yes. Yamada, he the bread and cake man. He learn." Lo How's tone was subtly jibing. The drawling emphasis he gave to the word "learn" brought him a glance from Yamada like a knife thrust.

"You make good bread, Yamada," Cindie stated. No reply. The Japanese stolidly continued his task of upending the cartwheels of bread upon a table against the wall. Lo How laughed softly and padded out of the kitchen.

Cindie followed him. She watched him prepare the primitive dining-room for the men's meal. For the white workmen and Funwala he set out the table tools and dishes in the conventional manner, but for the Kanakas he simply threw them on to the table in a heap.

Wandering further afield, Cindie found herself entangled in a stream of coloured men coming up towards the house for their breakfast. Her first impulse was to avoid them by striking out into the gardens, but on second thoughts, conjuring up a new boldness, she held to her course, ignoring the aloof glances of some, the interest of others, the sly lewdness of a small minority.

While yet at some distance from the shacks of the married couples she heard the shrill voice of Mary the Kanaka raised in anger. She slackened her steps. Was the black woman scolding her husband? Even as she asked herself that question Tommy came leaping through the doorway of the hut with his hands up to shield his head. A tin dish followed him, flying through the air to strike exactly where he had, evidently, antici-pated: on his head. At the sight of Cindie he arrested his plunging momentum, grinned shamefacedly, and mumbled: "She good shot, my Missis."

Mary herself followed the dish as far as the doorway. There, ignoring Cindie's presence, she flailed the air with her fists and launched at Tommy a fresh stream of invective in a hotch-potch of English and Island tongues. Tommy, assuming an air of dignity and long-suffering calm, raised his right hand and held it poised against her, a silent injunction to desist.

The picture the two of them presented, the virago of a woman thrusting forward from the doorway, her big body shaking with gusty fury, her eyes gleaming and wild, and the man in the guise of an admonitory apostle, sent Cindie off into a peal of laughter. At it, Mary shut up like a trap, then, drawing herself together, uttered a resounding, atrocious oath, spat in Cindie's direction, swung round and vanished into the hut.

Tommy dropped his hand, shook his head sadly and turned to Cindie. "Missie, I ask you excuse my Missis. She always the bush woman."

"You're a fool to put up with that," snapped Cindie angrily.

"Missie, I gotta put up with it." Tommy's head still wagged sorrowfully. "I marry her the Christian way. God, he look heart belonga me. He know I not happy. But He say: 'Till death do us part.' Maybe she die some time." Hopefully. "You think?"

"Yes. And maybe you'll die yourself. How would you like that?"

"Ah!" Tommy's head was now nodding. "Then I cross the shinin' river to the golden sands."

"Golly! You go to church, do you?"

Tommy drew himself up. "I preacher, Missie. Methodist man. This mornin' I preach to de flock. My spirit belong God."

"Oh! . . . All right." Cindie felt uncomfortable and wanted to get away. She moved forward. Tommy made her a sycophantic bow.

Minnie, the Aborigine woman next door, was waiting for Cindie with a happy grin wreathed about her blackened teeth and pipe stem. From within her hut there came the sound of a mouth organ softly played. Taking her pipe from her mouth, Minnie jerked it towards Tommy and cackled: "He Barney's boss. He boss the niggers in the paddocks. He preacher, too. He tell the niggers, the damn Kanakas, the glory road, and make them sing hallelujah. But Mary, she boss him. She teach him the glory road. . . . Say!" Like the flick of an eyelid she dropped subject and facetiousness together. "Say! You work in garden. She make you, that flash one?"

Sheer astonishment made Cindie stammer: "No! Of course not!"

Within the hut the music came to an abrupt end and almost simultaneously a young Kanaka, a mere youth, appeared in the doorway and stared at Cindie. She stared back. Minnie's eyes followed hers.

"He my husband," she stated, complacently. "He make damn good music."

"What!" Cindie was scandalized. "Your husband! He's only a boy!"

"He old enough," said Minnie, tersely. She dropped her eyes, smiled significantly, returned her pipe to her mouth and flashed a lubricous glance up at Cindie. With scarlet face the girl swung on her heel and hurried back towards the house. The old beast! She would take jolly good care to keep *her* at a distance in the future.

CHAPTER VII

AT THE BREAKFAST TABLE, HOWEVER, BARNEY PROPOSED THAT they all go down to the plantation to hear Tommy take the morning service. And in honour of her guests, as a sort of celebration, the Little Fella would take her violin and play a tune or two. "That all right, Mother?" Barney asked.

It was all right. "I usually play a tune or two for the Kanakas if anything special occurs," Mary told Blanche. "That's about all I can manage with the fiddle nowadays. Simple tunes to please simple folk."

"It pleases me, too, Old Woman," said Barney. Then to Blanche: "The only way I can get a tune out of her now is to share it with the niggers."

Blanche was amazed to find that the Callaghans arrayed themselves very smartly indeed before setting out for the service. Consuelo came from her room in flowing cream lace draperies that refined the clumsiness of her figure, lace mantilla about her head and high scarlet comb. In her hand she carried a jewelled rosary. Mary Callaghan put on a black velvet dress, boned to the figure, high necked, skirt trailing on the ground. Barney and Bert wore waistcoats, an article of apparel considered the prerogative of the "toff" and even by that class reserved for special occasions. Little Ricardo was dressed in a black velvet toreador suit, with a scarlet, silk-lined cloak thrown over one shoulder. Esme, the toddler, was to remain at home with Toby.

It was Ric's flamboyant appearance, preceding that of the adults, that apprised Blanche, as she lolled in a low chair on the front veranda, of what was toward. She shot out of the chair, called to Cindie, who was seated in the garden with a book, to bring the children, quickly, and made for her room. Mad, of course. Incomprehensibly stupid, but at least a chance to dress up.

She chose a frock of Indian muslin, a florid confection with every frill inset with fine torchon lace, a white straw hat of shoulder width with a side elevation and trimmings of ostrich plumes, a pair of white kid buttoned boots, and a long-handled white muslin parasol.

"Get Irene into her best mervelo, Cindie," she enjoined, as she tugged at the strings of her corsets to attain to her regulation twenty-inch waist measurement. "And Randy into his sailor suit."

When she made her appearance before the Callaghans, with her parasol daintily slanted in one hand and Titian-haired Irene held by the other, the plantation folk were startled by her superb beauty. Consuelo gave out little exclamations of pleasure and Barney held aloft his Sunday cigar to shout: "By God, you do look a snorter! A regular beaut. . . . Eh, Mother?"

"Yes, indeed." Mary laughed and took up her violin. "We must go. Where is Cindie?"

"Run and tell Cindie to hurry, Randy," said Blanche, graciously. And little Randy, reluctantly withdrawing his fascinated eyes from his mother, ran.

"Do you take part in this—er—service?" Blanche asked nervously, as the party walked across the back lawn. "I am not a Catholic, you know, Mrs. Callaghan," she added, her eyes on Consuelo's rosary. "I took it that we were only going to look on."

"The service is not Catholic, my dear. Tommy is a Methodist, but he conducts his service, I fear, much in his own inspired way. We believe, Barney and I, that our Faith is wide enough to cover all sincere approaches to God. And it is most important that we set the example of respect for all religion to the Kanakas."

Blanche, seeing a white workman preceding them, asked further: "And the white workmen also attend this Kanaka service?"

"No, by cripes, they don't, as a rule," Barney answered. "They are scoffers and heathens, the jokers. Bill there, I know what's bitten him this morning. He's got wind of our going. His mates have gone off to the hills with their guns long since and usually he goes with them."

Not only Barney's male Kanakas and Minnie the Aborigine woman were assembled in a grassy space between the huts on the bank of the stream, but Biddow's six Kanakas besides.

These, newly arrived in the company of a Palmer Estate native sent to escort them, made a little separate group, with Tirwana, like an ebony statue, standing with cold pride in their midst. The big Tanna was still clothed in singlet and trousers only, but to-day the singlet was new and the trousers white duck. All the Kanakas were dressed in their Sunday best, in the majority of cases slop-made dark trousers, white cotton shirt with collar and tie, and straw "sailor" or slouch hat. Some added a coat. All were barefoot.

As the house party came up, Tommy stepped forward to meet them and, concertina under one arm and Bible in hand, made them a sweeping bow. Those of Barney's men who had been seated on the grass rose up and with their fellows, hat in hand, chanted: "Good morning, Boss. Good morning, Mrs. Mary. Good morning, Mr. Bert and Mrs. Bert. Good morning, Mrs. Biddow. Good morning, Missie."

With each repetition of the phrase the whole lot of them swayed towards the person addressed. Cindie could not suppress a nervous giggle. Blanche was impressed and pleased with what she took to be a demonstration of semi-feudal fealty.

With their white superiors seated on wooden forms placed for them to one side, Tommy stepped out in front of his black fellows and shouted: "'Tention!" Slowly, with closed eyes, he began to sway the concertina. At first only negative strains came from it, soft and low, then it began to liven up, to take on volume, and soon there was pouring from it, in shivering ecstasy, the opening bars of the hymn, *Art thou weary, art thou languid*. The tune of one stanza Tommy played through to completion, then, after a pause, during which his eyes opened wide upon his congregation, he raised the concertina in his arms to their utmost extent, swept it down almost to the grass and round in a circle. And as one man, beginning softly and sadly, with feeling that gained and gained in intensity and a restraint that gradually gave way and built up to tremendous power and volume, the black men unloosed in song all the yearnings and aches of exiles who only in these moments of emotionalism became most deeply conscious of their limitations and woes. With exquisite harmony the deep bass voices mingled with the baritones and tenors, creating a

volume of rolling sound comparable to the music of a grand
cathedral organ.

Before it had gone very far Consuelo dropped to her knees
and began counting her beads. Tears rolled from beneath her
closed eyelids. Mary Callaghan gave a soft exclamation,
started forward to check her, then thought better of it and
drew back. She guessed that Consuelo, worried as she had
been lately about the effect of the revolution in Cuba on the
fortunes of her parents, and further distressed by her own
pregnancy, had yielded to nostalgic yearnings for her homeland evoked by the rendering of the old favourite plantation
hymn.

Blanche was amazed. She herself possessed a fairly good
contralto voice and had been trained to use it. Also, there
had been instilled into her by a teacher of note a respect for
musical gifts of any kind. But what impressed her most was
the common character of this considerable talent. *All* the
Kanakas could sing! All of them could harmonize! All but
one, anyhow, and perhaps he had a cold or something. She
marvelled inwardly and thought: the pity of it! If all this
group could sing, then all or most of their fellows must possess
the capacity, too. All that music withheld from the world!
With wondering eyes she watched the Kanakas, noting the
rapt looks, the natural dignity and reverence of their pose, and
suddenly it struck her that the majority of them were good
looking. That ebony giant, standing a little apart, the only
man among them not singing, he was *quite* fine-looking. But
surely she had seen him before! Why, yes, he was one of
Randolph's niggers! How like a Jew the fellow was! Had
sense enough not to wear those stupid shirts and hats. He
would have distinct possibilities on a concert platform. That
was, if he *could* sing. Impudent looking fellow, though.
Needed to be taught a lesson in humility, she'd say. Yes,
really they were a good-looking lot—must have brains of a
sort, too, to sing like that.

But maybe they sang like the birds, Blanche's thoughts ran
on. Yes, that was probably the real explanation. They sang
like the birds, with no real wit behind it. And all of one
species, too, again like birds. All canaries could sing. The
males, that was. Blanche laughed to herself as she thought

that crows could only caw and likened most whites to the carrion bird in that connection.

To Cindie Comstock the singing was a revelation. A revelation of things in existence on earth, if not in heaven, that added up to imponderables and mysterious dispensations. She was well able to appreciate the quality of the singing and, like her mistress, she was most struck by the catholicity of the gift. But, unlike Blanche, she felt humbled and chastened by the manifestation. Humbled by its intrinsic beauty and chastened by a sense of shame in her own hitherto natural and simple assumption of innate superiority to these black-skinned folk. Why, she thought, there must be something wonderful and unique about a people who *all* could sing! Tirwana! He did not sing. "I'll bet he *can* sing, though," Cindie told herself. There was a reason for Tirwana's silence, she would bet. There was something on his mind!

His mind! For the first time Cindie thought of the Kanakas as human beings like herself. People with minds. She thought of them as *men*, but in a manner divorced from the significance given to that presumption by Mary Callaghan. "They must think and feel like I do," she thought.

The startling nature and wonder of her conclusion reflected itself in a physical reaction. In a stiffening of her body and an irradiation of her face. Wonder and deep, pervasive pleasure in making what she thought was an original discovery kept her still as a forest pool till the rolling waves of organized sound died away. Here was something sweet and lovely added to the sense of growth and liberation she had garnered from her primitive contact with the soil. She would have liked the singing to go on and on, to go on yielding up those sweet and poignant messages of faith, hope and charity, of sorrow and love and pain.

And Tommy's preaching struck her just as forcibly, though with vastly different import. The hymn concluded, Tommy placed his concertina on the ground, and took his Bible from his pocket. He did not attempt to read from it. Tommy's scholarship, begun at an island Mission and self-continued ever since, was insufficient for that. He simply selected a text: "Know ye not that the unrighteous shall not inherit the Kingdom of God," repeated it three times, and then, keeping his finger at the place, used the Book to weight and accentuate his gesticulations.

To begin with, it seemed to Cindie that his discourse was like another form of singing. The "glory" words and phrases he used, shining river, golden sands, open your hearts to the Lord, lift your voices, sinful ones, be like unto a little child, and so on, these sounded to the girl like singing. But soon the sonorous declaiming lost much of its strength and savour by virtue of the fact that, from where she sat, Cindie could see Tommy's wife, Mary, at work in her garden, shovelling and digging, weeding and uprooting.

Further, as Tommy with mounting fervour sung the praises of the Lord, and added extempore injunctions to his fellows to be "thankful for da riches de good Lord has piled on to your sinful backs", and failed not to scarify laziness and sloth and foreshadow the after-death torments awaiting troublemakers and the ungrateful, as this sort of thing went on, Cindie began to feel a vague disquiet. She let her eyes dwell upon the company of Kanakas. Some stood, others sat on the grass, but all were deeply attentive to Tommy's emoting and orating.

Tirwana? Yes, he was attentive, too. But—— Now, what did that expression on Tirwana's face mean? His gaze on Tommy was sorrowful, and as Cindie watched him Tirwana shook his head in sad reproof.

There was no mystery about the expression on the white workman's face. As he sprawled on the bank of the stream his eyes upon Tommy were openly mocking. His lip curled in a cynical smile. Cindie's disquiet developed into reflection. There was something she did not like about this precious religion of Tommy's. Something Tirwana did not like. And that white workman, too. But she could not pin that something down, exactly.

Turning her eyes sideways, she carefully scrutinized the members of the house party seated beside her. Blanche was now bored. Cindie knew, though her mistress tried to hide it. The meaning of every nuance of that beautiful face was plain to Cindie. Consuelo sat with lowered eyes, her fingers moving devoutly upon her beads. Barney and Mary wore interested expressions, the expressions of parents indulging their children.

Bert? What was Bert thinking? He sat forward in an easy attitude, his elbow resting on a thigh, his fingers clasped round the stem of his pipe. He puffed away and watched Tommy with noncommittal eyes. Much as though he were watching a not too interesting experiment.

"Sinners and fornicators all," yelled Tommy. "Lay down you sins and come to Christ with me."

Cindie, her eyes again upon the white workman, saw him stretch his mouth and throw back his head in a gale of silent laughter.

"De black man and de white man, together they enter de Kingdom of Heaven. Be ye humble, be ye penitent, do da proper day's work in de vineyards of da boss and de Lord will reward you wid dishes of honey and golden harps and angel's wings."

Tommy stopped abruptly, took a bandanna handkerchief from his pocket, mopped his brow, then turned to Mary Callaghan and said simply: "Mrs. Mary, will you kindly play you instrument for dese humble brothers in sin?"

Mary began on *Nearer, my God, to Thee.* She played the tune right through, thinly but sweetly, and then signalled for the Kanakas to sing. Two more hymns followed, then she played *Home Sweet Home* with variations, and concluded with a rousing Irish Jig. Before she had finished, many of the Kanakas were bobbing and jigging about, their faces aglow, but once the violin was lowered they came quickly to order and stood with lowered heads, hat in hand, while Tommy led them in the Lord's Prayer.

On the way back to the house Mary Callaghan stopped beside the garden of Tommy's hut to have a few friendly words with the preacher's wife. The big island woman straightened her back above the yams she was training to climb a network of sticks and turned to them.

"How's the pig doing?" cried Barney jovially. "All right now?"

Mary snorted. "Pig like his boss," she sneered. "No guts in him." She raised her voice. "He eat all my kaikai but still no guts in him. I kick him into the bush." Then, her eyes on Barney, she appeared to come to a sudden decision. Taking a few steps towards him, she paused, and then, with authoritative gestures and manner, spoke a few terse sentences to Barney in her native tongue.

Barney uttered one deep chuckle, checked himself and turned to his companions. "You go on home," he told them. "I've got a bit of a problem to solve here."

The group moved off, but before they had gone very far Bert turned back. "Want to be in on this," he told his mother, smiling broadly. "The Old Man's got a problem all right."

Disclosures by Bert to Biddow, who had arrived home in time for lunch, soon found their way to Blanche's curious ears. Cindie was curious, too, even to the point of directly questioning Blanche, but her single blessedness, in Blanche's opinion, debarred her from being informed of the reason for what was obviously a crisis in the domestic affairs of Barney's head field man.

When, in the middle of the afternoon, Mary Callaghan went off with Barney to assist in arbitrating between husband and wife, Cindie, by now aware that the whole plantation was humming with joyous palaver over events, became so consumed with curiosity that she descended to making discreet approaches to Toby on the subject. And Toby, having been down to see Minnie for the express purpose of getting progress reports, gleefully rolled her liquid eyes, hopped about a bit and then made a pronouncement so bald and comprehensive that Cindie's moral concepts were shocked to their foundation. Her first impulse was actually to slap the Aborigine's face, but Toby, reacting like lightning to the effect of her words, cried out: "You asked, Missie! You asked!"

A shaken Cindie had the grace to mutter: "So I did. It serves me right."

Toby, however—they were preparing afternoon tea in the kitchen—did not choose to be ignored for long. With an assumption of childish innocence she said plaintively: "You think me bad because I say words white man say. If I say black man's words you no understand."

Cindie had to concede the reasonableness of that. Also, by this time the shock of hearing a spade called a spade, or rather, of hearing Black Mary's opinion of her husband's anatomical and amatory deficiencies plainly stated, had been partly absorbed by a new appreciation of the strangeness of her present conditions, a sense of her own complete ignorance of certain matters. She took care to be on hand with the tea when Mary and Barney returned from the plantation, her eyes and ears attuned to watch and listen.

Nobody objected to her hearing of the decision that had been made.

On the basis of Mary's flat refusal to maintain domestic relations with Tommy, Barney had ordered the Kanaka to move out of the hut they shared and take up living quarters elsewhere. His pig and few belongings would go with him. Mary would return to field work. Barney and his wife were concerned about the blow to Tommy's prestige, as man, foreman, and religious leader. He was terribly upset and probably would not be much good in the fields for some time.

"I wish you would take him over to your place for a few weeks, Biddow," said Barney. "If he stays here he will have a bad spin. The other blokes will poke fun at him. Mary will soon take up with some other bloke and then the affair will be forgotten."

Cindie put in, hesitantly: "But Tommy is married to Mary, Mr. Callaghan, isn't he?"

"Can't help that"—gruffly. "Should never have happened." He threw an accusatory glance at his wife.

Mary sighed. "Yes. I admit you are right, Barney. But Tommy wanted it so much. It will be terribly damaging to his religious beliefs to have the ceremony he set such store by disregarded by both his wife and us."

"But would you allow a married woman to take up with another man?" cried Blanche. "Even a black woman! And with the children around!"

"Mrs. Biddow." Barney spoke sharply. "These people have got their own ideas about marriage. They've got a high moral sense about these things. A damn sight higher than some whites I could name. Mary is honest. We should leave them to their own customs."

Blanche flushed and took him up in a spirited manner. "I can't understand you, Mr. Callaghan! These people, niggers as they are, are married. Yet you would allow the woman to live with another man. That's wickedness. It's sin."

"Allow her, be hanged!" Barney started forward from his

chair, his eyes bulging, his face red with exasperation. "Tell me how I could stop her, even if I wanted to."

"Tut tut," Mary intervened, laughingly. "All this fuss over poor Mary. "

But Blanche pursued the matter as though some secret chagrin, some personal resentment, were involved. "Poor Mary! *Poor* Mary!" she echoed. "Anything but *poor* Mary, I should say! The black trollop ought to be whipped. I can't imagine why you keep her on the place."

Dead silence. Silence and stillness. Biddow stared straight before him, tight-lipped with disapproval. Of the lot of them Cindie was least surprised. Beneath the pressure of her present unprecedented experience Cindie was beginning to assemble into some sort of coherence certain nebulous intuitions which had been laced through and through the six years of her intimate association with Blanche. Almost negligently, and with a little contempt, she told herself: "She's jealous. She doesn't know it but she's jealous, for some reason, of the black woman's rights."

Mary broke the silence. "We have very good reasons for having her about the place, Mrs. Biddow. But for Mary, our dear Consuelo might not be with us to-day."

Blanche, already ashamed and sorry, not for the sentiment but for her breach of good taste, looked startled. "I—I beg your pardon, Mrs. Callaghan."

"Mary is an excellent midwife, Mrs. Biddow. When little Ric was born the doctor was delayed on his way up from Port Denham by floods and, but for Mary, Consuelo would probably not have pulled through."

"Oh!—I'm sorry."

Biddow turned to Blanche then and quietly, but with that deadly note of finality she had heard but seldom and yet knew so well, told her: "You will have to realize that all you can do about conditions up here is learn to accept them. You should have sense enough to know that. You're no fool."

CHAPTER VIII

DURING THE FOLLOWING WEEK BLANCHE WAS TO FIND THAT Callaghan's property was by no means the king pin of Masterman sites for size and up-to-date conditions, though it certainly eclipsed all others for positional beauty. Mary Callaghan, for all her years, could handle her four-in-hand phaeton as well as Barney himself and now, through a succession of visits, she set out to make Blanche known throughout the country-side.

Across the Masterman river lay Glenelg, two thousand acre holding of Darcy Montague, his wife Ellen, and their family of five sons and four daughters. With two daughters-in-law, four sons-in-law, and the round dozen of offspring these could muster, the Montagues were a clan in themselves. The major part of their labour forces were one hundred and fifty Chinese, the remainder being fifty Kanakas.

As with all other holdings of any size in that area, until this present year corn had been the main crop harvested from the few hundreds of acres of cleared land on Glenelg: corn to feed the horses of the teamsters at Port Denham, and the mule teams, up to one hundred strong, that trekked from the coast up over the range to the Tablelands; corn for the provisioning of Pearltown and other settlements down the coast. After corn came extensive banana plantations, rice on the high lands, a little coffee, citrus fruits, mangoes and vegetables.

This year, one hundred acres of Glenelg territory had been planted with cane in preparation for next year's crushing by the mill, the machinery for which was even then on its way out from Scotland. And, again in company with most other holdings, since the ending of the "wet", in April, the Kanakas had toiled at felling the red cedar, pines, oaks and nondescript timbers, to make way for bumper plantations of cane in the ensuing year. At that time, white labour was non-existent on Glenelg, Darcy Montague's sons providing the necessary supervision of the work.

The majority of Glenelg's Chinese were putting in their last year on the estate. The Chinese were inferior to the Kanakas

in respect to work in the sugar. For plantation fruits, grains
and garden produce they were thorough-going agriculturists
and conscientious workers, but as wage workers in the peculiar
conditions of sugar cultivation they came out a bad second.
And, not being indentured, wage workers they must be. The
Chinese refused, in general, to accept contract work, for their
slowness, added to their conscientiousness, made contract work
unprofitable for them.

Montague's small army of Celestials in the main would
return to China, following in the wake of thousands of their
countrymen who, having been lured from their native land by
the promise of wealth from the Mountain of Gold—their homeland name for the mighty Queensland colony—had actually
realized their expectations and, with the goldfields gutted,
returned to their Flowery Land. The failures on the goldfields
had drifted down to the coastal farms, to serve as labourers or
housemen for the planters, or to take up their own plots of
land.

Many of these had settled in the Masterman area as far
back as the 'sixties, and these were now converting to cane
with the same eagerness as the whites. Some of Glenelg's men
would doubtless be employed by these old settlers, for the
Chinese consistently stuck to their own. The remainder?
For the last time on Glenelg they would this year flail the corn
on the drybeds and the rice in the mortars, and, when the
harvest was completed, gather together their meagre store of
possessions and go their ways from the barracks they had for
many years known as home.

Blanche Biddow's first visit to Glenelg took some of the edge
off her discontents. Glenelg had been settled for twenty-five
years and bore the insignia of what in that tropical country
was almost a venerable age. Great mangoes made an avenue
easily five hundred yards long from the outer gate of the homestead up to the gardens and lawns. Groves of the same fruit
trees made shade for a few cattle and several teams of horses
about a paddock that surrounded the long, low, trellised and
creeper-covered dwelling-houses. Two smaller and newer
homes flanked the parent home and all were connected by
concreted yards. Mangoes shaded the barracks of the Chinese,
the thatched huts of the Kanakas, the sheds, stables, and

flailing drybeds. And great poinscianas stretched their mighty curling limbs above the homes and the lawns.

The place was a hive of industry when Mary, with Blanche and the children, drove up. The swipple of the flails wielded by dozens of Chinese resounded from the drybeds, intermingled with outbursts of their Orientals' sharp cacophonous gabble. Two Kanakas were gardening. Black women cackled with laughter and soft intermittent talk as they strung snowy garments upon lines stretched across a side lawn. But as Mary Callaghan's phaeton swung round and pulled up on the concrete beside the steps of the front veranda, activities magically ceased. Brooms, garden scissors and other implements were held poised or dropped, the laundresses, fat and thin, came waddling or running to view at close quarters the new arrivals whose looks, manners, actions and business had been a main topic of query and conjecture in barracks, huts and kitchen for several days past.

Blanche learnt that a "visit" meant spending the best part of a day and often the full evening too, in neighbourly get-together fashion. There was nothing of drawing-room politeness about it. Oh no! The hearty welcome, the more hearty in that the visitors were not expected, was succeeded by removal of hats and gloves. Then came morning "tea", piles of scones, bread, meats, cakes and tarts set out on the dining-room table and partaken of by all those family members within hearing of a metal triangle resoundingly beaten. Followed a do-as-you-please routine that consisted chiefly of wandering about the house and grounds, in haphazard conversation with whoever happened to fall into line with your step at the moment. The children of the clan were given a day's respite from lessons in honour of Irene and Randy and to enable their teacher, a daughter-in-law, to participate in the dispensing of hospitality.

Visits to smaller farms followed. To homes of struggling settlers that were little more than huts. These appalled Blanche, who inwardly vowed that the inmates of such places would see precious little of her. There was a visit to Port Denham, a visit entailing jolting and jerking over twelve miles of rough bush track and the fording of the Little Masterman River.

The town of Port Denham, with its population of three thousand souls, sprawled across a low-lying narrow strip of land that thrust out into the waters of the Long Lagoon, and up the slopes of a small rocky hill that perched upon its snout. The northern beach of the strip curved to form a salt-water inlet, partly lined with crocodile-infested mangrove swamps. The southern beach, half a mile distant, gave on to woodlands comprised of mingled eucalyptus, casuarinas, and rain-forest trees, and was itself of a nature so wide, hard, long and alto-gether lovely as to function as a race-course and pleasure-ground for all the far northern settlements.

From Fort Denham a road cut inland through the forest to a teamsters' camp called the Fourmile. From there it thrust towards a second teamsters' camp situated near the base of the range, up a spur of which, the Rump, the teams of horses, mules and bullocks clambered to serve the mining settlements and incipient farming communities above. The Sevenmile, this second camp was called. There, the four-ton, four-wheeled wagons were prepared for the terrific climb. Sixteen horses to a team, sixteen to eighteen bullocks. Yet no one team could do the job. Two full teams, of horses or bullocks, were required to be harnessed together for the negotiation of the Rump by each wagon. Thus it was essential for the teamsters to travel in pairs. Mules were used, as a rule, for packs only.

In the country between Fourmile and Sevenmile, Barney Callaghan's initial holding, now occupied by his second son, Jack, was located. Not farmer only, but teamster-mailman for the coast and Tablelands besides, was Jack.

The round of calls Mary Callaghan made at the Port, on her own and Blanche's behalf, were without exception either boring or dismaying to the younger woman. The very appear-ance of the town depressed her. The weatherboard homes and business premises were shanty-like and unspeakably drab to Blanche, fresh from one of the smartest homes in Brisbane's smartest residential suburb. And the people! She was nervous and reserved with them. She tried not to be condescending yet hardly knew how otherwise to behave with people who appeared to be of the servant class or newly risen from it. Their casual manners and ways were to her a symptom of devitalization. The poor showing made in her eyes by the people of the Port, in comparison with the farming community, almost reconciled Blanche to a wilderness existence.

She would have been mightily surprised if she could have listened-in to some of the remarks and discussions corollary to her visit. Quite a number of the thirty-five hotel and pub bars made the family and political history of Blanche's father, "old Tom-bloody-Hilliard", the day's conversational relish. The main Brisbane daily, *The Courier*, and weekly newspapers besides, kept every man in the Port informed on political events. Hilliard, generally recognized to be the strongest influence behind the Premier in the then tory Cabinet, was more especially the target for local interest because of his and Barney Callaghan's joint historic strike on the nearby Palmer goldfields. More than one Port Denham man had worked on the goldfields with Hilliard. They had followed his evolution from fire-eating radicalism in his early mining and prospecting days, through the whole gamut of political hedging and apostasy which had culminated in his elevation to power.

Yet, through all the bitter and cataclysmic strike struggles of the early nineties, struggles between the tory Government on the one hand—acting on behalf of banking and pastoral interests involving its own members and supporters—and the shearers and other categories of workers on the other, throughout all those years "old Tom-bloody-Hilliard" had retained a measure of popular admiration for the very chicanery by means of which he had hidden his controlling hand. Though Ministry after Ministry had fallen into its own stink, borne down by the weight of graft and boodling so flagrant that even judges and the better elements among the employing class itself had sided with the workers in their struggles, "old Tom-bloody-Hilliard" had maintained a semblance of popularity even with many of the workers upon whom his unseen hand had enforced killing wage-cuts and conditions little better than industrial slavery.

With William Lane, idealistic, perfervid leader of the rising Labour Movement, Hilliard had maintained a friendly connection, inviting Lane to his beautiful home in Brisbane whenever opportunity offered, to discuss with him William Morris socialism, to listen to and blandly comment upon Lane's savage demands for the eradication from the colony of "every dirty skin, black or yellow". In short, to subtly "milk" the man who stood to the great mass of the Queensland workers as a newly-risen Christ, heaven-inspired to lead the colony out of the cesspit of tory-ridden corruption and repression into a decent way of life.

At this time of Blanche's visit to Port Denham, a commission of inquiry into banking scandals had been enforced by popular demand, and Hilliard's name figured prominently in connection with it. His public statement to the effect that he would guarantee a complete clean-up of any "unjustifiable proceedings" had been broadcast. To which the more seasoned men of the Labour Movement, still licking their wounds after their 1894 defeats, gave back the hollow laugh of furious and impotent understanding. . . .

Yes, Blanche would have been surprised could she have listened-in to some of the comment attendant upon her visit to Port Denham. While the clinking of glasses in the bars made musical accompaniment to cynical disquisition bearing old Hilliard's relation to national issues, the women whose "commonness" had repelled his daughter dived into each other's houses and canvassed her looks, her manners, her past, present and future with eager interest.

Laughter and good humour mingled with sly pokes at her high-and-mightiness. A leading dressmaker forecast innumerable "creations" based upon the model of Blanche's grass-lawn frock and little Irene's elaborate silk. Irene's red hair inspired prolonged rumination and conjecture till, on the following day, that puzzle was solved and relegated to oblivion by a bluff statement from one of the two Port doctors.

"Nothing in it. Common enough. When both parents are very brunette the offspring are often red-headed."

The sum total of her visit to Port Denham was that Blanche surveyed the dwindling orbit of her "possible" world and concluded that if things came to the worst, if the place became absolutely unendurable, she could always insist upon Biddow's selling out and their return to Brisbane. Dad Hilliard would simply *have* to come up to scratch.

Impulsively, when preparing for bed that same night,

Blanche communicated this conclusion to Biddow. And once again she was faced with that hateful note of finality, hateful in that it *only* cropped up, to her way of it, when what it portended was inimical to propositions immutably essential to her own convenience and comfort.

"Don't get ideas like that into your head, my girl," Biddow told her. "This place suits me."

"But what if it doesn't suit me?" she snapped back, on the defensive like a shot.

"I'd be sorry. I'd be very sorry about that, Blanche. I would hate to have to contemplate life here without you."

"But you *would*!" Blanche could scarcely get the words out, for the ghastly fear that again had put its strangling hand upon her heart. "You *would* live here without me! You *could*!"

"Yes. I could. But Love! Can't you try to like this life? These other women, they like it. Look at Cindie. She loves it. She's a farmer already."

"Cindie!" In that one little word was expressed a whole lexicon of scorn and resentment.

"Yes, Cindie." Biddow persisted, doggedly now. "And don't say anything derogatory to Cindie. I won't have it. Now wait a minute! It occurs to me now, Blanche, that it might help you to adjust yourself to the ways of the people here if I tell you something about my own people, my own origin."

"Who cares about your people?" she flamed. "Anyhow, I know about them. Your people were farmers, like these dolts around here." She began to busy herself with clothes, toilette articles, snatching at one thing and then another, keeping her back turned towards him. As he continued to talk her movements became enfevered, uncontrolled.

"Yes, they were farmers, in a way. You have never probed into the matter of my people, have you, Blanche? Frightened you might find something you wouldn't like. And since my parents were dead it didn't worry me. I told you they were market gardeners and I let you think they were in a big way. But they weren't, Blanche. They were in a very small way. My father peddled his vegetables in a basket from door to door. . . ."

Explosive interruption. As though he had been silent, Blanche suddenly burst out with: "Cindie! A farmer! And so she should be! She should be a farmer. She's a servant. My servant. Oh, that you should dare! Dare to compare me with my servant!"

Biddow's eyes upon her became filled with incredulity. His mouth opened. His jaw dropped. But as she continued to fulminate wildly and turn and turn herself about like a panther on the rampage, his features broke up into an embarrassed, naïve smile. He went close to her, followed her about.

"Blanche, don't be *silly*." His embarrassment made his speech aloof, despite his continuing little smile. "You're just being ridiculous. Jealous of Cindie. Blanche——!"

He got no further, for Blanche, uttering one voluptuous, passion-filled: "Oh!" flew to her dressing-table, snatched up a hair brush and whacked him over the head with it.

"That will teach you!" she panted. "That'll teach you to insult me!"

Biddow took the crack with a paralysing sort of amazement. His eyes blinked. His hand went up to his head. Then he stepped backwards and fell, rather than sat, upon the bed. "Cripes, you must be upset," he muttered. Then his voice and manner took on vigour. "But look here, my girl! You do that again and I'll hit you back. I mean it. I'll hit you back and like it."

"You wouldn't dare." Blanche tossed the brush on to the table and spoke curtly. Her knees were trembling, her thoughts were chaos. She got into bed and turned her back while he got in beside her. She lay perfectly still, separated from him, hardly daring to breathe, yet conscious that exultation was rising within her, a wild exultant sense of having hurdled some hitherto unacknowledged emotional barrier. She wanted to laugh. To laugh out of her the strange feeling of satisfaction which yet was exciting and good.

Biddow lay on his back, staring up at the ceiling. Up there two gecko lizards perambulated in search of insect prey. He waited. Waited for that which experience had taught him would surely follow an explosion. This time he would teach her a lesson!

But nothing happened. Blanche continued to lie quite still,

so, rather grumpily, he asked her: "You heard what I said about my people?"

"To the devil with your people." No more.

Biddow's lips tightened. He put out the light, turned on to his side, and prepared to go to sleep. But shortly he gave an involuntary start, turned his head swiftly. It couldn't be!—but it was. Blanche was humming. Softly, almost inaudibly, but none-the-less surely, she was humming to herself in the dark. Queer. Biddow frowned, dug his head into the pillow, pulled the sheet up over his shoulder and dropped off.

CHAPTER IX

CINDIE DID NOT FEEL LIKE A FARMER. SHE FELT, AS TOMMY the Kanaka might have expressed it, like a labourer in the Lord's vineyards. With the sweet potatoes all uprooted and the pumpkins all cut, she went right on into the cane and began chipping: cleaning up between the rows and piling up the earth around the stools.

Biddow laboured with the Kanakas in the saw-pit and at rough hewing the bean-tree slabs. The addition of a very subdued Tommy to his labour forces was to begin with a considerable asset. At week-ends Jeff Grey came over and assisted in the erection of the framework of the house.

Unlike the homes of most other planters in that area, low-lying structures standing upon piles not more than two or three feet high, Biddow's was to follow the pattern of house building general throughout the colony. It would be mounted upon eight-foot piles. That would allow the stabling of his buckboard, and the cart and sulky essential to farm life which were already on their way north, beneath the house until such time as he could manage to put up sheds. When the Kanakas had built their own huts he would use their present shanty for the shelter of his beasts.

By the present of a little extra tobacco and tea the Kanakas were easily induced to put in a fourteen-hour day. Only four months to the "wet", which, if a bad one, would effectively hold up all felling work in the "scrub", as the rain-forest was uneuphemistically termed. And Biddow, in preparation for the '98 crushing, felt obliged to have another fifty acres cleared and ready for the planting in '97, if normal and satisfactory progress was to be made. If his new order of Kanakas came to hand in November, which he hoped for, maybe seventy-five acres would be cleared.

Within a week of Cindie's participation in the work, the social relations between Biddow, the Kanakas and herself had drastically altered. She no longer kept herself separate from the black men, and Biddow from both, at meal times and rest periods. Acting on an impulse that stemmed from a rapidly developing sense of initiative, Cindie decided one morning to make the fire and boil the billy herself. And when that was done she went up and called the men to tea.

"Thanks, Cindie." Biddow appeared not to notice this departure from the normal. So without more ado the girl, having poured the mugs of tea, took up her own and, deliberately seating herself beside Tirwana, began to engage him in conversation. She noticed that Biddow looked mildly surprised, but, further, soon became sufficiently interested in their talk to come over and sit beside them.

The big Tanna answered her questions seriously and with restraint. Occasionally he permitted his eyes to rest upon her in a meditative manner. Where had he come from? How long had he been in Queensland? Why hadn't he returned to his island home at the end of his term of indenture? These and many other questions Cindie asked him.

And the story he told in reply? He had been stolen from his island home at the age of fourteen. And that had served him right, for the elders of the tribe had warned the youths against the blackbirding of the recruiters. They had been warned against approaching the boats and separation from the body of the tribe while the white men were in the vicinity.

"Some boats," Tirwana explained, "would ask for men properly from the chiefs. Would give the paper to sign and make honourable contract. Other boats, they would give the paper to sign everything all right but they would steal the men and women and children, too. Other boats fool all the time and steal all the time. They take with guns, with cheating, and give the drink. They beat men with ropes and starve them on the boat to make them sign the paper."

His own tragedy had resulted from his running down the beach to meet a whale-boat coming ashore and the offering of a coconut to an oarsman. He had been grabbed and hauled into the boat, which had been rapidly shoved off and rowed back to the recruiting vessel.

"My people, they run up and down the beach, crying out. I cried for two days and two nights. For my people and for my island. The food on the boat made me sick. I was sick with the bad smell of everything on the boat. I am afraid of everything. My bones begin to stick out so they cook me some yams and I eat them. I was brought to a town down south. I work there for four years. Always for one man. First six months I look after the women in the house. I sweep the floors, cut the wood and get the eggs, things like that. The Missis, she always good to me. Treat me like son. After six months the boss say to me: You ready to go in paddock now. I use the scarifier, with quiet horse. I liked that. I manage the horse quite well. I never swear at him. I just sing out: Go, horse, and he went. But the time came when the Government, they stop the Kanaka from using the scarifier and plough. They stop them long before, really, but the farmer, he do it all the same, till Government agent came round. He stop me using horses and plough. Say we only to do the labouring work."

"Could you speak any English when you came to Queensland?" asked Cindie, absorbed in his tale.

"No. No Missionary on my island, then. But I talk English in three months. I catch him quick."

"You haven't told me why you didn't return to your island, Tirwana."

"Me too young, at first, to know I could return. The boss, he never tell me. Missis, she always tell me to stay with her, be Christian and go to heaven." Tirwana smiled satirically, drained his mug of tea and took his pipe from his trousers pocket. Changing his tone to fit his contemptuous words, he added: "Heaven look very good to young Island boy lost to his people."

"But you could have gone back afterwards, Tirwana, when you grew older."

"Missie, I did go back." Puffing at his pipe, he rose and signalled to his fellows to get back to work. "I went back. When I was twenty I went back. And when I saw my island coming up outa the sea I cried. I cried to see my people. But the captain, he wouldn't let me go off the boat. He locked me down in the stinking hold, said he would shoot me and feed the sharks if I cry out. I not want to feed shark." A shrug. "I thought better to come back. After next three years I feel Australian. That my story, Missie. Now we work."

"Do you think that is true?" Cindie asked Biddow, who was looking after Tirwana with knitted brows.

"I think so. There's a lot of fuss being made about it. In England, as well as out here. It seems to be pretty general."

"It's terrible! A clever man like Tirwana! He is clever, don't you think, Mr. Biddow?"

"Yes. But at least they are well enough treated once they get here, Cindie. I should think this life would be preferable to savage life, head-hunting and such. But then again—maybe it isn't, to a head-hunter."

"I like this life," said Cindie slowly. "I like it because there's somewhere to *go* in it. It's doing things, it's building. But the blacks! Where are they going? Why should they like it, Mr. Biddow? Work all day. Sleep at night. No wives, no homes, no children, no fun——"

That was the day, as it happened, of Blanche's visit to Port Denham. On the following morning, after a protracted period of brown study on the veranda, Blanche told Mary Callaghan that she would like to ride over and note progress on her future home. And it seemed to Blanche, cantering up the track past the plant cane, that the group consisting of her husband, Cindie and the black men, seated at their morning tea, was quite unnecessarily and disgustingly cosy. A superb horsewoman, and a splendid figure in her riding habit and bowler hat, she cantered up until almost upon them and then drew rein. Upon Biddow, who rose to meet her, she bestowed an exclusive and uncompromising stare.

"Hullo," he said foolishly, made conscious by her presence of a tender spot on his scalp.

"Things seem to be going along very comfortably here," she remarked, unable to keep a tremor out of her voice.

Biddow threw a glance of trepidation at Cindie. "We are just having tea. I'm sorry I can't offer you some."

"Randolph Biddow, are you mad?" Blanche hissed. "Help me down." He moved around the horse and swung her from the saddle. "Now show me how far you have gone with this— this precious house I've got to live in. A hutch, more like." She lifted her long habit from about her boots and marched forward, a little ahead of the man.

She hung around till the Kanakas had started work and Cindie had returned to her chipping. She accepted Biddow's explanation of things without comment, slashing at her boots with her whip, biting her lip, occasionally nodding her head. But at length she asked abruptly: "When shall I be able to move in?"

"That depends on how much comfort you expect. The furniture arrives on the next boat. We are building the big living-room first, this week-end, to store it. Bert is coming over to help. And Grey."

"Yes, yes. And how long before the four rooms are up?"

"A month, probably. Three weeks at the least. But why all this sudden hurry? I thought——"

"I'm sick of hanging round the Callaghans. I want to settle down."

Eventually she rode off, to pull up beside the cane plot and call graciously to Cindie. The girl dropped her hoe and came over to her, slowly, pressing one hand into the small of her back.

"So your back is aching, Cindie. Don't you think you're a fool to carry on with this Kanaka work? You're getting all burnt up. I'm sure we could find something more ladylike for you to do at Palmer Estate."

"I don't want to be ladylike, Mrs. Biddow," Cindie replied bluntly. "And even if I did it doesn't look as though there is going to be much chance of my being anything but a farm-hand once we are settled down here." She looked around her calmly.

"All right. Have it your own way"—curtly. Blanche struck her horse a sharp blow with her whip.

Thereafter, almost every day found Blanche riding up the track. Sometimes she drove over and brought the children. And day after day she put in more time on the job. She began to make condescending remarks to the Kanakas. That is, with the exception of Tirwana, towards whom she adopted and maintained an attitude of steady disregard. Tommy she singled out for special attention. With the result that the man, already unpleasantly conscious of playing second fiddle to Tirwana, began to convert from an asset to a liability. The dignified melancholy and reserve consequent upon Tommy's banishment from the hut of his refractory spouse gave way, under Blanche's flattering preference, to a more sprightly aspect and an increasing measure of self-assertiveness. And one of the forms the latter attribute took was fawning upon Blanche, currying favour with her still further by himself engaging in her sight in prodigies of labour and adjuring the Kanakas under Tirwana to do likewise.

And interlaced with seemingly an integral part of his reborn vitality was a recrudescence of his evangelistic fervour. He laid the injunctions of the Lord upon the labour of his fellows like whips upon their backs.

Biddow saw only part of what was going on. He failed to relate Tommy's new orientation to the visits of his wife. But what he did see worried him, for Tirwana's reaction was obvious, and the other Kanakas, while responding to Tommy's urgings and objurgations to some extent, were yet taking on a sullenness of mien that boded ill. Biddow hated the thought of trouble over Barney Callaghan's Kanaka. He realized that something should be done but went along from day to day in the hope that whatever that something was, it would happen of itself. He felt helpless and tried to compensate Tirwana for the slight to his authority by himself deferring to him even more than was his wont.

To Cindie the trouble was not perplexing at all. Seldom in the presence of Blanche and the Kanakas together, she simply laid Tommy's mischievous behaviour at the door of jealousy of Tirwana and a naturally obsequious disposition. She saw, also, Biddow's weak and futile handling of a situation that called for firmness, whatever the cause, and this, in turn, worried her.

She saw that Tirwana's respect for his boss, up till now very real, was degenerating into a sorry liking. And Cindie, as familiar with the vicissitudes and personal affairs of the Biddow family as was Blanche herself, felt apprehension attack her like a goad. For in this new way of life her own destiny was bound up with Biddow's success or failure. She desired passionately to have this farming venture succeed, herself to be part of the building of a *place*, of a created thing with life and vitality of its own.

Then came a time when circumstances combined to give Cindie an inkling of the real cause of the trouble, and before an hour had gone by she had snuffed it out like a candle.

Blanche, who had been timing her arrival each morning to miss the rest period, on this particular day turned up just after Cindie had put on the billy to boil. With her usual exaggerated graciousness towards Cindie these latter days, Blanche greeted the girl and rode on towards the building operations. Cindie's eyes followed her, much in the way a cat would look after a king. How beautiful she was! The forest air had laid a sheen, a gloss, upon what already had been glowing loveliness, and Cindie sighed faintly as she pictured the two faces side by side : Biddow's and his wife's. A perfect couple. Perfect physically, that was. Funny that Biddow, who looked so good and talked so soft and on every possible occasion stuck his nose in a book, was yet so—so—so what? Cindie was stuck as, swift as light, her knowledge of Biddow flashed through her mind.

Then, her eyes still following Blanche, she saw something that put Biddow's peculiarities out of her mind. Tommy was running forward to take Blanche's bridle rein. He was stooping and offering his shoulder as a stool for her dainty foot. "Well, if that nigger's not a crawler!" Cindie ejaculated aloud. And she ought to be ashamed of herself! Mrs. Callaghan would be mad!

The billy having boiled, Cindie threw a handful of tea into it, lifted it to one side and went up to call the men. The thought of Tommy's submission and Blanche's acceptance of it still rankled. Biddow was a fool! That's what he was! Look

at him now! On to her tail like a kite. Why hadn't he told
that slimy nigger to mind his own business? Listen to the
crawler, shouting at the top of his voice, glorifying the Lord.
And Tirwana, too, made her mad. Why didn't the big fool
punch Tommy?

Cindie stalked up to the saw-pit and took a stand a few
feet away from Blanche, who had seated herself upon a log
within talking distance of her husband. Cindie was thus able
to gather that Blanche's early appearance was due to the
expected arrival, within an hour's time, of their furniture at
the down-river jetty. She was waiting for Biddow to complete
his present job, when she would accompany him to supervise
its unloading and carting to the selection. Tirwana was
assisting Biddow, directing him by example, in fact, in the
making and placing of iron barriers against the ravages of
termites at the junction of piles and house flooring.

Tommy, close by, was engaged in the saw-pit. He had
stopped singing. Probably, Cindie thought sarcastically, because he needed all his breath for the showmanship he was
exhibiting in the simple process of sawing wood. Showing off,
that's what he was doing. But what on earth for? . . .

And then Cindie noticed that Blanche was watching the
man, watching him with smiling approval. She caught
Tommy's sycophantic smirks in response.

"The billy is boiled." Cindie spoke slowly, thoughtfully.
"Smoko, Mr. Biddow."

"Just a minute, Cindie," Biddow replied. "We are nearly
through with this . . . I'll finish it, Tirwana. You go and get
your tea. I want you to come along with me."

Tirwana immediately dropped the snips with which he had
been working and hurried away. Cindie started to follow him,
but before she had taken many steps halted abruptly.

For Blanche had said, coolly: "We'll take Tommy with us,
Randolph. I don't like that black savage."

Biddow, concentrated on his work, said absently: "What's
that?—Ah! Got it!" He stood up and tossed down his tools.
"What did you say, Blanche?

"I said we would take Tommy with us. *Not* that black
savage."

"Nonsense. Tirwana could handle the furniture while

Tommy looked at it. And why this sudden interest in Tommy?" Biddow gave his wife a blank look.

"It's not a sudden interest. I think Tommy is a good worker. I've been watching him. He gets work out of others, too. He can't do enough to please."

"Oh!"—shortly. "You seem to have been seeing quite a lot. And missing a lot, too. Tirwana goes with us. Come on." He hurried off, passing Cindie, who now moved on again.

Blanche, chagrined that Cindie had heard the passage, caught up with the girl and, with deadly coldness, remarked: "There was really no need for you to stand and eavesdrop, Cindie."

Cindie's stomach turned over. She *had* eavesdropped. And Blanche had the power to get rid of her; to send her away from this toilsome Eden she had come to love. She could think of nothing whatever to say. Her face burned. With an insolent, understanding laugh, Blanche hurried ahead.

But when, in a few hours' time, the laden buckboard returned, Tommy had deserted the place. He had collected his Bible and his belongings and gone back to Palmer Estate.

"He simply said he was sick in the stomach and wanted to go home," Cindie persisted, in reply to Biddow's puzzled questions. And she called upon the other Kanakas to bear her witness.

"Yes, Boss," said Bill. "He just say he sick and go."

Blanche said nothing, but her eyes gleamed with smouldering suspicion. And throughout the afternoon—she had brought her lunch with her—while load after load of furniture was delivered and stored, she was very, very quiet.

Tommy, of course, had not been disposed of as easily as all that. Cindie, still shaken, had drunk up her tea in gulps. It steadied her, to the extent that while she ate her sandwiches she began to figure out if anything could be done. At length she said casually: "You like it here, Tommy? Better than Barney Callaghan's?"

"Boss Callaghan good man," Tommy replied. "Missis Mary, she fine woman, too. I go back, sometime."

Silence for a time, then Cindie, portentously: "You want to be careful not to make Tirwana mad, Tommy, or you won't get the chance to go back."

Every Kanaka stopped chewing and turned interested eyes on her.

"What did you say, Missie?" Tommy's eyes had widened.

"Haven't you heard about Tirwana, Tommy? Don't you know that if Tirwana gets mad with a man he just picks him up and breaks him on his knee? Like this." She took up a stick and broke it over her knee. "Tirwana is a great wrestler, Tommy. You know, great fighter. One, two, three men Tirwana broke over his knee. So you need to be careful, Tommy. I've seen Tirwana look at you real bad. He hates preachers, Tommy. He didn't sing at your church meeting, did he? You notice that?"

"Yes. I notice." The reddish tinge in Tommy's face skin turned to a sickly imitation of pallor.

Cindie took up another stick and broke it over her knee. "Yes, just like that, Tommy. All of a sudden he breaks out. Without warning." She glanced at the rest of the group. Some eyes were goggling fearfully, but two pairs met hers with dancing laughter in their depths. And because a touch of humour makes the whole world kin, to these Cindie dropped one eyelid in a wink.

No more, then, but when his fellows had stretched out in the shade and lit their pipes Tommy came creeping up to Cindie, one hand rubbing his stomach. "Missie, I sick," he said miserably. "I go back to Boss Barney's place and get the medicine. I real sick."

"Oh, that is a shame, Tommy. You had better tell Bill about it, too."

And so exit Tommy. Within a few minutes he was shinning it across the clearing to pick up a short cut through the forest. Cindie watched him disappear and then looked down upon the black bodies lounging on the grass. "Poor Tommy," she said guilefully to Bill. "He's sick, all right."

"Yes, Missie," replied Bill. And his tone conveyed nothing if not a vast respect. "He sick enough for the glory road. Missie, you *clever*."

CHAPTER X

BY THE MIDDLE OF NOVEMBER, BIDDOW'S PLACE, NAMED FOLK-haven by Blanche, after the Hilliard family home in Brisbane, had all the appearance of a rapidly developing plantation homestead. The unpainted square house, with its wide verandas, looked outwardly what it was, a makeshift; but within it there was comfort enough, measured by frontier standards.

Cindie had carried the real burden of settling in, of ordering, cleaning, cooking and laundry. If Blanche had secretly entertained notions of dispensing with the girl and carrying on with coloured labour once the routine of things had been established, she quickly found reason enough to forget them. Or at least to compromise with her desires.

She found that the "coloured labour", consisting of an Aborigine woman Mary Callaghan had procured for her at the settlement on Palmer Estate creek, required training and constant supervision. And Blanche was incapable of the first and resentful of the second.

Solely coloured labour, she soon realized, would throw upon herself the responsibility for the multifarious tasks connected with provisioning and superintending the Kanakas, whose close approach she could not suffer. Why the body of the Kanaka, especially when sweating, should be offensively odorous, and the Australian Aborigine, apparently much lower in the anthropological scale, smell sweet as a nut, puzzled her. But there it was.

Cindie learned the full meaning of the word "organization" during those first two months. To begin with, she had waited upon directions from her mistress, or deferred to her before undertaking a task. But Blanche's "I'm sure I don't know", or "How can I tell?" very soon palled upon the girl. So, quietly, without fuss, she went ahead and assumed responsibility for the affairs of the household and Kanakas. Imperceptibly she impressed herself authoritatively upon Biddow, so that he got to consulting her about things as a matter of course, without attaching any special significance to it.

There seemed no beginning to Cindie's day and no end. No end to the needs and demands of a household of such a nature. From daybreak to dark she laboured, her hands flying over cooking and baking, her tongue directing, her brain seeking ways and means. She seldom wasted a thought, word or action.

Cindie never took time to ask herself the meaning of her mounting obsession with Biddow's affairs. Before the first two months had gone by she could have been married to Jeff Grey and installed on a farm of her own. Willis Fraser, too, middle-aged planter from "over the river", had almost immediately made clear the "honourable" nature of his intentions.

Fraser, Cindie detested at first meeting. But Grey she liked and respected. His "What ho, there!" never failed to bring a smile to her lips and a friendly glance from her eyes. But his half-joking though sincere proposal of marriage she dismissed curtly as nonsense.

She encouraged Grey to friendship with Biddow, subtly influenced the latter to discuss his problems with the young man, who had paid two hundred pounds as a premium to a Pearltown planter for teaching him the science of cane growing. Barney Callaghan was always at Biddow's service for advice and discussion, but Cindie, by straining her ears and powers of assimilation through the furious discussions that raged whenever Barney and Fraser or Barney and Grey came together at Folkhaven, was rapidly acquiring more than an inkling of the vital issues confronting the cane growers of that day and consequently was coming to think that Barney's outlook belonged to the past.

Carried along by the deep rolling tide of her developing and as yet unrealized motivation, Cindie began to devote hours that should have been given to rest to poring over the sugar journal and pondering the political news in the papers that came irregularly from Brisbane. And through all the interminable confabulation attendant upon any grouping of men in that period of countrywide ferment, she came to wait upon Biddow's pronouncements. To wait, knowing that, though his confrères might have the facts, the knowledge of events, it would be Biddow who, between puffs at his pipe, in the fewest possible words and with sublime clarity, would sum up the issues placed before him and arrive at a logical conclusion. His pronouncements were, conclusive, his logic impeccable. So impressive was his ability to single out the main influential factors in political and economic developments, that it became customary for a number of growers to ride over to Folkhaven on Sunday mornings to have him adjudicate on issues they had thrashed over during the week. Biddow's utterances came to be regarded as oracular, and the two women of his household watched and reacted according to their temperamental moods.

The eternal discussions around the problems of the sugar industry, particularly acute in that period, the pros and cons of the proposed federation of all the Australian colonies, the mounting clamour anent the White Australia policy, which involved deportation of the Kanakas, three issues inextricably interwoven and intimately personal to these growers, drove Blanche to distraction at times.

Though reared in a highly politicalized atmosphere, Blanche had only skated round on the fringe of its serious aspects. In her wealthy Brisbane home, escape from irritating factors had been easy. Here she could not escape. The voices of the disputants, attuned to shouting across paddocks, filled the tiny house and its purlieus with noise. And her powerful intelligence could not brook the "stupidities" of some of these men. Nor the crudeness and rough manners of others. Biddow's soft tones and clear disquisition in comparison were like music in her ears.

Blanche's love for her husband, in these primitive conditions which revulsed her, grew more passionately possessive than ever. Or maybe the improvement in her physical condition, attendant upon the change from town to country life, stimulated her natural ardours which, too often baulked by Biddow's fatigue, under frustration became perverted.

The question of Biddow's success or failure in this venture no longer agitated Blanche's mind. She gathered from the inescapable discussions that success or failure in the sugar industry hinged upon issues outside individual control. The crucial issues mentioned above, which had long agitated the colonies, were sharpening up. "White Australia" was becoming a fighting phrase. Feeling for it in the southern colonies,

and even in South Queensland, was assuming formidable
proportions.   If White Australia carried the day, and the
Kanakas were deported—well, that, to Blanche, was that!
That meant the end of the sugar industry.   For the sugar
industry as she reckoned it, anyhow.   Homestead allotments
were good enough for these boors, a hundred and odd acres
worked by a couple of whites, but for her—no, thank
you!

Blanche's attitude towards life, over those first few months
in her new home, came near to a half-conscious sense of the
flow of normal life being arrested, of life hovering, of present
conditions being on sufferance.   She was determined that
when the new batch of Kanakas arrived Biddow would relin-
quish some of his incessant physical toil and embrace the
traditional way of life of a "big" planter.

From day to day Blanche jogged along, through a routine
strenuous enough in face of the growing heat.   The question of
the children's education had been resolved by the Montagues'
offer to have Irene and Randy share lessons with the young
fry of their own clan; so every morning Blanche took the reins
after Cindie had harnessed up the horse and, in the spanking
new sulky, drove the children over to Glenelg.   In the afternoon she brought them back.   Sometimes she stayed over at
the big plantation throughout the day.   For the rest, she spent
interminable hours at crocheting fine lace, hand-sewing
delicate underwear for herself and Irene, riding and driving,
visiting the Callaghans and a few other farms she thought
worthy of her patronage.

By the time November happened along Blanche would
have repudiated with scorn the idea that Cindie could ever
have caused her a moment's disquiet.

And, judging by appearances, her scorn would have been
justified.   Unlike her mistress, Cindie did not bloom under the
heat.   She wilted.   By November the natural gold of her skin
had deepened to a rich brown.   She was, and looked, jaded.
She sweated so profusely that drops constantly rolled down
her face, arms and neck.   Long ago she had discarded her
stays, stockings and long skirts, and now went about dressed
in a blouse and an old pair of dungaree pants that Biddow had
discarded.   With a shapeless pandanus-leaf hat fashioned by

the Aborigines on her head, she looked like a youth of the labouring class.

And the outward metamorphosis was symbolic of a revolutionary development within. Cindie had put down roots in this soil. And far from Blanche's renouncement of concern about Biddow's personal responsibility for the progress of his holding, she realized that on him and him alone hinged failure or success. Within the compass of those other extraneous circumstances she strove so hard to understand, Cindie felt there was room to manœuvre, to adapt, to adjust, and Biddow, beyond and before all other farmers she had become acquainted with, was the man to recognize the inner meaning and trend of events.

But, she saw, at recognition he stopped. The clarity of his mind was outmatched by the practical inutility of his temperament. He was able to recognize trends and conceive ideas but unable to put them into practice.

And this understanding fired in Cindie a whole train of dormant possibilities. As time passed, her eyes, resting upon Biddow, would take on misty softness, an expression of mingled indulgence and pity. This was particularly so when she noted his natural acceptance of the black men as human beings like himself. She saw that this attitude was inherent in him, not an arrived-at conclusion as was her own present point of view. *And* it was something vastly different from the kindness of certain other planters, the Montagues, for instance. And different, too, from Barney Callaghan's appreciation of the Kanakas as likeable chaps and good men at a job. It was part of Biddow's comprehensive "brains", as Cindie termed it, of his born cognizance.

And Cindie saw that the Kanakas, in general, recognized this difference in Biddow as well as she did. She saw that Tirwana was beginning to regain his respect for his boss on the basis of what the man was, irrespective of those things he might not find it in his make-up to do. Between Cindie and Tirwana a tie was being forged through their mutual understanding of Biddow, and their own joint desire and self-acknowledged ability to complement his talents.

Biddow had been notified that he could expect his batch of a dozen Kanakas, direct from the islands, early in November, so lately his present labour forces had been taken off bush-whacking to prepare for their arrival. Tirwana's men, working at week-ends, had built their own shacks, three men to a hut, and now they toiled till late at night carting pandanus and palm leaves and weaving these into the newcomers' dwellings.

Cindie waited for Biddow to make some move in respect of the provisioning of the larger body of Kanakas. It was plain to her, as to Tirwana, that the present method of supplying the blacks with provisions, which each cooked for himself, was wasteful of time and labour. Supply on the lines of Callaghan's household was urgently necessary, so, when only a few days remained before the expected arrival of the new men and Biddow still said nothing about the matter, she broached it to him.

"Yes, Cindie, I have thought myself that something like that should be done," he told her, frowning. "Have I left it too late? It's a big job, isn't it?"

"No, Mr. Biddow. It's not a big job. There are some sheets of corrugated iron left over from the house roof. Have the men use them to throw up a small cooking shed, at once. Tirwana can bring up from the Port a colonial oven for bread-making, three big boilers and other things I shall list. Then, when the new men come in, the first thing they can do is build a dining shed and store room. I will select the best man of the lot for a cook—or maybe you should approach the mill Board for one of these Japs they are indenting for that job. Mr. Fraser told me he was applying for one."

And so it fell out.

The Kanakas arrived earlier than expected. And the sight of them made Cindie more than ever thankful for Biddow's good luck in securing an overseer of the calibre of Tirwana. Her heart took several jumps when they scrambled out of the buckboard and cart and, in utter silence, looked around them. Wild they looked, their slop-made clothes an insult to the integrity of their birthright and making ludicrous the stylish dressing of their hair.

Men from Api among them, men who built their hair up high, one side black, the other side red. Men from Malaita, fierce and martial, whose eyes gleamed like black gems as with unceasing movement they took in their surroundings. And, most amazing and startling to the whole homestead, a woman among them. A strapping young woman, flat-nosed, round-cheeked, with full Cupid's bow lips. She was as tall as the man she accompanied, a stocky individual of extreme ugliness of face and piercing, concentrated look. Her long hair was parted in the middle and neatly smoothed back beneath the man's slouch hat she wore. Her shapeless frock, reaching to the ankles, was drawn in to her waist by a sailor's leather belt. Her name was Charity. Her presence posed an immediate problem of accommodation. Married couples must, of course, be segregated, and all the huts had been built on the usual pattern, three to a hut.

Cindie proposed as a solution the immediate walling-in of a section beneath the house, to be occupied by Tirwana. Blanche objected on the score of propriety since Verbena, the Aborigine maid, was domiciled there. But Cindie, with the unpredictable nature of the new recruits in mind, accounted that a good enough reason in itself for Tirwana to be installed near by.

Blanche grudgingly assented, her whole aspect indicative of affront and disgust at being compelled to acknowledge certain instincts and appetites of her own as common to humanity at large.

"All right," she conceded. "Though why you should expect better behaviour from that black savage than from the others I can't imagine. But see that you keep him *under* the house. I'm inclined to think that he doesn't know his place."

"What do you think of them, Tirwana?" Biddow asked, later. "Think they will settle down?"

Tirwana shrugged. "Got to, Boss. But, Boss——"

"Yes? What is it, Tirwana? I want you to say what you think."

"Miss Cindie, and Mrs. Biddow, they must learn to use the gun."

"What?" Biddow almost yelped the word.

"No, no, Boss! Nothing bad. Nothing wrong. In all the years Tirwana work for white man he see nothing wrong with Kanaka. But that down south, where houses, plenty houses, all round. No mountain, no bush, only far off. Here, bush close up. And these men new. Some Api and Malaite men.

They savage, yet, maybe. And some of them, Boss, maybe more savage for being stolen from their people. They talk the pidgin of the Missionary but—— New country, here. No women. Boss, you give me the little gun and let the white women learn to shoot the pigeons in the bush. That good. That make the Kanaka think if he want too much the wife he left behind him."

Biddow was shaken. He dreaded broaching the subject to his wife. Out of sheer funk he went first to Cindie and in his usual hesitant manner made known to her Tirwana's proposal.

"That's all right, Mr. Biddow," she said briefly. "There's nothing to be alarmed about, you know. Mrs. Callaghan told me long ago that all the women up here learned to shoot." She noted his lugubrious expression with half-smiling solicitude. "You needn't worry, Mr. Biddow. I know how busy you are to-day. You get along with your work and I will talk the matter over with Mrs. Biddow."

"You would, Cindie?"—eagerly. "Thanks. Thanks a lot."

Cindie went into the house and found Blanche absorbed in a dress catalogue that had recently come in with a bunch of papers from Brisbane. "Mrs. Biddow," she said bluntly, "I think it is high time that you learned to use a gun, now that these new Kanakas have come in."

Blanche frowned at her. "You think quite a lot around this place lately, don't you, Cindie?"

A mask closed over Cindie's features. Her reply was wooden. "Mrs. Callaghan told me long ago that all the women up here learned to shoot. These new men are wild. They are clean from the bush."

Blanche jumped up from her seat and threw the catalogue into a corner. "This is ridiculous! Learn to shoot! What for? Do you mean to tell me that these—these savages would dare to interfere with me?"

Cindie looked her straight in the eye. "I don't know what they might do. To them, Mrs. Biddow, you are only a woman. Just a woman like—like me." She caught her breath perceptibly on that last phrase, and the shock of some sudden aberrant emotion that gripped her turned her brown skin to a putty-like hue. Her eyes opened wide upon Blanche. The muscles of her mouth tightened and straightened her lips.

Blanche stared at her. "What's the matter with you? Are you afraid of these savages?"—curtly.

Cindie heaved a deep, abrupt sigh. "Yes." She almost breathed the word. "Yes, I'm afraid of them." But the mind behind her eyes was far away.

"Then you, too, are going to learn to shoot?" Blanche was now watching her curiously.

"Yes . . . yes." Cindie turned away but Blanche recalled her sharply. "Cindie!"

The girl halted. "Yes, Mrs. Biddow."

"Does Mr. Biddow know that you have spoken to me about —this gun business?"

"No—o-o. No, he doesn't know." Then, realizing that for some reason obscure to herself she had told her mistress a half-lie, Cindie's face was stained with a rush of blood. Her thoughts whirled. What was happening? Why was Mrs. Biddow looking at her like that? "That is," she blurted out, "he told me Tirwana said we must learn to use a gun."

"Oh, he did, did he! Tirwana tells Mr. Biddow, he tells you and you tell me. Is that it?"

"Mrs. Biddow!" A ghastly sensation of disaster was overwhelming Cindie. Instinctively she sought to divert the current of the other woman's thoughts. "It's just that—that——"

"Get out!" Blanche vented the words brutally, her intonation masculine with rage.

And Cindie got out. Out of the house beneath Verbena's curious eyes and in a daze made down to the gardens of pine-apples and papaws. There she sat down. And presently, to her surprise, found tears gushing from her eyes. A dreadful wounded feeling replaced the daze. To be spoken to like that! No woman had the right! And why? Why? What was it all about! What had she done! Suddenly she felt terribly tired, a condition that roused her to a sense of loafing in the midst of demanding interminable tasks. She got to her feet and looked around her at the fruit trees. Here, right here, was one job she would have to give attention to without one hour's delaying.

For some days past, the first drop from the mature papaw trees had been ready for the picking. Each day Cindie had taken the ripe fruits and packed them in bags for Tirwana to take down to the Port. And to-day he was supposed to have gone.

Now the unexpected arrival of the Kanakas would veto that undertaking. Tirwana would have to build his room and assist Biddow to supervise their settling in. Yet the ripening fruits must get away. Why hadn't she learned to drive, to be able to cope with emergencies like this? Maybe she could drive. She would *have* to drive. There was nothing else for it. She would harness old Billy, the big draught horse, to the cart and give it a go.

"What ho, there!" Cindie jumped, and swung round to face Jeff Grey. Sunk in the chaos of her thoughts she had failed to hear the plod-plod of his two-horse team up the track. He was drooped above a board seat on the front of his cart, the reins slack in his hands, eyeing her with quizzical good humour.

"Oh, hullo." Cindie went over to him slowly.

"Brought your suckers," he called cheerily. "On my way to the Port with a load."

Cindie's eyes turned inwards. "I wish you hadn't brought them to-day," she said worriedly. "The new Kanakas have come. There's a lot of work."

The quizzical expression vanished from Grey's face, to be replaced by one of momentary keen penetration. Then he hitched his reins to his seat and took out his pipe. "Yes, I suppose there's a lot of work," he said casually. "What's worrying you? You look upset."

"I'm not upset." Cindie went up to the cart and examined the bunches of pineapple and banana suckers she had asked the man to supply from his own beds. "I'll have to get to work on these."

"They'll keep. I'll put them in the bush shelter."

"Could you take a few bags of pines and papaws down to the Port for me, Mr. Grey?" Cindie shook herself back to normal. "Tirwana can't go to-day. Too busy."

"Of course. Are they ready?"

"No. But I will soon have them bagged. You have a yarn with Mr. Biddow while I do the job."

"Why? I'm always having yarns with Mr. Biddow. Why

shouldn't I help you to bag the fruit and yarn with you, for a change?"

"But—but they might need you up there, Mr. Grey." Cindie's manner became confidential. "These new niggers are terrible looking. They are clean from the bush."

"So I hear. Willis Fraser's got a bunch of them, too. Cannibals from Api." Grey grinned. "I'm wondering if he will be as handy with his fists with this lot as he is with his old hands. . . . Righto, then. I'll hop along while you do the job."

Cindie went ahead with knife and bag and soon had the day's harvest ready for market. And while she hacked the golden rounded oblongs of pines from their cradle of thorny succulent leaves, or stood upon a high box to twist the green, yellow-streaked fruits off the trunks of the papaw trees, she deliberately reviewed the scene with Blanche and set herself to figuring out exactly what her mistress's outburst might connote. Get out!

Get out of the room? The house? Did that order signify anything at all beyond a freakish flash of fury out of some mystical resentment engendered by her own—Cindie's—bungling of—of what? There it was again! Of what? Something in herself had roused Blanche to that eruption, but what?

Cindie let go that thread and lost herself in nebulous day-dreaming. Her fingers continued by pressure to estimate the degree of ripeness of the fruits, but beneath this overtone of functional activity she drifted on a sea of sensuous, rainbow-hued dreams. The steaming heat widened the pores of her skin till her clothing stuck to her body and limbs, outlining the slimness of her torso and the sturdiness of her thighs. At intervals, after the manner of the Kanakas, she raked the sweat from her brow with her fingers and tossed it from her.

She was dimly conscious of an instinctive reluctance to delve deeply into the subtleties of her encounter with Blanche. Nothing had happened. Nothing really. But now the bagging of the fruit was completed and she must return to the house and have that conclusion justified.

Blanche, lounging over the rail of the balcony, was watching the new arrivals eat their midday meal. Squatted about the newly-built cookhouse they shovelled the thick stew of corned beef, pumpkin, onions, sweet potatoes and green papaws into their mouths with nature's chopsticks. Beneath the house, Tirwana and Biddow, with Jeff Grey looking on, worked against time at nailing up bark slabs.

Cindie spoke a few words of thanks to Grey and then climbed the steps, which were at the back of the house. In the kitchen Verbena was busily preparing the household luncheon. A very good luncheon, all things considered. Cold corned beef, with tinned peas imported from France, and a salad of tomatoes, onions, cucumbers, lettuce, avocado pear and pine-apple. Biddow had secured a milking cow from Glenelg which Cindie, who milked it, kept tethered at the edge of the clearing below the orchards. Thus there was cream, which, with eggs from the settlement store, laid the foundation for a good mayonnaise. Papaw, pineapple, bananas and cream made a fruit salad for dessert. The diet was much of a sameness but it was wholesome and healthgiving and never palled even upon Blanche's fastidious palate. For the housing of milk and other perishables, a shelter had been built on the bank of the stream, and from its slab flooring the household butter, contained in a plaster cooler, was kept lowered into the perennially cool water.

Noting that Verbena had set the table in the living-room, which was dining-room too, Cindie brought a towel and a clean frock from the bedroom she shared with Irene—Randy slept on the balcony—and returned downstairs to the shower cubicle. Jeff Grey had now departed.

"Lunch is ready, Mr. Biddow," she called, then scrambled hurriedly through her bath.

Back in the kitchen she carved the meat, infused the tea, which customarily was drunk with the main course, and then with lowered eyes sat down to await Biddow's coming. No question of his changing his clothes for the midday meal. Such amenities the exigencies of pioneering life did not encourage.

Within a few minutes he appeared and simultaneously, as though timed, Blanche entered the kitchen through the living-room door. Saying quietly: "I'll take in the meat," Cindie rose and took up a tray.

And with the opening of her mouth she felt herself to be in

complete command of the situation, if situation there might be. The appearance of Blanche, cool looking, dressed smartly even at midday, had generated in Cindie a spontaneous contempt. Contempt for the coarse dull texture of a mind insensible to the absorbing interest of the creative activities going on around her. And interlarded with the contempt a reservoir of resentment and fury was tapped within her at Biddow's subjection to such nullity.

The contempt and fury together lent to Cindie's bearing a fiery self-confidence. She strode past Blanche with a clipped, clear "excuse me", and clapped the dishes from the tray on to the table. And no sooner were husband and wife seated than she said brusquely: "I told your wife that Tirwana thinks we should learn to use a gun, Mr. Biddow."

"You did?" Biddow gave Blanche an apprehensive glance. "I don't think there's anything to it, Blanche. It is only that— these new men, they are pretty wild-looking. Nothing to be alarmed about, of course."

"I understand"—with cold detachment. "I'll learn to shoot. I think it's a very good idea. I'd like to feel I was able to deal effectively with any encroachments upon my preserves." Momentarily her lip curled. Her eyes narrowed. Then she continued in her normal conversational tones. "What about this black woman? What is she going to do?"

"Tirwana tells me that in island life the women do all the field work, even the felling. But naturally I won't permit that. What do you think?" Biddow addressed Cindie, who sat at the bottom of the table, somewhat apart.

"I need her in the orchards and gardens. And she can help in chipping the cane. That would leave me free to take on Tirwana's job of trucking out the produce to the Port and the boats and bringing in the stores. Tirwana could do more felling."

"Would you undertake that work, Cindie? Think you could manage it?"

"Of course."

CHAPTER XI

THE STORM SEASON WAS RECKONED TO BEGIN IN NOVEMBER, BUT beyond an occasional rumble of thunder around the mountain peaks, accompanied by some heavenly displays of pyrotechnics, there was little enough, that year, to justify that belief.

The lack of much rain was especially gratifying to settlers who, like Biddow, were anxious to take down as much forest as possible for the following year's planting, but at the same time the enervating heat made conditions very trying. The skeleton of Cindie's face gave ocular evidence of the strain under which she laboured. She grew irritable of manner and speech. Without removing her clothes she would walk under the shower a dozen times a day. With the approach of Christmas, even Blanche succumbed somewhat to the heat, though, well protected from the direct rays of the sun as she took care to be, her skin retained its silken gloss, her cheeks and lips their rose pink glow. She insisted that Biddow spare men from more essential work to build a shed for housing the vehicles, so that some of the space beneath the house might be converted into a fernery, for coolness.

It was over the building of this fernery that Cindie was brought to break a lance with Blanche in a way that left little of the relationship of mistress and maid between them.

Biddow's assent to his wife's demand had been grudging to begin with, and when he found that the erection of the shed had engulfed more precious time snatched from felling than he had bargained for, he gave way under the stress of heat and fatigue to impatient anger and directed the Kanakas back to work in the forest. Blanche's protests he gave short shrift.

"If you want a fernery to loaf in, go ahead and make it yourself," he told her. "I won't spare a man from the felling another hour till the 'wet' sets in."

"Cindie and Charity can do it!" Blanche stormed. "Cindie's a man about the place, isn't she? She can build fences and hoe the gardens. Tell her to do it."

"If Cindie wants to do it, that's her business. I won't tell her to."

"Why shouldn't you tell her? She's not my servant any longer. She's your man, isn't she? Isn't she just a Kanaka these days?"

She knew she had made a mistake before the words were out of her mouth. Biddow gave her one look, a look of shock and distaste, and walked away from her. It mortified Blanche, but at the same time its implied criticism induced in her an upsurge of bitter hatred for the girl. That look had revealed to her the deep cleavage between a man's respect for ability to toil, to build, to help out, and his love for the merely decorative and exciting.

Though fully conscious of a further blunder in pursuing the matter in her then furious mood, Blanche sped across the clearing to where Cindie was working and launched her venom recklessly upon the girl. "Cindie," she shouted, "drop that business and come over to the house!"

Cindie, engaged with Charity in burning off that section of land on which the timber had first been felled, stared, then threw down the bundle of small shrubs she carried. "Whatever's the matter, Mrs. Biddow?" she cried.

"The matter is that I'm sick and tired of never having you on hand when I want you! What do you think I brought you up here for? To turn yourself into a Kanaka?"

"What do you want me for?" Cindie's progress along the road of self-sufficiency was marked by the coolness of her tone.

"Don't you talk to me like that!" Blanche was white-faced. The knuckles of her hands were white with the intensity of her grip upon her skirt, which she held high above her boots. "Cheek! Impudence! I've had too much of it, lately."

Cindie started forward. "Mrs. Biddow, I have never been impudent to you. I don't know what you are talking about. What do you want me to do?"

"Bring that—that nigger there and come back to the house." Blanche swung on her heel.

Cindie flashed a glance at Charity, an interested spectator of the scene. "Come, Charity," she called, then, with tight lips, she hastened to catch up with her mistress. "Mrs. Biddow!" Blanche tossed a fiery look over her shoulder. "Mrs. Biddow, if you'll take my advice, you won't use the word 'nigger' in the hearing of a Kanaka. It spells trouble."

"You keep your advice till you're asked for it. I'm mistress here. You get to work and build a fernery for me."

"A fernery! Mrs. Biddow, in another two days we'll have finished burning off this section. Let us finish that first."

But Blanche now had her eyes on Charity, who was dragging along by the tail a six-foot brown snake. "Is that thing dead?" she snapped out.

"Of course," Cindie replied. "It was sneaking up on Charity when I killed it. First time I've seen a snake go for anyone. Take the snake to your hut, Charity," she directed.

"What's she going to do with it?" asked Blanche, now rather glad of a diversion from the tempestuous channel of her wrath.

"She will cook it and eat it. . . . But this fernery, Mrs. Biddow. I don't know how to make it."

"You mean you don't want to make it"—shortly. Then, with an air of derision: "You wouldn't let a small thing like a fernery beat you, would you? After a cowbail and a chicken house. There must be something mightily inspiring to you about this place, Cindie." Blanche marched beneath the house. "Let's see you spread yourself on a fernery, Cindie. See here. Along this side. As far from that smelly black savage as you can get."

Cindie sat down on a box, wiped her brow and then proceeded to look steadily at her boots.

"Well, what are you waiting for?" from Blanche.

"I'm—considering."

"Considering what, pray?"

"Considering whether to do the job or not. Mrs. Biddow, what would you say if I told you to build your fernery yourself?"

Blanche was frightfully disconcerted. Nevertheless she answered with bravado: "I'd give you the sack."

"Very well. You build your fernery yourself, Mrs. Biddow."

But Blanche was a good loser in small issues when her basic interests were concerned.

She bit her lip, then with a forced laugh blurted out: "But this is ridiculous! You know perfectly well that I couldn't do

any such thing. But of course—if you don't want to do it——"
Assuming an injured air she lifted her skirts and left the field
to Cindie.

CHAPTER XII

CINDIE REALLY ENJOYED BUILDING THAT FERNERY. SHE HAD
enjoyed laying out the shrubbery and garden plots in front
of and about the house. Though, with the exception of the
gaudy exotic crotons, in most cases the actual planting must
wait upon the autumn. Set in the summer, most ornamental
shrubs and domestic plants would either be shrivelled by the
heat or drowned beneath the flooding rains of the "wet".

But the fernery! Apart from the joy of designing and
creating there were enchanting foraging trips into the cool
forest in search of ferns and mosses and orchids. In addition
to the boon of a much needed respite from the heat, these
introduced her to aspects of forest life marvellous and exciting. And before she was far on with the job almost every
Kanaka on the place was anxious to assist her.

Cindie could laugh, now, at her fears of the new batch of
Kanakas. The fiercest-looking among them, including Sow,
Charity's husband, turned out if anything to be the most
docile. All the same, she heeded Tirwana's warning, repeated
when one day he saw her going off into the forest alone and
unarmed, not to under-estimate the powerful impulses of
primitive souls frustrated and possessed of entirely different
moral standards to her own.

As she came to know the Kanakas individually, Cindie
recognized among them the same inequality of temperament
and character as obtained among whites. Some she liked, to
others she was indifferent, one she detested. This man, a
Solomon Islander named Melatonka, she thought of as oily.
With the exception of Tirwana he was the finest looking native
she had seen. His torso was magnificent, he had the same
reddish tinge in his skin as Tommy the preacher. His features
were blunt and as Aryan as Cindie's own. His frizzy hair,

of which he took meticulous care, was combed high and
wide to form a halo for his face and was more red than
black. And he had a very good idea of the extent to which
the slop-made white man's clothes detracted from his beauty
and grace. On Sundays he discarded them and wrapped
around his loins a sulu of multiple hue that set off his natural
colour scheme to perfection.

It was not the fact that Melatonka became sex-conscious
whenever she approached him that roused Cindie's ire and
dislike. It was his "slimy grin" and downcast eyes, his
wheedling too-soft "Yes, Missie", his pretence of not understanding her directions; for the purpose, she very well knew,
of prolonging her contact with him. She detested him for
his sharp detection of her own feeling about him and his
knowing, perverted delight in it. She linked him in her
mind with Willis Fraser, Kanaka-beater and -starver, whom
she had recently told to quit bothering her or she would put
a shot about his heels.

Melatonka was one who made no offer to assist her in the
building of the fernery. He never brought in ferns or small
mossy logs from the felling sites, as did most of his fellows.
And when these others, in the brief hour of tropical twilight,
got in each other's way in their eagerness to assist Cindie,
he would stand aloof, perpetually smiling, or squat on his
heels, his Mission-supplied mouth organ to his lips, making
soft and melodious music of hymn tunes, or startling the
forest with amazingly loud and rollicking sea shanties.

Irene and Randy enjoyed the building of the fernery, too.
The relation between the children and the Kanakas was in
general one of friendly acceptance on the part of the former
and of respectful, affectionate submission from the latter.

Randy in particular loved the plantation life. He was
brown as a berry, was sloughing off like a snake skin the
finicky ways he had brought with him from Brisbane. Tirwana, he had taken to regarding as the sum total of common
sense and wisdom. . . .

First of all, to make the fernery, Cindie, under Tirwana's
direction, built a lattice work enclosure beneath the house.
After that, boulders were carried from the creek bed and
rockeries built up. Mossy logs were disposed to a design,

and trunks of trees to form hosts for tassel plants, stagshorns and orchids. Then came the jaunts into the forests, which in big timber country was not too difficult for penetration. Armed with gun and tomahawk, Cindie and Charity would ford the stream and plunge into the cool, deep-green depths. Not a day but that they brought back wood pigeons for the table, or bush turkey or bush fowl. Cindie would tie the birds' legs together and dangle them from her belt. The tameness and domestic appearance of the fowl shamed her to shoot them, but her healthy appetite and desire for variety in table meats always overcame her hesitation.

Very few flying birds were to be seen in the depths of the jungle. The screech of the white cockatoo from the tops of the high trees was more common than his appearance; though from the clearing numbers of these birds were seen daily, floating like snippets of cloud about the hill-sides or slowly flapping across the gulleys. The long preparatory swish of the whip bird, ending in a sharp crack, was constantly about them, but seldom did Cindie set eyes on this creature.

It was when the forest was broken by the clearings and streams that the flash of the sun on parrot, lory, parakeet, held Cindie's eyes entranced by the richness of their colouring. The small birds, too, seemed to confine themselves chiefly to the open spaces.

By no means a small part of Cindie's absorption in this wilderness life was her interest, and often actual rapture, in the presence and doings of the birds. In September, the gorgeous little sunbirds—the yellow male with his deep indigo bib and his all-canary mate—had begun to build their nests. They dangled the long, cute structure with its tail and side opening, from any bit of rope or projection about the balcony and sheds. Cindie and the children had delightedly noted the depositing of the eggs, the incubation, hatching and provisioning of the family that followed.

The peaceful doves, yellow figbirds, twittering green-yellow honeyeaters, these, with the sunbirds, were Cindie's special pets. While she worked in the gardens among the fruits the honeyeaters, always paired, would flutter to within arm's-length of her face, upend themselves, and with crooked

claws and wildly gyrating wings twitter twitter twitter in a
paroxysm of scolding. . . .

It was the time of the year for the ripening of the forest
fruits, the blooming of orchids and, not as it turned out a
matter for congratulation, the mating and consequent increased liveliness of the snakes with which that area was
infested. The two women generally kept a sharp look-out
for these, but when their attention was caught by a glorious
cascade of the ivory-cream flowers of a pencil orchid on high,
or a cluster of the orchid called Lily of the Valley, or great
sweeps of the six-foot old-gold plumes of the golden orchid—
when this happened they would stand, mute with admiration, oblivious of such lowly things as snakes. And thus it
happened that for the second time in company they encountered one of the deadliest of the whole order of Sauria,
the great brown snake of North Queensland.

In that period, the ultra-venomous nature and ferocity of
this lovely greeny-brown horror was unknown. The identi-
fication and classification of the taipan (*Oxyuranus scutallatus*)
had to wait upon the time of Cindie's middle age. It was
known that many men in lonely places in the far north,
prospectors, miners, outlying settlers, died of snake bite.
Dead men were come upon in lonely huts, the phrase "snake
bite" scrawled upon paper or wood beside them. Sometimes
it was: "The brown bastard got me," or "Terrible agony.
Snake." But this reptile, despite the prodigious size to which
he was known to attain, because of his colour was confused
with the ordinary brown snake, which actually was not
native to that area. The taipan was considered not nearly
so deadly as the death adder, which was even more common.

Again it fell to Cindie to save Charity from certain death,
agonizing and swift. They had come out of the forest, unexpectedly, on to the southern boundary of Jeff Grey's
neighbouring farm. Immediately in front of them lay Grey's
twenty-five acres of plant cane, set among stumps and logs,
with beyond them a small plantation of bananas and other
tropical fruits. Grey and his two workmen—a fine old
Jamaican black named Ben Hart, a free emigrant who had
come to Pearltown in the 'seventies to work in the cedar
and had afterwards transferred to the farms, and a remit-

tance man in temporary employ—well out of earshot, were chipping along the drills.

With their first look around on emerging from the forest the women had espied a Cooktown orchid in glorious pinky-mauve bloom in the high fork of a silky oak. But alas, the lower portion of the trunk was smooth. No chance for Charity's agility in climbing to secure it. So, Cindie sat down on a log, placed her gun beside her, and rested. Charity, not one to worry over the unattainable, dumped the sack she invariably carried and poked about for ground orchids. Cindie idly watched her.

Suddenly Cindie leapt up with a shout. "Charity! Snake!" Behind the black woman, stealthily undulating through the rank grass on the edge of the jungle, was an enormous green-gold snake. As she leapt up, Cindie's hand automatically shot out towards her gun; then, succeeding to the initial shock of discovery, came a reaction to the reptile's size of a nature to immobilize her. Only a carpet snake could be that big! And carpets were harmless.

Charity swung round at Cindie's shout and caught sight of the monster. Galvanized by fright, she leapt on to a stump and screeched.

"It's all right, Charity!" Cindie called, with a laugh. "It's only a carpet."

But was it? Cindie's amusement was short-lived. For the reptile had halted, was lifting its head in Charity's direction. And this movement was continued, slow and horrible, until three feet or more of its thick body were reared in the air. It flattened out its neck, even its head, and hissed.

Cindie put her gun to her shoulder as Charity, emitting another shriek, leapt from the stump and ran. The first shot missed its mark, for the snake had taken off with astounding agility after Charity. It slithered over the logs, hardly looping its body, seeming to kick itself along with its tail. And Cindie had to re-load her single-barrelled gun. She could hear the shouts of Jeff Grey as he came running in response to her shot. And having re-loaded, she had to chase into the plant cane through which Charity was dodging and try for a clean shot.

The reptile pursued the black woman with a deliberation

as diabolical as its glare. Charity's screams seemed to threaten her death from fright. But the crisis steadied Cindie and made her eye needle-sharp. She got in a second shot as Grey, armed with a stick, came pelting up. The snake plunged convulsively, then its body, with shattered head, thrashed about in the cane.

Cindie drew a deep breath, dropped the butt of her gun upon the ground and leant upon it. Charity fell to the ground upon her face and began gibbering in her own island lingo. Jeff Grey tossed away his stick and gazed at Cindie with smiling admiration. "By the holy jumping Jemima, but you're a beaut.," he said softly. "You got him right in the head."

Cindie was breathing hard. Trembling, too, now that the danger was past. "What a brute!" she quavered. "What a horrible brute! He looked like—like the devil."

Ben Hart and the remittance man now came up and began to examine the snake. Cindie and Jeff joined them. They opened the extraordinarily deep gape and disclosed the sharp, long, curved-back fangs. They straightened out the body and stepped out its length. A little over ten feet.

In the well-modulated tones of the educated negro, Ben Hart stated: "He is big, but I have seen bigger snakes of his breed up on Cape York Peninsula. That snake puzzles me. No other snake I have seen or ever heard of will go for a man like he does. He's a natural murderer. You like the skin, Missie?"

"The skin? What would I do with it?"

"Nail it on the wall, as a memento," said Grey, promptly. "No one can say you're not a big-game hunter after this."

Cindie giggled. And because it was the first time that Grey had heard a sound so girlish from her lips he laughed too, with surprise and gratification. "Ben will skin it for you. Won't you, Ben? And now I'm going to drive you girls home. The nig. there is still sick, by the look of it."

That adventure put an end to systematic foraging in the forest. Nothing would have induced Charity to go out again for the time being and Biddow forbade Cindie to go alone.

But the fernery was now assuming the proportions of a

really fine summer retreat. Wire baskets made by the Kanakas and filled with growing ferns hung from the roof. Small palms transplanted to boxes made nooks of the corners. The floor was paved with stones. Creepers were planted to grow along the latticed walls and over the rockeries. The orchids, stagshorn plants and tassel ferns were artfully disposed. Cindie was secretly proud of the effect when the last orchid bloom had been tied on and she stood in the doorway to admire.

Blanche was charmed, too, and resisted her impulse to damn with faint praise. "It's very nice indeed, Cindie," she said, graciously. "Now if you will only bring down that old wicker chair———"

When Biddow came in he fell for the fernery to an extent that surprised both women. "Fine. Very good." He moved from orchid to orchid, touching the petals of the flowers, his odd eyes alight, his manner boyishly elated. He took his pipe from his mouth and put it in his pocket. "Tobacco pollutes a place like this. . . . You've done a good job, Cindie. But then, you always do a good job. I don't know what we should do without you, Cindie. Eh, Blanche?"

"I think it is just possible we would manage to survive," Blanche replied, tartly.

Biddow took her words as a joke. "Well, I hope we shan't have to try. I like this, Cindie. But don't make the homestead too attractive or the felling sites might suffer."

Maybe the singing in Cindie's heart was too much joy at the moment, or maybe it was her instinct to spur, to guard against relaxation, but however it was she blurted out: "The felling sites won't suffer, Mr. Biddow. Did you remember to order the eight-hundred-gallon tank?"

"No, by jove, I didn't! And if we miss the next boat———" Biddow started up. "I'll have to send a boy over to the post office with another letter."

"I'll take it, Mr. Biddow. I want to have a talk to the butcher about the quality of the meat he is sending in for the Kanakas."

"What's wrong with the meat?" asked Blanche sharply. "Our meat's all right."

"The Kanakas' isn't. Too much gristle and fat. And I

could see about the Jap cook, too, while I am in town, Mr.
Biddow. Bill is not much of a cook and he doesn't like the
job."

"Yes. Yes. I suppose that's all right, Cindie. But take
Tirwana with you. You would hardly get back before dark.
I'll write the letter."

Blanche followed her husband up the stairs and into the
living-room. She lingered beside the table while he wrote,
tapped it with her fingers, her face dark. When she spoke
her words were a trifle blurred. "Randolph, does it ever
strike you that Cindie pretty well runs this place?"

"Eh? What's that?" He swung round from his desk, pen
in hand, and looked at her.

"You heard what I said."

"Yes, I heard." He returned to his letter. "Cindie doesn't
do anything of the sort." He reached for an envelope. "She's
a good assistant, that's all."

"The kind of assistant who tells the boss what to do."

Biddow slammed the letter down upon the desk with a
nervous angry gesture. "What's all this about? Don't I do
enough for you, even here? Do you want another failure?"

Blanche's voice came throaty and deep with passionate
feeling. "Have I got to choose between another failure and
a success based upon a servant's domination of my husband?"

Biddow rose and stood with his back to her. Blanche
knew she had knocked him hard, but, beside herself with
jealousy, she sought in her mind for yet another weapon.
"Even the children notice it," she spat out.

Biddow turned so swiftly as almost to make her jump.
"What?" he shouted. He looked awful, menacingly awful,
and Blanche, the gustiness of her fury caught by the sudden-
ness of it and thrown back upon itself, jerked herself backwards and threw up a hand.

"Say that again!" Biddow thrust his face close to hers.

"You needn't get so mad!" she flung out. "I only meant—
even the children notice that Cindie acts as though she owns
the place."

Suspicion, anger and a deep inner hurt intermingled in
the look he bent on her. Then, with a deep sigh, he dropped
his head as though ashamed and, turning, took the letter

from the desk. He walked past her with his head averted and Blanche, on an impulse, put out a hand and caught hold of his arm. He dislodged her hand with an upward jerk and continued on his way. Blanche sank into a chair and dug her teeth into her lower lip. She folded her hands in her lap and tried to quieten the trembling of her body.

Shortly Biddow returned. With half an eye she saw him standing stiffly in the doorway of the room but she made no sign. He cleared his throat. "I can see there's something wrong with things as they are, Blanche," he said quietly. "But it's your fault, Blanche. It's your fault because you've refused to do your job. If you want an alteration here you must yourself do the jobs that Cindie does now. Those jobs must be done. And that's what I'm going to insist on your doing, Blanche. You've got to do your job on this farm."

"Don't be a fool," she said curtly. She kept her eyes on the floor.

Biddow thought silently for a while, then said: "Well, there's an alternative." He waited. Blanche had to ask: "What alternative?"

"You could return to Brisbane and stay there till we've got the farm in proper shape."

The colour slowly faded out of Blanche's face. At length, the words tumbling from her quivering lips, she said breathlessly: "You forget that it was *my* father who advanced you the money to put into this place."

A fleeting smile passed over Biddow's features. "I forget nothing. Least of all do I forget that you are my wife. I'm not dependent on your father. The mill Board, or the merchants, or Barney Callaghan, for that matter, would advance me the money to carry on. Have a bit of sense, Blanche. Evidently you are not satisfied with things as they are. I'm not going to stand for—for any more scenes."

"Get rid of that girl!" Blanche burst out. But too theatrically, for her hard-headed sapience could not be eclipsed by any amount of heroics. "I won't stand for her—her——"

"Her what?"—bluntly.

"Her doing as she likes! Her running the place! her——"

"Shut up!"

And Blanche shut up. More with surprise than anything else, that such a phrase should issue from Biddow's lips.

He came forward and sat on the table. "Now listen to me, Blanche. This business is just about the silliest thing that I can imagine but evidently it's serious for you. And what's serious for you is serious for me. So I'm going to tell you frankly that Cindie is too useful to me to be put off until there is somebody to take her place. She is just the sort of person I need. She seems—I've never thought about it till now—she seems to complement what little ability I've got. Yes, that's it. . . ."

His manner of thought became introspective and Blanche, watching him, felt as though she had put a noose around her own neck. "I've wakened him up," she told herself in panic. "He never realized till now how much the girl was doing." In a desperate effort to take his mind off the trend of his thoughts she cried out: "She just does her job as a servant! It's nothing! I could do it but I won't! I'm not a servant. I'll go my own way."

"Oh no, you won't. I won't stand for it, Blanche. I can't be satisfied with things as they are after this. You must choose between doing your job, at least some of the jobs Cindie does now, and returning to Brisbane."

Blanche laughed scornfully. "You stupid fool! As though you can make me do anything I don't want to do!"

Biddow slipped off the table. "I wouldn't try to coerce you. But, until you decide either way—I'll sleep out on the veranda." He walked out and down the stairs.

Biddow was upset. He sat on a stump at a slight distance from the house and filled his pipe with trembling fingers. Dusk was coming down. The air was filled with the evensong of birds. But the humidity was higher, if anything, than throughout the day. Biddow's face and arms were stippled with sweat. His shirt stuck clammily to his body. Over by the Kanakas' quarters, a distance of a hundred yards from the house, Melatonka was rendering *In the Sweet By and By* on his mouth organ, accompanied by soft vocalization on the part of his fellows. Irene and Randy sat among them, their childish voices raised in chorus.

A quiet and lovely scene, thought Biddow. He liked those

blokes. Most of them, anyhow. Companionable people.
A man could find real friends among them. Tirwana, now—
Biddow's heart warmed at the very thought of Tirwana. He
would ask little more from life if only—ah, if only——

Softened by the scene, the singing and his children's happy
presence in the midst of the Kanakas, Biddow felt his heart
melt to an immeasurable sadness and yearning. Misery,
too. For with his anger flushed away he knew he would not
let the children go. He wished he had not put up that alternative to Blanche. But what else was there? Send Cindie
away? Yes, he supposed it would have to come to that.
Funny things, women. Then, just as he rose to call the
children to come into the house, Blanche ran down the stairs
and stood beside him.

"Ranny," she said abruptly, "I've been a fool. I promise
there will be no more scenes."

Biddow looked at her, silently, and gradually his face broke
into a gentle, deprecatory smile. "All right," he said awkwardly. "I suppose I'm a fool—but you're one too many
for me, my girl."

CHAPTER XIII

RIGHT UP TO THE EVENING MEAL OF CHRISTMAS EVE, CINDIE
worked with an energy that, emanating from a new-found
reservoir of spiritual pubescence, as it were, triumphed over
enervating heat and exhausted muscular tissue. She tramped
the days behind her with exultant resolution, every minute
of every last one of them weighted with some part of her
toil. Her eyes began to shine with an evangelical light, the
very look of her was an exhortation to her fellows to push
ahead. The jaded look vanished. There was a sense of
joyous ownership in each thrust of her feet against the sod.
She leapt from log to log as though she were borne on
wings.

Said Tirwana one day, in the careful speech that Cindie
had been demanding from him of late: "What's got into
you, these days, Miss Cindie? You make everybody work,

work and want to work. That's new to me, Miss Cindie. To make me like to work."

"Go on, Tirwana! Of course you like to work. Everybody likes to work when he is getting something out of it. Something good."

"But what do we get out of it, Miss Cindie? This is not our farm. Not the Kanaka's farm. This is Boss Biddow's farm. It is Mrs. Blanche's farm."

"Tommy rot, Tirwana. This is *our* farm. Don't you know the sort of man Mr. Biddow is? He'll see that we are looked after, Tirwana. We'll have a good home here all the days of our lives. You, me, and all the Kanakas who want it."

"You a simple woman, Miss Cindie." Tirwana looked at her gravely. "You happy now, for some reason. Lately you are happy. And you are young. And because you are young and happy you like to use your hands and legs and everything seems good. But Tirwana, he is not young. And he's not white, neither. He remembers that Boss Biddow will not have the say about the future of Tirwana and the rest of the Kanakas."

"Oh!—I'm sorry, Tirwana. But don't you worry, Tirwana. I'm determined that even if every other Kanaka is deported you won't be. You will stay with us. I mean, Mr. Biddow will see to it that you stay with us. As a matter of fact, Tirwana—now don't let on I've told you this—Mr. Biddow is going to pay you wages, Tirwana. He's giving me a raise, too."

"I get wages now, Miss Cindie."

"Nonsense. You get the six pounds a year he is compelled by law to pay you. He's going to pay you a white man's wages. Twenty-five bob a week, Tirwana. And he's giving me fifteen shillings a week. What do you think of that, Tirwana?"

"Miss Cindie, is that true?"

"True as gold, Tirwana." She nodded her head naïvely. "That's the sort of man Mr. Biddow is."

"By gosh!" Tirwana swelled with pride and pleasure. "Twenty-five bob! I bet you told him to do that, Miss Cindie. You remind him, eh?".

"Well, yes, I suppose I did. But he was glad to do it. You see, he said to me: 'Cindie,' he said, 'you and Tirwana do

as much work as half a dozen of the rest of us put together.'
And I said to him: 'But I still only get ten shillings a week,
Mr. Biddow. And Tirwana only gets six pounds a year.'
See? It's good to work, Tirwana, but it is also good to
remember that, as our precious Tommy would say without
meaning it, the labourer is worthy of his hire."

"You're smart, Miss Cindie. You're a very smart woman."

"No, Tirwana, that's not smartness. That's principle,
Tirwana. My father, he is a blacksmith, Tirwana. And he
always told me: 'Cindie, the working man with principle
will always do a good day's work for the boss. That's something bred in the bone. But he will never work for less than
the proper wage.' See?"

"All the same, I think you're a very smart woman, Miss
Cindie. You say: This should be done and it is done."

Cindie brought home Takeo, the Japanese cook, and
initiated him into his job. No easy task, for Takeo had come
to Queensland with the expectation of some sort of mechanical
or contract work. He resented being relegated to a cookhouse
job. Worse still, he despised the Kanakas. One of his few
phrases of English was "Kanaka-pig". And he managed to
convey to Cindie his belief that he was as good as she. He
refused to occupy the lean-to that had been thrown up against
the cookhouse, demanding "barrack, barrack, for sleep."

All this happened within a few minutes of his arrival at
Folkhaven. Cindie was for a time nonplussed. Takeo
plumped himself down on a stump outside the cookhouse
door and, having made known his requirements, sat there
like a graven image. The only man about the homestead
was Bill, the Kanaka cook. And Bill, though normally an
amiable chap, with that "Kanaka-pig" in mind was now
lowering and sulky.

Cindie sat down on the woodheap and cogitated. Here
was a pretty kettle of fish. Waste of time! With all the
Christmas cooking for the household on hand and whips of
other extra work to get through. She stared at Takeo and
kept on staring and suddenly it struck her that she didn't
like his looks. She didn't like anything about him, least of
all his assumption of superiority to the black men. On the
instant her decision was made.

"Hey, you!" She jumped up. "You get to hell!" She flourished her arms. "You, Takeo! You understand? Go! Go!" She snatched up his bundle of belongings and threw them in the direction of the track.

The Japanese ran and grabbed his bundle. Holding it in his arms he began to jabber at Cindie, his face thrust towards her, his gimlet eyes blinking. Cindie picked up a stick and made towards him. He held his ground, still jabbering. She flourished the stick in his face. "Get out, get out!" she shouted. "Skedaddle!" Takeo stopped jabbering and looked at her calmly. She lowered the stick. "Well, are you going?"

Takeo's face broke into an ingratiating smile. "You boss?" he asked, brightly.

"Yes, I'm boss." Cindie was now smiling herself and thinking: "He's not so bad, after all." Takeo shrugged and began to walk towards the lean-to. Cindie followed him. "You stop, Takeo?"

"I stop."

"Then Kanaka not pig, Takeo. Kanaka good fella." She raised a finger at him. "No trouble. No fight. You and Kanaka friends."

"You like him?" Takeo looked at her in surprise.

"I like him very much, Takeo. All friends."

Takeo took a good look at Bill. "He black," he said simply.

"And you're brown," said Cindie, promptly.

A broad grin from Takeo. "You brown, too. Ha, ha, ha, ha, ha! You brown, too, Boss. Ha, ha, ha!" He cackled and shook.

"Yes, I'm brown, too," laughed Cindie. "Now to work, Takeo."

Thereafter no trouble with Takeo. Once Cindie was assured that he really could cook, despite his predilection for work around the mill, she smartened up his lean-to with some coloured prints out of a flower seed catalogue. At which Takeo beamed.

One evening preceding Christmas, Cindie got the Kanakas together to receive their quarterly issue of clothing: a singlet, shirt and trousers. Charity was given an old frock of Blanche's, for "best" wear, and two new print Mother Hubbards. On this occasion the natives also received their annual issue of a hat and blanket.

While Cindie was about this business Biddow strolled along, accompanied by Blanche and the children. "When you are finished, Cindie," he said to the girl, "I want to have a few words with the men. Come, Tirwana, you stand beside me."

Christmas, Biddow told the Kanakas, was a time for having fun. On the night of Christmas Eve some friends were coming to the house and he would like his men to sing for them. In return for this favour they would receive cakes and nice drinks. Their Christmas Day dinner would be of pork and plum duff. For tea jam and cakes would be added to their usual rice, bread and golden syrup. On Boxing Day, they might choose between accompanying him and Tirwana into the forest to hunt the wild pig and fishing down the river or at the beach. New Year's Day would also be a holiday for them.

In conclusion he thanked them for the work they had done for him in the past and asked if they had any complaints. No complaints, it seemed. Faces were wreathed in smiles at the prospect of variety and jubilation. So Biddow turned to Tirwana. "And you, Tirwana, are you satisfied with things?"

"Boss!" Tirwana stepped forward. Though he addressed Biddow, his face was turned towards his fellows. "Boss, can I speak?"

"Of course, Tirwana." Biddow looked dubiously expectant.

Tirwana's eyes roved over the group of Kanakas, then, giving an appreciable emphasis to each word, he began to speak. "Boss, it's like this. The work on this farm has been hard. Never before has Tirwana worked so hard. But, Boss, never before have I worked for a boss who talks to the Kanaka like a white man. I have had bosses who—who—who were *kind*, who gave good food, who liked Tirwana and gave him money, and a horse, and a good hut to live in. But you, Boss"—he turned directly to Biddow—"you may not like. You may not give like other bosses. But you place your foot beside the Kanaka's and you—you treat him as equal!" He grew excited, abandoned his fumbling for correct speech, waved his arms. "You look into Kanaka eyes and know brain behind same as yours. You know the skin"—he slapped his mighty chest—"the black skin accident. So Tirwana like to work for you all the days of his life. I like big wage, good hut, but that not the biggest thing. The big thing is to walk beside the white man as same man." He flung round again, to face the Kanakas. "What you say, you blokes? You like?"

Murmurings of approbation arose from the gathering like responses to a sermon: long-drawn "Ah-h-hs!"

Biddow's face was red with embarrassment. He could not think of anything to say, or do. He was obviously moved. He cleared his throat, gulped a little, stammered.

It was with a feeling of intense relief that he encountered Cindie's eyes. The girl was gazing at him through unshed tears, her whole aspect dissolved in adoring, encouraging softness. Biddow was too confused to read any special significance into the peculiarity of her regard; he was only glad to clutch at her presence as a means of extricating himself from the embarrassment of being praised to his face.

"Thanks, Tirwana," he got out. "Thank you all, men. But you really should be thanking Miss Cindie, as much as me. She looks after you, you know."

Abrupt change of humour in the group, at that, a general lowering of tension, release of feeling. Black bodies relaxed, black faces curved again into smiles. Murmurings swelled into loud phrases. "Missie Cindie all right", "Missie good", and so on. One very clearly expressed opinion, "She devil to work", was received with loud guffaws and clapping of hands.

On every day of the week preceding Christmas, Cindie drove into the township on errands connected with the coming festivities. She liked these outings. She was developing the outlook and habits of the average settler. Quite often she was to be seen chin-chinning with growers in the street, the stores, on the roads. Lately she had taken to wearing her mannish attire into town, and the sight of the shabby pandanus-leaf hat, dungaree pants and cotton blouse became a signal to the storekeepers to hurry out of the pubs and mind their business. For Cindie, on finding a store deserted, helped herself to goods, leaving no inventory behind.

Growers and townspeople alike were coming to regard her as Biddow's manager, and as a pertinent critic and judge of public affairs. Probably Jeff Grey was the only man who recognized Biddow's conclusions in her mouth. For Cindie's mind was moving as rapidly as her body these days, and by prolonged concentration on Biddow's disquisitions, through efforts to thoroughly assimilate and understand them, she was able to retail them in a form and style of her own, a style much simpler than the man's.

Masterman township was growing at a phenomenal rate. Three hotels now flourished in the main street, in line with other business premises such as saddlers, bootmakers and laundries. The mill machinery had arrived in October in the charge of a group of Scottish technicians and was being assembled on the southern bank of the river, at the seaward end of the town.

Cindie liked the air of business linked with lines of vehicles tied up to veranda posts in the street. She liked the "feel" of the town, more especially on Saturdays, when the main thoroughfare became a hive of activity with the week-end business and friendly gossip. Mingled with the whites would be a colourful community of Kanakas, Chinese and Aborigines. Some of the better-off, old-established Chinese would descend from their vehicles dressed in a fashion reminiscent of their native land: embroidered black satin tunic and trousers, satin slippers and cap.

The "antics" of these, as Cindie expressed it, when they chanced to meet in shop or street, filled her with amusement and wonder. Such courtesy, such bowing and smiling, such flowery long-winded compliments, as compared with the perfunctory greetings and crude manners of the whites!

Cindie was deeply shocked but no less agog when, running into a strikingly beautiful, half-white, half-Chinese woman in a shop one day, she received from the shopkeeper in reply to a query the information that the woman was "A stranger in the town. One of *them*, you know."

CHAPTER XIV

BUT MOST OF ALL, ON HER JAUNTS INTO TOWN, CINDIE LIKED to meet up with miners from the mineral belt. Men with a certain amount of money who had come down to the coast to investigate what truth obtained in the widely-propagated reports of anticipated prosperity in Masterman, indicated by the erection of the sugar mill.

Once she had discovered that these miners were a fount of new supposition and prophecy bearing upon the welfare and development of Folkhaven, Cindie took no account of her sex in seeking them out and engaging them in discussion and even dispute.

The outlook of the mining fraternity on the future of the sugar industry was a mixture of dubiety and hope. The mineral belt was traditionally forward looking and radical. William Lane's paper, *The Worker*, organ of the recently constituted Australian Workers' Union, circulated freely on the minefields. Lane's ideals in respect to the historical role of Labour, his ceaseless industry and perfervid journalism, influenced the miners without regard to his confused and outrageously subjective approach to the coloured labour question. Practically to a man they supported the White Australia policy he so zealously and provocatively espoused, the deportation of the Chinese and Kanakas, which involved working the sugar lands by whites.

But the principle of White Australia carried in its wake a whole train of economic and land law adjustments, and these, the miners considered, had to wait upon a powerful orientation towards Labour throughout the land. Also, in common with the sugar growers themselves, the miners were confused by the schisms within the ranks of the tories and liberals over this question of coloured labour.

One group among these, that to which Tom Hilliard up till now had been attached, stood for leaving the planters alone to work out their own destiny with respect to labour forces, while supplying the industry with agricultural education and scientific research. Did not the sugar industry keep the iron foundries busy, the shipping trade in full swing, enable development of the mineral resources of the country? while at the same time supplying a market for the wheat, maize and other farm products of the south, and for the horses, sheep and cattle of the graziers. And was not the sugar industry completely dependent upon the coloured labour forces? Was it not a fact that the better class of white man, whether in need of employment or not, simply would not engage in work in the sugar in any number? And even if white labour to the extent required offered, was not there the further fact that the rate of wages the industry could pay would not maintain them?

Then there were those among tories and liberals who deprecated assistance of any kind to the sugar planters, on the ground that the industry must inevitably collapse when the coloured labour, as it must be, they contended, was swept away.

Another section stood for all possible assistance for the sugar men, in conjunction with the gradual elimination of coloured labour and coloured alien ownership of land, based on questions of national import such as defence against the "teeming millions of the East" and the German threat in the Pacific.

And outside, but linked with elements of the above, there was the confused but vigorous policy of growing militant Labour under Lane, which demanded the extinction of coloured labour and ownership because of the disadvantages accruing to Australian white workers in economic competition with such.

It is true that Lane's fanatical diatribes were chiefly directed against the Chinese, who in their tens of thousands had, for decades past, played a leading part in the exploitation of the Australian goldfields—much more so in the southern colonies than in the far north—and in the immense pastoral and grazier areas of Queensland. His boycott campaigns among housewives, local bodies and trade unions, were entirely directed against the Chinese. But a White Australian policy had to be extended to the Kanakas, despite that the sugar industry, so far, had provided little scope for economic competition between white and coloured workers. The

white workers, no less than their employers, especially in the
tropic belt, had been content to leave the multitude of
Kanakas in full possession of work which they regarded as
unfit for "respectable" whites.

But from out of the midst of all these intertangling threads,
two main trends had recently been emerging as most vital:
the imperialist policy of the British overlords, their desire
to build a White Australia as a bastion of Empire, as an
outpost of British Imperialism in the Pacific, represented by
the most powerful of the ruling cliques of the colonies—and
the subservient agitation by the developing Labour Movement in opposition to coloured labour on the basis of the
need to protect and improve the white workers' economic
standards and conditions.

The miners, then, as a result of being dragged at the heels
of Lane's theoretical obfuscation and the hotchpotch of
opinion recorded above, mingled a certain scepticism with
hope in their desire to transfer from mining fields in process
of decay, to agriculture on the coast. They were well aware
of the rapid penetration of the sugar lands, both as labourers
and landowners, by thousands of Chinese, and at least some
of them anticipated a repetition of the furious hand-to-hand
battles with the Chinese which had been associated with the
goldfields in the past.

The Kanakas, confined as the bulk of them were to agricultural labouring, were in somewhat different personal
regard to the Chinese. The outlook of the sugar grower,
both actual and potential, to a class of men restricted to
menial employment in his service, had to differ from his outlook upon the Chinese, who bought into the land in a big
way and employed their compatriots under conditions which
defied the edict of the whites.

The Chinese brought with them from their homeland the
communal instincts of pre-capitalist feudalism. Employer
and employed often acted together to evade governmental
regulations. It appeared that legislation passed to shorten
hours, raise wages, improve conditions, would only, in effect,
enable the Chinese employer to compete with better advantage. In new settlements like the Masterman area, the
fraternization of wealthy whites with wealthy Chinese, their

conspiring together against the workers of both nationalities was not apparent as in the more developed and larger communities.

There was also arising a big body of opinion, among both large and small sugar growers and the more far-seeing of the general population dependent upon the sugar, that insisted that the Kanakas, in this period of developing agricultural machinery and science, were actually converting from an asset to a liability. They promised to become more expensive than white labour need be. The more intelligent of the planters, especially young fellows like Grey, believed that the future of the industry lay in breaking up the large estates, the cultivation of small areas by individual owners.

Many of the miners took this latter view and to that extent they hoped to dig in to homestead allotments and become part of the "backbone of the country". The dubiety of these was engaged with the stinking corruption of the successive tory administrations, which offered little hope for the small owner, and a knowledge of world conditions gleaned by means of the typical backwoodsman's appetite for all manner of informative reading.

Squatted on their haunches on store or hotel veranda, or lounging on the triangle of grass reserved at the top end of the main street for decorative purposes, these men discoursed on such subjects as mooted increased bounties on beet sugar grown in Germany, increases which could not fail to affect the bulk and price of the Queensland export product.

It was from a miner that Cindie learned that despite the continuing revolution in Cuba, the year on the wing had not been so successful from the Queensland grower's point of view as had been expected. The buoyant tone of the year's beginning had declined as the year advanced. Refiners had refused to buy on the small margin of profit offering. Invisible stocks had been wrongly gauged by speculators. Overproduction, misplaced confidence: these and other unstable factors had characterized the latter part of 1896.

Spurred on by her discussions with the miners, Cindie took to studying the financial columns of the papers. Every fresh item of news, every fresh happening in relation to sugar, she treasured as though it were a jewel, turning it over and over in her mind before placing it before Biddow at meal times, the only times she had the kind of contact with him that legitimatized abstract discussion.

To begin with, Cindie's questions and disputatious manner had caused laughter and mild ridicule among men. But her ignorance of to-day became shrewd commentary on the morrow and it was rarely that the same man laughed twice. And with inexorable persistence she attempted to reduce every item of news to terms of its possible effect upon Folkhaven.

CHAPTER XV

ON CHRISTMAS EVE, THE FALL OF DUSK FOUND DOZENS OF GAUDY Chinese lanterns imparting an air of festivity and gaiety to the home precincts at Folkhaven. Even the huts of the Kanakas were festooned. Irene and Randy were permitted the joy of dividing up a tubful of fireworks among the blacks and of supervising the arrangements for letting them off. Both children were wildly excited, Irene in accord with the rather quiet disposition she had inherited from her father, Randy after the manner of his recently acquired tendency to noisy display.

When the guests came streaming up the track in buckboard, buggy and sulky, or clopping along on horseback, the air of conviviality about the place was rousing and exciting. Even Blanche was stirred to laughter and talkativeness. Dressed to kill, as Biddow expressed it, she welcomed all and sundry, planters, Scottish engineers, even the white mill hands, with a gracious condescension that lost its sting in the glamour and sparkle of her beauty. She had insisted that Biddow dress up, too, in a tailored fawn silk suit she had brought up from Brisbane and, so immaculate, she was filled to overflowing with passionate love for him. She would scarcely let him out of her sight. As her guests dropped out of vehicle or saddle and stood about or made seats of the stumps left in the incipient lawns, she drew him after her, her arm within his.

Barney Callaghan only was present from Palmer Estate, for Consuelo, already in labour, was expected to be delivered of her child before morning. Mary the Kanaka and a doctor from Port Denham were in attendance upon her. Barney had been glad to escape from the atmosphere of strain. His own Kanakas, out of consideration for this circumstance, were attending the festivities at Glenelg that evening. Barney had brought over a case of French wines, and Cindie, at the sight of bottles of whisky and rum emerging from hip pockets and piling beside it, began to wonder how the evening would end. Mary Callaghan had also contributed the loan of two dozen glasses. Biddow himself had little taste for alcoholic liquors but he had not neglected to provide a case of wine for his guests.

With the assistance of Charity and Verbena, Cindie carried the burden of catering for the guests. Physically she was tired after an abnormally strenuous day and the frightful humidity of the midsummer night had her constantly streaming with sweat. But, though her over-taxed limbs tended to tremble with nervous exhaustion, she was buoyed up by a sense of a good job well done, with the secret jubilation at the reality of her own contribution to the scheme of things at Folkhaven. She had put on her "best" dress, a cream mervelo with tight lace neck boned to the chin, leg of mutton sleeves and a wide frill that swept the floor. The blue of her eyes was startling against her tan. They gleamed with fatigue. There was a gaunt sort of beauty, a beauty of bony structure, about her face, and Jeff Grey, coming up to the kitchen in search of her, watched her from the doorway for a minute, unseen, grimly appreciative of it.

"Oh, Mr. Grey!" Cindie welcomed him with smiles. "Do help me with these drinks. But no! Will you see the children first and ask them to let off some of the fireworks? They will love that. Then come and help me. Do you mind?"

Grey did not mind. He liked it and let her know it. Strings of crackers were fired. Rockets soared aloft. Buzzers roared. The virgin forest to the south of the house was illumined with flying sheets of flickering radiance. The guests cheered. The Kanakas shouted and plunged into wild island dancing, chanting and song. Melatonka's mouth organ added appropriate measures, long shrill notes in the treble, full-blown blasts in the bass.

The guests streamed up on to the balcony to watch the scene. Not the programme Blanche had planned, but, as she was well able to realize, in its spontaneous vigour more satisfying and vivid.

Shortly Sow emerged from the uproarious company of Kanakas and took on himself the office of master of ceremonies. Cheer leader, as it were. He danced out in front of his fellows and, with alternate leaping and handclaps and inspiriting cries, incited them to rhythmic action. Forming into double line, in the non-luminous light shed by paper lanterns and stars, they developed a dance entrancing and memorable for its grace.

Tirwana took no part. He stood in the shadows, watching, and when he thought fit, called enough. The black men subsided at his word and then Biddow asked Cindie to send the coloured women out to them with piles of cakes and stone jars of ginger beer.

Then the whites themselves began to dance, to Ben Hart's rousing accordion music. Blanche and the other three wives present led off with their husbands. Many men danced stag fashion. The balcony shook and shuddered to the beating of their feet. Despite the heat they waltzed and polkaed and lined up in square dances: the Lancers, the first set, the Alberts. In between dances they drank, the women, as be-fitted the moral concepts of the day, confining themselves strictly to a few drops of wine in ginger beer or water.

Cindie could not dance. But that fact was no deterrent to men who had learned to use their own feet by chance. But for Biddow's intervention she would have been dragged on to the floor against her will. "I think Miss Comstock should be allowed to decide for herself," he told a "hand" from the mill who showed a tendency to roughness.

There was singing. Old English favourites and some of Stephen Foster's too, sung by everybody present who could stick to a tune at all. The Kanakas gathered on the lawns and sang in chorus, hymn tunes and two or three sea shanties.

In response to Biddow's exhortation, Blanche herself con-sented to sing. She stood up on the balcony, one hand on her husband's shoulder, and in her deep contralto rendered *Annie Laurie*. Her guests were enchanted. The Kanakas kept their gleaming eyes turned upwards, their bodies perfectly still; and when the song was finished cried out their long-drawn "Ahs" of soul-felt satisfaction.

The Scotsmen almost wept in the fullness of their home-sickness and yearning, aggravated not a little by the fiery breath of their national spirit. They demanded more. *Banks and Braes*, *Loch Lomond*, *Scotland Yet*. The English insisted on *The Englishman*. More than a little excited, Blanche settled what promised to become a brawl by singing to please both groups.

Later, Jeff Grey offered to read a short story from a volume recently to hand from "a bloke down Sydney way". He took the book from his pocket and handed it round. *While the Billy Boils*, by Henry Lawson. Only been out a couple of months.

"I reckon it's good," Grey declared argumentatively, though no one present would have dreamed of querying his opinion. "There's one yarn, by cripes, 'The Loaded Dog', would tickle a bloke to tears. This dog, you know, this here dog, he goes fishing with some blokes, and he thinks the charge of dynamite they chuck into the water is a stick. He goes in and brings it out and chases the blokes all over the place with it. . . ."

Privately, Cindie thought Grey was a little drunk, as obviously were some of the other men. She wished he would desist from thrusting upon the gathering a type of entertainment not fitting to their mood.

But, all trace of self-consciousness burnt out by the un-accustomed consumption of much liquor, Grey read the story superbly, and before he had completed a couple of paragraphs his hearers were intent. Biddow was particularly pleased and afterwards begged to be given precedence to a long list of claimants for a loan of the book.

Supper then, laid out in the living-room in buffet style, the guests all standing around and helping themselves.

And it was while everybody was so engaged that Willis Fraser—who by reason of Cindie's violent rejection of his suit had kept away from Folkhaven for some time past—made an uninvited and dramatic appearance in the doorway of the room. He stood there for a few moments, looking in. Then: "Merry Christmas, Everybody!" he called.

Every pair of eyes in the room went to him. The beginnings of return greetings sounded, to be abruptly cut off. There was a slight gasp from Cindie and then dead silence fell. For, standing behind Fraser, peering around his shoulder with frightened eyes, was the part Chinese girl Cindie had remarked in the town. "One of *them*, you know."

Fraser's handsome, red-bearded face was alight with malicious humour and drink. A white topee hung on the back of his head. White drill trousers were belted low on his hips, his white silk shirt blousing out above them. His tie was unknotted and hung from his collar loosely.

"Merry Christmas," he repeated. "I'm late. You know why? I've been to a wedding. To my own wedding, by God! Let me introduce my wife." He turned, grabbed the girl by an arm and thrust her forward into the room. "Meet my missis, Blossom. Hurrah!"

Of the women there, Cindie alone knew something of the girl's way of life. What shocked and offended the other women, principally Blanche, and kept them silent, was the woman's mixed blood. But within seconds Biddow had gone forward to greet her, his hand out, his face smiling. "That's fine, Fraser. Congratulations. Come right in, Mrs. Fraser, and have something to eat. You've just come in time."

So stupefied was the girl by embarrassment and fear that Biddow had to fumble for her hand. But once grasped he held it firmly, then drew it through his arm and led her up to his wife. "My wife, Mrs. Fraser." His eyes were warning signals and Blanche, obliged to take note of them, gingerly put out a hand.

"How do you do?" she said stiffly. "Oh, Cindie! A cup of tea for Mrs. Fraser. And some sandwiches, please. Sit down, Mrs. Fraser. You look tired. Oh, and meet . . ." She named the other women in turn.

Those men present who recognized the girl—several could have claimed a comprehensive acquaintance—reacted according to their nature or to the amount of liquor aboard. There was a certain amount of goggling, of sheepish looks. A few

were joyfully intrigued, some were angry. Cindie looked
with contempt upon Fraser, who had come forward and
stood beside her. He gave her back bold, flaunting glances.
"A cup of tea for me, too, Cindie," he said maliciously.
"After you have helped my missis."   He laughed silently,
opening his mouth till a wide gap yawned between his curly
red beard and well-groomed moustache.

Cindie's lips trembled with rage. "You are lucky, Mr.
Fraser, to get such a nice wife," she spat out. "I can't congratulate her, though." She reached for a plate of cream puffs
and placed them in front of the girl. "Have some of these,
Mrs. Fraser. They are nice. I made them myself."

The little exchange was lost upon no one. And its significance upon few. Bush telegraph kept the community informed on personal matters equally with more material events
and Cindie's contemptuous rejection of Fraser's suit had been
well canvassed. Jeff Grey let out a loud guffaw of laughter.
"That was a good one, Miss Comstock! 'I can't congratulate
her.' " He mimicked Cindie's tone. "A good one for you,
Fraser." He laughed again.

Fraser's red brows came down like a thunder clap above
his big Roman nose. He wheeled towards Grey, his hand
clenching.

"That's enough," declared Biddow, authoritatively. "This
is Christmas. Have some supper, Fraser. Help yourself. The
night's getting along."

Barney Callaghan stood up. "Yes, and I must be getting
along. Might be a new chip of the old block to give the once
over when I get home."

That started a chorus of relieved talk and laughter, a
general move. The younger people returned to the balcony
to luxuriate in the bliss of a fair south-easterly that came
blowing in off the sea. The married folk followed Barney's
example and made for vehicle and horse. Eventually, Biddow,
Grey, the Frasers and Cindie were left alone, around the
ruins of the supper-table and a pile of "dead marines".
Blanche was downstairs, seeing her guests off.

Fraser voraciously helped himself to food and maintained a
stubborn, savage silence. The girl Blossom had not uttered
one word since her entrance. She ate daintily but with effort,

as though each morsel was difficult to swallow. Her eyes, when not downcast, were lifted in frightened stealthy glances to her husband.

Grey began to help Cindie pile up the dishes and remove them to the kitchen. Biddow puffed at his pipe, tranquilly observant. At length he cleared his throat and spoke, casually. "Seem to be a good wind coming up. Suppose the rains won't be long now, Fraser."

Fraser rose abruptly. "Sorry to have busted up your party, Biddow. . . . Come on, you! We'll be off."

The girl, with a startled movement, looked swiftly from him to Biddow, then rose. A red stain ran up from her throat over her lovely face.

Biddow, his face as red as hers, also rose. "We shall always be glad to see you, Mrs. Fraser," he said quietly. "Come over whenever you like. Good night, Fraser. And again, congratulations."

"Good night," replied Fraser, roughly. He stalked out of the room with the girl at his heels.

Biddow sank back into his chair. Jeff Grey ceased to help Cindie with the chores and followed suit. "Don't you know what she is, Biddow?" he asked.

"What she is? That's obvious, isn't it?"

"Aw, you don't catch on." Grey looked round to make sure that Cindie was out of earshot. "She's a prostitute. A new arrival from the south. She's been living in a shack behind the town."

On top of his words, Cindie and Blanche came into the room together.

"Well!" Blanche dropped the word like an explosion. "Of all the colossal impudence! Randolph, do you know what they are saying? That girl——"

"Yes," Biddow interrupted her. "Grey has just told me. I'll have something to say to Fraser next time I see him. And I asked her to call. Not that she is likely to do it."

"I'll show her the track if she does," said Blanche furiously.

"And will you show Mr. Willis Fraser the track, too, if he calls?" Cindie spoke up with spirit.

Blanche glowered at her. "Don't be impertinent, Cindie. Mr. Fraser is different. His bringing her here was unpardonable, but after all he is trying to make a decent woman of her."

"Willis Fraser couldn't make a decent woman out of anyone. And I'll bet he didn't marry her with that intention. She is better than he is, whatever she may be."

"She is certainly as good as he is," Biddow put in, decisively. "There can be no question of our receiving a man whose wife is unwelcome. I felt sorry for the poor little thing."

"Poor little fiddlesticks!" cried Blanche. "Whatever possessed the man! So handsome. A man with his looks could get almost any—well, lots of women."

"He couldn't get me," said Cindie flatly. "Do you know how he feeds his Kanakas, Mr. Biddow? He tips buckets of food on to bags on the ground and makes them pick it up with their fingers. Just like animals."

"What? Are you sure about that?"

"It's true enough," put in Grey.

"Where do you get all this information from, Cindie?" Blanche asked, coldly.

"I don't go around with my ears shut."

Blanche stalked out on to the balcony and Biddow followed her.

While he helped Cindie wash the dishes—Charity and Verbena had been dispensed with early on—Grey again asked Cindie to marry him.

"No, Mr. Grey——"

"Jeff," he corrected.

"No, Jeff. I don't want to marry anyone. Anyhow, what would Folkhaven be without me?" she asked playfully.

But Grey did not smile. "Cindie, sometimes I think that both Folkhaven and you would be——" He paused, glanced at her, then dropped that line. "Cindie, I've got a farm, too. A farm that would be yours."

"I'm sorry, Jeff. I just like this place."

"And you don't like me."

Cindie handed him a dry towel. "I do like you. I like you very much. But I don't think I'm the marrying type, Jeff."

"All right"—gruffly. After a time, as casually as he could make it, he added: "How you getting along with Mrs. Biddow, Cindie?"

"All right." Cindie shot him a keen glance. "What made you ask me that?"

"Just wondered."

"You know, Jeff"—Cindie's manner became expansive—"sometimes I think she does not like me. But she's been brought up to do nothing useful and so, even if she doesn't like me, she won't let me go. . . . Mr. Biddow thinks the sun shines out of her, you know. She's mad about him, too."

"Yes, I've noticed that. He's the cleverest man I've ever met, Biddow. Can't help wondering why he came up here. With her like she is. Anyone can see she's not suited to this place. Old Tom Hilliard for a father, too. He must be rolling in money."

"Oh, I don't know so much about that. He lost a lot of money in the bank smashes of 'ninety-three, did Mr. Hilliard."

"And picked it up in graft again, since. Say, Cindie, don't you ever get a day off? How about coming to the races at Port Denham with me on New Year's Day?"

"I'm sorry, Jeff, really sorry. The Biddows are going down to the New Year's Eve ball so I shall have to take the children on New Year's Day."

"Oh——!" Grey chewed that over. "Um——"

On Biddow's invitation Jeff spent that night at Folkhaven. He lay down on a rug on the balcony, a cushion beneath his head.

CHAPTER XVI

WHEN CINDIE CAME OUT OF HER ROOM ON CHRISTMAS MORNING, later than usual in deference to the holiday spirit, through Grey's offices the kettle was already singing on the hob. The man himself was downstairs with Tirwana and the children, admiring the visual consequences of a visit from Santa Claus. No Verbena in evidence.

Cindie called from the top of the stairs: "Tell Verbena to come up at once, Tirwana. She should have had the table set by now."

But Verbena was not in her room.   Nor were her few belongings. She had packed them overnight and decamped.

"That was to be expected, sooner or later," said Grey. "She's stuck things out here pretty well."

"But it's Christmas!" wailed Cindie.   "Look at all the work I've got to do!"

"Tell you what." Grey's eyes lit up. "We'll go round to the Abo. camp this morning and see if we can pick up another girl for you."

"Not this morning. There's Christmas dinner, poultry and everything, to cook. And Takeo doesn't know a thing about plum puddings. I'll have to keep an eye on him. But we could go this afternoon."

Charity grinned at Cindie when told that Verbena had disappeared. "She have baby one day," she said affably. No, she did not know who the man was. Maybe big Tanna man under house. This quizzically, with sly glances at Cindie.

Cindie refused to accept that. Tirwana would never do such a thing! Nevertheless, she bluntly put the question to Tirwana.

"Miss Cindie!" Tirwana shook his head, fluttered his eye-lids and smiled in the shy, charming manner of an amused and flattered child. "Miss Cindie, *no*."

"I'm glad of that, Tirwana. Who is it, Tirwana? I'll bet you know."

"Miss Cindie, that's not my business." His tone reproved her.

"You mean it's not my business, don't you, Tirwana? And I don't suppose it is, really. But, Tirwana, someone has to look after the child when it comes."

"The black people, they will look after the baby. Black people are not sensible like whites, Miss Cindie. They won't let the little baby starve because the father not known. They only savage." Tirwana's lips curved in a shadowy smile.

Immediately after breakfast Blanche and Biddow went off in the sulky to inquire about Consuelo's condition; to return with the news of the arrival of a fine baby boy. They brought also an item concerning Willis Fraser's marriage, contributed by Bert Callaghan.

When Bert, on the preceding day, had gone down to the Port for the doctor he had run into the couple in the street. Fraser, half drunk even then, had volunteered the information that they had just been "hitched up" by a Justice of the Peace and invited Bert to have a drink with him on the strength of it.

Bert had accepted, thinking that maybe the marriage would do Fraser good. He had been taken with the girl's looks, too. They had left her standing in the street while they had the drink, to find, when they came out of the pub, that two men were annoying her. She was in tears, just standing in the street with the tears running down her face.

"And what did Mr. Willis Fraser do?" Cindie asked, indignantly.

"He grabbed her by the arm and made off with her without a word. Bert took the blokes up on it and they told him what she was. . . . Hanged if I know whether to think good or ill of Fraser over this."

"I think I know," Cindie said, slowly. "That poor thing's in for trouble. Fraser's a bad egg. A girl like that couldn't build him up. I doubt if even a strong woman could."

"One never knows," put in Blanche, smoothly. "People do change, you know. They can be built up. And very rapidly, too, under a certain influence."

"Aw, hang Fraser!" Grey exclaimed loudly. "He's been like a skeleton at a feast."

Early in the afternoon, Cindie and Grey set out for the Aborigines' camp on Palmer Estate creek. At Palmer House, where they took the time to inspect the new baby, they decided that instead of cutting through the fields on horseback, they would proceed by foot along the bed of the creek: a decision Cindie had no cause to regret.

In places the stream widened to one hundred yards and more. Tangled masses of vegetation rose from islets dotting the bed and from earth lodged among blue granite boulders. The sun's rays easily penetrated to the water at these stretches, but soft air currents seemed to flow from the mighty beech, cedar, pines and oak trees rising from the banks, cooling and sweetening Cindie's flesh. The timber trees were blanketed with the ubiquitous wait-awhile or lawyer vine, and with innumerable other creepers. Many trees and vines were a riot of glorious blossom. The white and cream flowers of the creepers and lesser trees mingled with the scarlet of the great silky oak, with the cascades of ivory pencil orchids and long spears of the golden species. Ground orchids decorated the banks.

And, for the first time, Cindie learned something about the nature of the timber trees. And other things besides that set her thinking deeply.

"So many of these trees contain valuable timber," she repeated, after Grey.

"They would be valuable, if there was a market for them, was what I said. The cedar alone would be worth a small fortune. But we are too far north for the market."

"And Mr. Biddow has got seven hundred acres of timber country to fell. . . . All those trees will be left to rot."

"Nothing else for it, as things are."

"But the settlers are having to bring timber from Pearl-town to build their homes! That seems ridiculous to me."

"It is, on the face of it. But even if the market obtained up here for a saw-mill, there's no labour available. The whites won't stick because of the climate and the Kanakas are confined to agricultural labouring."

"What about the Aborigines?"

"The Abos.! D'ye think you could make saw-millers out of them?" Grey was amused.

"Why not?"

"Why not?" Grey ran a hand through his hair. "They are wild men, Cindie. They're just like animals. Belong to the bush."

"Oh? I thought we were going to their camp to try and get a woman to work for me."

"But—but Verbena went walkabout, didn't she?"

"Yes, but Verbena is not an animal. She is learning to cook as well as I can. And she is as clean as a new pin. I'm thinking, Jeff. All this lovely timber——" She subsided into deep thought.

A little further on Jeff said slyly: "If you were married to me, Cindie, you could try out all these schemes you get in your head."

"I'll try them out without being married to you, Jeff, if it is in any way possible. Seven hundred acres! There would be an awful lot of timber there, wouldn't there?"

"Yes, a hell of a lot of timber!" Grey exploded violently and pushed on ahead of her.

Cindie was not prepared for anything so primitive as that camp and the conditions of the natives inhabiting it. It was simply a collection of *mia mias*—shelters formed of branches, palm leaves, flattened kerosene tins and bags—placed in the shade of the trees on the edge of a Palmer Estate clearing.

The creek at that spot was particularly beautiful. The further side of it a long reach of deep water, on the camp side it rippled over boulders or circled white sandy islets. Few young men were visible. A number of youths and children were swimming or floating in the deep water. Old folk were in plenty, crones whose nakedness was barely covered by the ragged remains of "white" frocks, and aged men in tattered pants. Almost all of both sexes of these clawed at clay pipes. Several young women wore reputable garments, some being ludicrous in long frocks that swept the ground. But what stopped Cindie dead in her tracks was the sight of several young girls stark naked.

"Now don't be silly," warned Grey. "That's common. I told you they belonged in the bush."

"You had no right to bring me," Cindie exclaimed furiously. "I had no idea of this sort of thing."

"Then turn round and go back," he replied, coolly. "But there's no need to get mad. They don't feel any shame."

"No. They certainly don't. All right. Go ahead. Oh, there's Verbena, the little scamp!"

The whole camp, consisting of about four dozen souls, had concentrated its mild, curious gaze upon the visitors. Some dogs lying in the dirt got up and meandered towards them, snuffling and growling. Verbena grinned at them broadly but kept her distance.

"Verbena," Cindie called sharply. "Keep those dogs off us."

"They no hurt, Miss Cindie." Verbena picked up a stick and, running towards the dogs, sent them flying.

"Verbena," said Cindie severely, "why did you run away from me like that?"

Verbena seemed unable to take the grin off her face. "Too much talk, Miss Cindie. I tell you and you talk and talk. I tired of wash dishes, wash clo's."

"Oh! So you're not coming back?"

"You give me money I come back, maybe"—slyly.

"How much money, Verbena?"

"Money, money. Like you buy clo's with."

"She doesn't know anything about money," Grey said, in an undertone. "Promise her sixpence a week. Biddow wouldn't mind giving her that."

"I should think not! Sixpence! . . . Verbena, are you going to have a baby?"

Verbena's head nodded vigorously. "But long time yet. You give money?"—in a wheedling tone.

"If you come back with me, Verbena, I will ask Mrs. Biddow."

Verbena's manner grew furtive. She looked around her. With the exception of the oldsters the whole camp was encircling them. "I come bynby," she said quickly. "I come sure bynby."

Cindie hesitated. Perhaps she had better try one of the other women. But Verbena was trained. To start that all over again. . . . And she was fairly reliable, too. Another might be like Toby. "All right, Verbena," she said, at length. "You come to-night. I will ask Mrs. Biddow about money."

"You the boss," said Verbena, promptly. "Missis Biddow, she——" She emitted what might feasibly be claimed to have been the original and father of all raspberries. And as though it were a signal all the folk around, from old crone to pot-bellied toddler, screeched and cackled with laughter.

The demonstration scared Cindie. She felt glad of Grey's presence beside her. She wanted to get away quickly but instead, with simulated boldness, stood her ground and looked around. What a way to live! Yet everything seemed clean enough. And there were signs of fairly extensive cultivations near by. The stubble of corn, the dried vines of sweet potatoes. And pigs grunted from a sty at some distance from the camp.

"These people *do* work," she told Grey, triumphantly. "And these people are good-looking in their way, Jeff. Nothing like the miserable specimens I saw round Brisbane. What do they live on?"

"They cultivate in the winter, by the looks of things. For the rest, I suppose they depend on the forest foods they always lived on. There are plenty eels in the creek and fish in the river. They eat goanna, too, and wallaby, snakes, bandicoot. They needn't go hungry in this country, believe me. And they beg around the farms, do a bit of wood-carrying and—chopping."

"Well—we'll see." Cindie spoke enigmatically. "But listen! What's that, Jeff?—it's a mouth organ. Melatonka's. I'd know his tunes anywhere. There he is! Look!" Far down the clearing, coming up towards them, Melatonka was swinging along.

At the sound of the music Verbena began to register consternation. "Missie Cindie," she faltered. "You no tell?"

"So it's Melatonka, Verbena," said Cindie. "I might have known."

"She's not worrying about her condition," Grey laughed. "I'll bet there's been quite a few to blame, there. And she wouldn't dream of anybody objecting. She's worrying about old Melo's leaving the farm without permission, I'll bet."

"Maybe he got permission from Mr. Biddow before he left. I hope so. I don't like the idea of peaching on him."

"As long as he sticks to this camp he can't do any harm. But he looks a cheeky cuss. There have been a few yarns lately. A woman out at Backwater Creek was frightened by a wandering Kanaka. They say he grabbed her by the leg."

The handsome native himself did not seem to be concerned about the presence of the whites. He hopped up to the camp jauntily, his mouth organ now thrust into the folds of his fancy sulu, grinned at Cindie, made straight for the bank of the creek and threw himself down at full length upon it.

On their return to Folkhaven, Cindie and Grey scarcely had time to unsaddle their mounts when Louis Montague and his wife arrived, full of a yarn about a miniature battle that had raged that morning between Glenelg's Kanakas and Chinese.

"Can't let the beggars within cooee of each other at any

time without trouble," Louis declared, "and since this albino Kanaka came in, two months ago, a few of the Chinks have been looking for it. They reckon he's bad luck. He's cocky, this albino chap. Reckons he's a white man." Louis laughed. "He is, too, for that matter. White curly hair, fair complexion with big freckles. Got the black features, that's all. Funny. They say there's an island full of these freaks somewhere.

"Anyhow, it seems that a few of the Chinks—we haven't got many left, you know—celebrated Christmas Eve with a beano on papaw wine, and this morning they had the regulation hangover. It's the worst stagger juice ever invented, papaw wine. Takes days to get rid of the hangover.

"They tell us the row started when the albino chap comes strutting around the barracks and calls a Chinaman 'yella fella'. The Chinks took to him. He's been pretty badly mauled. We had to get out on horseback and scatter a few bullets around their heels."

After some deliberation, Cindie thought fit to approach Tirwana about Melatonka's conduct.

"You knew that Melatonka was to blame for Verbena's condition, didn't you, Tirwana?" she concluded reproachfully.

"Miss Cindie, Tirwana"—he corrected his infantile English —"Miss Cindie, I'm not interested in the black girl. But leaving the farm without a permit, that is different. Melatonka, he's not too good. Some Kanakas I trust to go anywhere. All of them, I think, but Melatonka. A man to be trusted would ask for the permit. There's something I didn't tell you, Miss Cindie, about Melatonka. He gets the drink. One night I went into the kitchen and I heard something funny in Takeo's hut. So I looked in and Melatonka's there with Takeo and they have a bottle of whisky to drink. Takeo said he got it but I know he lied. The Kanaka got it. It was written in the smile on his face. Bad smile. Not the crawling smile he always have but the bad smile of the deceiver."

"But how could Melatonka afford to buy whisky, Tirwana?"

"That's the worst of it, Miss Cindie. He can't afford. He must get it some cheap way."

"You should have reported that to Mr. Biddow, Tirwana. You know the danger of letting the Kanakas get drink."

Noting that Melatonka was in his place in the field dining-room as usual that evening, Cindie waited and accosted him as he was on his way back to his quarters.

"Mr. Biddow probably wouldn't object to your visiting the creek, Melatonka," she told him, "but you are supposed to ask for permission. We must know where our men are. Then if any trouble arises, like thefts, or Kanakas snooping around other farms, we are in a position to prove the innocence of our men. See? It's for your own good."

"Oh yes, Missie. I see." His face was wreathed in smiles. Then, with simpering, deprecatory manner he asked softly: "You get permission to visit creek, Missie Cindie?"

Cindie's eyes remained steadily on his. "Yes, Melatonka, I got permission."

The man was unable to conceal his chagrin at the failure of his taunt. The smile was wiped from his face, his head drooped. But he stuck his ground, sullenly waiting for Cindie to make the first move.

"You may go, Melatonka," she said graciously. "I am sure you won't make it necessary for me to complain and have you fined."

He moved off quickly, at that, but the glance he threw at the girl as he went lingered in her mind. That look did not predicate savagery. It had nothing in common with the wild fury of Sow when he rowed with Charity because she had not yet given him a child. Rows which usually ended in Charity's swiping her husband with anything that came to her hand. Melatonka's look was sophisticated malice. "Golly," thought Cindie, "I had better keep out of his way in the bush. He might chop my head off, cook me and eat me."

She mused curiously upon the background of many of the Kanakas. Headhunters and cannibals, at least in their youth. Yet here they were, apparently comfortably adjusted to civilized conditions. Charity had kept her absorbed, at times, with grisly yarns, though disclaiming anything in the nature of cannibalism in respect to herself. She had described to Cindie the manner in which the chefs of the tribe had prepared their choice repasts of human flesh. Had promised, indeed, that when the first wild pig was brought in Cindie would be furnished with a practical example.

That occasion presented itself within the following twenty-four hours.

CHAPTER XVII

UP TILL NOW, IN THIS CHRONICLE, ONLY BRIEF AND PERFUNCTORY reference has been made to what really constituted a serious menace to the interests of the pioneering farmers of the far north: the wild pig. For the very good reason, as it seemed to this chronicler, that since Folkhaven had suffered little from the ravages of this animal, the subject might well be left in abeyance until the Boxing Day hunt wove it naturally into the texture of the story.

The comparative immunity enjoyed by Folkhaven in this respect was by no means fortuitous. It was the direct result of a planned campaign waged upon the pigs over the preceding summer and autumn by the Callaghans, Biddow, Jeff Grey and some other neighbouring planters. Palmer Estate's losses in farm produce in 1895 had been so extensive that Barney had organized a team of Kanakas to patrol his fields nightly, in addition to two-day week-end hunts during which as many as fifty to sixty pigs would be disposed of. As a result, the remaining animals had learned to eschew the immediate neighbourhood. Only lately were they returning in any number. During several nights, recently, Biddow's cane patch had been damaged by the foraging of these raiders. He had been worried over his inability to secure a couple of good pig dogs for nightly service and week-end hunting. Eventually, through Bert Callaghan, it had been arranged that he would buy two serviceable dogs from Jack Callaghan while down at the Port at New Year.

Over Christmas, Grey had agreed to bring over his dogs for the Boxing Day hunt.

"You will come out with us yourself, Grey?" Biddow had asked.

"No. I have decided to take Miss Comstock for a ride. Show her something of the country." Jeff had cast a wary eye at Cindie as he spoke.

"Jeff Grey, I never said I would do anything of the kind," was Cindie's rejoinder to that. "Who's going to do the work here, do you think? Verbena might not return to-night and Charity has the day off."

"How conscientious we are." Elaborate sarcasm from Blanche. Then, with an assumption of indulgence: "You can leave something prepared for lunch, Cindie, and take the day off."

"The house is full of food," replied Cindie, shortly. "What time do you expect to be back from the hunt, Mr. Biddow? The Kanakas are going to cook a pig the way they cook men in the islands and I want to see it done."

Biddow was startled. "Oh, I say, Cindie! Rather crude, don't you think? The children——"

"I know all about it, Dad," cried Randy. "I'm going to help cook the pig. Sallerome has promised to lend me his flesh fork, that he used to eat long pig with in Api. Long pig is man, Dad. It's a lovely fork. All carved with men and animals. Sallerome says he got it from Fiji. Only the Fijians make them, he says."

Early on Boxing Day morning, a dozen Kanakas assembled with Biddow to take off into the forest. Biddow and Tirwana carried guns, the others were armed with tomahawks and cane knives.

Tirwana cautioned his fellows before they set out. "You be quiet. You be careful. The wild boar is savage, strong, quick. He won't run. He fights. The sow, she will run, but the boar will charge. You follow Mr. Biddow and me."

Eagerly the three dogs, cross between bull terrier and cattle dog, plunged into the jungle and began to search for the fresh rootings and droppings that indicated the recent presence of pigs. Impossible for the men to keep up with them, but every few minutes the well-trained animals returned to hand. Once the neighbourhood of a pig had been determined, the dogs would start up a furious barking and take the trail. The hunters would crash forward. When a pig was located, in addition to the barking, grunts from the boars and squeals from the sows and young as they took to their heels would guide the men.

As luck had it, the first pig that bailed up, after nearly an hour's hunt in the foothills, was a boar. The Kanakas, who all had slipped through the forest with less noise than Biddow alone made, received the throaty porcine grunts and loud barking with intense, though repressed, excitement. Instantly they dropped all recognizance of Biddow's authority and vanished from his sight.

Alone, the white hunter in this case would have moved very circumspectly indeed. For the boar with his fighting blood up was an adversary to beware of in the confines of the scrub. He might charge, any way, or double back. In these circumstances, however, Biddow plunged forward, concerned that the exultant Kanakas might underestimate his "nibs". One rip of the huge, knife-sharp tusks and, as had happened the preceding summer, a man might be disembowelled.

But when Biddow approached the scene of operations closely enough to note the proceedings he was too intrigued to elect to do otherwise than watch. The wild men had surrounded the pig, which, in slashing around, had flattened out the immediate undergrowth, but so silently and deftly that they were scarcely visible to Biddow and not at all, he felt sure, to the pig. The dogs realized their presence, for their barking became intermittent. They flirted their heads and darted expectant looks about them.

Screened by the undergrowth, he tried to pick out Tirwana from the momentary glimpses he caught of intent, peering faces. Ah! There he was, straining his eyes between the ten-foot fronds of a wild ginger. His expression was incredulous, his mouth agape. "What's got into him?" Biddow asked himself. Slinging his Snider rifle into an easy position he moved forward, curious but wary.

Simultaneously the forest came to life. With the exception of Tirwana, every Kanaka leapt up and with demoniac yells hurled himself towards the pig. At which blood-curdling outbreak the old boar, as evidenced by his scarred hide a veteran of many doughty combats, and game to the last

breath against any ordinary foe, was galvanized into an
activity entirely volitionless. With a short sharp squeal that
more than rivalled the frenzied clamour of his assailants, he
shot almost vertically into the air, vaulted a dog, knocked a
Kanaka flying, and was off up the hill in a crashing rush
that seemed to bring down the forest about him. The dog
he had vaulted let out an astounded howl, then recovered
his assurance and with a yelp set off in pursuit.

For the life of him Biddow could not have forborne lapsing
into a paroxysm of laughter at the exquisite humour of that
scene. The monstrous boar—quite the largest he had ever
seen, easily three foot high and six foot in length, with the
razor back and long snout of the "Captain Cook" breed—
launching itself into the air, the astonishment of the dogs, the
sudden checking of the brave warriors and their scrambling
scatter, the yowls of the winded Kanaka: though not given
to excessive mirth, Biddow's sides ached with the strain put
upon his muscles by his uncontrollable laughter.

But the lesson the Kanakas had learned from their first pig
was a good one. Tirwana gave Biddow a mortified look
and with a shake of his head promised: "Not any more,
Boss."

They never caught up with that particular boar, but several
other pigs fell to the guns, among them a sow who presented
Biddow with a bit of a physiological puzzle.

This pig was one of a trio the dogs started up on the bank
of a creek. A boar, the sow, and a young animal the size of
an average domestic pig, probably a yearling, stampeded as
usual with the dogs on their heels. Quite five minutes elapsed
before the modified tone of the dogs' barking assured the
hunters that a pig had bailed up. And bailed up, it transpired,
on the edge of Willis Fraser's plantation.

When the hunters came up, the boar and the youngster
had vanished into Fraser's well-grown cane and the dogs
were holding the sow in the centre of a triangle. Whirl and
charge as she would, one or other of the dogs would fly in
and rip her hindquarters. A snuffling grunting roar, a nasal
roar, compounded of exhaustion and terror, accompanied
her exertions. When brought to a standstill, her sides heaving,
the dogs flew in and attempted to bring her down.

Though distressed by the sight, fear of injuring the dogs kept Biddow's trigger finger relaxed until such time as a safe shot seemed assured. Eventually he hit her in the side of her solid, muscular neck, but with little result beyond the gushing of profuse streams of blood. Then Tirwana got in a slug behind the shoulder and the sow dropped instantly, quite dead.

Biddow decided to call it a day. What with the dreadful heat and the mounting exasperation of having to hack a way through the denser undergrowth, he felt that he had had more than enough. Also, Fraser's holding being separated from Grey's by a narrow headland only, the Kanakas would be able to make easier way in carrying home the heavy carcass by cross-cutting the farms.

So, a stake was inserted behind the tendons of the pig's hindlegs and she was hoisted and hung on a tree for disembowelling. Sallerome, who was something of an expert at butchering, did this job.

On slitting the belly open, Sallerome gave utterance to mournful cries. The slug, it appeared, had torn out the wall of the heart and shattered one lung. Blood, lung and heart tissue poured out of the thorax in a mess, and this, to a native who valued these organs as extra special titbits, was a matter for dismay.

And loud were the general protests when Biddow, following an accepted practice, supposed to stimulate the hunting instinct, rubbed the noses of the dogs into the bloody liver and then gave each of them a part of it to eat.

To see the Kanakas scrape with their hands among the viscera disgusted Biddow, but when Sow disentangled a longish, pale-purple tube and held it aloft for his inspection he found himself full of interest. Obviously an uterus, though not at all like what he would have imagined that organ to be.

From the womb Sow extracted a single fœtus of about four pounds weight. And what amazed Biddow, apart from the fact of a single birth from a pig, was that, though the sow had been dead for quite fifteen minutes, the fœtus still revealed reflexes. It quivered and jumped. Sow, with much grinning, told Biddow: "That for my missis. Maybe she breed now."

Eventually the carcass was slung up by the hind legs from a pole and the hunters, in procession, set out to skirt Fraser's cane in the direction of Grey's farm. They had not gone far when Fraser himself, brought out by the shots, came riding up. A few words of greeting and then Biddow was invited to go over to the house for a drink. Biddow calculated swiftly. To be neighbourly or not, that was the question. To accept meant that the die was cast for reciprocal overtures, and though he himself was now prepared to renounce the position he had taken up on Christmas Eve, how would Blanche take that? Hang it, he concluded, his face red with the knowledge that Fraser followed exactly what was passing through his mind, and hating the fellow's caddish amusement at it—hang it, a man couldn't refuse to give a woman a shove up.

"Righto," he said shortly. "I could do with a drink. You carry on, Tirwana."

Fraser tumbled from his horse and, putting an arm through the reins, walked along the headland with Biddow towards his house. The Kanakas proceeded on their way home and before long their voices, harmonized in joyous song, floated back across the fields.

Fraser's house was little more than a three-roomed shack, squatted upon the top of a small knoll. Its sides were slabs, its roof of thatch. But his farm, his outhouses, his gardens, were exemplary for order and condition. Not one of his twenty-odd Kanakas was to be seen, but two young Aborigine women pottered about the gardens. Biddow stiffened at that sight, for the status of Aborigine women in Fraser's household was a subject for lewd comment among men.

"Your 'boys' got the day off, I suppose, Fraser," he said stiffly, to make conversation.

"Day off, bedamned! They're bushwhacking. I don't spoil my niggers, Biddow. Hey, you!" he yelled to one of the Aborigine women, "come and take my horse." The girl came on the run and, with a grin, took the reins.

"Well, I'm still honeymooning, Biddow," Fraser spoke sarcastically as they walked up to the front door of the shack. They entered. "Hey there, Blossom!"

The girl came into the front room from the kitchen and

Biddow was again struck by her remarkable beauty. The pure oval of the face, the faint slant to the long brown eyes, the small nose, the rosebud mouth, the natural blush of the cheeks, all this was crowned with a mass of glossy black hair. And to make the picture perfect she wore an embroidered Chinese gown of turquoise blue silk, high-necked and slit to the knee. At the sight of Biddow she shrank back, startled, and crossed her hands upon her breast.

"Bring some glasses," Fraser commanded, tossing his hat upon one of the few rough chairs the room contained. There was little furniture besides: a home-made cedar table and cupboard, a couple of boxes, that was all. But upon the otherwise naked wall two conventional frameless Chinese prints had been tacked.

"Suppose you'll be building a decent home now that you're married, Fraser?" said Biddow, as he took a chair. Assuming a jocular tone he added: "Your wife will be wanting to entertain, I suppose."

The wife entered on top of his words and Biddow instantly rose and took her hand. He kept on his feet while she stood, shaming Fraser into following suit. But when the girl had brought the whisky bottle from the cupboard and arranged the glasses and water, Fraser told her, curtly: "That will do." She had scarcely disappeared when he added, cynically: "Better come off the high horse, Biddow. You can't fool me. Say when." He sank back into his chair, glass in hand, and abruptly changed the subject. "I've been wanting to have a yarn with you. Got any ideas about all this political shite? this talk of uniting the colonies?"

"Could hardly help having ideas about it, could I? You must have some yourself."

"This convention of representatives of the colonies to be held in Adelaide in March: looks pretty conclusive, doesn't it? No use shutting our eyes to what this federation business might mean for us."

"But our colony is not taking part in it. Not but what we would have to come in, I suppose, if the other colonies decided to federate and England agreed." Biddow mused and Fraser, his eyes upon him intently, waited.

"Seems to me," Biddow continued slowly, "we sugar men

would have to revolutionize our methods altogether. As I see it, the whole idea of federation is coming to be one of Empire build-up. Defence and so on. And the White Australia policy is the basis of that. Mistakenly, I think."

"What do you mean by 'revolutionize our methods'? If the Kanakas are deported we are done for. Bloody well done for."

"I'm not sure about that." Biddow made his words fit his hesitating thoughts.

"Hell, man, you can't grow sugar without labour! And we can't make a go with holdings of our size with a couple of dozen niggers, either. I need about thirty more niggers for the coming year and so must you."

"I think I can put about sixty acres under cane next year with the men I've got. That would satisfy me."

"You are pretty optimistic," Fraser said, grimly. "But you've only got ten acres to cut. I've got thirty. And that would mean you'd get no bushwhacking done till late in the year. . . . But hang that! What do you mean by revolutionizing our methods?"

"Well. . . . Look at Grey. He wouldn't indent a Kanaka for love nor money."

"That weasel! A tinpot miner bringing his tinpot ideas into the cane. A one-man farm's no meat of mine, Biddow."

"You might be left with little choice. We've got to realize, Fraser, that the defence of Australia would only be a joke without federal unity."

"They can have their federal unity!" Fraser slammed his glass upon the table. "The Kanakas are not concerned with that. They don't threaten us. It's the so-and-so Chinks they ought to deport and leave the Kanakas alone."

"Ah, but you've got to think in the broad, Fraser. How could a White Australia policy ignore the presence in the colony of about fifty thousand blacks? Our white population is only about half a million. The sugar industry promises to rival the pastoral industry in size and importance. If it continues to grow at its present rate and the importation of Kanakas were allowed to match that growth; well, where's your White Australia? I reckon the Chinese Government would resent its nationals being discriminated against."

"Who the hell cares about the Chinese Government?"

"The Mother Parliament cares. British imperialist interests are very much concerned with China, I imagine." Biddow rose. "But I hardly think things have got to the stage where we need worry overmuch. They can't sweep away the Kanakas at a moment's notice. And as I said before, our colony seems to be keeping well out of this federation business. We'll be able to get a better idea of things after this Adelaide Convention."

"Old Tom-bloody-Hilliard ever give you any pointers, Biddow?" Fraser asked bluntly.

Biddow's manner chilled. "Not at all. . . . Now, if I could say good-bye to Mrs. Fraser I'll be off. I'm getting stiff."

"Blossom!" Fraser shouted, and again the girl appeared. Biddow went forward and took her limp hand. "I'm off now, Mrs. Fraser. I wish you a happy New Year."

In response, for the first time she uttered a word in his presence. With a fleeting smile she said softly: "Oh yes. Happy New Year to you, Mr. Biddow."

Biddow, pushing along at a very good bat through a desire to be on hand at the cooking of the pig, was not long on the heels of the Kanakas in arriving home. Emerging from the forest near the homestead he had broken into a run and taken logs on the jump, for from the midst of a group of people near the quarters of the Kanakas a column of smoke was rising.

All the members of his household, not excepting Blanche, were congregated with Jeff Grey and the blacks around a shallow hole dug in the ground. Large stones from the creek bed paved the bottom of the hole and upon them a fire had been lighted. When the stones glowed red with heat the fire was raked out, some of the stones were placed within the belly cavity of the pig, armfuls of leaves swiftly thrown in upon the remainder, and the carcass lowered upon these. Then another layer of stones upon the top and a second fire built upon them. A couple of hours of cooking and the meat would be done to a turn.

The fœtus, Charity had put to roast in Takeo's oven. "Sow, he say I get baby, too, if I eat baby pig," she told Cindie.

"But that's nonsense, Charity. There is only one way you can get a baby."

"You say so, Missie Cindie? You think baby pig no help me to get baby?"

"Of course not, Charity. I'd sooner die than eat that horrible thing."

"Aw, baby pig, he good." Charity ruminated for a time. "But I think I get baby alla same. Sow, he no good. I get proper Kanaka."

"Oh no, Charity! You mustn't do that." Cindie was alarmed. "Do you hear, Charity? You must not do that."

Charity shrugged. "How you know? Verbena, she get baby with Kanaka. I tired of wait."

The pig, when taken from the hole and stripped of its skin upon a heap of palm leaves, was delicious. Biddow not only permitted the children to accept a portion but helped them to scoff it up, too. Those Kanakas who had gone down the river after fish arrived home in the nick of time to add a string of river perch to the repast.

The day's events seemed to have excited the Kanakas, for no sooner was the meal disposed of than they began to dance, heavy stomachs and all. Melatonka, who had made one of the fishing party, began it with a solo. Chanting and playing his mouth organ in turn, he got out in front of his fellows and stamped around in a circle, little steps and jerky stamping of his feet, monotonous and interminable to the whites watching from the balcony, but exciting to the black men. As he proceeded, first one and then the other of them began to take up his chant, to clap their hands and sway their bodies. Then two, three, four together until the whole group, Tirwana included, were rhythmically swaying, clapping and chanting.

As dusk came down a bonfire was piled and lit, and in its fitful light the Kanakas continued to dance and sing, their movements even wilder, eventually licentious, their singing and chanting gradually deteriorating into raucous shouts and ribald laughter.

Long before this stage was reached Tirwana had withdrawn and seated himself quietly at some distance. As black eyes rolled more wildly and movements became disordered he began to walk about. Intermittently he glanced up at the balcony, unease in every line of him. Biddow and Cindie and Grey also yielded to disquiet.

Blanche made no comment. She sat against the balcony rail, very still, her chin resting upon her folded arms, her face hidden.

Then, when Biddow and Grey were debating the advisability of going down to put an end to the exhibition, Charity, restrained till now by her sense of the white women watching, threw out a shrill laugh, pranced forward into the firelight and, pulling up her long frock—her "best"—till the major part of her legs was exposed, began to participate in the saltatory orgy. Tirwana came swiftly towards the house. Biddow and Grey rose at once and hurried down the stairs.

Together the three men made over towards the Kanakas. Tirwana's voice boomed out authoritatively. Charity's reply was to dance up to him, take hold of her dress, and flourish its flounces in his face.

Blanche laughed out loud. "That's one for your black savage," she declared maliciously. Then with contempt: "As though it matters what the animals do."

"I'll see whether it matters or not," cried Cindie, angrily. "Look at that! She's giving Mr. Biddow cheek!" Down the stairs she flew and over to the gathering. Without a moment's hesitation she grabbed Charity by the hair as she whirled, jerked her to a standstill and slapped her face with all her weight behind it.

The leaping and shouting stopped like magic. Black bodies seemed turned to stone. Then arose a long-drawn angry: "Ah!" On top of it came Cindie's furious voice. "Get to bed, the lot of you! D'yer hear? Christmas is over. No more dancing. No more song. Bed now, for work to-morrow. Put out the fire, Tirwana. You, Charity, come with me."

"What's the meaning of bringing that black trollop up here?" Blanche met Cindie and the black woman at the top of the stairs and barred their passage. "Take her downstairs at once!" Her voice trembled with rage. Her face in the semi-darkness was flower-white.

"Mrs. Biddow," said Cindie firmly, "it wouldn't be safe

to leave Charity alone with all those men to-night. I think
she should sleep on the balcony."

"Alone! What do you mean by alone? She's got a husband, hasn't she? You stop your interfering between husbands
and wives! Take the slut back where she belongs."

"Mrs. Biddow, you don't understand——" But Charity, already thoroughly intimidated by Cindie's blow, at this to her
other strange and unfathomable conflict between the two
white women, grew terrified. She turned and bolted down
the stairs. Cindie swung round, made to follow her, then
halted. Biddow, coming back to the house with Grey, called
to Charity as she ran. The girl stopped and, crouching a
little, her head bent, waited for the men to come up to her.

"I told Charity," said Biddow, as he came up the steps,
"if anyone attempts to interfere with her to-night she must
shout for help."

"Of course." Blanche was triumphant. "The proper thing
to do." Husband and wife went indoors. Cindie sat down
on the stairs and sighed deeply.

"Time I was getting along, Cindie," Grey said. "I'll saddle
up." He lingered, nevertheless. Cindie said nothing. He
cleared his throat, then laughed softly. "You certainly scared
'em, my girl. Not a sound."

But there was a sound. A sound that made Grey bend
swiftly and peer into the girl's face.

"Cindie, Cindie," he whispered. "Why, Cindie, you are
crying. . . ."

CHAPTER XVIII

AFTER BOXING DAY NIGHT CINDIE'S MANNER WAS THAT OF A
woman withdrawn into herself and a little fearful. It was
the manner of one recovering from an emotional shock. The
joyous urge to work had gone, supplanted by a dogged, tight-
lipped determination. When Verbena returned on the morning following Boxing Day and straightway asked about
money, Cindie told her, morosely: "You don't deserve any

money for not coming back when you said you would. But you can ask Mrs. Biddow. She's the boss."

Verbena instantly turned sulky. "I go to camp again, you no give money."

Cindie raised her voice. "I tell you I'm not the boss! You can ask Mrs. Biddow."

"What is she to ask me?" Blanche, well pleased with herself that morning, came out of her room.

"About being paid some money for her work."

"Why didn't you tell her?"

"Because for the future, Mrs. Biddow, I should like you to run the household yourself."

"Oh!" The smile vanished. "But that's what you are paid for. That's what Mr. Biddow increased your wages for."

"No. It was for doing a man's work on the farm."

"Really, Cindie, you are insufferable"—plaintively. "But never mind. I know you are tired. Miss Cindie is tired, Verbena. You were a bad girl to run off and leave her your work to do." With that, Blanche returned to her room and shut the door behind her.

Cindie, her lips pressed tightly together, her expression hard, thought for a few moments, then, with a frigid smile, told the girl: "Mr. Biddow said he would give you a shilling a week, Verbena. Now get to work."

Christmas was over, but the year still had to drag along to the anti-climax of the New Year festivities. The strong strain of Scotch blood in the pioneers ascribed to New Year's Day a paramount importance. From all over the far north, from mountain, tableland, and coastal settlement, miners, farmers, tradesmen and fishermen converged on Port Denham for the races and Caledonian sports. Horses came up by boat from Pearltown and Townsville, to compete with the local product.

On New Year's Eve Blanche drove herself and husband down to Port Denham to attend the ball. When Cindie set out in the buckboard with the children the next morning, the track was a stream of vehicles, ridden horses and footsloggers, the latter mostly Kanakas and Chinese workers who regarded the long walk each way as not too high a price to pay for the

pleasure of seeing the horses run and hearing the music of
the Port band.

The town itself was crammed with visitors. The dozens
of pubs and hotels and stables overflowed. When Cindie
swung her two-horse team into the main street the band was
already blaring beneath an hotel veranda. Groups of men
squatted on grass plots and played cards. Other groups
canvassed the relative merits of the horses. Betters called the
odds.

Cindie drew rein outside the hotel the Biddows had booked
in at and bade Randy descend and go in search of his father.
Biddow soon appeared. He took the reins himself and directed
Cindie and Irene to join his wife upon the hotel balcony.

Blanche, lounging in company with the women of the
Montague clan, was very gracious to Cindie but refrained
from introducing her to her friends. Old Mrs. Montague,
however, her sharp eyes upon the girl, bade her sit down
beside her. "Come here. Sit by me. I want to talk to you.
I've heard a lot about you, my girl. They say the farmer
who succeeds in hooking you will be a lucky man. I've got
no more sons, myself, worse luck." She chuckled like a
kookaburra, took hold of Cindie's knee with a skinny claw
and shook it.

Cindie looked at her calmly, then, liking the old lady,
smiled and said: "Worse luck for me, too, I think. You are
Mrs. Montague, aren't you?"

"Tut tut! Where's our manners? We forgot to introduce
you. . . ."

By the time a general move was made towards the beach
racecourse, Cindie had been put so much at ease by the old
lady's friendliness that the lonesome soreness of her heart over
the last few days, though not altogether dissipated, was filmed
with brightness. Again, as at the Callaghan home, she felt
herself to be a personality. She felt that she was liked, and
accepted on equal terms, by people who themselves performed
useful social service.

When the group of women and children went down into
the street, Biddow, Barney Callaghan—his wife had remained at home with Consuelo—Bert and Grey detached
themselves from the crowd around the hotel doors and joined

them. Grey at once constituted himself Cindie's escort and throughout the day stuck to that position.

The day was not a financial success for our party. Influenced by parochial and personal loyalty they put their money on Callaghan and Montague horses, which let them down badly. But nobody minded, for, apart from the insignificance of the bets, the colour and gaiety and infrequency of such gatherings more than compensated for the losses.

At four in the afternoon, Biddow proposed that he take the buckboard and accompany Jack Callaghan to his home for the purpose of collecting his dogs. But Blanche, her mood out of the day's comparatively townified events one of mellowness and sensuousness compounded, felt that she could not bear to loose even for a few hours the ribbons of loving intimacy which had bound her for the past week to her husband. She slipped a hand beneath Biddow's arm. "Let Cindie go for the dogs, Randolph. Mr. Grey would be only too glad to go with her, I'm sure."

Biddow squeezed her hand against his side and gave her a fond look. "I don't doubt that he would. But Cindie might not like to go."

Cindie did like. She was tired, now, of the scurry and bustle and wanted to go home. Grey was delighted. So, with Jack Callaghan, a younger replica of his father, riding alongside, they took the buckboard and set off through the forest.

Four miles out from Port Denham they came on the teamsters' camp known as Fourmile. There they reined in for a while, so that Cindie might assimilate her first view of a backwoodsmen's camp. A few weatherboard homes comprised the settlement, with two pubs, a store, and stables. Dozens of working bullocks foraged in the clearing or chewed the cud beneath exotic tamarinds. Dozens of corn-fed horses browsed. Palms and poinscianas, papaws and rain trees, the latter an import from India, made the spot delectable. In the absence of all its usual inhabitants quiet and stillness reigned. And as they lingered there, up through the forest came the faint, sharp crack of a whip.

"Your luck's in," Grey told Cindie. "There's a pair of teamsters on the road. About a mile off, by the sound of it."

And a mile further on they met up with the teams, watering in the bed of a creek. The four-ton wagons each had two sets of shafts and its sixteen-horse team. The drivers had been preparing to move on, but when Callaghan and the buckboard pulled up alongside they settled down for the usual roadside yarn. Their talk was of mines, of nuggets, of tin, of beginning dairy farms among "the cedar" on the Tablelands and inevitably, in the end, of politics and graft. . . .

So virgin was the forest along the further track that Cindie was astonished when suddenly they ran out of it on to a semi-cultivated clearing of some eighty acres. The road skirted its southern boundary, separating the forest from the back gardens of the original Callaghan home. This was a fine, cream-coloured house with green facings surrounded by the usual gardens and outbuildings of a plantation homestead.

"Seems a remarkably well-kept place for a bachelor's home," Cindie remarked to Grey, as they followed Callaghan to the kennels behind the house. "Who looks after it for him?"

"His Chinese cook is the boss of the house Kanakas. For the field work he has a Javanese foreman."

Cindie was not interested in the dogs. What took her eye to the point of absorption was the lay-out of the farm, and a strange crop climbing the gentle slope of a foothill. No cane here. He and his neighbouring farmers, Callaghan told her—yes, there were other holdings behind the curtain of rain forest—hoped shortly to secure a tramline from the Port to the mill at Masterman which would enable the transport of cane. Presently, in addition to the usual corn, tropical fruits and vegetables, he relied on coffee and rice. Coffee! Was that that peculiar-looking crop on the slope? Cindie asked. Yes. Would she like to see it at close quarters? An interesting crop, coffee, a ticklish one, too. A specialist's job, really. Callaghan had found that out over years of more failures than he liked to think of.

On the return journey to Port Denham Cindie was thoughtfully silent. At length, with a bantering glance at her, Grey remarked: "Another bee in your bonnet, Cindie?"

"Jeff!" To his surprise she put a hand upon his arm, the first suggestion of intimacy she had ever permitted between them. "Jeff, I do wish I could marry you. I would love to build a farm of my own. Jeff, what a difference building things makes to people. Doing things that matter."

Grey smiled wryly. "Cindie, everybody makes things. All the time. Even Verbena makes things."

"I don't mean that. I mean—it's making things you are interested in. Building up things that matter. Like farms."

"Well, the Kanakas build up farms, Cindie. Better try again."

"Don't make fun of me, Jeff. But even the Kanakas would feel better, and bigger, more important, if they were building the farms for themselves."

"Ah ha! Now you're talking! You see, Cindie, it's not the building that makes people grow. It's the purpose of the building. If a man—or a woman"—he kept his face averted from her and chose his words carefully—"if you are building anything for yourself, or for someone you love, or for an ideal, that purpose, that unselfish purpose, naturally helps you to grow bigger and better. But if you are building for a mere crust, or for someone you hate, or despise, that sort of building may cramp your style, your mental and emotional life, quite a lot."

"Yes. . . . Yes. . . . Thank goodness I don't hate anyone, Jeff"—fervently.

"That so?"—quietly.

"Oh yes! I think I may—despise someone." Absorbed in a labyrinthine train of thought, her manner was simplicity itself. "But I wouldn't allow that to—to really influence me. Not away from the course I had mapped out. Not from a *job* I had taken on. A big job. Doing something for someone. . . . If the purpose is big enough, Jeff, if it's high, it can overlook meanness and uselessness. Look at all this growth around us, Jeff! Everything springs so, up here. Everything goes up high, to the sun. The sun is so hot, the rain is so heavy. It's been like a door opening to a new life, the way everything springs up here, Jeff. I wish I could tell you just what I mean."

"You're not doing so badly. Just be quiet for a time now, will you, Cindie? I'd like to have a go at figuring out something for myself."

So Cindie sat quietly and found that thought was much more potent than speech when it came to hair-splitting analysis. She knew what she meant but lacked words to communicate her ideas: a high purpose in the mind had the same effect as humidity in the latent life of the cane plant. It called into germination and growth the latent powers inherent in every normal human life, caused them to grow and flower and fruit, to pullulate throughout society as healthy plant life throughout the soil.

Yes, the mainspring of forward-moving life was high purpose. What Jeff had called an ideal. Cindie was solemnly glad that Biddow had made this opportunity for her to jog along quietly through the forest and let its essences creep into and purify her mood. And Biddow became linked in her mind with the softness and tranquillity of her thoughts, just as though he had known of her mood and done it on purpose.

CHAPTER XIX

AND NOW THE RAINS. FIRST THE SKY WAS FILLED, DAY IN, DAY out, with lowering clouds. Heavy drops fell and belied their promise. Till one night with a surge of wind and fury the heavens tipped over and deluged the earth with beating rains. The creeks and rivers climbed their banks and overflowed. The low-lying lands became quagmire.

Before a week was out the house at Folkhaven smelt musty. All leather goods, even clothes, had to be cleaned daily of mould. Bedding was perpetually damp. Great fires were kept raging on top of the colonial oven in house and field kitchen, to counteract the rotting effect on flour and rice.

But how refreshing the coolness, the change from humidity and heat! It built up the body to withstand the oppressiveness of the atmosphere when, between the showers, and sometimes for days together, the sun shone torridly and drew the moisture from the sopping ground.

Biddow occupied himself through the first weeks of the rains by keeping the children to their lessons and reading.

Impossible, most days, for Randy and Irene to go over to Glenelg. Blanche would sew, read, or merely sit or lie beside the man while he read. But she chafed that now he had the leisure she had longed for there was little to do with it. And little to her pleasure that Biddow wanted to do. The man was physically tired to the bone of him and needed the relaxation provided by the "wet" to recoup his vitality. A few weeks, he stipulated, of rest for himself and the Kanakas and then work must be resumed despite the rain. Another shed must go up, a fence constructed, "peasant" fashion, to enclose a couple of acres around the house as protection for gardens and shrubberies.

Biddow grew testy, at times, over his wife's incessant sensual approaches. He got to the stage where he told her bluntly: "Look here, my girl, a man can get too much of a good thing. Just leave me alone for a while, will you."

At which Blanche felt ignominiously insulted. "You needn't talk like a Kanaka!" she fired at him, furiously.

"Why not? I work like one, don't I?"

On the first fine day after that Blanche took herself off to Port Denham on horseback, and on her return exploded a bombshell by announcing that she had bought a piano she had seen advertised for sale in the Port paper.

"Where did you get the money?" Biddow wanted to know.

"Out of your desk."

"The money for the wages and the quarter's bills! Are you mad?"

"You can replace it from the bank. It's Dad's money."

"And it's money that has to be repaid, don't forget."

"That rot," she retorted coolly. Then burst out upon him with: "What do you think I'm going to do with myself? Confined for months to this rabbit hutch!"

"You could have sent for your own piano to come up from Brisbane. You had only to mention it and I would have sent a telegram."

"Randolph Biddow, you know perfectly well that my big grand would not fit into this hutch."

"We could have made it fit in. And not so much of this hutch business, if you please. I and the children and Cindie live in it, as well as you."

"Yes, and you're getting more like a farm labourer every day! Or maybe like a small-time market gardener who peddles his own carrots."

"Or maybe like a small-time prospector who has the luck to find gold and then heaves himself into prominence by tricking his mates and political thuggery."

At that they stood glaring at each other. Both, it must be said, more than a little astonished at the exceptional trend of this mutual objurgation. Then, suddenly shamefaced, Biddow mumbled: "There's no sense in this sort of thing. Anyhow, you can start teaching Irene how to play. It's time she began."

But once the piano arrived—Cindie and Tirwana had to go down to the Port and fetch it—Blanche scarcely touched its keys. And Biddow was not sorry, for in music, as in literature, he demanded the best and consequently found the rather tinny instrument a trial.

Cindie carried on through the "wet" with never an idle moment. After the first few days she ignored the rain, taking no heed of constant soakings. She scarcely ever put on a coat, except for warmth against the chill that resulted from prolonged riding or driving when wet through. Before January had been washed away all trace of her sunburn had vanished, leaving a patina of natural gold upon her cheeks. Relief from the heat gave her flesh a chance to pad her bones becomingly.

Physically, the Kanakas thrived upon idleness; but shortly the confinement in their quarters, remarkably snug and rain-proof for all their thatched roofs, began to irk them. Their lounging and singing of the first few days began to develop into impatient movements and quarrels. Tirwana had to be constantly among them, threatening, coaxing, adjudicating. At length he advised Biddow to permit them to visit the town occasionally, and to go fishing at will. This, Biddow was at first loath to do, for lately another report of a woman frightened by a wandering Kanaka had gone the rounds; but he came to see, as Tirwana pointed out, that the problematical risk involved in humouring them was preferable to strife which might result in broken bones, or worse.

So it came about that, except through the heaviest downpours, the Kanakas would go off with their improvised spears, to invariably return with fish of some sort. Fish that was appreciated by the white household as much as by themselves.

But the least suggestion of fine weather meant work at piling up the small logs and branches for burning, and shortly Biddow got them busy on the shed and fencing, rain or no rain.

He came to doubt the wisdom and humanity of this, however, for several of the Kanakas went down with fever and other complaints, chiefly chest troubles. Though Tirwana insisted that not the work but the miasma arising from the rotting ground was responsible, Biddow remained uneasy. The death-rate of the indentured Kanakas in the older-settled areas, chiefly from malaria and measles, was appalling and it worried him to think that he might contribute by undue pressure to its incidence.

Cindie dosed the patients with brandy and Epsom salts, the latter being as acceptable to them as the liquor. Indeed, they were most docile and trustful patients, obediently swallowing anything proffered them in the way of medicine. The panacea of the newcomers from the islands for all ills was a copious draught of sea water, and heads were shaken dolefully over the lack of this. Fortunately, no illness was really serious. Serious sickness meant that the victim simply resigned himself and waited quietly for death.

The worst trial of the few dry spells over the three months of the "wet" was the mosquitoes. Joss sticks burned day and night in every room of the house. But these sunny days brought joy as well, especially to Cindie and the children. Joy in the butterflies that fluttered their pennants of green and blue, of yellow and red and black, from leaf to flower. Joy in the myriad birds, the several species of finches, crimson and multi-coloured, the mistletoe bird, the rainbow bird, the fig bird, the white-breasted wood swallow, the spangled drongo, the cuckoo shrike: these and many other species topped the rain forest and glided down to inspect the fruit trees and gardens and make the clearing ring with their whistle and song.

With April came fine weather that could be depended

upon to last. The "wet" was past, and also the worst of the heat. The days were now halcyon. On moonlit nights the clearing shone with silver; in the absence of the moon emerald stars sparkled from an indigo sky. The dark forest rustled and sighed.

And with the first heat of the sun after rain the clearing became redolent with pungent scents that streamed out from the plant life. Certain forest trees came into bloom, clothing themselves with mantles of cream or pink or scarlet.

Within a week Cindie had browned up again. She gloried in the comparatively mild heat. And how she worked! From dawn till dark, helping a gang of men to log up, and, as soon as the vegetation was dry, to burn off. Biddow's ambition had come down to fifty acres of plant cane for the succeeding year, in addition to which there would be ten acres of ratoons to follow upon this year's harvest. He had ordered sufficient cane sticks for fifty acres from the mill Directorate, which in turn got them from the big planters down at Pearltown.

And while she did a man's work in the fields, Cindie directed Charity and Verbena in the home and at the job of building up the domestic gardens.

Verbena was now growing very stout. Blanche had objected to her presence about the house. "She will have to go," she told Cindie. "There are the children to consider."

"But Charity will soon be getting stout, too," Cindie told her. "And you can't send Charity away."

Chagrined, Blanche had accepted the situation and made the two black women frocks as shapeless and unrevealing as possible.

Verbena took her pregnancy with the utmost unconcern. Charity's condition, which she had announced to Cindie with giggles into her hand and which Cindie refused to discuss, was Sow's pride. For a week after he knew of it he went about with a circlet of pigeon's feathers in his hair.

Cindie could not refrain from ruminating on these manifestations of natural phenomena. How had Charity managed the business? Who was the man? Then, one day she came upon the two black women with their heads together, gossiping and laughing.

"What's the matter with you two?" she asked indulgently, thinking how pleasantly companionable they were, how colourful their shining black skins. They glanced from her to each other, giggled a little. Charity put her hands on her hips and swayed her long, lithe body uxoriously. Then up spoke Verbena, her mirth dissolved in curiosity.

"She tell me Melatonka give her baby, Missie Cindie. How? How man give baby to woman, Missie?"

Cindie was thunderstruck. "Verbena, don't you know?"

Verbena shifted her feet uneasily. "Baby," she patted her stomach, "baby, he out of bush. He come when I dream one night."

"That right, Missie Cindie," Charity put in, complacently. "She not know. She just savage."

Cindie took her incredulity to Blanche, but all she got from that quarter was: "She's a little liar. Of course she knows."

But Cindie knew Verbena was not lying, so she placed the problem before Tirwana.

"Ah, Miss Cindie, that's true, what Verbena says. The Abo., he hasn't been taught how babies come. Before the trader and the Missionary came to my island my people, too, thought babies came from spirits. My people, they used to get the prize pig off the boats and let it run in the bush with the skinny sow. My people, they thought only the mother and the spirit got the baby. The father, he was there only to get food. That's why the mother, she's the boss in my tribe. Then the whalers, the traders and the Missionary, they came and told us about the father."

"Oh!—Whoever would have thought it! Tirwana, if Melatonka keeps on at this rate he'll have a tribe of his own about the place."

"Pity he's so good to look at, Miss Cindie. He's a very pretty man. He's like the cock bird in the fowl yard."

Now came the time of planting. The small logs and branches had been piled and burned. Each Kanaka was assigned to a portion of land and began to dig holes, two feet apart, in rows. About three thousand five hundred holes to the acre. As they went along, the small roots were removed from the soil with a grubber. Two cane sticks were set in each hole, well apart to prevent rotting from contact, and covered with two inches of soil.

And as the planting went forward, the dream in Cindie's mind took shape. Plenty of time. Patiently she waited on her opportunity to broach her ideas to Biddow. It came when, towards the end of the planting, in May, Biddow received a letter from Tom Hilliard, in itself an event.

The seven days a week activities of the planters following upon the rains had precluded visiting and discussion. But the papers coming up from Brisbane had acquainted them with a certain knowledge of occurrences at the statutory Congress held in March in relation to the adoption of a Bill to establish a federal constitution for Australia. The proceedings had been adjourned, one reason being the obligation of the Premiers to set out to attend the old Queen's jubilee in London, another being the expedient desire to submit to the electorates and the Parliaments of the colonies the contentious issues the Convention had been unable to resolve.

Until the receipt of Hilliard's letter, Biddow had given little thought to these matters, chiefly through fatigue, though it had not been possible to ignore altogether the reflection in the press of the ferment the federation proposals had created in the southern colonies and to a lesser extent in Queensland. Hilliard's letter roused him to really serious contemplation of the probable far-reaching effect upon his own future of political events.

"My boy," wrote Hilliard, "I think it is only wise to give you fair warning of the possible trend of events.

"As you know, up till now I have kept an open mind about this question of the federation of the colonies. My Government, for various reasons, held aloof from the recent Convention. And possibly, I might state, may remain aloof indefinitely. West Australia also is uneasy and fractious about affairs. New Zealand refuses to commit herself in any way.

"However, little doubt now remains that the southern colonies will eventually bring the scheme to at least partial fruition, for the imperial Parliament certainly favours unity. In such a case, failure to realize the pressure Queensland would be called upon to sustain would simply be to ignore the obvious.

"The last thing I wish to do is to alarm you, Randolph, but you must be well aware of the implications of federation. Though the powers and privileges and territorial rights of the existing colonies should remain intact, such being the unalterable basis of the Commonwealth Bill, nevertheless the surrender of certain powers would be essential to the authority of the federal Government. And one of those powers would be defence. The defence of Australia, its military and naval forces, would certainly come under federal control, and the whole question of defence seems to be bound up with the White Australia policy.

"Frankly, I am beginning to think that the imperialist demands, and the claptrap agitation of the rising Labour forces together, will in time submerge the case for the retention of coloured alien labour. Naturally, I feel concerned about your and Blanche's welfare." ("Not forgetting that his own money is involved," Biddow told himself, cynically.) "At the same time I feel that maybe I have been too insensible, in the past, to the just claims of Empire consolidation. To the fact that, as Sir Henry Parkes pointed out in '91, the crimson thread of kinship runs through us all." ("The wily old devil," was Biddow's silent comment. "He sees the writing on the wall and is getting out from under, as usual.")

"What I desire to do, Randolph, and what it is incumbent on you as a sugar man to do, is to try to grasp the implications of the White Australia policy in respect to our economic affairs. Forewarned is forearmed. So, will you kindly supply me with a considered statement on the question of labour in the canefields. Is there truth in the contention that whites are unable to stand up to the work in the sugar paddocks? What other factors would you consider operative? . . ."

Biddow read the letter through and then handed it to Blanche. "But you knew all this before," was her comment on it. "He's not telling you anything you didn't know, is he?"

"Perhaps not, fundamentally. But when the old boy starts to worry about his position it means that things are approaching a crisis."

"Well, I'm not going to worry. I'm not married to this place."

"I am. This life suits me."

"Whether it suits you or not, you will have to get out if the Kanakas are deported."

"Not at all, my dear Blanche. Grey is doing very well on his holding."

Cindie, who had been listening, at this juncture decided impulsively to intervene between the two, a thing she had never before had the temerity to do.

"Has anything special happened, Mr. Biddow?" she asked.

"Only that Mr. Hilliard, Cindie, seems to have come to the conclusion that the Kanakas must eventually be deported, and he is worried about the effect upon us."

"Oh! . . . Mr. Biddow, now that this has come up. . . . I have been thinking. . . . Would you mind if I put an idea I've got before you?"

"Of course not, Cindie. Go ahead."

"Oh yes, by all means go ahead," said Blanche smoothly.

"Mr. Biddow, have you ever thought of all that timber out there going to waste? The cedar, pine and maple."

"Of course. Naturally I've thought about it."

"Mr. Biddow, I think that timber could be turned into money. No, no, let me finish! I have gone into the matter, Mr. Biddow——"

"Hey, just a minute! What do you mean?—you've gone into it?"

"I mean I've inquired about the price of timber, and ways and means."

Biddow stared at her. Even Blanche displayed interest.

Cindie continued: "I find that as much as fifty pounds can be got from the Forestry Department for a big log of cedar. Our creek runs into the river. A team of horses could haul the logs down the creek into the river. From there they could be poled down to the jetty, made into rafts and towed by steamer to Port Denham. They could go south by lighter.

"Now, suppose the freight on a log was five pounds or more, there would still be an enormous profit. Logs might even be sold to the mill at Pearltown."

Biddow, who had listened with raised eyebrows, now smiled slightly. "That reasoning sounds all right, Cindie. It is all right so far as it goes. But what you haven't thought of is the labour, Cindie. I would have to get another couple of dozen Kanakas, and with this talk of deportation—— No, by jove, the Kanakas couldn't do it. Couldn't handle the logs, anyhow. Not in the category of agricultural labouring."

"I have thought of the labour, Mr. Biddow." Cindie still spoke quietly, but suppressed excitement revealed itself in the clasping and unclasping of her hands. "The labour I have thought of is not Kanaka labour."

"Oh? What is it, then?"

"It is Aborigine labour."

"Aborigine? Do you mean the Australian Aborigine? But that's ridiculous, Cindie."

"Thought there would be a catch in it somewhere," Blanche put in, with a sarcastic smile.

"Mr. Biddow, why is it ridiculous? What do you know, really, about the blacks? Our blacks, I mean."

"I know what the old-timers say about them, Cindie. That they are unreliable, won't work at anything steady."

"Mr. Biddow, I've been talking to people. To Jeff Grey, to Verbena, people in town. I don't think the Abo.s have had a fair trial. They don't like settling down. But what— what——"

"Inducement." Biddow gave her the word.

"Yes. What inducement have they had to settle down? I feel that if they were treated properly, if they were given reason to think they were working for themselves, they might work all right."

"They go walkabout, Cindie."

"Let them. Let them go walkabout. There are plenty of them, goodness knows. Mr. Biddow, do let me have a go at the logs."

"Let you have a go, Cindie? What do you mean?"

"I am prepared to organize the whole business of getting the labour and seeing that the logs are delivered to the jetty, if you will provide me with a team of horses and arrange the business end of it, the selling end. Teams are cheap now, you know, Mr. Biddow, with the railway up the range taking away their freights."

"Cindie, you are putting a tough proposition up to me!" Biddow began to stride about the room. "It would need some thinking over. Suppose you did get the Abo.s to work, what about payment for it? What do you propose there?"

"I have thought about that, too. I wouldn't pay them in money, Mr. Biddow. They wouldn't know what to do with it. They would spend it on drink, be cheated out of it by the whites. I would give them good food, buy them clothes, give them plots of ground and huts to live in. Things like mouth organs, too, things they could get pleasure out of. But the main thing would be to be friendly with them, to treat them as friends."

"Full of ideas, aren't you?" Blanche put in, grimly. "Stuff and nonsense, I call it."

"I'm not so sure." Biddow's eyes were glittering. "If we could get a good man to work the team. . . . It might pan out all right, Cindie."

"I think it has every chance to work out. I'm not absolutely sure, you know. There's a risk, but the chances are so good that I would be ashamed if it wasn't a success."

She spoke so artlessly, yet withal was so earnest, that Biddow found himself smiling at her with appreciative affection. Blanche saw this. A tigerish light leapt into her eyes. But wariness, or maybe some saving sense of shame, bade her crush back her swift impulse to fly at the girl and strike her.

"Well, I'll think about it, Cindie," said Biddow.

"Think about it but don't talk about it, Mr. Biddow," the girl said, sagely. "Everyone will laugh at the idea of the Aborigines working. I would rather they laughed when they see the logs going down the river."

"I can see you've got the job in hand already, Cindie." Biddow laughed. "And, by jove, I'd like to see you make a job of it. I've half a mind to write to the mill at Pearltown right away. Could use my own timber, perhaps, to build the house."

"That's right! That's the way to do things! Make up your mind now, Mr. Biddow. Then I could visit the blacks' camp on Sunday and see about the prospects of labour. It might take me some time to talk them into it."

Biddow was very perturbed. The two women waited, Cindie willing him to a decision with the force of her regard, Blanche sitting very straight, her eyes on the floor. "The fool," she thought savagely. "The fool, to hesitate. Anyone could see the girl could do the job."

At length Biddow turned to his wife. "What do you say, Blanche?" he asked sharply.

"Make your own decisions. I won't accept responsibility for your hair-brained schemes."

"Very well, then, I will. You go ahead, Cindie. See what's doing about the blacks and if there's a chance——"

"Thanks, Mr. Biddow. Oh, thanks! And there's something else——"

Blanche burst out laughing, shot up from her chair and swept her trailing skirts from the room.

Biddow gave way to acute embarrassment. "That will be enough for to-night, Cindie," he said swiftly, his tone distant, his manner withdrawn.

But to his surprise Cindie did not acquiesce. For some moments she stood quietly, her body stiffening, her face paling with rage at the jibe of that laugh. Then, as Biddow's frown deepened at her stand, she said throatily: "No, it will not be enough, Mr. Biddow. I demand that I be treated with respect in this house."

Their eyes locked. Cindie's were blazing. The colour flooded her face. The idea of some tawny beast of the field at bay flashed through Biddow's mind as he stared at her. Then his inalienable sense of justice overcame him, mingled with a sickening hatred of Blanche for involving him in this predicament. "All right," he said coldly. "You shall be treated with respect in the future. Now leave me, please."

Cindie whirled round and flew out of the house. So tremendous was the force of her anger that she felt she must explode if some release was not vouchsafed her. She set off running, down the track, running, running, running. Tirwana, seated on a stump, crooning softly to himself in the beauty of the afterglow of sunset which persisted and illumined the gossamer dusk, jumped up and stared after her in shocked surprise. When her figure was merely a blot on the blue-grey shadows he started after her.

Blanche, from the balcony, had heard Cindie's words and her husband's reply. Immediately the two personalities within her began to war. The jealous virago fought with the calculating drone. "How I hate her! How I hate her!" she breathed through shut teeth. But common sense—Blanche's particular brand of it—won, and swiftly, for Biddow had to be faced. She hurried back into the living-room. "I heard what she said, Randolph," she snapped. "It's all nonsense. Can't I even laugh in my own house these days?"

"You promised there would be no more scenes."

"But she makes the scenes, Randolph! Oh, Ranny, can't you see the—the *humour* of that girl, that servant who couldn't say boo to a goose twelve months ago, talking like a—a man, like a——"

"What I can see is that you have made things impossible as they are. This time Cindie will go."

"Oh!" Blanche flattened out. "What about—the logs?"

"The logs can rot in the paddocks."

Not the logs, however, but the same old routine considerations, the household, the work, were in Blanche's mind. "Oh, I suppose I shall have to give in, as usual!" she cried. "I give in! I'll tell her I'm sorry! Nice state of things, when I've got to apologize to my own servant!"

"I don't want you to apologize to her. You are my wife. She must go."

"Damnation!" shouted Blanche. At which the children, engaged with their lessons in the kitchen, came running in. "You've got me into this mess, Randolph! No, no, I didn't mean that! Go back to your lessons, children! All right. I won't apologize. She's gone down the track. I saw her. If she says nothing we won't. And this time I mean it, Randolph. She can bloody well do as she likes!" She brought out the oath with startling vehemence. She began to run about the room, her hands in her short curls, fuming, ferociously splendid. Biddow, watching her, felt his anger melt away before the flaming vitality of her. She was like a magnet to his loins. He moved towards her and confronted her, reached out a hand.

"All right," he said thickly. "It's not a hanging matter, I suppose."

CHAPTER XX

WHEN CINDIE CAME OUT ON TO THE MAIN ROAD IT WAS QUITE
dark. She felt better for the run. Not so bottled up. But
the draining away of her fury had left her physically spent.
She began to dread her return to the house. Sighing deeply,
she wandered on, bitterly reflecting that this time, surely,
the end had come to all her hopes.

How she wished she had held her tongue! Long ago she
had mapped out her course. Had not she told Grey? Hadn't
she decided that the chance to build, to create, to help
Biddow, more than compensated for that woman's hateful
behaviour? Hadn't she even felt sorry, at times, for the
poverty of a mind that could remain impenetrable to the
uplift, the exaltation to be found in serving, struggling, in
bringing under control the natural riches of the soil? And
at a mere jibing laugh her well-thought-out design had
crumbled. Why?

Cindie sat down on a log on the side of the road and
grimly faced the question that honesty demanded she resolve.
And she flushed in the dark as she answered it squarely.
Self-respect, maybe, had been the basic urge, but it alone
could not have been responsible for the surge of elemental
fury that had set every nerve in her body tingling with a
desire to attack, to rend.

Jealousy! That was the whip. Jealousy allied with self-
respect. For the first time in her life she had been, like
Blanche herself, jealous. Yes, Blanche's jibing laugh had been
inspired by jealousy, Cindie told herself painfully. She could
see that now. But Blanche was his wife. She had a right to
be jealous. Oh, in the future, if there was to be a future,
if she had not cruelled her pitch entirely, how she must guard
herself against a repetition! He loved his wife. . . .

Pain, pain unutterable, assailed Cindie. She actually
groaned, her hands pressed against her breast, eyes closed
upon the mocking loveliness of night. She rocked her body.
He loved Blanche. But even if he did not, he would never
love her, Cindie. A man so beautiful as he.

"The old draught horse in the buckboard, that's me," she said aloud. And opened her eyes to see Tirwana standing a few feet away from her. Not recognizing him at once Cindie sprang to her feet with a cry. "Who are you?"

"Miss Cindie." Tirwana came close up to her. "What are you doing out here by yourself in the night? That is silly, Miss Cindie."

"Yes, I suppose it is, Tirwana"—wearily. "But sometimes a woman has to think things out, Tirwana."

"That may be. But next time you want to think things out, Miss Cindie, you tell me so I can walk with you."

"But that's just it, Tirwana. I had to be alone."

"Can't be alone in the night, Miss Cindie. Not in the bush. Go. You go. Tirwana will walk behind. The black man, too, sometimes likes to be alone."

"Thanks, Tirwana." Cindie took him at his word.

When the dark had fairly settled down and Cindie had not returned to the house, Biddow, himself again, became worried. He walked about the balcony for a time and then slipped downstairs with the intention of sending Tirwana down the track in quest of the girl. No Tirwana in his room, but Verbena, who had Charity for company in her quarters, was able to tell him that the Tanna had followed Cindie.

Biddow felt more relieved than he cared to acknowledge. He wished Blanche had not chosen that particular time to play the piano. And the gayest of tunes, at that. Sounded harsh, brazen, somehow, on top of that scene.

Nor could Biddow feel proud of his own recent conduct. Made him an accessory to the insult to the girl. Listen to her! Singing, now. The first time she had sung since Christmas. Wretchedness fell upon the man. The whole thing was so unfair! He should tell the girl to go. The only decent thing to do. . . . He would, too. Try and get her fixed up with some other farmer in the district. Slowly he mounted the stairs, his purpose strengthening within him. With his hands in his trousers pockets he stood in the doorway of the living-room and looked in at Blanche. She flashed him a dazzling smile, stopped singing and crashed her hands down upon the keys.

"The runaway not returned yet? Don't worry, old dear.

Our Cindie is more than a match for anyone she is likely to meet around here. . . . Oh, there she is!"

Biddow swung round. Cindie stood at the top of the stairs and at the sight of her the man felt thankful that Blanche could not see her face from where she sat. The girl's eyes, as they stared at him, seemed twice their normal size. About them, about the whole of her, was a lost, stray cat sort of look that wounded Biddow to the heart. "Oh, there you are, Cindie," he said swiftly. "I was getting worried about you."

Her features broke into a smile that stabbed the man afresh. In it there was joy, joy he knew in a flash that was born of his thinking about her. Commingled was resignation, childish resolve and quite natural sweetness.

"You don't have to worry about me, Mr. Biddow," she said cheerfully. "Tirwana was with me. Now I'll go to bed."

"Just a minute, Cindie." Suddenly Biddow knew exactly what the situation called for. Far above and beyond the services she had rendered to the farm, the personal significance his wife attached to her gave Cindie importance. Very well, then. Unto her importance he would render the things that were hers. "Just a minute, Cindie. My wife and I want you to know that we thoroughly appreciate all that you have done for us. Any—lack of respect—you have suffered has been due to the peculiar manner in which you have— have grown on to the farm. But from now on there will be no question of your position at Folkhaven. From now on you will not be here as a servant but as an equal. In this matter of the logs, if you succeed in putting the business through you will receive a fair percentage of the profits in addition to your salary. My wife concurs with me in this. Isn't that so, Blanche?"

Dead silence. Again to Blanche, sitting at the piano, there came that sense of having tied a noose around her own neck. But Biddow was looking full at her and in his look there was that old, inexorable seal of finality, so, with stiff lips, she got out the best way she could a shaky: "Of course."

CHAPTER XXI

"THE CONTENTION THAT WHITES LACK THE STAMINA TO STAND up to work in the sugar paddocks is nonsense," Biddow wrote to Hilliard. . "It's a fairy tale imported from the older sugar countries by the early pioneers whose traditions, and profits, were bound up with cheap coloured labour.

"I have yet to experience a cutting season but I doubt if it could offer me more strenuous toil than that I have stood up to over the last two years. And as you know I was not accustomed to hard manual labour.

"In general, the refusal of the white workers to engage in the sugar fields must be attributed to the poor wages and conditions the industry offers. As things are, only the ragtail and bobtail among whites, men without family and ambitions, will volunteer for this work.

"But these poor rates are unjustifiable. The big planters can well afford wages and conditions to enable family life. The profits in sugar for the big men have been fantastically enormous. That's taking the good years with the bad. But, apart from that aspect of things, sir, I am inclined to think that Kanaka labour is tending to become far from the cheap proposition it used to be, and still is to a lesser extent.

"In a pioneering area like Masterman, where the felling of the timber provides work all the year round, the Kanaka is still unequivocally an asset. But once that period is past, the sugar industry will need large numbers of men during the crushing season only. Fewer men are needed for the planting and the chipping. And this condition must develop progressively with the application of science and invention to the soil and cultivation and extraction methods, a process that is even now beginning to speed up.

"The cost of landing a Kanaka in this country is around thirty pounds. His wages are six pounds annually plus housing, food, clothing, tobacco and medical attention. And he must be maintained all the year round. Add to that the extremely high death-rate and no great discernment is required to see that the time must come when the employment of a white gang, even at fairly high wage rates and shorter hours, for the seasonal work of cutting, and the use of an extra hand or two to supplement family labour and machinery for the rest of the year, will be cheaper by far than the maintenance of Kanakas all the year round. So the long view, as I see it, is that the day of the Kanaka, as *cheap labour*, must terminate, quite distinct from the implications of your 'crimson thread' theory, sir.

"The general viewpoint of the younger men who are coming into the industry up here is that its future is bound up with the small farm principle, the subdivision of the large estates and the development of family production. As a matter of fact, the largest plantation in the Pearltown district is presently being sold to the monopoly sugar concern, the Colonial Sugar Refining company. And it is common talk that this concern intends to make the estate available to tenant farmers. Bona fide farmers are to be supplied with tools, implements, horses, etc., given every incentive to produce cane, which will be bought from them by the C.S.R. company.

"All these things considered, I am not inclined to add my voice to the clamour raised by a section of the big planters over the threatened deportation of the Kanaka. I do not believe that any dire results will accrue from such action. It would certainly dispose of the old school of 'aristocratic' planters who have lived like princes on the backs of black labour; it would mean the extinction of large estates, but on the other hand it would make way for the settlement of the country by white farmers under good conditions.

"Personally, I hope I shall have my land cleared before the measure becomes operative, but whether or not I feel that you need have no misgiving about the safety of the money you have placed at my disposal.

"As for the White Australia policy, I must confess that except in respect to the question of the colour of a man's skin, I am confused about it. The infamous methods that appear to be still engaged with the recruitment of the Kanakas are the only valid reason I can adduce against their employ-ment here. Certainly I am sympathetic to Labour's demands that the coloured aliens be not allowed to depress the conditions of Australians, but I feel that the remedy for that lies in the realm of domestic legislation and its rigorous enforcement. I refuse to subscribe to any racial discrimination. If anything holds me back from allegiance to the cause of Labour, it is these shameful diatribes of a section of the Labour leaders against aliens on the basis of colour.

"It is when I depart from the colour question that I become confused. Is the White Australia policy tenable? Is it economically sound? Again taking the long view, which is the more reasonable assumption: that the future of this country, a Pacific country, is bound up with the destiny of far-away Europe, or with the countries at our back door, the countries bordering on the Pacific—countries inhabited by coloured peoples?

"It seems to me, sir, that if Australia is ever to become a great power she must build up as a manufacturing nation. And where would our manufactured goods find the readiest market? In industrialized Europe? Or in the non-industrialized countries to our north, which in turn can supply us with products, such as tea and silk, and other raw materials we would need in manufacture?

"The short view, I take it, is that we are at present a pastoral and agricultural country and sell our products to the Mother Country. We also depend upon Britain for defence. I repeat, I am confused about these aspects of Empire policy. The only thing I am convinced about is that whether the immigrants to this country are coloured or white, European or Asiatic, their allegiance to Australia in the event of armed combat would be determined, not by their origin (as witness the American War of Independence and Britain's use of colonial troops against their own peoples') but by their assimilation or non-assimilation, as equals, into the normal life of this country. Not racial distinctions would determine the loyalty of our immigrants in the event of war but social relations. My experience with my own Kanakas convinces me of this."

Biddow did not mention, in this letter, the logging project, nor Cindie's further proposal to grow coffee. These were still in the air.

CHAPTER XXII

YES, COFFEE!

In the dignity of her new position Cindie had lost little time in preferring her desire to include coffee among the plantation's products. Coffee, she pointed out, was a crop not subject to the many vicissitudes which appeared to be threatening the sugar industry. And being a long-distance crop, as it were, once the forest was felled it would not require a great deal of labour. For this, too, she reckoned on Aborigine labour. Female Aborigines, she told Biddow. And he, with the example of Verbena before him, could find no reason for doubting the validity of this. But the coffee, they jointly agreed, must wait upon the succeeding year.

With the confidence of the enthusiastic tyro Cindie embarked upon the business of recruiting Aborigine labour to work the logs. In addition to the camp on Palmer Estate creek there were, she knew, many roving bands of natives in the area whose members wandered in and out of the township. Since the conception of her project she had been taking stock of these people, with the object, if need be, of later making contact with them. But first of all, she relied upon establishing goodwill with the semi-settled folk. And for this Verbena was the intermediary she employed.

When, on Sunday morning, the two of them arrived at the camp on the creek, Cindie carrying a brace of pigeons she had shot on the way, Verbena had been primed to act as ambassador and go-between. Not a satisfactory go-between, from Cindie's viewpoint, for the girl could not be roused to grandiloquence about the scheme. When Cindie told her, urgently: "You do understand, Verbena, what a good thing it would be for your people to have plenty of good food and nice clothes and mouth organs and things, don't you?" the reply was a matter-of-fact "Much better have gun, to shoot wallaby and birds."

However, there they were in the camp at nine o'clock in the morning, with Cindie very pleased at the sight of the several young men present. The gun beneath her arm and

the purposefulness of her visit together inhibited disquiet.
Besides, by this time her experience with the Kanakas had
taught her that looks were no criterion in respect to character
and motives.

She threw the pigeons down beneath the nose of an old
crone who was cooking a mess in a kerosene tin above a tiny
fire and spoke a cheery greeting. The old lady gave her a
fleeting, deprecatory smile, picked up the birds, examined
them and then, in an oddly shrill voice, shouted something
to nobody in particular. In a moment Cindie was surrounded
by smiling feminine faces and disjointed murmurs.

Verbena squatted down and began to talk. And Cindie
noted with apprehension that as she proceeded a sharp
wariness succeeded to the smiles. "Verbena," she said quietly,
"don't they like the idea?"

"They just listenin', Miss Cindie. You wait."

So Cindie left the gathering and sat down on a log. Shortly
some old men wandered over and attached themselves to the
gins and lubras. Lastly, the young males joined up. There
was little talk among them and what there was seemed dis-
connected. Then, one by one, the assembly melted away.
Its units settled down as before.

Verbena came over to Cindie, whose heart had sunk.
"Two young men, they work in the timber before, Missie
Cindie. They say it all right for little time but they want to
know who boss."

"Oh! Good, good, Verbena! Tell them Mr. Biddow is
the big boss, Verbena, and I am the little boss. No,
I'll do it myself. Show me the men who have worked
before."

The upshot was that Cindie set Folkhaven in a dither of
excitement by turning up before noon with half a dozen
young bucks trailing her. With pride she made them known
to Biddow and Tirwana by name. Takeo refused to feed them,
so, while Biddow attempted the difficult task of conducting
a conversation with them in their infantile English, Cindie
herself prepared for them a big meal. By one o'clock she,
Biddow, Tirwana and the Aborigines were making up the
creek, selecting likely trees.

"You think they can be depended on to turn up to-morrow, Cindie?" Biddow asked dubiously as they made back to the homestead.

"Now that they are here I would keep them here, Mr. Biddow. You know they don't expect much in the way of accommodation. We've got a store of blankets in. They can sleep on blankets in the field dining-room to-night and to-morrow make themselves some mia mias out of palm leaves and slabs. They could start work on Tuesday. Just leave it to me."

And so it turned out. Intrigued and amused by the life of the homestead, the Aborigines agreed to all Cindie's pro-posals. The blankets, she told them, would be theirs when so many logs went down the creek. She doled out food, plenty of it, which they cooked for themselves on small fires. On Monday morning she was up betimes and away to Port Denham for, among other things, new axes.

"They must have new axes, Mr. Biddow," she had de-clared. "Our axes have all been handled. They are good axes still, I know, but I've got a hunch that the shine of new blades will appeal to these blokes."

"That's good psychology, Cindie," he smiled.

And telegrams Cindie sent from the Port. Letters could not keep pace with her enthusiasm. Telegrams to timber agents in Pearltown, in Townsville. Then out to Fourmile she flew to inquire about a team. No obstacle there, either, though, despite their publicized cheapness, the price asked set her back on her heels a bit. But that was Biddow's business.

That same night she was back at the Port to receive the replies to her telegrams. At Pearltown, as she had feared, the mill was engaged to its fullest capacity with local timber, but Townsville could take cedar, maple, oak, in any quantity.

Biddow tried to damp down the fire of excitement and elation that consumed the girl. "Cindie, you are asking too much too quickly. Try and bear in mind that these Aborigines have never cut timber yet. Even the pair who have worked before have only used pick and shovel to help get logs out. And even that only for a few days at a time."

"They can learn." She was splendidly, exuberantly con-fident. "If the Kanakas can cut timber our Aborigines can.

Mr. Biddow, haven't you noticed that our blacks are more
powerful than the Kanakas? Most of the Islanders are soft
and flabby in comparison with our blacks. They will be
better axemen. You'll see."

And Biddow himself felt a little exalted to realize that
she was proud of the Aborigines. Proud that they were
Australians, like herself. She *wanted* them to be superior.
"And, by jove, if anyone can bring out what qualities they
possess it is Cindie," he told himself. Nevertheless, he felt
bound to repeat his warning. "Cindie, if you expect too
much you will get hurt."

"I don't expect more than they can give, Mr. Biddow.
They are bushmen. They must go walkabout now and
again. I've gone into that. I understand about people,
Mr. Biddow. I don't know why or how but I do. These
people must know all sorts of things that we don't know, Mr.
Biddow. Have you thought of that?"

On Tuesday morning she insisted that Biddow himself
accompany her and the Aborigines into the forest. The big
boss himself must teach the blacks how to fell the trees.
"They might not like to be taught by the Kanakas, Mr.
Biddow. We must consider them in every way. We must
not allow feeling to develop between them and the Kanakas.
. . . Now, about the price of those horses."

Within a few days the Aborigines were taking the timber
trees down.

"They are so darned intelligent," Biddow told Grey, who
with other planters could not get over to Folkhaven quickly
enough when the word got around of what was in the wind,
"that once is enough to tell them anything. But six men are
too many for felling, so I am taking Cindie's advice to let
them handle the team and raft the logs down the river, too."

Grey said very little. But Fraser—his marriage had by
now fallen naturally into the category of accepted things—
the Montagues and others shook their heads and prophesied
disaster. Louis Montague warned Biddow: "You wait!
They'll be with you for a few weeks and then they'll be
off. You'll be left with the team on your hands."

Barney Callaghan gloomed portentously. "You are letting yourself be led by the nose, my boy. Eight horses at ten quid a time is no joke."

"But I don't see how the scheme can possibly fail," protested Biddow.

"You'll see well enough when the boongs light out on you."

"D'ye know, Callaghan, if the Abo.s lit out I'm willing to bet that Cindie would find some other way to get those logs down the river. I'm putting my money on Cindie." Biddow spoke with quiet smiling pride.

"Huh," Barney grunted, with a flick of the eyes in Biddow's direction. Then heartily: "Maybe it would encourage the girl if I took on a bet or two on it."

Not only Barney but throughout the district, men got to laying odds on the success or failure of the venture. The teamsters and Jack Callaghan carried the news up over the range to the mineral belt and miners around the pits and prospectors on the creeks swore with pitying admiration or cursed the girl for a fool. The boongs were good horsemen. Everybody knew that. Out on the plains of the west they had carried the graziers on their backs from puny beginnings to wealth, but these bushmen were different. Treacherous beggars. And they didn't need to work. Too much tucker in the bush. They would have to be stood over with a gun.

But the influence Cindie brought to bear upon the Aborigines was infinitely more effective than a gun. That was: commonplace acceptance of them as they were, coupled with a deliberate policy of give and take in respect of things to be learned. She found no man among them who could reasonably be selected as a leader, so she adopted the practice, on her daily visits on horseback to the felling site, of sitting down with them and discussing the work and procedure with them jointly.

First of all, there was the question of hours. Since the Aborigines normally rose from sleep at daybreak, after eating it was natural to them to take their axes and make off into the forest. But their hours of work were erratic. Cindie often found them sleeping when she arrived at their work site. She would let them have their sleep out. The thing was: the logs came down.

Early on, she got a fright that set her heart in a flutter.

Not one Aborigine to be seen at the work site! The axes gone, too. She sat down, pale and shaking. But, shortly, indeterminate sounds came filtering through the trees, and when the six black men emerged from the jungle and threw a youngling pig at her feet, their faces abeam with delight, she could have cried with joy. "Fine, fine!" she cried. "Good, good!" She insisted on their enacting the whole business of chasing and cornering the pig. With wide-mouthed laughs they danced around and mimed the action of separating the young one from its mother, of knocking it on the head with an axe. "But axe no good like spear," one concluded.

When Cindie took up with them the matter of the team they displayed a naïve pride in being requisitioned for work forbidden to the Kanakas. The handling of horses appealed to them tremendously. Indeed, for the sake of peace, Cindie had to promise that they would work the team in turns.

And once a number of trees were down she set them to building a stockyard to enclose the corn-fed horses at night. This done, she went down to Fourmile and arranged for the delivery of the team. Before two months were out, several rafts, each comprising a dozen logs of red cedar, had been towed down to Port Denham for transport south.

Naturally, all had not been plain sailing. Two of the Aborigines disappeared after three weeks but Cindie had no difficulty in replacing them. One night, inexplicably, the rails of the stockyard had been let down and the horses, after destroying a goodly section of the vegetable gardens, had wandered down the track. The following morning the Aborigines had picked them up on the roadside, half-way down to Port Denham, browsing their way back to their original home.

We may anticipate by stating that as time went on the profits from the logs dwindled in proportion as the felling sites receded from the banks of the creek, making the snigging of the logs from the jungle a lengthy and onerous task. But the venture remained to the last more than merely lucrative. Only three of the original gang of Aborigines became permanent work-men and these Biddow at an early stage put on the same cash and subsistence basis as the Kanakas. Before that year was out one of these, named Billy, had settled down with Verbena and her baby in a shack of their own.

The fame of Cindie's exploit spread throughout the far north. She became a kind of Amazonian figure. When she made her appearance among men in the town, at the jetty, at the Port, she was greeted as one who possessed not only the ability of a man but, beyond that, some secret magic of her own in the handling of "boongs". For though some others, eager to emulate her success, made a bid at consistent employment of the Aborigines, they had little to show for it.

And why, they could not fathom, for Cindie, so far as they could judge, by observing her manner with the blacks, was not particularly kind to, nor thoughtful of them. She was often heard to rate them soundly when they had slipped, as she considered, on some job.

"What's the secret, Cindie?" Grey asked her. "We would all like to know. The old-timers say there was a bloke up on Cape York Peninsula who got the blacks to work for him pretty consistently but he used to live like a black. Was adopted into the tribe. Others get a bit of work out of them occasionally by belting them. But you seem to have a magic formula of your own."

Cindie's brow wrinkled. "There's no secret about it, Jeff. I simply treat them exactly the same as I treat white men. The same as Mr. Biddow treats the Kanakas."

The opportunity arising, Grey questioned Verbena's Billy, though not with much hope of satisfaction. Between the average white and the Aborigine a well of distrust and reticence yawned. But Billy, having noted the friendship between Cindie and Grey, spoke up without hesitation.

"Missie Cindie, she always do what she say. She to trust. And she like us. She just—she alla same boong."

CHAPTER XXIII

IN JULY, A LOCOMOTIVE, TRUCKS, MILES OF PORTABLE TRAM-line and other essential iron goods came into the mill. The tram-lines were laid out to the various farms in order determined by the importance of the crop of cane grown, and in August the crushing began. The first cane grown in the Masterman area, grown on Glenelg, to be exact, was fed to the rollers in the mill.

Three months the season lasted. At the end of it three thousand tons of raw sugar were purchased by the Queensland National Bank and transported down the coast to be refined at Bundaberg.

Biddow's ten acres yielded four hundred tons of sugar, a good crop with the canes then in vogue even from rich virgin river flat soil. The price paid the farmers by their mill was the comparatively small one of nine shillings a ton, but since each succeeding year's increased quantity of cane would allow crushing at lower figures with a higher margin of profit for distribution among the growers, this was considered satisfactory.

That so slight a quantity of cane took so long to run through the rollers was due partly to some refractoriness displayed by the new machinery but chiefly to the unreliability and incompetence of the white labour to which work among machinery was confined. Despite that the wage paid was twenty-five shillings a week and keep, a rate above that generally paid throughout the colony, and that in addition the mill Board promised a bonus to workers who saw the season through, there were very few whites who failed to pass on after a fortnight's work.

This fact, as can be imagined, led to fast and furious argument and even to bouts of fisticuffs between the proponents of a hundred per cent White Australia policy and its opponents. What chance, the latter group demanded to know, had planters of recruiting white labour for the more arduous work in the fields when whites would not stick to the few weeks of comparatively easy mill work?

Biddow's first experience of cane harvesting left him even more enamoured of the planter's life. There was something peculiarly picturesque about the black bodies of the Kanakas as they worked with rhythmical and leisurely movements to take down the green-gold cane. Those days, the trashing of the sticks was done preliminary to the cutting. A group of Kanakas, preceding the cutters, would grasp the tops of the sticks with their hands and tear off the leaves by dragging them down. A number of them working together made a sound like the swish of the sea at a distance. A musical measure, which, to ears that had time to listen, filled the golden days of winter and spring with drowsy enchantment.

Only Blanche fell into this category. And she did not fail of complete appreciation. The whole winter, for that matter, with its shining calm days and just sufficient bite in the air at night to make sleeping pleasant, had not found her lacking in appreciation. But for the fly in her ointment constituted by her self-enforced forbearance towards Cindie, Blanche would have been content, that winter.

For Biddow, relieved of immediate financial pressure by the success of the logging venture, took time off to go about with her, to accompany her to house parties at Glenelg, at Palmer Estate, to dances at the Port. On some Sundays excursions were engaged in, but Blanche's enjoyment of these was restricted by the presence of the children, Cindie and Tirwana.

One such trip, down to the mouth of the river, served to introduce the party to the great salt-water crocodile that infested the estuaries along the far northern coastline.

On this day, following their usual practice, Blanche and Biddow made use of the sulky to go out from Folkhaven. The others jolted along in the buckboard. Leaving the vehicles at the mill, they walked along the tram-line to the jetty, where they took to a borrowed dinghy and rowed down the river. Down till the jungle dropped behind them and great cottonwoods lined the banks, tumbling aslant to sweep with their masses of large flat leaves the surface of the water. Further still, till the cottonwoods were lost in river tea trees. These were succeeded by low-lying swamps.

From the mouth of the river white sands stretched out on either side, wide and miles long, fine and glittering in the sun, curving scimitar-like within the embrace of rain forest, palms and casuarinas. So flat was the bed of the Long Lagoon, enclosed by the twelve hundred miles long Great Barrier reefs, that at low tide the sea shallowed out for hundreds of yards before a depth sufficient for swimming was reached.

Our party found the tide at ebb. In the shallows dozens of Kanakas were stalking fish with spears. Three white men were dragging a net. Since many of the blacks were naked, Blanche, Cindie and Irene remained at some distance. Biddow, Tirwana and Randy joined the white fishermen. These already had secured many fish, among them being a fine specimen of the king of North Queensland edible fishes, the barrimundi. Quite twenty pounds in weight, this fish.

The women sat down at the junction of coarse sand and grass and absorbed the loveliness of the marine panorama. The sky was softly deep with blueness and swansdown clouds were puffed about the horizon by light breezes. North, rocky headlands jutted from the mainland. East from them a mountainous island humped itself out of the sea. Nine miles due east a lighthouse on a reef island made a white chalkmark against the sky, and a mile beyond that again, a wooded island drew a thin black line.

It was on the way home, drifting up the river on the tidal flow with an occasional lazy dip of the oars, by Biddow and Tirwana, that they came on the crocodile. About eighteen feet long, a shining jet black, the monster emerged from the scrub a few yards above them and slithered down the sloping bank towards the water. The women and children saw him first, for the oarsmen had their backs presented to him. At four simultaneous cries the men flung round. Biddow let out a sharp: "Hell!" Tirwana vented a loud "Huh!" threw up his hands, then grabbed the oars again and back-paddled madly. Since Biddow did not follow suit the boat swung round.

The crocodile was more startled than they. Rushing forward, he plunged with a great splash into the river. The boat rocked . . . the women screamed.

But that, of course, was the last they saw of the brute. Before many minutes had passed, the encounter had taken on the aspect of an exciting and pleasing adventure.

Later it was learned that that particular saurian was regarded by the Aborigines with awe and superstition on account of his phenomenal colour. Other croc.s were grey, green or yellow. He alone was black.

INTERLUDE

I

EARLY ON IN SEPTEMBER THE ADJOURNED INTER-COLONIAL
Convention resumed its sittings in Sydney to consider the
numerous amendments proposed by the representatives of
the colonies to the Commonwealth Bill and to receive the
reports of the Premiers on their discussions with the Secretary
for the Colonies, Mr. Joseph Chamberlain, in London. A
further adjournment resulted. At the end of that same
month Congress met again, in Melbourne, for a final session
of that year. Here, the opponents of federation fought deter-
minedly against the Bill, but their efforts could not prevail
against the tide of popular feeling.

In January of the following year the longest and most
important session took place. At it, arrangements were
made to submit a Constitution Bill, proclaimed as the most
democratic ever conceived in history, to a referendum, to
the decision of the electors of the colonies.

Queensland remained aloof. The Government of West
Australia, on the assumption that its isolated position would
render it liable to neglect in the event of federal union, also
stood out. From then on until the referendum was taken, in
June, an Homeric battle raged in the most powerful of the
colonies, New South Wales.

Campaigns virulently slanderous to the point of madness
were waged between the ultra-conservatives on the one hand
(the old Sydney Party, who hated "like hell" any kind of
union with any other colony) and the pro-federation tories,
liberals and Labour supporters in opposition. Unity upon
this over-riding measure generally took precedence over all
other differences among these latter groups.

The main retarding factor in the New South Wales swing
to federalism was the yes-no policy of its Premier, Reid. His
support for the Commonwealth proposals had never been
more than lukewarm and now, when their fate hung in the

balance, he publicly stated that though he would himself vote for the Bill, he refused to advise others either way.

Sydney's *Sydney Morning Herald* and *Evening News* supported the Bill, the *Daily Telegraph*, with inflammatory fanaticism, opposed it. At a late stage Reid's Government appointed a commission which presented a report so noncommittal that both sides were able to claim that it supported their case.

But the thunder of the big guns of the federalists roused and stirred the continent from north to south, from east to west. No occasion was accounted too small, no audience too meagre, no country sheet too obscure, to serve as a medium for spreading the fundamental principles of federation. These were: Implementation of the White Australia policy, the defence of Australia as an integral part of the British Empire—both by organizing the manpower already in the country and the introduction of a conformist and suitable immigrant type—the linking up of the nation so defended with its fellow-nations and the Mother Country by preferential tariffs, the building of necessary industries by protective duties and by bounties, and their control by compulsory arbitration!

More British than the British themselves because of their dependence upon the imperial navy and military forces for defence, the imperialist-minded among the federalists expounded their dreams of an Australia the dominant power in the Pacific, an Australia the great manufacturing country of the Pacific! And Labour, while in the main repudiating the imperialists' aspirations, trailed legitimate ideals, intertangled with chauvinist confusion, in their wake.

Mad scenes of excitement tore Sydney asunder on the night of the poll. The first figures thrown on the screens in the streets showed federation the winner. The crowds seethed. Yes-no Reid got the fright of his life. Then it was found that an error had been made in the counting and dismay succeeded to triumph. The federalists, though polling well over a majority vote, had failed to poll the eighty thousand minimum required for affirmation by an Act of the previous year. Victoria, South Australia and Tasmania had polled high for federation, but, with New South Wales lost and

Queensland and West Australia holding aloof, the battle for union appeared to have been lost.

The anti-federalists, thinking their victory conclusive, rejoiced. But then Yes-no Reid, noting the majority and in danger of being discredited and shelved in his own colony, now got off the fence and invited a conference of Premiers to consider an amended Bill.

In January, 1899, the Premiers met in Melbourne to consider amendments proposed by New South Wales and West Australia, and here Queensland, too, was represented.

That Convention decided to place an amended Bill before the electorates, a simple majority vote to be decisive. In the middle of 1899 a second referendum was taken, with West Australia alone holding aloof, and this time the proposals were sanctioned.

In West Australia a battle royal was now joined. The goldfields of that colony rioted, declaring that their Government was leading them to ruin. They petitioned the Queen, asking that the goldfields be allowed to separate from West Australia and be included in the fold of federation.

The final stage came with the praying to the imperial Parliament to pass the Commonwealth Bill into law. And to this end a delegation from the colonies accepted Joseph Chamberlain's invitation to visit England and be present when the Bill was presented to Parliament. The West Australia Government, reluctantly dragging at the heels of popular clamour, participated in this delegation.

The intense drama of the titanic, unprecedented struggle waged by certain members of that Australian delegation against the bull-dozing determination of Chamberlain to show these "damned Australian agitators" that though the imperial Parliament welcomed federation the measure had to conform exactly to British desires and control, has no place in this chronicle. The upshot was: with West Australia brought into line and New Zealand standing out, in July, 1900, the Queen's assent was given to the Commonwealth Bill and the stage at long last set for the march of the Australian people towards nationhood.

II

Queensland's participation in the proceedings towards federation did not exclude attempts by her Government to obtain from the Convention assurances of protection, in the event of federation, for Australian sugar in Australian markets, against bounty-fed sugar from abroad. And throughout Queensland planters conferred, declaimed and protested against unfair competition on Australian export sugar by the bounty system of European countries. Demands were advanced that the United Kingdom and other British colonies act in their favour by imposing countervailing duties. The fact that London had recently placed Australian wines upon a dutiable basis equal to Continental was a spur to this demand. The reply they got from Chamberlain? "Impertinence, by God!"

However, despite the hostility of leading sugar planters and millers to federation, hostility based upon the proposed measures against black labour, they were finding themselves in the position of having to choose between the devil and the deep blue sea.

For their hatred of the rising Labour forces was even deeper than their hatred of the White Australia policy. If a change to white labour was inevitable, then a tory administration was their need. For such would be amenable to their influence in respect of wages and conditions. White labour with Labour in political control, the obscurantists contended, would spell their doom! In December, 1899, the first Labour Government the world had known had been formed in Queensland. This Ministry had petered out after only four days, but that it should have assumed office at all predicated a stable Labour administration in the colony in the near future.

But in the federal sphere Labour appeared to be very much at a loss. In the elections for delegates to the Convention, no Labour man had been even considered. So, an overriding federal Government to which "a dozen or so of our more enlightened statesmen have been transferred", was infinitely preferable to a Labour Government in Queensland, with its ability to give legal sanction to the white workers' demands for improved conditions, shorter hours, higher wages. The moaning and fury of the big planters and millers became submerged in a battle for whatever plums could be picked from the inevitable political and economic trends.

At the same time, these men did not neglect to prepare for readjustments. They began to speed up the process that the more enlightened among them had been engaged upon for some time: the subdivision of large holdings. The operations of the farmers' co-operative mills had revealed that small farmers, working beside their employees, on farms they could claim to be their own, were more eager for success than when labouring or overseeing for others. The control of mills by directorates of farmers was also more economical than in the hands of planters or managers with semi-feudal ideas and the old-fashioned organization that demanded large administrative staffs.

So the big men set out to modify their production methods to hand the work of growing cane over to small farmers and producers. By the time federation became an accomplished fact the process was well begun by which, in its further development, farmers' homes would break up the long vistas of cane.

But not yet. For, concerned only with their own interests and not at all with the White Australia policy, the transfer of the sugar lands was in the main to Chinese. In a southern Queensland district, this transfer to Chinese, who bought in eagerly with the object of using their compatriots for labour, reached the stage where every stick of cane supplied to one large mill was grown by Chinese. In the Pearltown district, half the cane-growing lands came under the ownership of Chinese.

PART TWO

CHAPTER XXIV

BY THE YEAR 1902, FOLKHAVEN WAS A FINE PROPERTY IN good order. That year four hundred acres was put under cane, half of it by "cultivation" methods. Two hundred acres had reached the stage where the big logs left lying, burned year after year with the trash from the cane sticks, had rotted into the ground and thus made cultivation possible. Another two hundred acres had been sublet, with a clause in the purchase in the contract, to a farmer named Chris Martin.

In 1898, Cindie had gone ahead with her scheme for putting thirty acres of sloping ground under coffee. A venture, it had transpired, which involved subleasing the coffee plantation to the girl. For in 1899 the mill Board had transferred its custom from the Queensland National Bank to the Colonial Sugar Refining Company, which made purchase of raws contingent upon the exclusive production of sugar by the growers supplying the mill.

Only forage for the teams and vegetables and fruits for home consumption would be generally permitted.

Some of the farmers shook their heads over this clause, contending that alternating maize and hay with cane would improve the land. There were also objections raised on the ground of its being a monopoly imposition. But the majority of the mill Directorate were agreed on the basis of contentment on the part of the industry in general with the price paid by the C.S.R., for both standing crops and sugar.

Queensland had proved by experience that intra-colony competition for the colonial markets, the markets of the other Australian colonies and New Zealand, was bad business. On the other hand, the monopolist company, by scientific methods, profitable investments and reliability in the fulfilling of engagements, had built itself into a position so strong that it was able to offer encouraging terms. Ex-

pansion was its need and its motto. More sugar from the lands
already planted, new lands to be opened up. . . .

Normally, Biddow would have left the timber on the
foothills standing to the last, since high land, from which
in the dry season all soakage ran away, tended to produce
poor cane. But so confident had he become of the success
of any undertaking of Cindie's that he had given her a free
hand in the further recruitment of Aborigine labour for the
clearing of that section she had selected as suitable for her
purpose.

Sloping ground, it seemed, was best for coffee, in that it
prevented surface water from lodging and souring the soil.
Good friable soil was essential, too, and great depth not
required.

Cindie's first job had been to build a nursery, ten acres
in extent and running parallel with the bank of the creek,
in which to raise the plants. Keeping pace with the felling,
she employed her logging gang to haul off the slope any
saleable logs. Other logs and stumps were left to rot. At
the same time she brought in two Aborigine girls to assist her
in burning off.

Followed trenching of the ground and its lay-out in beds.
Less than half a bushel of "cherry", yielding about twelve
thousand seeds, was then pulped by a process of squeezing
through the fingers in water from the creek. The seeds were
then planted in beds, nine inches by nine apart and thinly
covered with earth.

From the time the seedlings appeared above ground until
they were four inches high, watering every morning and
evening was essential. A job, Cindie found, fraught with
more difficulty than she had bargained for.

For the Aborigine girls could not be persuaded to work
except through the day. To Cindie's seductive offers of
reward they merely gave teasing laughs. Chagrined at this
unexpected limitation of her power to cajole them, and loath
to admit it to the Biddows, Cindie for the first day kept her
failure to herself. That evening she slaved mightily at hawk-
ing great tins of water from the creek and along the beds.
But she was forced to give in. By dusk she had not covered
one half of the plots, and though a full moon shed ample

light for her to complete the task, she dared not linger in the fields. As it was, Tirwana came striding across the paddocks to look for her.

"You silly, Miss Cindie, to worry about the water," he told her. "I will help you!"

"I feel I'm not as good as I thought I was," she replied ruefully. "Those young brats wouldn't stay even for money."

"Won't hurt you, Miss Cindie, to be knocked back. You think you are a little god, you know." Tirwana smiled at her fondly. "What we'll do is make a slide. Hammer some slabs across a forked log, harness up a horse and cart the water round the beds."

When on the following evening Tirwana turned up with his slide, the Aborigine girls were disposed to remain and assist him, but Cindie sent them flying. Once the plants had reached four inches, watering on alternate evenings only was sufficient; by which time Cindie was so enamoured of her nursery that each evening she left it, life hardly seemed worth living till in the morning she returned.

While the plants were growing, the remainder of the land was cleared. With the assistance of a succession of Aborigine women, Cindie in this period cut thousands of fifteen-inch wooden pegs. With these and a rope marked off every six feet by a rag let into the twist, she laid out the cleared ground in straight parallel lines six feet apart. Logs and stumps were jumped. Ranging rods, called wadd sticks, were used to keep the lines straight. At intervals of six feet along the rows, holes eighteen inches deep by eighteen wide were dug. Then the surface soil around the hole was mixed with ashes from the burning off and heaped back into the hole. A peg marked the spot.

Four months had passed by the time the thirty acres were prepared for the nursery plants. It was now August and Cindie prayed for the rain needed for the successful transfer of the plants. A big job, this, and particularly arduous. When the places marked by the pegs had been re-dug, the plants had to be lifted, alternately, with a ball of earth adhering to the roots, and carried to the planting field on trays.

Care in the replanting was also required, for too much

depth tended to strangle the plants. The best method was to plant a little deeper than required, then, with a foot on either side of the plant, apply a steady pull upwards to straighten the root. Failures would be replanted during following wet weather.

Morning after morning Cindie had risen from her bed and raked the heavens with anxious eyes. With what delight she had welcomed the drizzle that began in the middle of the month and persisted intermittently over several days!

But on the first day of the transplanting the eight Aborigine women she had enlisted, decamped, disgusted with the heavy toil and meticulous care involved. Cindie was left disconsolate in the field, watching the flying figures of the black women as they took off into the bush.

A few minutes of scowling thought, then with grim determination she started back to the homestead on the slide. No use at all in considering the Kanakas. The cane cut that year covered seventy acres and not a man among them could be spared. But the logging gang, unlike the cane cutters, did not work in the rain. Some of them, at least, she would have!

Hitching the horse to a post, Cindie strode over to Verbena's shack, in the doorway of which Billy was lounging, minding the child. Two other Aborigines, she found, were within.

Not a word from the three in response to Cindie's straightforward request. They stared woodenly at the dirt floor. Down among them Cindie squatted. Their eyes came to her. She smiled. "I can't get on without you," she said, simply. "Aren't you my friends?" She waited.

Soon the trio became uneasy. They scuffed the floor with their feet.

Cindie raised her voice. "You are not my friends? You would let the boss tell me I'm no good? You let me leave the farm?"

"But, Missie, it wet," Billy protested.

"Coffee, it needs the rain." Cindie, who long ago had apprehended that even though the natives might not understand some English words, they appreciated having it taken for granted that they did, began to explain about the planting, using exactly the same phraseology she would have addressed to a white. But the reaction of her listeners was not promising. Her heart was sinking when suddenly an idea struck her, a wonderful and irresistible idea. These people loved the dance! And were not their dances mimo-dramas of the origin and development of natural phenomena? She sprang up from her squatting position.

"You like coffee, don't you?" she cried. "You take care, when you grind the beans I give you between the stones, not to lose one single grain! Well, those coffee beans grow in a special way or they are no good. They must be treated kindly, like you treat your piccaninny, Billy." Liquid black eyes were now beginning to kindle on her and Cindie, warm-ing up in response, set to and mimed, there in the little dark hut, the process of coffee farming from the felling of the timber up to the stage she had arrived at.

She fired the dark men, fired their love of drama, of the play. To each of her actions in turn they began to utter sounds expressing its effect upon the body. When Cindie bent down and made pretence of watching for the first tendril of leaf to appear, three inspired faces bent with her.

"It comes!" she cried, scarcely less carried away by the sincerity of her own imagining than they. "See, Billy! See, Jimmy! See, Joe! The piccaninny plant! It comes up out of the earth and says hullo to the sun."

"A—a—h!" soft voices concurred.

"And then it sings out for water. Miss Cindie, Miss Cindie, it cries, in a tiny voice like a bird's, give us drink, drink, drink."

Up she sprang and mimed the carrying of water from the creek. Tirwana bringing the slide. The logging up and burning she enacted. The men chortled with glee when she mimicked their individual mannerisms with the team. Then came the trenching, the laying out of the beds, the flight of the black girls, her dismay. The whole chain of events, she unfolded, giving a representation natural and true, till in the end she was left alone, deserted, disconsolate, with the plants calling wildly, shouting in a voice like the curlew crying his sorrows across the cane fields at night.

"And only you can save them," she concluded. "You, my friends."

They responded like lambs. Not only did they persuade their three mates to follow their suit but that night they visited their own people in the forest, with the result that next morning at daybreak another half dozen young bucks came trooping out of the bush and offered to work.

Cindie wept when she saw them. But even as she dashed a hand across her eyes she was calling to Charity to come help her feed them! Calling upon Biddow for utensils, bulldozing Takeo, by now absolutely under her thumb, to the production of an enormous stew, a whole boilerful of rich, thick stew, for a mid-morning meal for "her workers".

"If I can hold them for a week, Mr. Biddow," she said breathlessly, "and the rain continues for only three days, just three short days, I'll have the whole thirty acres in plant."

"You'll hold them, Cindie," was his quiet reply.

CHAPTER XXV

THE WEATHER, AS WE ALREADY KNOW, WAS OBLIGING ENOUGH, and the natives were willing workers; but Cindie, noting their weariness after a few hours on the job, decided that the risk of committing them to a long day was too great. So after six hours she called a halt, fed them mightily, and then offered them their choice of fishing, shooting or pighunting, for the afternoon. The horses she placed at the disposal of those who chose the river, her own gun and services for the bush. Biddow had cautioned her against putting a gun into the hands of these bushmen who only now, after decades of infamous treatment at the hands of the whites, were learning the lesson that resistance to encroachments upon hunting grounds which had been theirs from time immemorial, did not pay.

A fortnight went into the planting of the coffee but the job was well done and Cindie herself did little but superintend. Once the Aborigines were shown what to do they rarely bungled. They took pride in their capacity for neat-

ness and dispatch. At the completion of the job Cindie, with
Biddow's consent, took horse to Palmer Estate creek and
invited the whole shebang of Aborigines at the camp to
come over to Folkhaven that night for a feast. The young
men in the camp she sent off into the forest to procure a pig.
A good big pig, she stipulated, or in default of that two or
three first-year young.

On her return journey to Folkhaven she visited the Callaghans and asked for the loan of boilers, tin dishes and mugs.

"Cindie, my dear girl!" Mary Callaghan threw up her
hands in dismay. "You don't know what you have let yourself in for! Goodness me! Oh, dear me! We shall have to
help you out! Consuelo and I will get to work at the ovens
straight away. You may expect us over in the late afternoon
with the utensils and provisions. Oh dear, oh dear! Suppose
the Kanakas and the boongs start to fight, Cindie?"

"No chance of that, Mrs. Callaghan," Cindie laughed.
"But, Mrs. Callaghan—you wouldn't consider bringing your
violin and playing a tune for them, I suppose? Some jigs,
lively stuff, you know."

"Of course I would, Cindie! I think it's wonderful, what
you've done."

Cindie hastened home to fill the hours with the baking of
tarts and cakes. Charity and Verbena, wildly excited,
cleaned piles of yams and sweet potatoes. Blanche, pro-
fessedly disgusted with the "turning of the place into a
niggers' camp", drove off to Glenelg with the children and
spent the day there.

At Glenelg, however, Blanche found nothing but admiration for Cindie's latest exploit: the pulling off of the planting
of a coffee plantation at the cost only of the feeding of her
workers, some presents and a feast. The old lady chuckled
and again deplored the fact that she had no more sons. She
intended to be present. And help out with the food, too.
She flabbergasted Blanche by prophesying that every
Aborigine within a radius of ten miles would that night
converge on Folkhaven. Oh yes, there'd be high jinks!

"You tell Biddow to keep his guns handy to-night," she
warned Blanche. "My men will bring a revolver or two."

Before lunch time the Aborigine bucks came out of the

forest with two half-grown pigs. An hour later, three strange
blacks turned up from coastwards with a wallaby slung from
a pole. And during the afternoon, an old, rheumy-eyed but
terribly tall black headed a small procession up the track.
Three gins trailed him, one of them aged and bent, the other
two young, carrying babies draped across their backs and
with very little in the way of clothing to cover their most
intimate parts. Half a dozen chubby little youngsters at their
heels were stark naked.

The three gins almost tottered beneath the weight of an
eighteen-foot rock python. Biddow, who had nursed the
precincts of the homestead all day with a view to keeping
an eye on events, was startled by the sight of the giant snake,
the first of its species he had seen. And hardly less startled
by the naked hanging breasts of the gins. The old man,
with a childish elfish smile, squinted down at Biddow and
said softly: "Corroboree, Boss. We bring snake."

That was the beginning. By the time Blanche arrived
home with the children, Biddow was both speechless and
helpless before an inundation of primitive nude and semi-
nude humanity. They came out of the bush, up the track,
men, women and children. Some of the bucks carried
spears. The women dangled babies and dilly bags from their
necks.

Though quaking somewhat at the formidable dimensions
the festivities threatened to assume, Cindie was neither
speechless nor helpless. With Mary Callaghan and Consuelo
assisting, she raided the storeroom again and again. To
Biddow she laid down the law.

"This is the test of our attitude towards these people, Mr.
Biddow. If it cleans us out of foodstuffs they must be fed.
These are our own people, Mr. Biddow. They are Australians.
They can't be deported. We can't expect to have them to
fall back on if we lose the Kanakas unless we treat them
right, now."

Her words made Biddow uneasy. "Maybe you are right,
Cindie," he told her, carefully. "But there's something I
don't like about it. It's even cheaper labour than the Kanakas.
I feel that we are exploiting these people unjustifiably. There's
something wrong about it."

"No!" Cindie's reply was imperative. "I've thought all that out. It's a stage in the pioneering of this country, Mr. Biddow. To give them money would be ruinous to these people, as yet. Not only they but the whites must be educated to that. But it is also ruinous to the blacks to be neglected, to be forced to live like bushmen once the conditions have deprived them of their old way of life. The proper thing to do is to bring them among us, to teach them to live like whites, stick to a job, send their children to school."

"I reckon you ought to have been a Missionary, Cindie." Biddow smiled and sighed. "Very well. I certainly have nothing better to offer them, at this stage."

Realizing the impossibility of catering for the crowds that were turning up, by normal cooking methods, Cindie got ground fires going and had piles of potatoes, yams and onions cooked in the ashes. So interested were the Aborigines in the Kanakas' manner of cooking wallaby and pig—for this job Biddow had called in Tirwana—that they adopted it in respect of the great rock python.

By sundown the scene of operations presented a memorable sight. One hundred and fifty odd blacks had come in. Mostly they squatted in groups about the fires, silent, or talking together in low tones. Even when the meats were removed from the cooking ovens the bulk of the Aborigines made no move. Only the children crowded round.

From the Aborigines the Kanakas held aloof, in the main contemptuous of a people whose physiognomy they derided and whose technique they regarded as appallingly primitive. The word "myall" was spat out by some of them in disgust, weighted with a significance quite foreign to its simple "bush native" meaning.

With cane and sheath knives the carcasses were hacked to pieces on the field dining-table and heaped on to as many plates as were available. The vegetables were raked out of the ashes, the contents of the boilers tipped on to sheets. At that stage, Mary Callaghan expostulated with Cindie. "There's no sense, Cindie, no sense at all in attempting to regulate a meal of this nature. Call the blacks around you and invite them to help themselves. They will do it orderly enough."

And they did. The black women came forward, gathered up food and presented it to their menfolk. Not until the men were satisfied did the women divide up the remainder of the meats and vegetables among themselves and the children.

But when tubs filled with cakes and tarts were handed round among them their delight overcame their shyness. Muted laughter and soft cries accompanied the sinking of their splendid teeth into the sweet delicacies.

By now, not only the householders from Glenelg and Palmer Estate had arrived but many other whites besides. Planters and townspeople alike had been roused by bush telegraph and sped Folkhavenwards to see the "doings". From the balcony a dozen women looked down. Downstairs the white men stood about in groups, not all of them compliant with this "toadying to niggers" so recently brought to heel in respect to outright hostilities and who yet refused to surrender the labour of their hands and their freedom of movement to their oppressors. Jealousy rankled in the hearts of many. Cindie found herself the recipient of black looks.

"What's the matter with you?" she said sharply to Chris Martin, at that time a banana and citrus fruit grower and a self-appointed leader in local Labour politics.

"It's what's the matter with you, I say," was his forceful response. "What you ought to be doing is showing these niggers the barrel end of a gun." He took his pipe from his mouth and spat.

"Oh! Any more talk of that kind around here, Chris Martin, and I'll show you the barrel of my gun."

"If I had my way I'd run you out of the district," he gave back, savagely.

Willis Fraser, who had stepped up to listen-in, now intervened. "There's no sense in that sort of talk, Martin. What I say is: Biddow's damned lucky to have a woman to manage his business better than he can manage it himself."

The tone, rather than the words, the subtle silky nuance of expression, sent a wave of red over Cindie's face. She flared up. "It wouldn't be difficult to find a woman to manage your affairs better than you can manage them yourself, Willis Fraser, if all I hear is correct."

She left them and hurried up the stairs of the house, agitated, her heart thumping. Was it possible that people —said things? No, no! That couldn't be! It was only Fraser's filthy mind. She sought out Mary Callaghan and asked her to play now, while the Aborigines were still eating.

Mary, who had herself been involved with much the same kind of critical comment from a couple of women present, guessing the cause of the girl's obvious agitation, said shrewdly: "Don't let anybody's jealousy get you down, Cindie. . . . Yes, I will give them a tune."

The music floated down from the balcony, bringing a hush upon the gathering below. Not even a child stirred. When Mary took the instrument from beneath her chin Cindie whispered to her: "Mrs. Callaghan, do ask Mrs. Biddow to play for them, and sing. She wouldn't do it for me."

"Now, Mrs. Biddow, it's your turn," Mary laughed. "How about bringing the piano out on to the balcony?"

Blanche loftily assented.

Down below, Grey wandered among the menfolk, listening and pondering what he heard. Funny business altogether, this White Australia business, he thought. Funny how its advocates ignored the presence in the country of tens of thousands of original black inhabitants. It was tacitly accepted that the Aborigines did not count. Sub-humans, they were accounted. No longer shot on sight and tortured with approbation, it was true, but . . . Darned if he could make head or tail of what the future could hold for them!

Verbena's husband, Billy, came up to him, a broad grin on his squat, ugly face. "We want to show Miss Cindie the dance she make, Boss. You tell her?"

"Dance? What dance?"

"She make dance in hut. Dance for the coffee planting, so we go out in the rain and work for her."

"Well, I'm jiggered." Grey took off his hat and scratched his head. His eyes went up to the balcony to seek Cindie. There she was, leaning over the rail beside Consuelo. "Hey, Cindie!" he shouted. "Your blacks want to do your dance for you."

"All right, all right. Tell them to go ahead." Cindie

glanced around her warily, her face again flaming. Whatever would these people think? A dozen pair of eyes were
upon her.

"I asked the blacks to make me a dance around the planting of the coffee," she explained hastily.

"They will make a dance for us all with spears in our
backs, if this nonsense is not put a stop to," Chris Martin's
wife vociferated.

"Rubbish, Mrs. Martin." Blanche, torn between a desire
to defend a policy that put money in her pocket and her
detestation of Cindie, made acidulous reply. "Those creatures
know what's good for them."

Two dozen Aborigines, all males, were now forming into
line. This done, with inimitable grace and gesture they
mimed the process of coffee planting as Cindie, clumsily by
comparison, had done it before them. But in addition they
enlivened it with vocal expression that, added to the gesticulations, had vivid and entrancing effect. The true ballet!

At this demonstration of an art they themselves excelled
in, the Kanakas no longer held aloof. They pressed forward
towards the dancers. They exclaimed and argued with one
another. And scarcely had the dance of the coffee planting
ended than they broke into their own peculiar style of terpsi-
chorean expression. . . .

The only threatening incident for which the coloured folk
were responsible occurred when Melatonka, parading with
his mouth organ in all the glory of his carefully-treasured
sulu and flower-adorned coiffure, made up to a comely
young lubra already plighted to a buck. But when suddenly
confronted with a spear supported by a menacing glare from
a pair of gimlet eyes, Melatonka's ardour precipitately
cooled.

By nine o'clock Cindie had distributed among the gins and
lubras a tubful of cakes she had kept back for this purpose
and manœuvred the small army of visiting blacks into a
retreat down the track.

The whites, however, did not prove so tractable. Political
arguments woven around the core of the evening's festivities
festered into jealous conflicts and early in the evening only
the general recognition of the desirability of an appearance

of unity among the whites in face of so large a body of dark people, kept the peace. But once the Aborigines had drifted into the night and the Kanakas had retired to their quarters, a small group, with Chris Martin their leader, made a frontal attack upon Biddow.

"What's your game, Biddow?" Martin demanded. "I speak for the small farmers who stand for white labour in this country under white man's conditions. Isn't Kanaka labour cheap enough for you?"

Biddow, who had recognized with something of a shock the factional current of opinion flowing around him, had waited downstairs among the men in expectation of things coming to a head. Before replying he put a match to his pipe and in the light it shed allowed his eyes to dwell upon Martin. "I'm not playing any game," he said evenly. "You are open to get the Aborigines to work for you the same as I am, Martin. If I don't pay them in money it is because I know there are plenty of bloody mongrels among the whites who would steal it from them and debauch them into the bargain."

"Debauch hell!" shouted Martin. "First I ever heard that niggers could be debauched! I'd shoot the whole bloody lot of them, if I had my way."

"Now, Martin, you're going too far," put in Fraser oilily. "I reckon Biddow's lucky. Wish I knew his secret." He laughed.

Biddow ignored Fraser. "Then I take it that the trouble with you, Martin," he persisted, "is that I reckon the blacks have a right to live in their own country."

"The trouble with me, Biddow, is that I reckon you are aiming to use the boongs as cheap labour when we've got rid of the Kanakas."

"Well, that's your opinion." Here Biddow took his pipe from his mouth and stepped towards the other. "And in my estimation it's as rotten as your general outlook upon the black people. It doesn't interest me." He swung round to face Barney Callaghan and Fraser. "I'm not aiming to perpetuate cheap labour in this country. When we can get white labour to come up here and work I will employ it. And any black labour I employ besides will receive the same

wages for the same work done. Until then I will manage
my own business and thank other people to manage theirs.
. . . Now enough of this. We'll go upstairs."

The group of men broke up. Martin, Grey, Callaghan and
Fraser followed Biddow upstairs. The others took horse or
vehicle and made down the track.

But when all the guests had gone and Biddow, Blanche
and Cindie were left alone, Blanche lost no time in questioning her husband. "What happened downstairs to-night,
Randolph? We heard Martin shouting. And anybody could
see there was something wrong when he came up."

"Nothing that need interest you."

"Oh? Then perhaps it's something that would interest
Cindie," she flashed.

"Maybe it would interest her but that's beside the point.
I'm off to bed."

"You were quarrelling about those blacks! I know. We're
the talk of the country-side! Our name is mud!"

"Our name's not mud, my dear Blanche. At least, not
through anything I have done or am likely to do."

"That *you* have done! Nobody is fool enough to
imagine——"

"Mrs. Biddow!" Cindie intervened, swiftly and bluntly.
"Don't say anything you might be sorry for. There's some
jealousy about the blacks. That's all there is to it. But
I've got coffee planted. That's more in your interest than in
mine. Now I'm tired. I want to sleep. I'm taking a day
off to-morrow, Mr. Biddow. I need it. Good night."

"And it's daybreak for me," said Biddow. "Come,
Blanche."

Blanche did not follow him immediately. With clenched
hands she leant against the table, staring down at it, but
blind to everything else in the world but her twisted mental
vision. "Cat! Bitch!" she hissed. "You wait! Wait till
the logs are all out and the farm in order! Then it will be
my turn."

From then on Cindie had experienced no difficulty in
getting sufficient Aborigine labour for the maintenance of
the coffee plantation, continual weeding and the work
essential to the eventual harvesting of the beans. Within a

month of the completion of the planting two commodious shacks had been built on the bank of the creek for the housing of her workers, and she had made it known among the nomadic dark people that these were at their disposal. This latter move was essential, for Blanche had flatly refused to countenance the constant drift of Aborigines to the homestead that followed upon the night of the feast.

If many blacks were in camp, Cindie would hunt with the young men, bringing in pig, wallaby, bush turkey and fowl. In the winter months she supplied seeds and plants and insisted upon the camp dwellers cultivating the ground around the shacks.

And gradually she taught those who worked for her the value of money. Instead of handing out a pair of pants or a dress, she would give the price of the garment and then take the recipient along to the store and supervise the purchase. She got to dreaming of a school, a separate school for natives only, for as yet the little black pigeons of the bush were too wild and shy to intermingle with the whites, even had the parents of the latter been forward enough to permit this.

CHAPTER XXVI

THEN, EARLY IN 1899, HAD COME THE MILL BOARD'S ARRANGEments with the Colonial Sugar Refining Company. Biddow brought the news home from a night meeting of the co-operative farmers, and so it happened that he had thrashed out the matter with Blanche, in their bedroom, before Cindie heard about it in the morning.

At first hearing it was a bitter-sweet triumph for Blanche. Bitter for the financial loss it augured, sweet for the blow it portended for Cindie.

"So that's what our precious Cindie's schemes have come to!" she cried, hatefully. "All that ground and work wasted!"

"I don't think so," was Biddow's equable reply. "There's a way out. I shall sublet the coffee plantation to Cindie."

"But that would mean handing her over most of the profits!"

"A proportion of them, certainly. But I should see that she got her fair share, in any case."

"Her share! You talk as though the woman had put money into the place! Randolph, don't do this thing. Randolph, can't you see that as a lessee the girl could never be got rid off? She'd be on our hands for ever! For ever!"

Biddow, who had been preparing for bed, sat down and gazed at her for some time without speaking. At length he nodded his head. "So you've still got that bee in your bonnet. Very well. You can still make your choice. It's always there for you to make. I will come to some financial arrangement with Cindie to-morrow, if you want it that way, let her go and lease the coffee trees to someone else. But you know what that means, Blanche."

"You know damn well that's not what I want! Simply lease the coffee to someone else and let the girl go on as usual. I don't mind you making her some—some recompense for the work she's done. Besides, we need her for the blacks. You know that."

"Yes. I know that." Blanche's glance wavered before the scorching condemnation in his. Biddow said no more but she knew that she had lost again. For hours she lay, sleepless, seething with impotent fury. But she knew better than to interfere when Biddow, at breakfast, put the proposition before Cindie.

"I am sorry things have turned out this way, Mr. Biddow," said the girl, after brief cogitation. "But since that's how it is I can see that it is best all round for me to be your lessee. The terms you offer me are the usual, I suppose?"

"Much better than the usual." Blanche could not refrain from caustic comment.

Biddow gave her a fleeting glance. "Maybe a little better than the usual, Cindie. They are based on the low production costs, which I owe to you."

"Very well. That's fair enough. Business is business, Mr. Biddow."

Later, in conversation with Grey, Biddow retailed with amusement Cindie's attitude towards the transaction. "What

I like about Cindie," he said smilingly, "is her lack of sentimentality and hypocrisy. She takes on these schemes out of
idealism. Personal aggrandisement never enters her head.
But she always knows when to draw a line between idealism
and practical issues. There's no mock modesty about her.
She doesn't hold herself cheaply."

"That's it," Grey concurred. "She's what I call square-
headed."

Twelve months after the coffee plants had been bedded
they were sufficiently grown to be topped. To facilitate
the lateral spread of the trees as against height—to ensure
easy cropping—from three to four feet of the tops were lopped
off. By the third year, when the maiden crop of beans was
ripe for harvest, a pulp house, storeroom and platforms for
drying the beans had been erected beside the creek. A water
wheel had been installed. Disc and pulper had been imported
from Ceylon at the negligible cost of seventeen pounds.

The maiden crop ran to between two and three hundredweight per acre, which when sold realized a staggering profit
above production costs. From then on, the crop would show
an annual increase in weight till, in the sixth year, when the
trees would be in full bearing, up to fifteen hundredweight
an acre could reasonably be expected.

Since London, at that time, was paying five pounds per
hundredweight for plantation coffee, it can well be understood why Blanche, despite occasional convulsive outbursts
against the woman who had made this exceptional affluence
for Folkhaven possible, never reached the stage of forcing a
showdown on the issue of her hatred versus Cindie's initiative
and powers.

Blanche could not help but become aware, not only of
Biddow's increasing dependence on Cindie but also of an
essential depreciation of the man's physical and spiritual
make-up. Fundamentally antithetical to ambition, he slid
into the groove of subservience to Cindie's energetic drive
with a tranquillity of spirit that tended year after year to
become matched by sensual inanition. Less and less he
responded to the seduction of his wife's sustained ardours.
And this condition, interpreted by the illogic of her blazing
desires as symptomatic merely of her failing attractions for

him, simply drove her to a cynical re-assessment of her whole position.

Blanche in those years was at the height of her physical and unspiritual bloom. Sensually satisfied, she could have made out indefinitely in a stormy, inchoate sort of way. But with her passions mounting in proportion to their denial and subject to the influence of the perennial lustiness of the natural world around her, she could see nothing for it but to lash out at life with the whip of her desires and take what relief she could from the blood-letting.

In 1900 she took the children down to Brisbane and put them to school there. Took them from Cindie's tacit influence upon them with a tigerish joy that yet was interlarded with bitter jealousy over the necessity of leaving Biddow alone with the girl. For weeks she strove to persuade the man to accompany her. She went to the length of proposing that he make Cindie manager of the whole property and reside with her, Blanche, in Brisbane. But all she got out of that was his counter-proposal that she remain in the south herself if that was what she desired.

For four months, while her new home at Folkhaven was being built, Blanche sought to drown her smouldering hates and frustrations in a whirl of gaiety in Brisbane. But she found that city life, after the first week or two, had lost its charm. The wide sky, the forests, the mountains, the free and exotic life of the tropics had imperceptibly set their seal upon her. And the psychology of her own people, more than ever confounded with political opportunism in that year of Labour upsurge, profoundly bored her.

The very first night of her return to her parental home her mother had demanded, in the domineering manner she had bequeathed to her daughter, an account of "this chit, Cindie. The children talk as though the girl runs the place."

"And that's about what it amounts to," was Blanche's calculated reply. "Cindie turned out to be a genius at organization. She's got brains."

"Is that all there is to it?"—shrewdly.

"What else could there be to it?"

"One never knows. . . . These outlandish places. . . . But I can scarcely see you taking second place to a servant."

"She's not a servant"—shortly. "She's a sort of over-seer."

"Oh!—I can see there's something, Blanche. You had better send her back down here."

Blanche burst out laughing. She laughed and laughed till her mother became a little alarmed. At length, wiping her eyes with a bit of flimsy muslin, she declared: "You may as well know, Mother, that our Cindie is not only the boss of Folkhaven the second but the admired and adored of the whole country-side, besides. The bitch! Now we'll talk of something else."

On the receipt of the news that her home was nearing completion, Blanche made ready to return north. She rejected with decision her mother's offer to accompany her. "You would hate it, Mother," she stated. "You would hate the long trip. I know what is in your mind. But there's no sense in your thinking you could do anything about Cindie's position. It suits me to put up with her. She stands between me and the niggers. She means money."

"Well, Blanche," replied the sophisticated old woman, "I suppose you've got your own standards. I confess I can't understand them. The young women of to-day seem lost to the old-time decencies."

Stung by a shaft from the meagre arsenal of her conscience, Blanche blushed, at that. For within the last few weeks she had essayed the desperate expedient of seeking solace in an extra-conjugal excursion. Once only, for, like many a woman before her and since, she had found the brief intercourse snatched out of chance contact barren of satisfactory results.

But the incident, seemingly the fruit of impulse and chance contact combined, had been actually a milestone on a road already mapped out by cynical rationalization.

Settled down again at Folkhaven, Blanche continually assessed and re-assessed her position. Fate was damned hard. If only in determining her preference for this plantation way of life. But since she had to stick there—well, she would see. One thing, there was no real shortage of money now. And the district was growing rapidly, providing more oppor-tunities for social life. An entertainment hall had been erected in the township. Dances were held regularly and balls not too far apart. Her standards had been lowered over the years. Blanche no longer despised the company of small farmers and traders. Or rather, despite her contempt, she was prepared now to "squeeze" it for pleasure.

By the turn of the century she had had a new stable built on ground behind the homestead. Had installed two young colts bred from good stock, and, besides, animals for her four-in-hand phaeton. The racers she trained herself on advice from the Glenelg and Palmer Estate stables and ran in events at Port Denham.

In 1899, the banks of the lower Masterman River had begun to cave in, limiting navigation by the sugar lighters and thus necessitating the building of a tram-line down to Port Denham wharf. This led to much passenger traffic between the two towns and assisted in the settlement of the country between them. White settlers came flocking to the area from impoverished lands of south Queensland. On race days train loads of these poured down to the Port for enjoyment. In addition to the carriages for whites, special Jim Crow cars were attached to the engine for the use of the coloured alien population.

So, as time went on, and Blanche's outlook on life became ever more brittle, it was not difficult for her to fashion events in a way to her cynical liking. Often she stayed overnight at the Port. The hotel chambermaids came to note her arrival with whispers and giggling. In Masterman itself, there came a time when Blanche took to riding out along the road that had pushed across the river many miles to the north, and it was accounted no coincidence by many who saw them, that Willis Fraser, too, found that lonely locality of interest.

CHAPTER XXVII

IN THE AFTERNOON OF THE FIRST SATURDAY IN JUNE, 1902, the gardens of Folkhaven were filled with gaiety and colour. Blanche was holding a garden party in celebration of the ending of the Boer War. We see her against the background of her pleasant home, brilliant, glittering, a laugh never far from her lips, her voice loud. "A little like a king parrot," Jeff Grey told himself when, in need of a messenger, she hailed him and flamboyantly ordered him to undertake the duty.

On Grey, too, the pressure of the intervening years could be noted. There were crinkles about his eyes, a tight line to his lips. Years ago, Jeff had got to the point of telling himself that he was no longer in love with Cindie. Love was a fire requiring at least a minimum of fuel and not so much as a stick had been vouchsafed him. And an austerity existence had not benefited Grey. Passion too long denied had taken toll of his virility.

"Yes," he repeated to himself this afternoon, as he obeyed Blanche's injunction to run into the house and tell Cindie to send out more lemon squash, "a bit like a king parrot, the Missis. All colour and splash. Decorative, though."

The house he entered was no part of the original building. When, in 1900, Biddow had at length felt justified in spending the money on a permanent residence, Blanche had demanded a home to herself. Cindie, she declared, could occupy the old place.

Blanche's new home was built to her own design, on the then front garden site. Sufficient of the plantation of citrus fruits and papaws had been disposed of to provide for a wide, sloping lawn and flower gardens. A curving avenue of mangoes was planted beyond them to serve, when grown, as a drive.

The house was set low, not more than three feet from the ground. Broad concrete steps led up from the front garden path to spacious and deep verandas. Lattice work enclosed the frontage, a support for rioting wild creepers and bougain-villea. To-day, behind this cool, leafy wall, small tables were set out, loaded with bottled drinks and trays of cups and saucers.

Along the full length of the southern side of the house the veranda had been glassed in and made into a fernery by the transference of the plants beneath the old house and the addition of new treasures. Part of the other side veranda had been furnished with louvres, and was used by Blanche as a sleeping porch.

The interior of the house was very simple. A drawing-room ran along the whole frontage. In it, Blanche's grand piano and other samples of good furniture forwarded from Brisbane added dignity to the charm of the flooring of unpolished North Queensland maple. Wallaby rugs graced the floor.

From the drawing-room, a hall-way ran through the house to the back veranda, one section of which functioned as a kitchen. A dining-room and a breakfast room stood to the right of the hall-way, two bedrooms were opposite. Plunge baths were unknown in the far north as yet, but Blanche had succeeded in getting a workman sufficiently skilled in plumbing to rig up excellent showers.

Distinct from the front lawn, two acres of green sward dotted freely with native trees, palms and shrubs, surrounded the house. To one side of these a croquet lawn was laid out and recently a tennis lawn had been added to the attractions of the place.

At this afternoon's celebration, Blanche was intent on initiating the younger people among her guests into the mysteries of the game of tennis. Biddow, physically somewhat stouter, more set, his handsomeness a little coarsened, was dutifully acceding to her demands—Blanche always "demanded" these days—for assistance in her tutorship.

Not that Biddow felt equal to much running about. What with the farm work and the forty-four years behind him, his limbs were stiffening up. But he did his best. Standing on the tennis court, racket in hand, waiting patiently for Blanche to assign him a partner, Biddow watched his wife and idly ruminated.

Blanche must be nearly thirty-eight now. Looked it, too, he reckoned, for all her smooth face and supple limbs. Look at her now! Darting like a red shank from one to another, trailing skirts and all, instructing, bullying, laughing. She was directing young Caroline Montague, Louis Montague's girl, to join him. And taking Willis Fraser to partner herself.

Biddow frowned. Funny how she had taken to that bloke.

Funny, too, these yarns about the fellow's wife. Nobody ever saw the woman. Except the Kanakas and Aborigines, that was. Never even visited the town. Not too good, Fraser always said, when asked why she did not accompany him to Folkhaven. Or busy with the children. Fine youngsters, she had given Fraser. Two fine-looking sons.

Biddow's frown deepened as he recalled some remarks Grey had once dropped about a visit he had made to Fraser's home. "Something funny about the woman over there. When I rode up to the back of the house she was washing clothes. When she saw me she threw up her hands as though I had given her a terrific fright and then bolted inside the house."

Yet Fraser himself, everybody agreed, had settled down a bit since his marriage. Seemed proud of his youngsters, too. Perhaps the woman was a bit queer. . . .

When Grey entered the kitchen, Cindie was there directing the preparations for the afternoon tea. Verbena and Charity—the majority of his Kanakas had been signed on by Biddow for a second term—were gossiping and laughing as Cindie hustled them around. Charity's latest baby, her third, crawled upon the floor in company with Consuelo Callaghan's fifth. Consuelo herself, having come in to the kitchen to prepare a bottle of milk for her offspring, sat around contentedly, desultorily chatting with Cindie. These two women were tacitly friends, a fact that had as tacitly alienated Consuelo from Blanche.

Grey delivered his message from the kitchen doorway and then entered and sat down. He eyed Cindie reflectively. By contrast with the Missis, a muscular and stringy old crow, he decided. But he had to "hand it to" the two of them for the way they had integrated and maintained a situation that had bristled with jagged loose ends. They seemed friendly enough. Of late Cindie had grown close with him, though. Maybe there were currents underneath.

Of the two he shrewdly suspected that Blanche would be the least content. She asked for so much. Cindie, he knew, had asked for nothing of a personal nature from fate, had expected nothing. Probably she felt that everything possible had come her way. She did not look discontented. She simply looked gravely and competently at grips with life. And Grey knew that the farm was her pride. Maybe part of a larger pride in her build-up and complementing of Biddow's capacities. Yes, he could understand that Cindie might take secret joy to herself in that she, and not Blanche, was responsible for the direct, undeviating march of the man to material success.

But could any wife, let alone Blanche, be complacent about such a situation? Grey felt intensely curious, all of a sudden. When Consuelo drifted away he said casually to Cindie: "The Missis is teaching the bunch to play tennis."

Cindie glanced at him and said merely: "If you are going to stay up here you can help me to squeeze these lemons."

Grey got to work. "Can't help thinking, Cindie, seeing things as they are, what Folkhaven would have been like to-day if you hadn't come north."

"Silly. I did come north."

Grey smiled ruefully. "Always the realist, Cindie. But now that the farm is shipshape, what of the future? You will find things pretty dull, won't you, with no big schemes on hand?"

"Jeff Grey, you're a fool. . . . I got a letter from Randy yesterday." Warmth crept into her face, her voice softened.

"You did? And what did he say?"

"He hates Brisbane. He wants to leave school. Come home and work on the farm."

"Oh!—and will he?"

"I don't know"—abruptly.

"The Missis intends him to be a lawyer, doesn't she?"

"That's enough, I think." Cindie swept the squashed lemons aside and took up a bowl of juice. "Charity, clean up this mess, please. And then the both of you start carrying out the food to the veranda. You can take out the jugs of lemon drink for me, Jeff, if you like."

"You come out, too, Cindie. For God's sake have a bit of pleasure."

"Pleasure?" Cindie grinned at him. "That's not my idea of pleasure, Jeff."

"What is your idea of pleasure? Go on, Cindie, tell me. I'm curious about you to-day."

"Well, reading, for one thing. That's something I owe to

you, Jeff. Riding. Music. Listening to the Kanaka choir,
that is. Fishing, shooting. Visiting at the Callaghans'.
Writing to the kids. Oh, I've got lots of pleasures, Jeff."

"Don't resemble the Missis' pleasures much, do they?"

"Why should they? People are different."

"Cindie." He spoke warily now, though with an appearance of bluntness. "These yarns about the Missis. Think
there's anything in them?"

"What yarns?"—curtly.

"Don't gammon. The yarns about—her and Fraser. And
others, too, for that matter."

"Be quiet!" she said, stridently. She added sugar to the
lemon drink, her manner flurried, then, slamming the tin of
sugar upon the table, turned squarely to him. "All right.
If there's yarns, you tell me. Who talks?"

"Aw, just anybody——"

"Tell me the truth, Jeff. Is it serious? Is Mr. Biddow
likely to get to know?"

"Good lord, no! I should hope not. Who would tell him?"

"Someone might. But I don't believe it. She's still in love
with Mr. Biddow."

"Maybe. But life has a way. . . . Biddow's a pretty quiet
cuss, these days, isn't he?"

"What else could you expect? He always was quiet. And
he has a right to a rest, after all these years of work."

"Um. . . . That's the trouble with her ladyship, I suppose.
Idle hands, you know, Cindie."

"Yes. Idle hands. Idle brains, too." To his surprise her
voice took on a deep chesty note. "Jeff, how can a woman
be content to neglect a good brain? Tell me that! She's
got more brains in her little finger than I've got in my head."

"I can't tell you. Maybe her beauty has got her side-
tracked."

"Stuff and nonsense! Most of the really big women in
history have been good-lookers. So they say."

Grey shrugged. "Must be her bringing up, then. Train
up a child in the way he should go, you know."

"Fiddlesticks to that, too. Look at Barney's wife and
Mrs. Bert. Both of them brought up in wealthy homes and
both of them always busy. Busy at real things, I mean."

"What are you trying to prove, Cindie?"

"Me? I'm not trying to prove anything. I'm just wondering, that's all. There must be a reason for everything."

"Just so"—quietly. Grey dropped the subject but it stuck in his mind till it came to him out of the blue that Cindie's "reason" for wondering was a subconscious attempt to prove to herself that she had no part or parcel in responsibility for Blanche's shortcomings.

After Jeff had left her, Cindie alternated gloomy meditation upon Blanche's "mad fool" behaviour and its possible consequences with supervising the toilettes of Verbena and Charity preparatory to their waiting upon the guests at afternoon tea.

Both black women were now mothers of three children. Gone were the Mother Hubbards of their early training days. Verbena's still skinny form and Charity's now rotund shape were clothed in nicely made print dresses and white frilly aprons. Verbena's shaggy mop of hair and Charity's long smooth strands were kept neat, and on festive occasions like to-day adorned with bows of red ribbon.

Satisfied with the appearance of the maids, Cindie went out on to the lawns and intimated by a word here and there that refreshments awaited the guests. But even in the midst of the sociable gathering a forbidding undercurrent of thought persisted and ascribed to her manner a suggestion of impatience and irascibility. She went over to the tennis court and stood among a crowd of onlookers to watch the play. Blanche and Fraser against Biddow and Louis Montague's girl, Caroline. Cindie's brow came down like a thunderclap at Blanche's loud laugh when she and Fraser collided as they made a simultaneous dive for the ball.

The yarns about those two were true! She had known it for some time. And before Fraser there had been Florenz Bardia, the slimy blackbirder whose name, even among the hardened ranks of his colleagues, had stunk to the degree that his licence for recruiting Kanakas had been revoked. "But of course she would have to fall back on the scum among men," Cindie muttered fiercely. Decent men wouldn't respond to her wiles.

A resolute, indomitable figure in her prim dress of white

muslin, Cindie marched up the boundary line of the tennis court and called sharply: "Mrs. Biddow, the tea is waiting."

"You see to it, Cindie," Blanche gave back. "We must finish this game."

"I've had enough, Blanche," Biddow called. "I'm blown out." He walked off the court and Caroline Montague, after hesitating, followed him.

"I'm pretty blown myself," Fraser told Blanche. "This game's too strenuous for hard-working farmers."

"It's not too strenuous for me," replied Blanche, coolly. "Come on. We'll get some tea."

Fraser obediently paraded his cream flannel trousers and silk shirt beside her.

Cindie moved among the guests upon the veranda with the assurance of a hostess among friends. She saw to it that the elders were well served, the tea constantly renewed and kept hot. When the refreshments had been dispensed to her satisfaction she gathered up the remnants of cakes and tarts and herself carried them up to the field dining-room to regale the Kanakas when they came in from the fields.

As she went, she thought with regret of the recent departure to his homeland of Takeo, the Japanese cook. He had been replaced by two cooks, Suzuki and Ching Ling, Japanese and Chinese who quarrelled incessantly. Two cooks were essential these days, with thirty Kanakas and a varying number of Aborigines to be fed.

After delivering the comestibles to Suzuki, Cindie climbed the stairs to her own quarters and, taking Randy's letter from her bedroom table, made herself comfortable in a canvas chair upon the balcony and re-read it.

"Talk to Dad, Cindie," the boy had written. "Tell him I can't stand this place any longer. I will *not* be a lawyer. I want to be a farmer. I want to go home."

No problem at all, ran Cindie's thoughts, grimly, but for his mother's goings-on. But which was most important? the boy's whole future life or the possible loss of respect for Blanche?

It did not take her long to decide. Dear Randy! Cindie's whole being softened and glowed as she lost herself in sweet

remembrance of the companionship that had developed
between herself and the boy during the last year of his sojourn
at Folkhaven. She brought to mind the photograph that
stood on Blanche's dressing-table: the boy's shining golden
eyes, the colour of his father's light-gold one, the black waving
hair which, strangely, in that year of pubescence had taken
to itself a strand of spun gold that, mingled with a broad
lock, fell rebelliously across the forehead.

The boy was beautiful, but not to a fault. What might
have been accounted feminine beauty was redeemed by a
certain ruggedness of contour and by full masculine proportions of the body. Even at fourteen Randy had been man-
proportioned, tall as his father, heavy-boned. Now, Cindie
reflected, in his seventeenth year he would probably be
physically mature.

Eleven years younger than she! Cindie sighed, then
roused herself and shook off her dreaming mood. The boy
would have his way. That she would see to. All this fine
property: what use to have put such loving care and ambition
into its building if eventually it must go to strangers?

She went over to the veranda railing and looked out over
the fields. In the declining afternoon sunlight the broad
acres of yellow-green cane lay perfectly still. The mauve
plumes of their tall arrows gave a silvery, shimmering effect.
And snaking through the canefields was the creek, with a
substantial breadth of virgin forest left to bulwark either side.
The deeply indented mountain range slid steeply down to
the foothills and against it there flickered like aluminium in
the sun a scattered flock of white cockatoos. The dark flat
spread that was Cindie's coffee plantation merged into the
virginal rain forest.

But alas! The blacks' camp beside it, upon which she had
built so many hopes, had vanished. In 1901, shortly after
the harvesting of the first crop of coffee beans, a young gin
had been shot dead in the camp. The bullet, it had been
generally surmised, was a stray from the gun of a hunter,
but no direct evidence had supported this. Then, within a
few weeks a charge of gunshot had whistled through the
camp and by nightfall of that same day the place had been
deserted. Helpless in her fury, Cindie from then on had

housed her single Aborigine workers beneath her house.
Billy, with Biddow's consent, she had schooled in the use of
her gun and had broadcast far and wide that any further
accidents to her workers would ensure at least a scouring of
the forest by her blacks. And woe betide any skulker that
was caught! She had bearded the police, both the newly-
appointed officers in the Masterman area and the headquarters down at the Port, and laid this ultimatum before
them.

Now, her glance came down to the environs of the homestead. To the wide spread of the huts of the blacks, now
numbering fourteen. Well-cultivated garden plots ringed
many of them. Born cultivators, the Kanakas; and Verbena's
husband Billy, and the old Aborigine couple Cindie had
installed in a shack for stable and garden work, had followed
the example of the Islanders in this respect.

Beyond the natives' quarters were the stables and other
outbuildings erected over the years. Beyond them again,
the horse paddock. On the seaward side, the citrus fruits,
papaws, bananas and vegetable gardens, at the behest of
the mill Board's contractual commitments, had been reduced
to proportions sufficient to meet household needs only. The
one cow which the innutritious, swashy nature of the coastal
grasses permitted, still grazed within the range of its tether
rope.

And as Cindie gazed upon the domain the mild winter
sun dipped down to the great gorge through which the river
came tumbling over a granite foundation to find the sea.
A deliquescent golden light poured through the gorge, a
heavenly regenerating light that purified the girl of her lachry-
mose mood and replaced it with a sense of spiritual fulfilment.
And the bird song! The air was drenched with it. And from
afar over the fields, from the distant felling sites now reduced
to little more than fifty acres, and from the coffee plantation,
the black men came streaming home along the headlands.

Streaming home! The sight of them diverted Cindie's
mind to the fact that another two months would see all but
Tirwana of Biddow's original group of Kanakas *en route* for
their island home. Several more of the second lot, who had
come in in 1896, were repatriating this year, too. The

thought of it saddened Cindie. So many of them were her friends. She sighed and, going into her kitchen, kindled a fire upon the top of the colonial oven and placed a kettle of water upon the bars above it. Usually Verbena did these domestic offices for her, but this evening there was much cleaning up to do down at the big house. But Cindie was pleased, now, to be alone. Verbena and Charity, with whom at meal times more often than not she shared the kitchen table, were inveterate chatterers.

By the time she had finished her meal the fleeting twilight of the tropics had dissolved into night. She cleared away her tea things and then, taking with her some linseed oil, went up to the hut that functioned as a hospital to see a sick man.

Cindie and Biddow were worried about this Kanaka, a recent arrival and, like Tirwana, a native of Tanna. The doctor, called from Port Denham to report upon his condition, had pronounced him sound enough physically. He was sick in mind. Homesickness and longing for his people and island were his trouble.

Sitting beside his rough bunk, in the light of a candle thrust into the thatch wall, Cindie noted the wasted condition of his body, the illimitable sadness in his sunken eyes. He averted his head when she offered him the oil.

Tirwana glided into the hut and stood silently watching the prone man.

"Tirwana," said Cindie suddenly, "ask him to tell us about his island home. Ask him to tell you in his native tongue and then you interpret for me. I hate trying to make out that horrible pidgin."

Tirwana drew up a stool and sat beside her. Neither noticed that Biddow, too, had come in. He stood near the doorway, listening.

To begin with, the Kanaka would not talk. Suspicion partially lightened up his dulled eyes. But as Tirwana persisted, the very sound of his own liquid tongue had a pacifying effect and soon, his body raised upon one elbow, he was talking, hesitatingly but with growing strength and excitement.

He had no wife. He could not pin his longings down to

any definite thing. It was just that he had visions, of his people spearing fish on the reef, of tribal life. And in his breast and stomach always a pain. There was a weight upon his shoulders, his legs had lost their spring. Food turned rotten and sour in his mouth.

"Tell him, Tirwana," urged Cindie when, at last, he fell back, exhausted, "tell him that when he gets well enough to walk we shall take him out to the reefs, where he can spear fish and bring in coral to make manure for the paddocks."

Tirwana obeyed her. And the prospect he glowingly painted had an immediate effect. The whole aspect of the patient, exhausted as he was, became enlivened. He turned wide eyes directly upon Cindie. "You say: no cut cane?" he gasped. "Me get canoe?"

"That you shall, Sonsie," she replied. "You and Tirwana and me, we shall go out to the reefs. You shall do the work you want to do. No cane."

"Not a bad idea," said Biddow, as he and Cindie left the hut. "I believe it will work out. And we must certainly do something about the manuring of the cultivated paddocks next year. They are pretty well worn out."

"The lime from the coral may be a help. But never mind that, now. That poor devil, Mr. Biddow, is sick because he has been rooted out of the way of life that suits him. The kind of life he likes. And the same thing applies to white men. White men, too, can get sick, spiritually sick, and have life go rotten on them if they are forced into a groove they hate."

"What are you getting at?"

"I had a letter from Randy this morning."

"Yes, I know." Biddow thought grimly that he had reason to know. He had had to put up with his wife's tantrum at seeing the boy's letter among the mail Tirwana had brought in.

"Randy wants to come home. Doesn't he tell you that in his letters?"

"Yes, but——"

"No buts about it, Mr. Biddow. The boy is pining for his home. He hates town life. He hates his school. He hates the thought of the legal profession."

"Did he say that—in those words?" There was mortification in Biddow's tone.

"Worse. Much worse."

"Oh!" Biddow halted as they neared the few steps that led up to the veranda of his home. "I didn't think it was as bad as that. The situation is—is rather difficult."

"It's not difficult at all. The boy wants to come home. He wants to learn to be a farmer. Anything peculiar about that? You like farming yourself, don't you?"

"Yes, yes. Of course. But—I had something else in mind."

"I should think that the first thing a man would bear in mind would be the welfare of his children."

Biddow shrugged uncomfortably. "You are pretty definite about things, aren't you, Cindie?"

"Not more definite than Randy. Mr. Biddow, can you give me one good reason why the boy should be tormented? Isn't this property good enough for your son to take pride in?"

"Yes, yes"—irritably. "But there are other things in life, Cindie, a man has to consider. I'll think about it. Come in."

About to refuse, Cindie checked her tongue and accepted the invitation. For at that moment a burst of laughter sounded from the drawing-room, laughter Cindie recognized though she had not heard it for some time. It was followed by the crashing of the piano keys into the sea shanty *Whisky Johnny Whisky* and the breaking of a lusty baritone into song.

Cindie halted in the doorway of the drawing-room to survey the room. Special friends among the afternoon's guests had stopped over: the Callaghans, the Louis Montagues, Jeff Grey. In addition there were present the young Church of England parson, John Melody, a new incumbent, and, at the piano, the notorious blackbirder, Florenz Bardia.

"Now, what is he doing back here, I wonder?" thought Cindie, as she seated herself upon a couch and let her eyes linger upon Bardia. "It's like his cheek to turn up here." Surely Blanche would not want to see him, in view of her present intrigue with Fraser, and as for Biddow, he detested the fellow for his beastly reputation.

But after noting Blanche's demeanour Cindie began to feel that Bardia's presence was not unwelcome to her. Blanche was looking exceptionally handsome and vital. Bardia was accompanying his own singing, his style in both respects spectacular, and Blanche, sitting bolt upright in an easy chair at a little distance from him, tapped her foot and blithely hummed in unison.

The song concluded, Bardia swung round on the piano stool, rose, and with mocking gestures salaamed Blanche. There was faint applause. Cindie noticed that Biddow's brow was bent, his eyes averted from the man.

"Where did you spring from, Mr. Bardia?" Cindie asked. "I thought you had gone south."

The man, in appearance the antithesis of the traditional blackbirding type, came over and sat down beside her. "Dear lady," he purred silkily, "I did go south. But I have returned, as you see."

"What for?"—bluntly.

"If you must know, I have brought back a schooner, a nice schooner, in which I intend to fish the reefs for bêche-de-mer."

"Making Jamestown your headquarters, I suppose?" put in Grey.

"Making Port Denham my headquarters, my dear chap." Bardia leant back and, swinging one leg over the other, settled himself comfortably.

"You don't look much like a fisherman," said Cindie, critically, boldly trailing her eyes over his sleek, oiled head, his finely-moulded features, soft gleaming eyes, waxed moustache, trim beard, slim body and tiny feet.

"Ah! Appearances are often deceptive, dear lady."

Eighteen-years-old Caroline Montague, who had been gazing in fascinated wonder upon this pleasant-looking man whose evil deeds she had heard canvassed over years, here spoke up eagerly: "Mr. Bardia, did you ever meet the pirate, Bully Hayes?"

Bardia laughed softly. "Yes, my dear, I have met Bully Hayes. In fact—but tales about Bully are not for your pretty ears. I can tell you a story, though. Would you like to hear about something tremendous I saw on my last trip to the

islands? No, no, my dear Madam!" He deferred to a deprecatory movement on the part of Caroline's mother. "Nothing
offensive, I assure you. Simply a fish story."

"Oh yes! Do let him tell us, Mother."

Flashing a white-toothed smile at the girl, Bardia began:
"It was when our schooner was anchored in the lee of a small
island. The ship's mate and I had put out in a dinghy and
pulled into a lagoon to do some fishing. We were about to
throw down the anchor when we were attracted by the
shouting of a mob of Kanakas on the reef. We rowed over
to them, to find that they were madly excited about something that was going on below the ledge of coral rock upon
which they stood, in about twelve feet of water.

"Down there was a coral cave. And in it a fairly large
shark, a twelve-footer, I judged, was swimming frantically
to and fro. Frantically swimming, my dear girl, because at
the mouth of the cave, blocking his exit, a great squid was
lying.

"I had never seen anything like this fellow before. His
body must have been anything from four to five tons in weight.
A great mass of gristle, with two enormously long feelers,
easily twenty feet long, and eight shorter ones, protruding
from his head. So powerful-looking were these tentacles
that they gave me the impression that nothing could possibly
withstand them.

"The body was an unwieldy thing. Like an overfed beast
with feelers all around the front of it. More like the body
of a crayfish than a fish. That's a poor description but I
can't do any better. With some of his feelers the squid was
clinging to the coral rock, the rest of them were directed in
front of him, lying in the water, perfectly still, yet full of life,
waiting to pounce.

"At last one of these long feelers streaked out and encircled
the shark's body. It leapt in the water and struggled like
mad. Then the second shot out and got a grip. The shark's
struggles became so terrific that the body of the squid bounced
about. But he had no hope against those tentacles. Slowly
but surely he was drawn in towards the monstrous beak of
the squid. He was drawn in just like you would take a length
of india-rubber hose and bend it in so that the middle portion

curved towards you. And when he was drawn in close enough the squid began to chew his body, while he was still struggling, like a cat chewing meat.

"We left the spot at that. We were afraid that the shark might not be enough for a meal for the brute. He might get the idea of throwing a feeler over the dinghy. Yes, he was a pet, all right. I had seen plenty of his kind before but nothing nearly so big."

"And do these squid inhabit the Barrier reefs, too?" Cindie asked.

"Not to my knowledge. Cayman, I think the brute is rightly called."

CHAPTER XXVIII

ON THE FOLLOWING MORNING CINDIE, AS HAD BEEN HER CUSTOM of late, rode into the township in order to accompany to church those Kanakas who attended Melody's morning service.

Not that Cindie was religiously inclined. Her main reasons for attending were to hear the Kanaka choir Melody had got together and to keep an eye on the contributions the Folkhaven men made to the offertory. This, because Melody had confided to her his reluctance to accept the florins and shillings the dark brethren would drop in the plate.

"Pretty nearly the whole of their weekly wage," he had declared, worriedly. "But what's a man to do?"

The more staid among Biddow's Kanakas, on his representations, permitted him to bank for them the major portion of the money they received. In addition to their legal six pounds annually, for the last two years Biddow had been paying his men an equal sum in cash. Tirwana, besides his wage of twenty-five shillings weekly as general overseer, had been given a horse and saddle, and to half a dozen other exceptionally reliable Kanakas Biddow, after the custom of most decent planters, besides the increased money payments made periodical presents of extra clothing and odds and ends of personal requisites.

There was no occasion for worry in any quarter over
Tirwana's disposal of his money. He never attended church
And over years, relying on Biddow's promise to do all in his
power to prevent his deportation—despite the Federal
Government's Pacific Island Labourers Act of 1901 which
enabled the summary deportation of any Kanaka found in
Australia after the end of 1906—Tirwana had been banking
practically all of his money with the object of buying a bit
of land for himself.

It was Cindie's practice to marshal the Folkhaven Kanakas
into church in a body and then seat herself in a position
from which she could direct a stern eye upon each worshipper
in turn at the approach of the plate. Despite their promises
to "be sensible" beforetimes, she knew that the religious
fervour engendered by the singing and the enchantment of
their own responses to Melody's passionate praying, would
without her supervision induce the Kanakas to bestow their
meagre all.

It seemed to Cindie this morning that Melody's reading
of the text was particularly intense. And in response the
Kanakas, by far the major part of the congregation, made
ever louder and heartier obeisance to the Lord. The voices
of the few whites present were scarcely audible. Cindie was
surprised, however, and felt her face redden when, during
the sermon, the parson sternly chided the whites for their
lack of grace and praised "those who talked a foreign tongue
yet spoke out clearly and heartily, sounding their praises to
God". She was further surprised when Melody, at the conclusion of the service, beckoned to her to come up to him.

The parson was worried by the failure of the Biddows to
attend church. "I visited Folkhaven last night," he told
Cindie, "intending to bring this matter forward, but the
time, in view of the presence of other guests, did not appear
to be propitious. Miss Comstock, I am sure you can realize
the bad effect of the masters failing in respect for the church
to which the servants give allegiance."

Having in mind her own reasons for attending Cindie was
flustered and perplexed. She liked John Melody. And respected him besides for refusing to tail behind the general
policy of the churches, which defended the indenture system

of the Kanakas on the ground that their recruitment brought them more closely within the influence of Christian ethics.

"I don't see that I can do anything about it, Mr. Melody," she said, frankly. "The Biddows are not religious, I think."

"Ah! It means nothing to them that the—that other denominations flourish while their own Church decays!" He had removed his surplice and now walked with Cindie down the aisle.

Outside the church a real shock awaited the girl. For near the steps, an arm through the reins of his horse, Willis Fraser was standing; plainly in expectation of seeing the parson. He frowned on Cindie's presence, threshed his leggings with his plaited kangaroo-hide whip.

"I'll get along, Mr. Melody," Cindie said hurriedly. "Mr. Fraser wants to see you."

"No, don't go, Miss Comstock." Fraser made a sudden decision. "Maybe you can help. Parson, I want you to go out to my place and visit my wife. She's got me worried."

"Worried?" Melody looked grave. "You mean—you want me to offer her spiritual solace?"

Fraser made an impatient gesture. "I can't say anything about that. My wife is not well. There's been something wrong with her for the past year or two but I can't persuade her to see a doctor. Says she will shoot him if I take one out. But I've got to think of the youngsters! Will you go out and see if you can get her to listen to reason?"

"Of course, of course. I'll ride out with you immediately, if you like."

"Not with me. I'm on my way to the Port. You wouldn't get to see her if I were with you. Damn it, the woman seems to be going off her head! Shies off seeing anyone. But maybe a parson . . . And you, Miss Comstock, she used to talk about you. Would you mind going along, too? Maybe you and the parson together . . ."

Cindie was looking at him keenly. "Just what do you think is the matter with her, Mr. Fraser? Is she bedridden?"

"No. She gets about all right. Works all right. But she looks funny. And she's as scared as a rabbit of seeing people. Damned if I know. . . . Beg pardon, Parson. You'd have to sneak in on her. Quiet-like. Might be able to do something." Fraser took out a handkerchief and wiped his brow of the sweat that had gathered on it.

"We shall do our best. You may depend on that." Cindie spoke decisively. "She's probably all nerves through living alone so much, Mr. Fraser. You get your horse, Mr. Melody, and we'll get going."

"Yes. I will tell my boy to postpone the midday meal."

During the two-mile journey out to Fraser's homestead, Cindie kept silent. The parson, beyond a sympathetic ejaculation or two, also kept his thoughts to himself.

But when they came to the big gate that opened on to the gardens, Cindie drew rein. "We had better tether the horses here, Mr. Melody," she said, "and walk up to the house. The mother and children will probably be having their dinner, so we'll have a chance——"

"But don't you think——?" The parson was embarrassed. "I am sure the man was exaggerating. Surely we do not have to—to sneak up on the house."

"Mr. Melody, if you knew Willis Fraser as I know him, you would realize that only something of an extremely serious nature could bring him to approach you. And more particularly me. The woman is probably going off her head."

She led the way up the trim pathway through the orchard and vegetable gardens, where even on Sunday a Kanaka was busily weeding. He saw them, abandoned his work and stared. A dog began to bark at the back of the house, the same old framework of years agone with the addition of weatherboard wings.

They had almost reached the front door when it opened slightly and a small boy peeped out. "Mum!" he shouted, then slammed the door in their faces.

Cindie ran forward and threw the door open. "Anybody here?" she called. "You home, Mrs. Fraser? It's Cindie Comstock come to see you!"

There was a stir in the back regions, then Fraser's two boys came to the inner door and stared at the visitors. "Mum says go away," the elder said solemnly.

"Nonsense," cried Cindie, cheerily. "That's no way to treat visitors. I'm coming through, Mrs. Fraser! You wait here, Mr. Melody," she whispered. Without more ado she walked through the front room, gently put the little boys aside and found herself in the kitchen.

As she had expected, the family had been interrupted in the course of their midday meal. Mrs. Fraser was sitting at the top of the table, her back to the fireplace. At Cindie's entrance she crouched down in her chair. Her eyes dilated with unmistakable terror. Cindie stared at her. The children scrambled back on to their seats and, never taking their eyes off the intruder, began shovelling food into their mouths.

"Mrs. Fraser." Cindie's voice quavered on the name. For something, some indefinable suggestion of horror, of dread, had been conveyed to her like a flash by the sight of the woman she remembered as lovely as a flower. It set her heart thumping. It was like ashes upon her spirit, blown by a chill blast of wind. The loveliness? All gone! In its place was a queer, thickened, blotchy countenance, with wrinkles plainly drawn upon the forehead. "She looks like a cat," Cindie thought, shrinkingly. She shuddered slightly, then pulled herself together. What nonsense was this? She took a step forward.

"Mrs. Fraser, dear, why are you looking so frightened? Don't you remember me, Cindie Comstock? The parson and I have come to see you, Mrs. Fraser. To see you about —about the children coming to Sunday School." The lie came glibly.

"I know you all right." The other woman obviously fought to control her fear. She drew herself upright but kept her face averted and lowered. "But I don't want to see people. I want to be left alone."

"But why, Mrs. Fraser? Why?" Cindie dropped into a chair. With thankfulness, for her legs were trembling. Her first sensation of horror had passed but dread remained. As she spoke she stared with ever-increasing apprehension, thrusting her head forward. For away at the back of her consciousness filaments of memory were stirring, memories of talks with Consuelo. They stirred but they did not come to the surface.

"It is not good for you to be always alone, Mrs. Fraser. It's not good for anyone. You are not well, Mrs. Fraser. You are all nervy."

"Did Fraser send you here?" The voice was muffled, the head bent lower.

"Well, to be truthful, Mrs. Fraser, he did ask me to call upon you. And why not? We have all been worried that you have not come to see us."

"What did he tell you?"

"Tell me? Only that he would like me to come and see you."

"And now you have seen me!" Mrs. Fraser sprang up, wild and distraught. Her hands were clenched, her arms held stiffly against her sides. "Now go away! Go away, do you hear? Leave me alone!"

Cindie rose, too, hurriedly. "But, Mrs. Fraser!" she appealed. "You are ill! You can't stay out here like this!" On an impulse of loving sympathy she put out her arms and moved forward, offering an embrace.

"Go away!" the other shrieked. She fell back precipitately. Step upon hurried step, her hands out-thrust behind her. "Get out of my house!" The children began to cry in unison, loud sudden yelps.

And as the woman fell back, the fingers of one of her hands came into contact with one of the iron bars that bridged the high colonial oven hobs. A bar that glowed dully with heat from the mass of lambent wood coals beneath it. The fingers rested upon the bar—*and they were not withdrawn.*

Cindie did not see this monstrous thing. Her move towards the woman had been arrested by the shrieked command and the expression of heart-rending terror. She stood still, her arms dropped, her face blanched with pity for this mother who, she now felt sure, was quite mad. She heard the parson step into the room behind her, heard his exclamation of mingled horror and compassion. Then he was striding swiftly past her. He was crying out: "Mrs. Fraser, your hand!" He was grabbing at Mrs. Fraser's arm!

Panting like an animal she wrenched it out of his grasp and, with convulsive strength, shoved him back. He fell against Cindie, who braced herself unconsciously to take his weight. The children screamed. The smell of burnt flesh permeated the room.

Then Mrs. Fraser looked at her hand. Held it up before her face and looked at it. She gave a cry, half scream, half roar, flung her arm out from her body as though striving to disconnect it from her body. Then her head shrank down between her shoulders, her eyes closed. She moaned, then suddenly flew around and out of the back kitchen door. It slammed behind her.

Cindie also had seen the significance of that hand. Sickness fell upon her like a stroke. One moment of paralysis and then she was dragging at Melody with main strength and crying hoarsely: "Come away, come away!" With a veritable shouting she continued: "Mrs. Fraser, we are going away! Come back to your children, Mrs. Fraser! We are going!"

Once through the front door Cindie began to run. She picked up her skirts and tore down the garden path as though Old Nick himself were at her heels. Outside the big gate she collapsed on the ground. She began to sob. With her arms limp, her hands palm-up upon the grass, she bent her head towards her knees and gave way to frightful sobs.

Melody, with deep, agitated breaths, had come after her at a rapid walk. Coming up to his horse, he unhitched it and then leant his head against the saddle. His face was white. His lips twitched. "Miss Comstock!" He tried to speak sharply. "Stop that! Stop it, I say! The Kanaka is watching. Get up."

Cindie scrambled to her feet. Still sobbing, she unhitched her horse and with masculine ease swung up into the side saddle which on Sundays of late she had affected. Digging in her heels, she set the horse into a gallop. Melody followed suit.

Neither lessened that pace till they were approaching the Rectory. Then Cindie drew rein and motioned to the man to do likewise. "Well, what's to be done?" she queried, dully.

"We may be mistaken. After all—I pray to God. Those children!"

"Praying to God won't help. We must make sure. But it's true! It's true! You saw her hand! *The tips of her fingers were white.* They burned, they burned! You smelt them, didn't you?" Sheer mental agony tore at her again and twisted her features into a grimace. "Hell! Hell!" she groaned. "Oh, hellish fate!" She rocked in the saddle. Her eyes closed.

The strangeness of her words, the paralysing nature of her grief, awed the parson somewhat and at the same time puzzled him. She acted as though she were racked by an extremity of personal anguish. "Miss Comstock," he said gravely, "you are letting your emotions run away with you. I am surprised. After all, God in His goodness——"

Shivering in the mellow noontide heat, Cindie fought to get a grip on herself. She shook the reins and started her horse into a quick walk. At length she made up her mind. "Mr. Melody." She turned to him. "Will you leave this matter to me for immediate attention?"

"What do you propose to do?"

"I will ride down to the Port this afternoon and consult a doctor. See what he says. Then Fraser must be told. I can't understand it!" She smote her forehead with her hand. "He should have known! Why didn't he realize it?"

"Very few would know, I fancy. I am surprised at your knowing. It was part of my Missionary training."

"The Aborigines have told me about it. I saw one, once, in an Aborigine camp. And Mrs. Bert Callaghan told me about a Chinaman they had to send away in eighteen-ninety-three. She told me all about it. Mr. Melody, maybe, if it is true, the business can be handled without—people knowing."

"I hope so, Miss Comstock, I sincerely hope so."

When Cindie rode up to Folkhaven her stomach was like water within her. She could not control the trembling of her limbs. Pity for Blanche alternated with mad rage in her breast. The woman had to be told! But when? How?

Ah! There was Biddow, lounging with his pipe upon the front steps of the house. And at the sight of him, all the deep abiding love that Cindie had harboured in her heart over years, a love that had slumbered for long because of its irremediable nature, surged up from the secret recesses of her being and overwhelmed her. She turned her head aside from him as she rode past. Merely to look upon him, then, she felt, would betray her.

Biddow looked after her speculatively. Must have stayed

somewhere for lunch, he reflected. She looked well in her riding habit. A loose seat on a horse, but good. His thoughts wandered in the fields of drowsy rumination. He felt placidly content. Thank the Lord Blanche had grown out of her jealousy of the girl. Mostly, that was. The little scene over Randy's letter had been the first in months and that, Biddow told himself, had nothing to do with him. The natural resentment of a mother, he supposed.

Naïvely Biddow cogitated. She really was not a bad sort, Blanche. She had stuck to him. And, by cripes, with her looks and temperament and his increasing insensibility she might easily have kicked over the traces. He was glad she had taken to getting around. Eased his conscience a bit. Her going off to the Port that morning had given him a quiet day.

Yes, all things considered he had done pretty well for himself. There was only this question of Randy. He would ask Blanche to compromise there. Keep Cindie's name out of it. Give Blanche a free hand with Irene and let him decide about the boy.

CHAPTER XXIX

AS SOON AS CINDIE PUT FOOT INSIDE HER HOUSE VERBENA, WITH sly giggles, told her about Blanche's visit to Port Denham. Cindie closed her eyes on the terrible vision the news conjured up and, refusing lunch, threw herself face downwards on her bed. She must think, think, think! She must make no mistake. She must get to Blanche before her return to Folk-haven. Between them they must keep the truth from Biddow.

Pity again surged uppermost as Cindie pictured the effect upon Blanche of the blow. She retched as she faced the fact squarely that she must be the one to tell her. Her stomach contracted, forced its contents upwards. She had just time to make the balcony rail and lean over it before she vomited.

Biddow, now strolling around in company with Tirwana, saw her and started up to her house.

"I'm all right," Cindie called down to him, quaveringly, handkerchief to her mouth. "Just a bit of biliousness, Mr. Biddow."

But he kept on coming, up the back stairs and round the balcony to where she sat. And in the moments of his coming Cindie decided, impulsively, that to attempt to keep him in ignorance might in itself be fatal. He would almost certainly find out. The parson, the doctors, all friends. How keep hidden her own part in the business? No, he must know. And know now. Now was the time to tell him.

"Sit down, Mr. Biddow." She tried to smile. "I'm sick. Sick because of something I found out this morning."

"Oh?" He looked at her with surprise, which converted to curiosity and concern.

"Yes, Mr. Biddow." Cindie clasped her hands and swallowed. "Mr. Melody and I went out to see Mrs. Fraser. And, Mr. Biddow"—her voice fell to a tense whisper—"Mr. Biddow, we think she is a—a *leper*." Her hands went up to her face and covered it. She couldn't bear it! His wife! His wife!

But in the few moments during which she crouched before him as though bent to a blow, the turgidity of Cindie's thoughts was washed away by a swift outpouring of womanly sympathy for Blanche. For Blanche who, though loving this man, might never know him as husband again. The irrevocable met and encompassed the merciful in Cindie's mind so that when, after a stillness, there came Biddow's almost inaudible "Hell!" she was able to drop her hands, straighten up and speak with heavy calm.

"Yes, that's what it is, right enough. She's got the lion face they talk about. Her fingers rested on the red-hot bars above the oven and she didn't feel it. They sizzled. I smelt the burning flesh. Her hands were thick, too. Her breath was hateful. There were patches of whitish skin on one cheek. It all comes back to me, now! But worse than anything, Mr. Biddow, was her—her fear. She knows! The poor soul! She knows!"

Biddow had risen from his chair and was taking agitated steps to and fro. "But that means . . . What about Fraser? The kids?"

And again, at his words, Cindie wilted. A feeling of suffocation sent her hands up to her throat. "I don't know just what it means. But I'm going down to the Port now to find out. I'm going to see a doctor. It might not be so bad." She fled from him to her room.

"Sure you wouldn't like me to go with you?" he called out. "It's tough on you to have to do this, Cindie."

"No, no! I'll go alone. I'm upset. I want to go alone."

Find Blanche, find Blanche! The words became a refrain keeping pace with the galloping hooves of Cindie's horse. And when suddenly it struck her that maybe she couldn't, maybe the woman had not gone to the Port at all, maybe she was even then skulking in some secluded valley with her lover, the blood seemed to drain from Cindie's heart. She *had* made a mistake. She had told Biddow prematurely. What if Blanche got home before her? Biddow would spring the news on her and then what? Biddow was nobody's fool.

When she pulled up at the hotel Blanche invariably patronized, her horse was in a lather of sweat. The crowd of men beneath the hotel veranda—though the front doors of the pubs closed on Sundays the back doors remained invitingly open—eyed her curiously. She hitched her horse to a post and went into the hotel.

Yes, Blanche had lunched there. With Florenz Bardia and his mate. Her present whereabouts? The proprietor called a waitress.

The calculating gravity of the man's manner and the smirk of the girl when she came had a salutary effect on Cindie, constrained her to outward calm. And the information vouchsafed by the girl, that Blanche had gone riding with the two men, chilled her sympathy till only implacable judgment was left.

She wandered out of the hotel. Plenty of time, now. And in the street she ran into Fraser!

"Saw your horse," he said briefly. Their eyes met, Cindie's filled with fright and consternation, his probing and dark. "Well?" he asked, curtly.

Cindie put a hand to her brow, closed her eyes, and lied. "She wouldn't see us, Mr. Fraser. I'm not well. I've come down to see the doctor." She walked off, leaving him staring after her with scowling brows.

The doctor she went to, a middle-aged Englishman recently transferred from Melbourne, listened to her story with frequent impatient interjections. Incessantly he fiddled with his watch-chain and raised and lowered his shaggy eyebrows. To Cindie's question: "You think it is leprosy, Doctor?" he coughed a little, pushed back his chair and replied: "We shall see. We shall see. But why are you so worried about the matter, young woman?"

"I'm worried about the children. There is Mr. Fraser, too." Her face flamed. "The disease is infectious, isn't it?"

"Ah!" His manner chilled. He gave her a stern look and then lowered his eyes. And Cindie knew, as surely as though he had told her, that he suspected her. Instinctively she opened her mouth to protest her innocence, but on second thoughts closed it again. Let him think what he liked! She must protect Biddow, Randy, Irene! He began to speak, judicially, coldly. "The theory is that it is infectious. Yes, but only by close contact. By intimate contact, I might say. We have not as yet sufficient data. . . . I should say that almost certainly the children will not be infected. The disease is rarely congenital. So far as we know. The husband——" He coughed. "Maybe yes, maybe no."

"How long would it be before the disease revealed itself in—a husband?"

"I can't say"—vigorously. "I can't say. There are different forms. A year or two with one form, many years with another. The incubation stage is uncertain. But now, young woman"—he rose and stood above her, grimly resolute—"that husband has got to be told. I'll go out there immediately."

"He's in town." Cindie rose. "I'll find him and bring him to you. You tell him."

"Very well." He glanced at his watch. "Ten minutes? Fifteen?"

"It depends. If he is still in the street, ten will do."

As it happened, she almost missed Fraser. He was riding down the street, making back home, when Cindie came out of the doctor's front door. She had to chase after him. He turned his horse and came back to her, deliberately. He looked from her to the doctor's residence. "Thought there was something bloody funny about you. What is it? Spit it out."

"Mr. Fraser, the doctor wants to see you."

He sat motionless for a few moments, looking stonily before him, then swung off his horse, threw the reins over its head and went straightway into the doctor's house.

Cindie picked up the reins, hitched the horse to a fence and then made slowly back to her own patient nag. She stabled it behind the hotel, saw that it was fed and then went upstairs and sat on the balcony. She awaited Blanche.

When, an hour later, Blanche and Bardia came cantering in a twosome up the street, with a third man a few yards behind them, Cindie's anger at her "brazenness" flared up and eclipsed every other emotion. One thing her news would accomplish, anyhow: it would put an end to this contemptuous flouting of propriety. She leaned over the balcony so that Blanche could not fail to see her. She saw the sudden scowl that drove the light smile from the beautiful face, the surprise of the man that preceded the flash of his white teeth and the flourish of his hat in her direction.

They rode round to the back of the hotel, to the stables, and Cindie walked round the square balcony till she was in a position to call down to Blanche. But her tongue, now that the crisis was upon her, clove to the roof of her mouth. She could only stand and stare, the frightfulness of her mission locking her in an invisible vice.

Not until Blanche had disappeared into the hotel beneath her could Cindie move. Then she went into the main corridor linking the rooms and watched the top of the stairs. Blanche came up humming to herself, humming defiantly, Cindie knew, and again deadly fear overtook her. Her eyes stared starkly and Blanche, refusing even to acknowledge her presence till almost upon her, at her first glance was shocked into an exclamation.

"What's wrong? Anything wrong at home?"

"No. Not at home." Cindie's words dribbled out of her. Her glance travelled down the corridor. "Where is your room?"

"My room?" Blanche stared at her, then, realizing that

something momentous was behind Cindie's harrowed look, marched on, flinging words back over her shoulder. "Follow me." What occurred to her instantly was that someone had been blabbing to Ranny, and a thrill of fear intermingled with her detestation of Cindie's intervention. Cindie followed her into her room.

"Well, what's up?" Blanche sat down on the side of the bed and spoke sharply.

"Something dreadful has happened." Cindie walked over to a window and looked out of it. "Mrs. Fraser—Mrs. Fraser —is ill."

Silence. At the mention of that name Blanche stiffened. Her eyes narrowed. "Oh," she said coolly. "So Mrs. Fraser is ill. And what's that got to do with me, pray?"

Cindie clasped her hands. Her whole body contracted. She was positively unable to utter another word and as Blanche continued to stare at her, at the bent crouching shoulders, a premonition of disaster stole upon her and made her shiver. She licked her lips. "Cindie!" She cried the word. "What the devil is it?"

"Mrs. Biddow, Mrs. Fraser has got a—a terrible disease."

Their eyes clung together. Then Cindie closed hers, clasped her hands upon her breast and stood like a statue.

"What disease?" It was just a breath. "Syphilis, Cindie? Is it syphilis?"

"No, Mrs. Biddow. She's—she's a leper."

The ramifications of that word did not immediately penetrate to Blanche's understanding. There was, if anything, a let-up of the dread which had laced the train of thought a few moments agone set in motion. Blossom! The former prostitute! Syphilis!

Then, swiftly following, memories of stories she had read crowded into her mind. A story of a mysterious inmate of a mysterious house. A mad, naked figure that danced on a lawn in the moonlight. A snow-white figure. A living putrefaction. Biblical stories, too, flitted bat-like through her cognition. But still she hovered on the sidelines of recognition.

"A leper," she repeated slowly. "Oh! She's Chinese, isn't she. I see. Bad for the children."

"Mrs. Biddow, it's bad for—for Mr. Fraser, too. It's—it's *catching*."

Then Blanche got the full significance of the thing. And she took it superbly. She could not control the physiological processes that whitened her face and seemed to liquefy her whole body, but the momentary relief of her first dread had given her time to gather her forces for an instinctive defence.

Give nothing away. That woman there was her enemy. Time, time to think! Procrastination, that was her need, now. She drooped her head and began to fumble with the buttons of her riding habit. "Catching, is it? Do you mean that Mr. Fraser might have caught it?"

But Cindie was not deceived. She turned her back again, unwilling to look upon this dissolution of a world of sophisticated dreams. "He may have. It is not certain, the doctor says. It may take years to develop. But—but anyone who has had—relations—with her is in danger. She will have to be taken away."

"Yes. . . . Yes. . . . I suppose so. . . . I . . . I think I'll have a shower." Blanche's voice trailed away.

Cindie, warned by a sixth sense, swung round and rushed forward. She was unable to prevent Blanche's fall but managed to break it so as to avert a crash on the flimsy board floor.

With unrestrained sobs Cindie bathed the lovely face with water from the bedroom jug. If this were only death! Cindie prayed to a God she only half believed in. "Let her die, God! Please, God, let her die now!" For all sorts of problems crowded in upon her that Blanche alive might give rise to. Worst of all, the woman's own state of mind.

Blanche soon came to and sat up. Cindie handed her a towel to wipe her face and then, simply, because she could not see any other way to deal with things, said: "Mrs. Biddow, we must discuss ways and means of keeping the truth from the people. From Mr. Biddow. We must plan for the sake of Randy and Irene."

"What do you mean?" Blanche took hold of the bed and pulled herself on to it. "What's it got to do with Mr. Biddow and the children?"

That was too much for Cindie. The bald cynicism of it

shattered her control. The woman dared still to play the
fool! Dared to go on with her play acting! Maybe she would
even dare——

An avalanche of rage descended on Cindie. Took control
of her actions, her tongue. Her hand shot out and smote
Blanche's cheek with a resounding slap that sent her, because
of her unpreparedness, sprawling sideways upon the bed.
And Cindie's tongue was unloosed in a torrent of denunciation, in a summation of all Blanche's shortcomings, as wife,
mother and woman. Words came to her tongue that normally
she would have scorned to utter, but which now seemed
appropriate and peculiarly moral. Rage invested her with
a blistering clarity of thought that made her sentences
licentiously lyrical. And when she was spent she concluded
by laying down the law.

"You will tell me here and now what you intend to do.
Whether you will leave the farm, go down to Brisbane, or
stay on and think up some yarn to tell Mr. Biddow."

"And suppose I won't." Blanche had remained asprawl
on the bed. One cheek flamed with the mark of Cindie's
hand. "Suppose I tell you to mind your own business, Miss
Cindie-bloody-Comstock? What would you do?"

"I would tell Mr. Biddow all about it."

Blanche sprang up. "Yes, I bet you would! I bet you
would glory in the chance! The only reason you haven't
told him already is that you know he would despise you for
it. Oh yes, you'd have a chance to get him if I were out of
the road."

A wave of sickness washed over Cindie. But she knew
that Blanche was babbling out of despair. She was sorry,
now, for her outburst, and said wearily: "There's no sense
in talking like that, Mrs. Biddow. You know better than
that. I'm sorry for what I said. Come now. We'll ride home.
The fresh air will cool our brains."

But she had to wait for the storm of tears that burst from
Blanche to subside. Then they took their way down the back
stairs of the hotel, mounted their horses and clattered down
the street.

Cindie's thoughts as they rode, with Blanche keeping a
little to the fore of her all the way, moved in strange, quest-

ing channels. Maybe there was a way the ultimate could
be avoided. She wished she knew more about sex relations.
Why—how—had the Biddows limited their family to two
children? Most other women about the place kept on having
babies. Consuelo was with child again. Did this aspect of
things present an avenue of hope? She pushed her horse up
beside Blanche and called: "Mrs. Biddow, pull your horse to
a walk."

Blanche complied. The misery of her face stabbed Cindie
afresh. God Almighty! The woman couldn't go home
looking like that! "Mrs. Biddow!" she cried. "Isn't there
some way that things could remain as they are. Why don't
you get in the family way, Mrs. Biddow? Your mother, too.
She only had you."

Blanche smiled pitifully. "I've thought of that myself.
But I can't see. . . . No, I don't know enough. . . . But what
the hell does that matter, anyhow?" She put heel to her
horse.

And Cindie was left to ask herself: Indeed, what did it
matter? What could it matter to Blanche, caught in the coil
of horrific speculations involving her own fate?

She spurred on her horse. "Mrs. Biddow, you must try
and pull yourself together. You look awful."

Blanche gave her a terrible look then lifted her whip and
cut her horse with it. It leapt forward into a furious gallop.
Cindie tore after her, afraid, her teeth set. They looked like
two mad women, desperately straining forward in their
saddles, their horses' tails streaming, hooves clattering on the
hard clay of the track. Kanakas walking stared in astonishment. A couple of whites riding down to the Port drew rein
and looked after them. "Rummy," one of them remarked.
"They didn't seem to see us."

But Blanche drew in her horse to a steady trot as they
approached the turn-off to Folkhaven. When Cindie came
abreast she told her calmly: "I'll be all right. You don't
have to worry about me."

Cindie had not the heart to voice the query on the tip of
her tongue, but Blanche sensed it. "You needn't worry
about anybody else, either," she added, with grim decision.
"I'm not quite mad."

"If you will be all right I'll ride on to Fraser's place," said Cindie. "They might need me over there."

But there was not much she could do when she arrived at Fraser's place. For Fraser and the doctor had found the two little boys locked outside the house in the care of a group of scared Kanakas and a dead woman with a bullet through her brain on the kitchen floor inside it.

Within a week Fraser had transferred his holding to a couple of Chinese and shaken the dust of Masterman from his feet.

CHAPTER XXX

TO BEGIN WITH, BIDDOW ACCEPTED AT ITS FACE VALUE Blanche's declaration of the development of some internal trouble that inclined her to frigidity. He did not like it. He thought it queer that anything of the kind should manifest itself without warning. Worried by her haggard looks he exhorted her to get medical attention. But so far as his own sensual comforts were concerned, he transferred from the sleep-out on the veranda to an indoor bedroom with a slight feeling of relief.

Biddow was not looking for trouble himself these days. The tragic death of Fraser's wife had jolted him quite a bit, and on the top of that he was forced to realize the urgent need to resolve some knotty problems in respect of the affairs of the farm.

Subsequent to the decision of the Federal Government to forbid the employment of alien coloured labour after 1906, the sugar industry was offered a bounty of four shillings per ton, calculated on cane giving ten per cent of sugar content, upon all sugar produced in Queensland with white labour. And Biddow, in company with other forward-looking growers, now that the expiration of the indenture term of many of his Kanakas was approaching, began to debate the advisability of letting all this number go and making a bid for white labour while he had the remainder to fall back on. The

particularly good position he occupied, due to Cindie's enter-
prise with the logs, coffee and Aborigine labour, encouraged
this. Should that experiment prove successful, by the time
his remaining Kanakas were due for repatriation, in the following year, with the assistance of Aborigine labour which,
being Australian, was exempt from the provisions of the
White Australia Acts, he would be in a position to register
Folkhaven as a white labour holding and receive the bounty.

As usual, however, having got the idea and acknowledged
its practical value, he lacked the initiative to proceed with
its implementation. That waited upon Cindie's judgment,
and she, influenced first one way and then the other by the
seemingly myriad complications and contradictions that beset
the industry on all sides, was unable to make up her mind.

Cindie's original hope of the employment of Aboriginal
labour to an ever-increasing extent had year by year of
necessity been whittled away. For with the closer settlement
of the district the natives had been proportionately despoiled
of their hunting grounds and compelled to retire to distant
areas. Now, she could only rely on the old hands who had
come to look on Folkhaven as a permanent home.

Throughout the State, fast and furious debate waxed
around the question of the limitation and deportation of the
coloured alien population and the problems of import duties,
excise and bounty these propositions involved. Between the
leading white sugar growers of North Queensland and those
of the southern areas of the State a bitter feud raged. A
section of the growers of North Queensland, comprising all
trends of political thought, spilled acrimonious wrath upon
the heads of the growers of the south, whose different conditions had prompted a different policy in respect of black
and white labour. In the sub-tropical areas of the south,
where in addition to the less trying climatic conditions the
planters were connected by rail with the centres, white labour
was now becoming freely available with the provision of
good wages and conditions. Their demand upon the Federal
Government, therefore, was for heavy protective duties which
would enable them to meet the demands of white labour.
A high protective tariff would increase their profits and have
little effect upon the difficulties of production.

But with the far northern planters, the problem was not one of getting sufficient protection to enable them to meet the demands of white labour, but one of getting white labour under any conditions.

With the rapid decline of the mineral belt then taking place, the entire population of the far north was becoming dependent on sugar. And even though, as in the Masterman area, the majority of the growers in general favoured a White Australia, yet at the same time, seeing their ruin in the deportation of the Kanaka, the big planters with few exceptions were hot for a compromise in this particular field. The general outlook was that the humidity and enervating heat of the tropics demanded coloured labour. In their experience, the only class of whites who would volunteer for labour in the tropics was a type lacking the requisite stamina.

One rabid Northerner, speaking at a conference in Townsville, declared passionately that "God had only sent thick-skulled men like Kanakas into the world to do such work as cane cultivation. The best use the Kanaka could be put to was to create wealth for the white man. Those who advocated bringing white men down to the level of the Kanaka had a false conception of what white men should and could do."

He was countered by a Southerner, one of the few who already had embarked upon a policy in conformity with White Australia tenets. The white workers he had engaged under contract for the cutting of his cane had given eminent satisfaction. In the fields at daybreak and out of them at dark, these whites had earned for themselves the "munificent" sum of nine shillings a day. Compared with the expenses of the all-year-round Kanakas, contract white labour was indisputably cheaper. Whites cut the cane more adroitly, moreover, the result being better ratoons. And they both trashed and cut the cane.

Northerners attempted no refutation of a self-evident fact. Their trouble was an inability to secure white labour to do "niggers' work". White Australia, they recognized, must come. The people had declared for it. But in the attempt to realize that state of affairs, there was a tendency to ride a principle to death. A modification of the Act to conform with their special conditions was all they asked.   By all means exclude the Chinese, the Japanese and other Asiatic aliens, by all means forbid the further recruitment of Kanakas, but those Kanakas already in the country should be allowed to remain. Confine them exclusively to field work by stringent regulations, forbid their intermarriage with whites, adopt every provision of human wisdom to prevent them acquiring a strength and status in any way inimical to the well-being of the whites, and the principle of White Australia, but *allow them to remain.* By the granting of this boon the White Australia principle, without being ridden to death, would be given practically the effect its most ardent supporters could wish. Decrease by death must eventually extinguish the Kanakas. Such a gradual extinction of the blacks would enable the State to determine in a statesmanlike way whether the field work could be done without black labour, or whether the loss of the industry, with all that it meant to the country, was really preferable to the continued existence of the Kanakas in their midst.

This narrowed the question down to a very simple issue: to ruin the industry or adopt the alternative: retain the Kanakas and exclude all other aliens.

From another quarter came a loud lament anent the barbarity of returning these people, who had enjoyed the "benefits and refinements of civilization", to their native state.   Groups of Kanakas were organized to petition the Governor-General against their repatriation.   These men, mostly married, many of them to white women, had reared families in Queensland, acquired property and differed from whites only in the colour of their skin.

The reply to this was an Amending Act to enable the avoidance of injustice, consideration to be given to exceptional cases.

Against this, from yet another quarter came a savage outcry to the effect that the "degradation" involved by the union of black with white in marriage was a puissant argument in favour of deportation.

Cindie, furiously resentful of the chauvinism that characterized these political fireworks, was yet torn this way and that in her estimation of events.   Whatever the morality of the arguments in favour of the retention of the Kanakas, it was not in her to view the essential issue other than objectively in its relation to the welfare of the farm. For the imperialist issues at stake she had nothing but contempt. She, no less than Biddow, believed that the defence of Australia against foreign aggression did not hinge upon a population composed exclusively of whites but upon the feeling for country developed and fostered in both black and white populations by social conditions. The facts of life as she saw them proved conclusively that the Folkhaven Kanakas, the Folkhaven Aborigines, accepted on a basis of equality with whites, would put down roots of loyalty and love into the soil of the land and, if need be, die in battle for its defence!

She wanted passionately to retain the Kanakas. Not as cheap labour, but as a matter of vindicating the integrity of her beliefs. The sugar industry, she could not help but be aware, in general was paying dividends at terrifically favourable rates. It was able to give decent wages and conditions and still reap enormous profits. She was determined, if the arguments for the retention of the Kanakas prevailed, to use all her influence with Biddow to have the Folkhaven Kanakas placed upon the same footing as white workers.

But would those arguments prevail? That was the question. The Prime Minister, Sir Edmund Barton, had stated that he did not intend to make hard and fast laws in relation to sugar. On the other hand, the Labour Party in the Federal sphere, which, contrary to the hopes of the big planters, had polled heavily in the federal elections, was known to be held in great favour by Barton and, in fact, held the balance of power. Barton had included many Labour planks in his programme, even accepted the principle of equal pay for equal work on behalf of women: he had granted to women the right to equality with men in status and pay. And elected Labour, despite much diversity of opinion among its followers in the sugar industry, was one hundred per cent in favour of White Australia.

September came. The planters were now in the midst of the crushing season and still Cindie shillyshallied. Still Biddow waited upon her decision. But now, Cindie realized,

further procrastination would be fatal.   For, if an attempt
to secure white workers was to be made, either she or Biddow
must go south to do the job.   Herself, for preference, she considered.   Biddow was too easy.   White workers for this area
must be picked men.   None of these social derelicts who
wandered into Masterman occasionally and worked till they
got the wherewithal to get out and hang around the street
corners in town.

Cindie's love for this far northern country was bulwarked
by her common sense.   To go ahead it needed a settled
population.   It needed an influx of workmen who would look
on it as a permanent home.

The operations of the Masterman mill over the previous
season gave decisive support to this supposition.   Exclusively
white labour was employed inside the mill.   To get the
one hundred and fifty men necessary for the crushing the
company had had to engage four hundred men.   And even
the one hundred and fifty selected from the four hundred
had not constituted an effective staff.   They were simply the
best available.   After pay day the mill repeatedly had had
to begin the new week with a shortage of workers of from
fifteen to twenty-five per cent.   For the more arduous work
in the fields, therefore, Cindie realized that the provision of
good wages and conditions would be of little avail unless
the men selected were of the solid settling-down type.

But what finally made up her mind was a factor uncon-
nected with political and economic issues.   That was the
development of a crisis in the jealous rivalry that existed
between the two field cooks, Suzuki and Ching Ling, and
an unsavoury incident arising from it involving Blanche.

It happened on a day when the oven which had been
built in the horse paddock for the burning of coral was being
put to its first use, under Cindie's direction.   Her given
word to Sonsie had materialized in the chartering of a small
launch for trips to the Great Barrier reefs and the bringing
of loads of coral.   Sonsie, whom Cindie had attached to herself as man of all jobs about the homestead, had built the
clay oven and now both were engrossed in the job of burning
the coral preliminary to its pulverization in the fields.

The first intimation Cindie received of untoward events

at the cookhouse was a faint sound of vocal clamour wafted up to her on the light sea breeze. She easily recognized it for what it was: the cacophony of Oriental voices raised in violent dispute. She was not surprised, for over the last few days Suzuki had been morosely nursing a supposed injury in that she, Cindie, had insisted that the baking of bread for the future must be solely the job of Ching Ling, a remarkably efficient baker.

Beyond a frown and a shrug, Cindie took no immediate action in the hope that the trouble would blow over. To the contrary, however. The faint clamour suddenly converted to wild shrieks. Cindie began to run. And down below the stables she met Verbena tearing up to fetch her.

"Missie Cindie, come quick!" Verbena screamed. "Suzuki, he dead! And Missis beat Ching Ling! She hit him with whip!"

Cindie flew down through the quarters of the Kanakas, to meet Blanche, dressed for riding, whip in hand, coming out of the field kitchen. Her eyes gleamed with triumphant satisfaction. Wailing filled the room behind her.

Ignoring Blanche, Cindie shot into the kitchen. To find Suzuki lying like one dead on the floor and Ching Ling crouching against a wall, his head clutched in his hands. He it was who wailed. Across his face were several livid weals. Cindie dropped on her knees beside Suzuki and swiftly looked him over. Nothing wrong with him that she could see. "Stop that noise!" she shouted at Ching Ling. "What happened to Suzuki?"

"Missis, she whip me!" Ching Ling howled. "I tell the bobby! I tell the perlice!" He howled again.

"Shut up!" Cindie rose from her knees. "What happened?" She questioned Charity and Verbena, who hung together in the doorway.

"Missis, she find the Chink bashing Suzuki's head on the stone floor," vouchsafed Charity. "And she whip him. She lash and she lash." Charity's body shook with excitement. Her eyes rolled.

"Is that all?" Cindie sighed with relief. "You villain, Ching Ling. . . . He's coming to." Suzuki began to groan and move his limbs. In a few moments he sat up. Nobody spoke. Ching Ling, not so sure, now, of the soundness of his grievance, sidled round the wall and out through the door.

Five minutes later Ching Ling was pelting down the track with his bundle bouncing in his hand, and Suzuki, in the midst of collecting his own odds and ends of belongings, was telling Cindie: "You tell the yellow basta he make good bread. You tell him he better man than me. You make bread yourself. That suit me." And there he stuck. Shortly he set off down the track and Cindie was left with an empty kitchen and the feeding of forty adults on her hands.

Putting Charity and Verbena on to the job, she sat down and considered the situation. Difficult to find cooks in the midst of the crushing. Here was one instance when Aborigines could not fill the bill. After a few minutes' cogitation she went down to the big house.

Blanche, now dressed in cool muslin, reclined at full length on a couch on the front veranda. Her arms were clasped behind her head. She stared straight up at the ceiling, her face like stone. Cindie walked up the steps and took a chair a few feet away from her. Blanche ignored her.

"The cooks have gone. Cleared out." Cindie spoke casually. No reply. Cindie continued: "You and Mr. Biddow will have to eat the food from the field kitchen until new arrangements can be made."

"And why, pray? There are plenty of men in the paddocks. Bring one of them in."

"The men are needed in the fields. The mill can scarcely be kept going as it is."

"Then what about yourself? Have you forgotten how to cook?"

"I haven't forgotten." Cindie still spoke quietly. "If the field cooking doesn't suit me I shall cook for myself. It wouldn't hurt you to do the same."

Blanche threw herself upwards. "Listen here, Miss Cindie Comstock! When Randolph comes in from the paddocks he will be told mighty quick to bring in a cook."

Cindie rose. "Please yourself. You will also tell him that you whipped the Chinaman."

Blanche's gaze upon her became malignant with hate.

She knew very well that the time had gone by when such things were looked on with equanimity. She was afraid to have Biddow know. "But surely," she dribbled, "you wouldn't let Mr. Biddow eat Kanaka food, Miss Comstock?"

Cindie looked at her squarely. "That sort of thing doesn't get anywhere with me, Mrs. Biddow. . . . You know, you're a fool. What you need is something to take your mind off things. You need work."

"What I need is my home freed of a blight," was the thick reply.

"Well, if I'm the blight, you can be free of me any day," said Cindie, levelly. "There never has been a day when you couldn't have been free of me. Do you want me to leave Folkhaven? I'll go this minute if you say so. And you haven't the excuse of thinking that I would pimp to Mr. Biddow, either. I wouldn't. You see, Mrs. Biddow, I trust you. I believe that you love your husband, Mrs. Biddow."

Naïve Cindie! The paroxysm of hate that seized upon Blanche and made her leap forward from the couch with talons crooked to rend, shocked the girl more by the unreason of it than anything else. The why of it stunned her. Good heavens! what more could the woman ask of her? Of anyone? Cindie was lost in the labyrinthine coils of human psychology. "She couldn't hate me more," she reflected, "if I had done her a mort of injuries."

Cindie was not proud of her precipitate retreat in face of Blanche's charge, either. She promised herself that she wouldn't stand for a repetition of that. But later, when she came to review the events of the day calmly, she felt terribly worried about the future. Randy! She had shown his latest letter to Biddow, to induce him to act, but now she wondered if bringing the boy home was after all the right thing to do. Surely his mother was not right in the head. Why the devil didn't the woman go down to Brisbane? There she might get more information. . . .

But presently there was the prosaic problem of the field kitchen to face. She saw to it that special little dishes were prepared by the black women for the table at the big house.

Kooka, the ancient male Aborigine, was brought into the field kitchen to peel potatoes and yams, to bring wood. His wife, Cindie sent to do Blanche's housework as best she could.

CHAPTER XXXI

THE FIRST COOK SHE MANAGED TO SECURE WAS A CHINESE addicted to opium. He could not get himself out of bed. The first morning of his engagement chaos reigned. Cindie shunted him off down the track and reverted to the maids. After scouring the country-side throughout the day she brought home a Chinese who, though pleasantly indefatigable at his tasks, for two days running, three times a day, produced a tremendous stew and nothing else. To Cindie's protests he gave a chortling: "Yes, Missie, yes, Missie. All li, all li," then went ahead with the making of another vast stew. So on the third morning, aghast at the sight of yet another sickening mixture and faced with rebellious mutterings on the part of the Kanakas, Cindie told him flatly: "You're a liar, Hi Low. You told me you could cook. You can't cook. You haven't cooked a thing but stew since you came here."

To which Hi Low replied: "Yes, Missie, I no cook. I blacksmith. You give me 'nother job?"

Cindie laughed. "You're an old devil, Hi Low. No more job. Clear out."

It was the exit of Hi Low that led her to a decision in respect of the white labour issue.

"God only knows how long we'll be messed about with this kitchen trouble," she told Biddow. "I could train Aborigines but they would likely walk out on me just when we need them most. And I don't like the women in the field kitchen. It leads to trouble. Verbena's Billy is after Melatonka's scalp right now. I think you should sign up as many Kanakas as will stay for a short term, Mr. Biddow. Say: six months. I don't see a possibility for either of us to leave the farm at this juncture to look for white labour."

"I don't see why I shouldn't go," said Biddow, judicially. "Tirwana could manage the farm as well as I do it myself."

"He could if you took Mrs. Biddow with you," Cindie said bluntly. He frowned. He gave her a chill look "Oh, there's no sense in evading things, Mr. Biddow," Cindie added, harshly. "You know perfectly well that your wife hates Tirwana like the devil. I've got enough to do without— I'm getting a bit fed-up, Mr. Biddow! I'm—I'm nervous!"

Suddenly conscience-stricken, Biddow bit hard on the stem of his pipe. "You make me feel a bit of a rotter, Cindie. You've not had a holiday in six years, have you? That's no good. I'm afraid we all take you too much for granted, Cindie. We'll have to do something about it."

"Do? What can you do? I'll take a holiday when things have settled down."

"I'll tell you what I'll do!" For the first time in years that old note of finality was evident in Biddow's tone. "I will bring Randy home."

Cindie's heart leapt. "You will?" she cried joyfully. But instantly a lugubrious uncertainty succeeded to her joy. "But, Mr. Biddow," she added, hastily, "maybe you shouldn't."

"What!" He bent astounded eyes on her.

Cindie's eyes drooped. She flushed. "I—I only thought that perhaps Mrs. Biddow would object."

"You certainly do need a holiday," Biddow said coldly. He left her and, immediately seeking out Blanche, informed her of his decision.

"Why?" she asked, her lips trembling with uncontrollable agitation.

"For two reasons, Blanche, both of them, I think, imperative. Randy wants to be a farmer and I need him on the farm."

"And what I want doesn't matter."

Biddow looked at her without speaking for a time. A look mildly thoughtful. At length he asked: "Don't you think the boy's interests should come before your silly prejudices?"

But Biddow was not really interested in the subject of Randy just then. He was really seeking in his mind for an answer to a question he had asked himself many times lately. What was the strength of this peculiar trouble that had so suddenly revealed itself in his wife? Any fool could see that she was wretchedly unhappy. Maybe the whole thing was some sort of neurosis that had descended on her out of the blue. He let the stream of her wrathful disclamation and protest roll over him and then stated: "I think you should go south and get some expert medical attention. You're going to pieces."

"You want to get rid of me!" Her utterance was half wail, half tameless fury. And with it tears fountained from her eyes.

"Darling!" In a trice Biddow was at her side, taking her in his arms. "Darling, what's wrong with you?" He attempted to kiss her, was mortified and harried when she twisted her lips away from his and slipped out of his embrace. "Don't touch me!" she cried. "Keep away!"

"Keep away! Good heavens, what *is* the matter with you?" he shouted, then drew in his breath sharply and added: "I beg your pardon." He sank on to a chair apart from her. He was trembling. His guts felt like jelly within him.

For in that instant during which he had clasped her to him and she had yielded, even clung to him, Biddow had felt her desire for him searing hot. And it was borne in on the man, ineluctably, that her rejection of him, the manner of it, her refusal of her lips, all together weighed up to some dark riddle the meaning of which was deliberately being withheld from him.

"Look here, my girl," he told her, his manner a mixture of dignity and menace. "You had better tell me what's at the bottom of this mysterious trouble of yours. It's gone far enough."

"You know very well. I told you what the doctor said. I've got a prolapsed womb."

"Huh. . . . I'm not a fool. Why don't you go down to Brisbane and have it fixed up?"

"And leave you here with that—that bitch!" But this time it did not do. Blanche knew instinctively that her shaft had missed its mark. She knew that her words had rung false. Inwardly she cursed. She was tired. Her head ached.

Biddow rose precipitately. "I'll have Randy home as soon as I can get him," he said coldly, and left her. Left her there in deadly fear.

It was the middle of October before Cindie managed to secure two satisfactory cooks. Things had muddled along. But Cindie would have been happy those days, in anticipation of Randy's imminent arrival home, had it not been for concern over Biddow. The corrosive spirit of oppression which had hung over Blanche seemed to have extended itself to her husband. Biddow's native air of tranquillity had converted to stern, tight-lipped repression. To any little problem of farm management he brought acute impatience, even angry irritation.

And Cindie, thinking she knew the reason, began to actively hate the woman who would not go away. By the light of her reading and those other normal channels by which information on matters of sex is gleaned, she could understand, she thought, the strain on the man of living with an opulent beauty like Blanche, a woman he loved, in enforced continence.

And Biddow seemed to have conceived a dislike for his home, for whenever possible he kept out of it. Except, that was, when it was filled with visitors, which came to be very often.

Following upon the death of Mrs. Fraser, Blanche, in accord both with her pretended physical disability and her actual spiritual sickness, had settled down to a quiet life. But after the incident reported above she felt herself unable to sustain that role. Biddow's consequent air of chill suspicion, alternating with moody introspection, added yet another prong to the tenterhook of her frustration and fear. The pressure upon her became such that nature herself conferred relief by plunging her into fits of reckless desperation during which, consigning Biddow and her own destiny to hell, she would get into her riding habit and tear about the countryside on horseback.

To begin with, the instinct of self-preservation was enough to the fore to constrain her to confine her jaunts to those hours when Biddow was busy in the fields or away from the farm. But inevitably the element of chance defeated that precaution and she had to face the man's black, voiceless suspicions.

For the hour of leisure between the evening meal and dark, Biddow those days usually took his old-time favourite seat, the stump below Cindie's dwelling. There he would sit and yarn with Tirwana and Verbena's Billy, the latter now a man of affairs by virtue of his job as ploughman.

Cindie, physically relaxed upon the balcony above them, her eyes on Biddow, would ponder unremittingly the abnormality of the coil in which Blanche's frivolity had embroiled herself and the man they both loved. And at times, spurred by the loveliness of the canefields in the afterglow of sunset, fields set like blocks of topaz in the heart of the jungle green, she would stiffen with sour hate of the woman who had been unable to effect a compromise between her overwhelming desire for absolute domination and the general well-being of family and farm.

Again, the ache of her reflection would yield to the realist's common sense and she would ask herself impatiently: What the devil did such things matter, anyhow? Did they amount to any great shakes? A worthless woman, a man deprived of his "horizontal pleasures", as Jeff would have it, what the odds? Why couldn't people face up to the facts of life? Why was she, herself, shielding Blanche, shielding Biddow? What did this so-called sense of decency amount to, that constrained her to do it? One such evening she got so far as to declare, loudly: "I jolly well ought to go down and tell Mr. Biddow all about it. Then they would have the business out, come to some arrangement and get over it." She wavered for some minutes but at length renounced the idea. "No," she muttered morosely, "for some idiotic reason I can't do it. Things will go on and on, with her getting madder and madder and him closing up on himself till something dreadful happens. Till Randy is made to suffer. . . ."

But no! There Cindie stuck. She'd be damned if she'd stand for the boy being made to suffer! If the interests of Randy ran counter to her sentimental indulgence of his parents, well, there would be altogether a different kettle of fish.

CHAPTER XXXII

ON THE EVENING PRECEDING RANDY'S ARRIVAL, WITH BLANCHE not yet returned from a day's visit to Glenelg, Biddow surprised Cindie by joining her on her balcony without the excuse of pressing farm matters to discuss. He sat down and smoked, his eyes on the paddocks stretching out before them.

Cindie put aside the sugar journal she had been scanning and let her eyes follow his. On the cutting sites the trash was burning. Billows of black smoke were slowly rolling up from the ground, with tongues of non-luminous flame whisking out from it here and there, and vanishing almost at birth. A flock of white ibis, heavy and dumpy with the weight of the grubs they had consumed, rose from the horse paddock and winged their way over the forest to roost in the great fig-trees on the coast.

For quite a time they sat there in congenial silence. Realizing that the man had come to her for companionship only, Cindie's spirits soared. Her mental processes mounted to an optimistic plane. Perhaps things would work out all right, after all. Perhaps Randy's coming would suffice to give his father content. Perhaps Blanche, too, would find new maternal solicitude derive from her wretchedness and trouble. Poor Blanche! How poor in spirit to be immune to the peace and satisfaction that stemmed from the tree of voluntary service!

As the film of dusk began to obscure the white sky a desire came upon Cindie to talk to the man in the speech of companionship. And since between them there had never been any kind of talk unrelated to family and farm, her words, though warm, had a utilitarian meaning.

"I'm thinking we should bury the trash in the paddocks next year, Mr. Biddow." She took up the sugar journal again and ruffled its leaves.

He rose, spat over the railing, resumed his seat and gave her a laconic: "Why?"

"It says in this journal that burying the trash renders soil looser, airs it. Listen! 'Supplies carbonic and organic acids.'

. . . Um. . . . And here. 'After a few years gives soil consistency and the freedom of virgin lands.' Wouldn't do any harm to try it. Question of more labour, though."

"Yes. More labour." He sighed. "Everything gets back to a question of labour, Cindie. But maybe burying the trash would act as a substitute for green manures. I had thought myself of doing it this year."

Cindie gave him a fleeting, fond smile. He had thought of it! Trust him to think of things. But as for the doing of them . . .

The plod of hooves coming up the track turned their heads. Four horses reined up beside the big house. Biddow sighed again as he rose. "Coming down?" he asked.

"Yes, I think I will." Caroline Montague's laugh had rung out and Cindie liked the girl. She was curious, too, about the other visitors. Most farmers were too busy to be gadding on weeknights at that season of the year.

"Tirwana!" Blanche's voice called peremptorily as they went down the stairs. Tirwana came out from beneath Cindie's house and joined them. "Take my horse, Tirwana" —sharply, from Blanche. "Oh, there you are, Randolph! No lights in the house. It looks like a tomb."

Cindie replied to her. "I'll get the lights going. Hullo, Caroline. Hullo, Jeff. Where did you spring from, Mr. Bardia?"

"My dear young lady, that seems to be your stock greeting so far as I am concerned." Bardia offered his hand to Cindie, then to Biddow. Neither took it with any great enthusiasm.

"And you've got a stock answer, perhaps," was Cindie's reply.

"Come on, come on," Blanche intervened. "We don't want to hang around here all night."

Cindie lit the hanging kerosene lamps in the drawing-room and corridor and then seated herself, very upright, beside Bardia. "Now answer my question." She turned her eyes, faintly derisive, full upon him.

In his turn he faced her with smiling malice. But as he stared at her the malice was gradually supplanted by admiration and suddenly he laughed, richly, and slapped his leg. "By the jumping Jemima! Want to know where I came from,

eh? From the Port. Just brought my schooner in with
forty tons of bêche-de-mer, my girl. How's that for money?"

Cindie's eyes narrowed. "How much a ton? How long
to take up?"

Bardia laughed again. "Interested, are you? Thought
that would get you. Four months to take it up. Average price
nearly one hundred pounds a ton."

They were now looking at each other straightly. Cindie's
eyes were filled with alert curiosity, Bardia's with a bright
flame of interest. "What's left after you've paid expenses?"
she asked.

"The best part of it. The schooner was the big expense."

"What about the crew?"

"The niggers? A mere bagatelle." He laughed again.

"Just what I'd expect from you." Cindie relaxed and took
her eyes from his.

Biddow smiled. Grey laughed and Caroline, possessed
by the wonder and shine of an adolescent passion she was
only now discovering for Jeff, emitted a shrill echo. Blanche,
pouring wine, remarked sarcastically: "That's upset your
applecart, Mr. Bardia. Don't you know that our Cindie is
the champion of all niggers?" She brought a tray of drinks
and proffered it him.

"Yes, I knew it. First time I heard of money entering
into her relations with them, though." Bardia spoke jeer-
ingly and, taking up a glass, offered it to Cindie. "Ladies
first, Miss Comstock." With a mocking bow. But a note in
his voice, a suggestion of embarrassment, of mortification,
even, brought Blanche's eyes back to him. She offered the
tray to Biddow and Grey, Caroline, of course, being debarred
by her youth from the sophisticated practice of wine drink-
ing.

When Blanche had taken up her own glass, Bardia cried
laughingly: "May I suggest a toast? To Miss Comstock's
championship of niggers. She sweats 'em her way, I sweat
'em mine."

He tossed off his wine at one gulp. Blanche followed suit
but Biddow and Grey, holding their glasses untouched, began
to converse. Cindie carried hers to the table and put it
down.

"I hate this stuff," she said amiably. "Well, Caroline, Randy comes home to-morrow. I suppose we'll have to put up with a bunch of youngsters round the place from now on."

"I'm not a youngster," Caroline replied hotly. She shot a glance at Grey, the significance of which Cindie could not comprehend.

"Oh!" she said lamely. She felt as though she had been winded by a blow in the stomach. Caroline and Jeff! Was Caro really grown up? A stab of loneliness shot through her, a sense of loss. She stared at Grey. "What brought you out on a weeknight, Jeff? Pretty busy, aren't you?"

"I had to go over to Glenelg about some corn and Caroline pushed me into escorting her over here. And that reminds me." He rose, drained his glass on his feet. "Come on, Miss. Time little girls were home."

"I'm not a little girl. I'm a grown woman." Caroline stuck to her chair.

Grey put his hands beneath her arms and lifted her to her feet. "Want to be slapped?"

She dragged herself away from him, her face flaming. "I'll slap you! Mrs. Biddow, am I a little girl?"

"Of course not, Caroline. I was thinking of getting married when I was your age. Ask Mr. Biddow."

"All right. You're not a little girl. But you're going home now, all the same, because I'm tired."

"You go, then," she said sulkily. "Mr. Bardia can take me home."

Silence. Out of it came Bardia's amused voice. "Thanks for the compliment, Miss Caroline, but I've got a long ride back to the Port."

"You can stay with me for the night, if you like, Caroline," said Cindie gently. "Jeff can ride over to Glenelg and tell them. Then you would be here when Randy comes."

"I'll go now! Good night." Caroline flew across the room and out through the doorway. Grey lifted one shoulder, shook his head comically and followed her.

Biddow rose. "Afraid I must ask you to excuse me, Bardia. Daybreak for us farmers, you know."

"Sure. Sure." Bardia, too, rose.

"You needn't run away," Blanche cried, giving Biddow a furious look. "I'm not tired."

"Neither am I," said Cindie swiftly.

Bardia glanced from one woman to the other. His eyes sparkled. His teeth flashed. "Sorry, but I only came up to get the feel of a horse between my legs again. Just chance I ran into you, Mrs. Biddow. But Miss Comstock, I know, is interested in the bêche fishing. Suppose we have a business talk some day, Miss Comstock?"

"Maybe we could." Cindie eyed him speculatively. Then with vigour: "But you'd have to turn your carcass inside out, Florenz Bardia, before I would do business with you."

He flung his head back and laughed, a ringing ha-ha-ha of mirth to which Cindie could not help but contribute a smile.

"You don't want to do anything foolish, Cindie," counselled Biddow, as he walked across the floor.

"You needn't tell her that," flashed Blanche. "She always knows what she's doing. . . . Put out the light when you've finished your talk"—venomously. "Good night." She darted after Biddow and banged the door behind her.

"You go out, Mr. Bardia," said Cindie equably. "I'll turn out the lights."

He was waiting for her on the front steps. "A lovely night, Miss Cindie," he said cordially. "But early, early. No use suggesting that you invite me to visit your humble abode, I suppose."

"Why not? I'm a business woman, Mr. Bardia. You can come up on to my balcony and tell me the ins and outs of this fishing business, if you like."

Blanche, now regretful of her flight, sat on her bed in the dark and strained her ears. At the sound of their making up to Cindie's house she darted on tiptoe out on to the veranda. The little trull! Well! . . . Randolph should hear of this! She sank into a chair and set herself to watch. In a few moments the two came out on to Cindie's balcony and sat down. The murmur of their voices percolated through the night.

It was symptomatic of the disintegration of Blanche's intrinsic self beneath the grind and strain of constant fear that, sitting there watching that confab. between the woman she hated and her old lover, not once did the homecoming of her son nor his image obtrude itself. She welcomed and hugged to herself the pain of jealousy, for by it she was relieved from those other, ever-recurring horrific thoughts.

And shortly, on the wash of that profound and inseparable unity of the sexual impulse and pain, out of the heat engendered by swarming mental pictures of hours spent with Bardia in the past, an idea crept into Blanche's mind that, though at first rejected with a slight thrill of horror, yet recurred and in gradually shaping itself into the possibility of materialization, at length settled itself in her twisted cognizance as objectively fine and, from the point of view of her own interwoven needs and hates, eminently permissible.

Cindie could not possibly know of her affair with Bardia. So ran Blanche's thoughts. Her first adulterous venture in the district, she had taken every possible precaution—so she imagined—against detection. Yes, a pretty good idea, Blanche exulted. She achieved a vicarious semi-satisfaction for her own lustful urges in putting the two of them, up there, in imagination, to bed. All ways, all ways, this plan, if successful, would meet her own needs.

The quickening of her mind, her exultation, demanded physical action. Down the veranda steps beside her sleep-out she crept. She knew him! Knew the meaning of his "business talk" with the slut. Fishing! As though he needed anybody's money! And she had suspected it before. More than once he had given her reason to suspect his interest in the girl. She recalled his hesitations, his evasions, in respect of her own sneers and contumely.

She walked down the track in the deep violet dark, the warm, fragrant dark of star-lit, forest-encircled night. And before she had gone far she was halted by the approach of a figure, a figure which, even in its first shadowy appearance, she recognized as that of a Kanaka. She stood still.

Melatonka, for it was he, did likewise. Then, taking it for granted that the feminine form must be Cindie's, and fortified with liquor against a scolding, he grinned and came on.

"What are you doing out at this time of night?" Blanche rapped out.

Taken aback by her identity, Melatonka dodged around her swiftly. "Just go walk, Missis   Just go walk in the night."

The fumes of liquor streamed back to Blanche as she stood looking after him. "Beastly niggers," she muttered. But the encounter decided her against going further. She stepped off the track on to the grass that lined it and waited in the shadow of an isolated forest tree.

Melatonka, vastly curious about this lonesome walking of "the Missis" in the night, hurried up towards the homestead with many looks behind him. Up at the house, he was just in time to see Cindie and Bardia making ready to leave the balcony. And this circumstance, combined with Blanche's presence down the track, incited him to snooping investigation. He slipped aside into the shadow of the trees on the edge of the creek and waited, his eyes flitting, his ears twitching. And when Bardia came down the stairs alone, unhitched his horse from a stump and mounted it, Melatonka grinned in concupiscent relish of a situation he was certain he now thoroughly understood. Bardia set his horse slowly jogging down the track and Melatonka, his natural lustfulness inflamed with liquor, screened by the shadows, jogged along after him.

Yes, there was the Missis, waylaying the man! Melatonka softly clapped his hands and teetered. Bardia slipped off his horse. But to Melatonka's disappointment the two merely stood on the track and talked. Nevertheless, marvelling, the Kanaka waited. . . .

Bardia had had the same idea as the native when he saw Blanche emerge from the shadows. "Ho ho," he cried softly. "So I'm in luck after all."

"Get down," said Blanche curtly. "I want to talk to you."

He dismounted with alacrity. "Only to talk?" he asked jocularly.

"Yes. Only to talk. Florenz, are you—interested—in Cindie Comstock?"

The man started, then peered at her intently. "What's the idea?" he asked roughly. "Jealous?"

"No. . . . I want to get the chit married."

"So? . . . What if I am interested? I haven't got much of a chance, judging by her own account."

"You have, you have! I can help you."

"Look here, Blanche, what are you up to? You don't like this girl."

"I hate her. I tell you I want to get her married."

"To me?" Curiosity blended with scepticism.

"Yes. To you. Nobody else would have her." Blanche laughed, in a gloating, feverish way that made the man move restlessly and frown.

"All right. Spit it out. What's on your mind?"

"I only wanted to make sure that you wanted to marry her," she said offhandedly. "And to promise you that she would have you, if you do."

"What devilish thing have you got in your mind? You're talking in riddles."

"Well—I'm afraid that if I told you you wouldn't want to marry her," she said cunningly.

"What? Spill it, I say! I'm no saint. I don't want any goddam virgin to break in. But I know. You'd tell me she's carrying on with Biddow. I guessed she was in love with him." Angered, jealous, mortified and disillusioned together, Bardia grabbed at Blanche and pulled her towards him. "Now what about you and me? You've got me going."

Blanche pushed him away. "Get away. That's all finished."

"Got somebody else, eh? Fraser still, is it? I'm up to your tricks."

Blanche gasped. "Stupid, silly rot! I never had Fraser! I—I'm going to have a baby, that's what."

"Oh!" Bardia fell back from her. "Sorry," he muttered. He turned to his horse and swung into the saddle. "If you can do me a good turn with the girl I'd be obliged. But no dirt, mind you. I want her willing." He struck the horse with the flat of his hand on its neck and made off.

Blanche looked after him for a few moments, then, lifting the skirt of her riding habit, set out briskly for the homestead.

Straight up to Cindie's house she went, up the stairs and into the bedroom which formerly had been her own and Biddow's.

Cindie was getting ready for bed. Hearing Blanche's steps she turned with surprise and, when she saw that flushed face with the eyes gleaming and the flesh of it seeming to quiver with triumph, a dreadful feeling of evil and disaster over- whelmed her. She sank down on to the side of the bed, sucking in her breath.

"It's all right, Cindie." A sibilant murmur. "I just came up to tell you how pleased I am that you are taking up with Florenz Bardia. That suits me, Cindie. It would suit us all. It would solve a lot of problems if you married Bardia, Cindie. I would be able to go down to Brisbane without worrying about you and Randolph."

Cindie's mouth dropped open in sheer astonishment. "But —but I am not going to marry Bardia," she stuttered.

"But I want you to marry him, Cindie." The voice was still silkily soft. "In fact, I insist on your marrying him, Cindie. And why not? He's handsome. He's got money. He could help you in your money-making schemes, Cindie."

"The woman's mad," Cindie told herself, fearfully. "Mad as a March hare. Careful, now. Careful."

"You had better go home to bed, Mrs. Biddow," she said aloud, gently. "We can talk about this in the morning."

"No. We shall talk about it now, Cindie." The soft- ness suddenly gave way to a harsh grating note. Blanche's eyes shot fiery hate. "You will marry Bardia or I will go back to Mr. Biddow's bed, Cindie. I will let him take his chance. Or make you tell him, Cindie. Or make you tell him!" Her voice rose. "Make you break up his home, Cindie! Make you explain to Irene and Randy, Cindie!"

Cindie brushed a hand in front of her eyes. She clutched at a bedpost for support. "Mrs. Biddow, you are mad," she whispered. "Things like this can't happen."

"But they do, Cindie, they do. Make up your mind. Make it up now, you bitch! Or I go into Biddow's bed to-night."

Cindie went to the toilette stand and poured herself a drink of water. She drank and then, pulling herself together, turned to Blanche. "All right," she said, quietly. "You go into his bed. And I won't tell him, Mrs. Biddow, *I won't tell him*."

An awful stillness fell between them. All around them. Their eyes were locked. Not more than half a minute went by but Cindie, beating out of life with her indomitable will the vaunting, madly-arrogant assurance of the other, felt herself a-swing in breathless space for time unlimited.

Then Blanche began to crumble, in body and mind. Her hate, her rage, seeped out of her. The colour drained out of her face. Her eyes closed. She swayed, put out a hand as though to steady herself against the air. And Cindie stood and watched her, knowing that she had scored again, scored finally, her stomach fluid, her breast filled with pitying anguish. Then Blanche turned and went from the room. Cindie listened to her steps, feeble and fumbling, upon the stairs. She resisted the impulse to run out to the balcony and watch. No. She must not look upon that horrific defeat. She threw herself upon her bed and clasped her hands over her eyes. But still she could hear those fumbling steps. . . .

But the avidly curious mind behind another pair of eyes knew no reason for scrupulous avoidance of Blanche's shambling progress down towards her home. Melatonka watched her come down the stairs and, after pausing at the bottom, shuffle off. And the difference between the steady swiftness of her walk a few minutes agone, when making up to Cindie's, and her drunken gait now, made his eyes bulge to pierce the darkness in search of a solution. She couldn't be drunk. He knew that. The boss's Missis did not get drunk. Then she was sick. But why was she wandering alone in the night? Ah! She had tripped over her habit. She recovered herself with difficulty, stood swaying for some moments and then sank down on to the ground.

Now, had Melatonka been in his normal coolly calculating senses, not befuddled with drink, he would have made off in this pass and hidden his head beneath his blanket. As it was, his halting progress towards Blanche was dictated by nothing more than consuming curiosity interlarded with a faint desire to help. Blanche sat so still. She had folded up limply, sat perfectly still, her head sagging.

"Maybe she dead," Melatonka muttered. He moved forward softly till he was standing beside her.

And suddenly Blanche's head jerked up, as though she had come out of a coma. The Kanaka jumped back with fright. He turned to fly but Blanche's voice, low but urgent, halted him. "Come here! Help me up!"

Melatonka went all a-tremble. "Not me, Missis!" he begged. "Not me!"

"Yes, you, you fool! Help me up. I've hurt my ankle."

Melatonka came close. "Me get Missie Cindie, Missis," he urged. The idea of touching this white woman gave him the creeps.

"You'll do nothing of the kind. Put your arm around me and steady me. Lift me. . . . That's right." Erect, Blanche put all her weight upon one foot and leant heavily upon the man. "Now help me to my room. Quiet, I say!"

It was Blanche's contempt for the black man, far more than her distracted condition, that led her to commit the ultimate stupidity of ordering Melatonka to carry her up the steps to her room.

"She alla same flash girl in back street." The thought ran like fire through his mind as, at the bottom of the steps, he put his powerful arms about her body, lifted her and ran up them.

Through the open louvres of the sleep-out the starlight plainly showed him the big bed. He put her down carefully, but when Blanche whispered fiercely: "Now get out!" he continued to bend down to her.

There was a cataclysmic silence.

The man loomed above her. The pain of her ankle, her perverted hates, the exotic exhalations of Melatonka, all focused into one central point in her brain and flamed into ravening desire.

That she had reached the end of her tether Blanche knew. She must leave Folkhaven, leave Ranny. Leave Cindie in possession of the field. So be it, then. Her eyes closed. A prodigious sigh floated from her lips, a realizable renunciation of everything in life that she had hitherto cherished. . . .

CHAPTER XXXIII

THE AFTERMATH?

After a sleepless night Cindie rose at daybreak determined to put an end once and for all to the whole affair. How, she had not yet decided. Let events shape their own course. A few days' companionship with Randy and then somehow, some way, she would compel Blanche to go south.

But on descending to go about her usual morning round she was met at the foot of the steps by Tirwana, his whole aspect ill-omened and forbidding. One glance at him and Cindie asked wearily: "What is it now, Tirwana?"

"Miss Cindie, Melatonka's not here."

"What do you mean: not here?"

"I mean what I say. Melatonka has gone."

"Well, what of it? I suppose the wretched man has stayed out with one of his women. He'll turn up. I'll have something to say to him, too, when he does." She turned away impatiently but Tirwana stepped along with her.

"Miss Cindie, it's not so easy. Oh, God damn, I don't know what to say!"

"Why, Tirwana!" Cindie stared at him. His face had gone the colour of putty. "There's something really wrong! Tell me, Tirwana, quick."

The man took a red bandanna handkerchief from his pocket and mopped his brow. His eyes rolled. "I don't know how to tell you, Miss Cindie. Melatonka, I think he's gone for good. I think he's gone bush."

"What? Tell me the truth, Tirwana! Stop fooling."

"Miss Cindie, you know I go up to the hospital hut to give the quinine to Tabby at nights. Well, Tabby was very sick last night, so sick that I stayed with him for long time. And when I am coming down here to bed I see—I see— Miss Cindie, I hate like hell to tell you this—I see Melatonka come out of—out of——" He swung round and pointed towards Blanche's sleep-out, "*out of that room.*"

"Oh no! Oh no!"

"Hold on to me, Miss Cindie. Hold my arm. I saw it."

"Tirwana!" Cindie's voice sounded hoarse in her own
ears. "He must have gone to steal. Mrs. Biddow, she slept in
the house last night."

"No. She slept there. I waited. I waited to make sure.
I hung round and in two, three minutes, the light went on
in that room. Melatonka, he's not a thief. And now he's
gone."

"All right. . . . You see to things, Tirwana."

As Cindie walked up the steps to the sleep-out she ran
her tongue over her dry lips. The door was closed. She
opened it without knocking and went in.

Blanche was still sleeping. Her lovely face was cradled in
the hollow of one arm. Her short black curls were tumbled.
Blue-black fingermarks lay in the hollows beneath her eyes.
Her pink lips were pressed tightly together. Even in sleep
there was an air of strain about her, and as Cindie stepped
within the room and quietly closed the door behind her,
tears sprang to her eyes and ran down her face unchecked.
Gingerly she sat down on the bottom end of the bed and let
her eyes, drenched with tears, dwell upon the photos of
Irene and Randy that stood in silver frames on Blanche's
dressing-table. But now they did not seem to be so important, those two. The extremity of their mother's predicament woke in Cindie a faint resentment against the settled
and secure. When Blanche at length moved and on the
moment of full wakefulness uttered a cry of pain, Cindie
turned a face full of humility and sympathy towards her.

"Get off the bed," cried Blanche. "My ankle!"

"What's the matter with your ankle?"—quietly.

"I sprained it last night. . . . What are you doing here?"

"I don't know." Cindie nodded her head with the action
of an old, tired woman. "Unless it's to tell you that Melatonka's cleared out."

Nothing more was said by either for some time. Both
were emotionally exhausted, incapable and contemptuous
of further heroics. Neither felt curious about that which
lay between them, unexplained. Blanche spoke first. "I
can't go down to the Port with Randolph to meet the boy.
I'll have to lay up till my ankle is better. Then I'll go down
to Brisbane."

"Yes. That's the best thing to do. Maybe you could learn something about—about the time limit of things. A year or two there and maybe you'll be back. Let me see your ankle." Cindie tossed the covers aside and examined the swollen blue ankle. "I'll tell Mr. Biddow. And bring some hot water and bathe it."

Shortly Biddow stood in the doorway and looked in. "How did you come to do it?" he asked aloofly, without interest.

"Tripped over my riding habit. No need for you to bother. . . . Oh, Randolph, I've decided to go down to Brisbane, after all. As soon as my ankle is better."

"That suits me." He turned on his heel.

Since the exact time of the arrival of the steamship bringing Randy could not be computed, Biddow left for the Port immediately after breakfast. "If Melatonka doesn't turn up before lunchtime," he told Cindie, before driving away, "you had better notify the police."

"Much good that would do," muttered Cindie, looking after the four-in-hand phaeton as it swung down the track. "Poor devil."

Saddling her horse, Cindie took her way across the paddocks in search of Verbena's Billy. Him she sent off to search for Melatonka. No doubt in her mind but that the Kanaka had taken refuge with the Aborigines. "Just tell him that Miss Cindie wants him to come home, Billy," she advised. "Tell him I'm not angry with him for staying away. Bring him straight to me."

Before lunchtime Billy came riding up the track with Melatonka astride the horse behind him. Cindie, informed of their approach by Verbena's little boy, ran out on to her balcony and called to them. "Thanks, Billy. Melatonka, come up here to me."

At the top of the stairs she met the man and without preamble began: "Melatonka, I want you to go out and work at the coffee mill for me. Come into the kitchen and I will give you your dinner. Then we shall go out together." She pretended not to notice the shifty, frightened eyes, the trembling hands.

Before she left him, at the mill, she gave him stern instructions. "Melatonka, you realize that everyone on the farm,

Mr. Biddow included, knows that you stayed away last
night because you got drunk and forgot to come home. And
that you've got to live out here for a fortnight as a punishment. So you had better stop here, Melatonka. You don't
want to be shot, do you, Melatonka?"

"Missie Cindie, I do as you say. I pleased to stay here,
Missie Cindie. Me pleased."

"All right. In two weeks' time you may come back to the
homestead."

"No, Miss Cindie. Me never want to go back. Me
'fraid."

At about five o'clock in the evening the four-in-hand came
bowling up the track. Cindie, whose natural resilience had
rapidly disposed of her mental and physical fatigue once
things had been straightened out, for hours had been restlessly waiting. Blanche had lain all day on a couch on the
front veranda, still, worn-looking, taut. Not once did she
mention to Cindie the name of her son.

At the approach of the vehicle Cindie called out to Blanche
and then ran down the track to meet it. She laughed aloud
with excitement when she noted, from a distance, how the
boy had grown. Boy? That was no boy! The *man* sitting
beside his father was the taller of the two. He was waving
to her, shouting. Biddow's face was beaming.

The horses, spanking along at the behest of Randy's desire
to be home, maintained their speed till almost upon Cindie
and then were pulled up with a jerk. They flung their heads
high, champed their bits, stamping and shaking their collars
as though they, too, were imbued with the excitement of
events. Now Randy was leaping over the wheel. He was
crying: "Cindie! Old Cindie!" He was clasping her in his
arms. She felt he was close to tears. "Oh, Cindie, it's good
to be home!"

Biddow drove on towards the stables.

"Your mother, Randy." Cindie gave the boy a reminder.
"She is waiting for you on the veranda."

"Mother! Yes, Mother!" He flew up the steps.

Cindie waited where she was for a time, assimilating with
joy the picture of the boy. He must be nearly six feet. And
he only seventeen! Big boned and raw, but when he filled

out—what a man! The perfect bony structure of the face, the great golden eyes with their black lashes, the big chiselled nose, the wide, clean-cut mouth. Everything about him was big.

She shook off the enchantment of the moments of reunion. She must have a word with Biddow and then superintend the preparation of the evening meal at the big house. She had herself cooked the meal, special delicacies for Randy. She followed up Biddow, to meet him hurrying back from the stables.

"What do you think of him, Cindie?" he asked, giving her shy, proud glances.

"Hasn't he grown!" She laughed. "He's miles bigger than you, Mr. Biddow. He's a man." She walked back beside him. "But I came up to tell you, Mr. Biddow, that Melatonka is back. I have put him out at the coffee mill for a fortnight as a punishment for staying away. Billy can take his place in the cane."

"All right. The farm can go hang to-night, Cindie." He went up the front steps of the house and Cindie went round to the back.

"Now, Charity," she cried blithely, "we've got to do ourselves proud to-night. Our Randy's home."

With everything prepared, she went up to her own place and, waited on by Verbena, ate her own meal in happy solitude. No more misery. Of that she was determined. No sense in worrying about "might-bes". It was too much to think that Biddow, at third-hand . . . In any case he could take his hurdles when he came to them.

Her simple meal over, she went on to her balcony, as usual, and sat there. Ah! There was the boy, standing with his father on the steps of the big house, looking over the place. Cindie leant over the railing and called out: "What do you think of your farm, Randy?"

"I'll be able to see it better from there," he called back and without more ado came hurrying up the rising ground. Biddow followed at his leisure. When he came to his favourite outdoor seat, the old stump, he halted, looked down at it, then seated himself on it and took out his pipe.

"Cindie, it's too good to be true, to be home again."

Randy lounged beside the girl and scanned the fields. "Listen! What's that call, Cindie? I don't remember ever hearing that." The whooping call of a coucal had sounded from the cane.

"It's a new bird, Randy. Only recently came down from the Tablelands to the coast. A big brown bird with a beautiful tail. The Englishmen say it's like the English pheasant. That's what they are calling it, a pheasant."

"Oh! . . . I feel I can't get started on the farm work soon enough, Cindie. . . . Let's pick up Dad and go up to see the Kanakas. . . . But what's all this, by cripes!"

Up the track came a procession. Several vehicles preceded by a cavalcade of young men and women.

"Looks like a surprise party, Randy," laughed Cindie. "There's Caro Montague and Jeff Grey in front. Come on!"

CHAPTER XXXIV

BY THE END OF 1904, THE WINDY POLITICAL SPARRING OF THE sugar industry in general around the White Australia policy had languished. Even the big sugar planters of the far north had bowed to the inevitable and, despite an aggravation of their mortification by a hardening of the sugar markets all over the world, due to the abolition of bounties to European beet sugar and the recent failure of the European crops, nursed their anger and disgust in comparative quiet.

The Federal Government, from which they had hoped so much, "had sold them a pup by its crawling to the Labour scoundrels" the big planters, with few exceptions, hated and despised. They still urged their demands for the right to retain indefinitely those Kanakas already in the country but mostly their efforts were directed towards procuring an extension of the bounty on white-grown sugar to cover a further ten years beyond its present time limit, the end of 1906.

Latterly, too, the political history of Queensland had included some stirring events which accentuated the worries of those planters who regarded any diminution of the privileged position they had occupied in the past as unwarrantable and disastrous. Due to internecine party strife, the tory Government of Queensland had collapsed, and from the resultant elections, in August, a coalition tory-Labour Government had assumed office. Immediately following, the pressure of Labour had secured certain progressive legislation affecting wages and conditions, a bitter pill for the employers of cheap labour to swallow.

Throughout these happenings, these same big men played safe by sub-leasing more and more of their land to Chinese. Short term leases, for the White Australia policy was aimed first and foremost at the tens of thousands of resident Chinese.

In the Masterman area, the remainder of the available land suitable for cane growing had been parcelled out among white or Chinese selectors. The whites, with rare exception, were families who, with the assistance of a few Kanakas and odd remittance men, toiled and moiled to put the pioneering stage behind them before the deportation of the Islanders became due. Thenceforward, family labour on its own, in the event of white labour failing to materialize, could hope to carry on. The Chinese pursued their time-honoured policy of semi-feudal communal production.

Barney Callaghan had accepted the inevitability of the passing of his Kanakas with bitter anger and, in respect of some of his old hands, grief at the prospect of losing men who had stood to him as trustworthy friends. So far as was possible he took advantage of the compassionate provision made to cover the cases of Kanakas who had acquired property and settled in working occupation upon it. His foreman, Tommy the preacher, had long ago returned to the islands to undertake Missionary work among his brethren. His successor, who had married an Aborigine woman, and Mary the Kanaka and her second husband, Barney had settled in freehold tenure each upon a few acres of good land. For the rest, he was allowing his Kanakas to repatriate as their terms of indenture concluded, and gradually leasing out the major portion of his land.

With the couple of dozen Hindus Barney had indented
he had formed no sentimental attachment.   The Hindus
lacked almost entirely the emotional appeal of the fun-
loving, musical Islanders.   The Islander, with his wild
freedoms, told the white man plainly, by his manner if not
by speech: "You're the boss. You've got me down. But
I'm not ashamed to be black. I like to be black. I spit and
I laugh." The Hindus were standoffish. As Barney himself
expressed it, they acted like black white men, neither one
thing nor the other. They were filled with the corruption
of self-pity.   They acted *wounded*, which roused Barney's
ire.

On Glenelg, the same process of leasing, often with clause
of purchase, was taking place, but to a lesser extent. For
the Montague clan, what with sons, sons-in-law and their
offspring, in themselves were capable of encompassing the
husbandry of the major part of their two thousand acres.

Folkhaven was one of the first far northern plantations to
engage white labour to an appreciable extent. During the
"wet" of 1903, Cindie had gone down the coast to the main
south Queensland sugar centres and brought back a picked
gang comprising a dozen white workers. The high wage of
thirty shillings a week and keep, with good accommodation
and work all the year round, were the terms of engagement.

On the receipt of an intimation from Cindie of the promised
success of her mission, Biddow had set the Kanakas to work
building two-bed huts in barrack form on the seaward side
of the orchard and vegetable gardens. These he furnished
simply but comfortably and into them the white workers
settled on their arrival.

Minor troubles during that first year had been profuse.
During the first week of the cut one man died of a bite
from a death adder. Almost all the white workers became
addicted to boils, attributed by some to the dust in the
cane, by others to the eating of an inordinate quantity of
mangoes.

There were also drunken quarrels among the whites and
much strife, both open and covert, between a certain type
of white workman and the Kanakas. But on the whole,

the second year of the employment of white labour revealed a profitable result in comparison with that of the Kanakas. The better ratoons got in 1904 from the cleaner and lower cut sticks more than compensated for the extra shilling a ton the white labour cane cost to harvest.

By the end of December, 1904, not more than a dozen Kanakas remained on Folkhaven. Men selected by Biddow on the basis of friendship engendered by long association and retained on exceptionally favourable terms. Melatonka was not among these. Sow was. For his own sake and also because of Cindie's affection for and valuation of Charity, his wife. For the past eighteen months Sow had been established on an acre of freehold fenced off from the horse paddock. To Tirwana, Biddow had sold his last ten acres of virgin land. The working of these was carried out as part of the farm routine, Tirwana taking the profits and his keep in lieu of a salary from Biddow.

With the exception of Sow and Tirwana, Biddow intended that 1905 would see the last of Kanaka labour on Folkhaven and its registration as a white labour holding. He had no qualms whatever about the result. He had long renounced all sympathy with those of his neighbours who persisted in trotting out the bogy of inevitable ruin with compulsory white labour.

To Tom Hilliard—whose favourite pastime of late years had been trying to crawl back into the Labour fold he had in the first place deserted—Biddow wrote: "These grumblers simply will not acknowledge any sort of justice in the reduction of enormous profits. I have proved that sufficiently reliable white labour will settle down up here with the provision of good wages and conditions and, furthermore, that in respect of cane cutting, white labour is cheaper than coloured. All-the-year-round work, lacking machines, is a horse of a different colour. But with the air full of rumours of double- and triple-furrow ploughs, of a planting machine to replace hand labour, I'm not going to worry about that. The Callaghans hear from Cuba that the Louisiana planters are even trying out a cutting machine.

"What the big chaps fear is the capacity for struggle of the white workers. They are afraid to see duplicated in the fields the tendency among the mill workers to strike and struggle for better conditions.

"Take the position in our local mill. It has been able to continually effect improvements, at own cost and out of earnings, till to-day the capital invested represents not merely the original loan of sixty-six thousand pounds, but something much closer to one hundred thousand pounds.

"The price our mill pays for cane at present is fifteen shillings a ton. I averaged nearly twenty tons an acre for my four hundred acres this year. You can estimate the cash returns for yourself.

"This present good position cannot, of course, be maintained. A slump in production must accrue to the change over from black to white labour and white proprietorship. But the main factor in this slump will be the elimination of the Chinese, as proprietors and workers.

"For those of us who are securely settled, the main concentration from now on must be upon the procuring of field machinery, the encouragement of scientific cultivation. Science will have to show us how to return to the soil some essential growth factors the crops take out. This is the road of real progress and it will offset the cumulative process of higher wages and shorter hours. Obviously the sun is about to set upon this twelve hours a day business. . . ."

Not that Biddow, these days, found himself in command of a great deal of ready cash. Blanche, on behalf of herself and Irene, made heavy demands upon his resources.

For the first few months of his wife's absence, despite the companionship of Randy, Biddow had been forbiddingly close and reserved of manner. His hair had greyed and tended to thin at the top. He formed the habit of going off for long walks by himself. But time, coupled with the healing influence of youthful exuberance around him, brought a drowsy tranquillity of mind in its train and he had gradually reverted to his former mellowing approach to life. Randy's eagerness to come to grips with the problems of cane farming, during those first few months a bit of a strain on Biddow, came to be at once his pride and chief pre-occupation.

Early on, both Cindie and Biddow apprehended that the boy was not particularly clever. But allied to a radiance, a brilliance, of manner, he evinced a remarkable persistence in the pursuit of what he wanted, whether that was the knowledge of farm technique or some personal satisfaction. He had Blanche's persistence without her arrogance. He had intellectuality without being specially intelligent.

Cindie, lynx-eyed with her ever-growing love, came to feel, with deep joy in her ambition for him and anxiety for the farm, that Randy was exactly the type suited to the requirements of the then stage of development in cane farming. He was, in fact, a younger edition of her own creative spirit, with the added advantage of at least the beginnings of an organized, educated approach.

He held Cindie enthralled with interest and pride in his expounding of the odds and ends of information he had acquired, and soon had her immersed in the contents of the small library he had brought home with him. Yes, here was an outlook singularly fitted to deal with those problems upon the solving of which the intrinsic value of cane farming rested. Problems of pests, of improved canes, of improved cultivation methods.

Randy's interest in these things was intellectual and æsthetic. That financial success was corollary to achievement in these fields he took simply as a matter of course. His eager expectations were all bound up with an inherent demand for personal fulfilment in what was for him creative effort.

"It's like painting a picture or writing a book." Unburdening himself to Cindie became as natural to him as eating. "I know all about these big artist blokes. They find it hard work producing something big. They have to sweat and grind, Cindie, just like we do building the farm. Beating the borer, the grubs, selecting and experimenting with canes, the soil, it's like an artist trying out different combinations of paints, or a writer working out his problems. I reckon that to be a good farmer, Cindie, is as good as being a fine artist. That's how it looks to me. I bet no artist ever painted a finer picture than our paddocks of cane present in the sunset, Cindie."

"Ah, yes, Randy," Cindie had replied wistfully. "But replacing the Kanakas by whites means taking the most

colourful thing out of cane farming for me. The black
bodies of the Kanakas amongst the golden cane: there's a
picture for you, Randy! Black skin is so velvety and shining.
And their singing! Randy, what shall I do without the
singing of the Kanakas? Our whites are so—so dry! There
seems to be no joy or romance in them.

"The blacks have educated me, Randy. Our own Aborigines and the Kanakas. Their talk of the earth, the sea, the
sky, of bird and animal life, their spirit worlds. I can't
bother with the white workers, somehow. I suppose they
know about—things. I suppose they must have interests.
But if I speak to them about nature they look at me as though
I were mad. Once I asked a white worker: 'Don't you take
any joy in life at all?' And what do you think he said?
'You bet! Ever stuck yer nose in a pint of beer?' Now, if I
mentioned something about nature to a black he would tell
me more about it than I already knew."

"Yes, I know. I realize that, Cindie. But when the
whites were savages they must have been like the blacks are
now. I reckon that cuts both ways, Cindie. The blacks
have something the whites haven't got and vice versa.
There's something twisted in what's happened in between.
It's as though the primitive appreciation of nature and
beauty has been wrung out of the whites by civilization, like
wringing out a rag."

Yes, the three of them together, Biddow, Cindie and the
boy, built up an association that for the last two, at least,
for quite a time spelt something very near perfection. Sexual
desire had never played a part in Cindie's love for Biddow.
Her love had been kindling awaiting the application of the
torch of opportunity and physical contact. Revitalized by
the anguish of events pivoting upon Blanche, her love had
subsided again with Biddow's return to a semblance of contentment and by the end of 1903, had she taken time to
analyse her feeling for the man, Cindie would have had to
describe it as one of indulgent affection.

But Cindie did not take the time from the routine flow
of her days for self-analysis of any kind at that period. She
was drifting along, for the first time in her life a dreamer,
an impractical adolescent. When Biddow, Consuelo, Grey,

commented upon her gaiety, her easier, more elastic approach to things in general, she would laugh and insist that it was time she learned to laugh, time she "came unscrewed".

CHAPTER XXXV

BY THE MIDDLE OF 1904, PROBABLY BIDDOW HIMSELF, OF THE whole country-side, was the only man entirely uninformed on "what was going on at Folkhaven".

Cindie and Randy came to be together continually. In the beginning, Cindie had refrained from overmuch intrusion upon the company of the boy and his father, but on all counts that policy was soon overridden. For Randy would come yelling: "Cindie, hey, Cindie!" and if she failed to go down he would come up to her house. So, for Biddow's own sake, she had perforce to make one of a threesome at the big house. It was Biddow himself who suggested that she take her meals there. "Might as well act sensibly, Cindie. Silly to make unnecessary work for the maids."

Over a period, Cindie and Randy formed an even more efficient team than she and Biddow. The absence of any conventional ban upon their freedom of association meant that first impressions never got the chance to be lost. Nor were arguments limited. They spurred each other on, each stimulated the other's thought. They argued and fought things out in a way impermissible between her and Biddow.

Sometimes they clashed, and at such times feeling on Randy's part would tend to run high. More than once Biddow administered a quiet but effective rebuke to the boy for his lack of restraint in expressing his exasperation and rage over Cindie's restraining authority.

Really serious dissension arose over the matter of the disposal of the trash from the cane sticks. It will be recalled that Cindie and Biddow had tentatively agreed to experiment by burying the trash instead of burning in the hope of effecting an improvement in the soil.

However, immediately preceding the 1903 cane cut, a
flurry of argumentation broke out among sugar men around
that very subject. One group contended that burning helped
to keep the pests down, the grub and the borer which were
the chief destroyers of the cane. Others claimed that burning proved no deterrent to their increase.

Biddow and Cindie, already alarmed by the fact that
these pests, which in the pioneer years of that area had been
non-existent, were now in evidence, in fear revoked their
intention to bury the trash. The risk was too great. Green
manures for the cultivated fields were becoming a pressing
problem, it was true, but the threat of an increase of pests
was frightening. On the older-settled lands their ravages
had been in many cases ruinous.

Randy, one evening at the dinner-table, argued this
point. "Look here, Dad, I don't agree! The pests have
only recently come into this area, haven't they? Right.
And all you farmers have consistently burned the trash.
Right. Stands to reason, then, that they will keep on multi-
plying whether you keep on burning the trash or not. You
are on the wrong track. By burning we will get the grubs
and we won't get the benefit of burying the trash. I reckon
we should bury it, for one year, at least."

"We get some benefit from burning, Randy," said Cindie.
"We get the ash."

"But not the equivalent of green manures, which are the
problem in this area. You say the cow pea has proved a
failure up here. The soya bean almost as bad. And anyone
can see the deterioration in the cane on the cultivated
paddocks. I say: give burying a go for one year at,
least."

Biddow, partly through pleasure in the boy's interest,
would have acquiesced. But Cindie grew a little impatient.
"Randy, your father intends to plant the Mauritius bean
this year. According to reports from down south there's
not much chance of failure with that crop. We can't afford
to take risks with pests."

"But you've got to take risks, Cindie! I'm interested in
this grub business, I am. Dad, you've *got* to give me a chance
to experiment!"

"What about it, Cindie?" Biddow looked to her.

But Cindie, seeing in Biddow's willingness to indulge the boy merely another aspect of his characteristic passivity, and appearing in a really dangerous guise, stuck out for her point. "I say no, Mr. Biddow. You are letting yourself be influenced by your feeling for Randy, instead of by your own common sense. When I proposed last year to bury the trash the grub had scarcely made its appearance in this area. I had to wait on this argufying to connect the two things. This year above all we should take no risks. By next year we might have learned something more definite about the matter. It's a crying shame, I must say, that with the sugar now worth more to the State than all its other industries put together we can't get a first-rate entomologist trained in sugar work and an experimental station to help us solve these problems."

"There you are!" Randy exclaimed. "You say it yourself! We've got to do our own experimenting! Dad, do this much for me. You are cutting the cultivated paddocks first. Let me bury the trash on them and burn the volunteer crops."

"You will have to persuade Cindie, Son."

Flare up from Randy. "Why? Tell me that! Why should I have to persuade Cindie? Aren't you the boss of this place?"

"I am. And I'm telling you you will have to persuade Cindie." But Biddow's manner was soft and uneasy. His eyes were downcast. Cindie knew it hurt him to resist the hotly entreating eyes of the boy. Her own heart smote her as she looked from one to the other of them but she was inherently incapable of subjecting rule by head to the unreasoning appeal of any less reliable part of her anatomy. Burn or bury, she thought now, was not here the basic issue. That was Biddow's subjection of his judgment on emotional grounds, to Randy's "caprice".

With a furious glance at her, Randy flung away from them and went off by himself. Biddow started up to follow, then sunk back.

"Don't worry about him, Mr. Biddow," Cindie said gravely. "I'll talk it over with him."

"You will? Thanks, Cindie. I don't like to knock him back."

"I won't knock him back, Mr. Biddow." She flashed him an affectionate smile. "But I'll have to keep my head, you know. You would let him run away with you."

He gave back a shy, half-guilty glance that warmed Cindie. They sat on together, silent, in comfortable companionship.

But Randy's anger was as adolescent as everything else about him. It soon cooled and gave way to guilty trepidation. Cindie, sitting with Tirwana on her balcony in the twilight, saw him mooching down from the Kanakas' quarters, his head bent, his hands clasped behind him, the picture of disconsolation. She felt terribly sorry for him.

"Randy, Randy!" she called. "Come up here."

His head went up. His face flashed into a beaming smile. He paused for a moment, then set out with gigantic strides and flew up the stairs. He threw himself down at Cindie's feet and leant his head against her knee. "By cripes, I thought you'd be mad with me," he said naïvely.

Cindie ruffled his hair, smoothed back the errant lock with its swathe of gold that as usual sprawled down over his brow. "I was, too," she told him, with a semblance of severity belied by the twinkle in her eyes. "But maybe we shall compromise on the burning after all. You may burn the trash on the cultivated paddocks, if you like. That's if your father hasn't altered his mind."

"Aw, Father!" Randy snatched at the hand Cindie had dropped from his head and put it back there. "I like that, Cindie. You're the boss of this place."

"I am *not*. You tell him, Tirwana."

"Your dad's the boss, all right, Randy," said Tirwana. "You will know that if anything big happens. But he knows that Miss Cindie has done wonders for this farm. You had better know it, too."

"I do. I'm sorry, Cindie." He caught her hand and pressed it against his cheek.

Randy set to work to study the habits of the grey-back cockchafer and by that time the following year there was little he had yet to learn about it. 1904 saw an alarming spread of the ravages of the grub, but by 1906, by application of the knowledge he had acquired by means of observation, study and experiment, the pest had almost completely disappeared, not only from the fields of Folkhaven but also from those of the neighbouring farmers who had anxiously watched and then emulated his methods. The burning of the trash, he established, was no deterrent, because the grubchafer, as the beetle was then called, laid her eggs not on the leaves but in the soil. Besides, she laid in late December and January, by which time the crushing season, which gave the trash, was generally ended.

Cindie and Biddow followed the boy's activities with absorbing interest. 1903 was a dry year, which meant that the beetle, which needs rain to loosen the soil and permit of its tunnelling up from the depths beneath the cane sett, did not emerge from the ground until late December and January. Over the previous six months, by breaking open the soil beneath the ruined cane setts, Randy had followed the evolution of the grub through the chrysalis condition and when, late in December, the transformation of the pupæ into the beetle began to take place and he saw their emergence from the ground, his excitement knew no bounds.

The beetles had been about for some days before this eagerly expected event, a fact that puzzled Randy and exasperated him. Hot with botherment, he smote his brow and appealed to Cindie and his father. "How did they get out without my seeing them! Tell me that, Cindie! Tell me that, Dad! I've dug and seen them ready to emerge. I've sat beside their tunnels from dawn to dark and yet they've beaten me. How, how?"

"Try sitting beside their tunnels from dark to dawn, for a change," suggested Biddow. "There's no law to establish that they must emerge in daylight, I suppose."

"Why, no! Gosh, Dad, why didn't I think of that?"

Accompanied by Tirwana he went out at dusk to his chosen place of observation, and by the light of a frost-bright moon and two hurricane lamps set himself to observe. And dusk had scarcely deepened into dark before a veritable multitude of beetles were swarming up out of the ground about his feet.

Once on the surface, they crawled about excitedly, their antennæ quivering, trying out their elytra and large membranous wings. Finally they launched themselves into the air and flew about haphazardly. They swarmed about the artificial lights.

Tirwana was almost as excited as the boy, who was in ecstasy. But after an hour of watching Tirwana proposed that they go home. "You've seen now, Randy. What about bed?"

Randy was disgusted. "Tirwana! It's only begun. I've got to watch what happens now. They will *do* something, Tirwana. What they do next counts a lot."

What they did, after a time, was fly off to the nearest forest trees and settle on them at a height less than twenty feet from the ground. Little difficulty in following the general direction of the swarm. Not long after they had settled themselves on the branches and twigs a general copulation began to take place, after which the beetles again took to the air.

"Now what?" cried Randy, rushing around in attempts to keep some of them in sight. "We're losing them, Tirwana! They're going!"

And gone they were for that night. Vanished into the darkness of the trees.

But at dawn Randy was back in that area, this time accompanied by Cindie. Together they searched the trees. They found the beetles clustered in hundreds on certain types of trees, particularly species of fig, apparently asleep. Even when handled they showed little sign of life, simply dropping to the ground when released.

"See what that means, Cindie?" cried the boy. "These, evidently, are their food trees. They have fed themselves sick. See how easy to kill them when they are in this state?"

The upshot was daily excursions of organized groups in pursuit of the beetles. Experience revealed that an overcast sky at early morning gave the best results. The beetles were shaken or tapped from the trees on to hessian sheets spread beneath them, taken to the homestead and killed by being immersed in boiling water.

"Seems that the young fella is putting your nose out of

joint, Cindie," commented Grey, who had been one of the first to turn up to watch events.

"And don't I like it," was her rapturous response. "Our Randy's the real goods, believe me, Jeff."

"I believe you"—dryly. "You are thoroughly taken up with the boy, aren't you, Cindie?"

"You bet." Her manner became confidential. "Jeff, life is good, now. It's not all work. Not that I don't like work. You know I do, but a woman needs something else besides, Jeff. She needs to—to love someone, Jeff." Then, noting his discomfited eye, she blushed and added swiftly: "I mean —a woman needs to be—to be affectionate, Jeff, to be able to *show* affection for somebody. Not be shut up in herself all the time."

"Of course, Cindie, of course." Irrelevantly he added: "He's a big chap, isn't he? Quite a man."

"He's a man in size, Jeff, but in heart he's only a boy."

"Yes?—Biddow's Missis ever write about coming home, Cindie?"

"Well—no—not exactly. She wants to stay and keep Irene company."

Randy did not stop at collecting beetles. He devised field traps of a mixture of molasses and water placed beneath a light and found that these served a double purpose. They trapped the borer moth in addition to the grub beetles. To Biddow's proposal to chop down the food trees in the vicinity of the plantation, he opposed the argument that to leave the near trees standing was a better design, in conjunction with other methods of destruction commonly pursued by southern growers.

In 1904 and thenceforth, all cane revealing signs of grub infestation was cut before it matured. The roots were removed and the larvæ which bored beneath them taken out. After this, the cultivated lands, always the worst infected, were ploughed, replanted, uprooted, ploughed again, fallowed for a season, then ploughed over and over till the ibis, crows, egrets, magpies, butcher birds, kookaburras and hawks which customarily followed the plough, ceased to do so. The land was kept on the go.

CHAPTER XXXVI

THEN, IN THE EARLY SUMMER OF 1904, THERE CAME THE DAY when Cindie was blasted out of her world of happy security by having her eyes opened to Randy's more than friendly interest in Caroline Montague.

In the past, it had been the boy's habit to give Cindie a shout whenever he was about to set off for Glenelg; but recently he had taken to disappearing quietly. He had dropped his week-end practice of accompanying Cindie and Tirwana on fishing and hunting trips. To Cindie's guileless questions he gave such foolishly noncommittal answers that she was bound to recognize dissimulation, but so lost was she in her fool's paradise of self-delusion that the line of her suspicions veered in any direction but that of the truth.

"Randy's up to something," she said worriedly, to Biddow, on one such occasion. "I don't like his going off by himself constantly like this."

"I wouldn't worry," was Biddow's equable reply. Cindie gave him an impatient look but forbore to tell him that she suspected the boy was involving himself in the gambling practices of the whites.

Bardia, it was, who at length jolted her into realization of the truth.

At intervals since Blanche's departure Bardia had made unsolicited appearances at Folkhaven. He was impelled to this course more by the pricks of mortified vanity than by any hope, these days, of finding favour with Cindie in either a business or personal capacity. Some time, somehow, if he only stuck around, a ray of light might be thrown upon the dark and puzzling happenings of that time when his hopes in relation to the girl had been raised, fantastically, by Blanche and then as fantastically blasted. For on his succeeding visit to Folkhaven, undertaken less than a week later, Blanche had been "ill", and Cindie had curtly begged to be excused. Some funny business was the core of that whole queer bag of tricks, Bardia had cunningly conjectured.

The more recent rumours connecting Cindie's name with Randy's gave him to cynical chuckling but at the same time to a reluctant disbelief. Impartially deliberate, out of his own experience and ability to estimate character, he surmised Cindie's innocence of sexual intrigue. Up to date, at any rate. He knew the look, the "feel", of virginity in woman, did Bardia. The "old girl", for some devilish reason of her own, had put it over him that night about Biddow and the girl. His own heat had beguiled him into accepting something his mind, in cool deliberation, rejected.

At the same time, a very few minutes in the company of Cindie and Randy together apprised him of the real nature of her absorption in the boy. So, when it happened that on a Sunday morning he saw Randy and Caroline together at the Port in circumstances that permitted intimate observation, he took to the saddle with alacrity and satanic anticipation of "getting a little of his own back".

He bided his time until he had Cindie and Biddow together under his eye at the table before launching his arrow at the woman's heart. And then he did it so swiftly that Cindie had no time to cover up, even had she possessed the artifice to enable her to do so.

"Looks as though there's going to be a wedding in the family, Biddow," he said genially, with all his effeminate charm to the fore.

"Wedding? What family?"

"Why, yours, old man. I saw Randy down at the Port with Caroline Montague this morning and anybody could see with half an eye that he is nuts on the girl."

Biddow laughed. "That's news to me. To you, too, isn't it, Cindie? . . . Why, what's up?" His face straightened with consternation. For Cindie's face had gone chalk-white, her eyes on Bardia dilated with a kind of staring pain, her mouth was slightly open, and stiff, as though her lips would not close.

"Cindie, are you ill?" Then, assisted by the malice of Bardia's gnome-like grin, Biddow took the full force of the truth. He jerked his head back, then, his expression harsh, even fierce, he leant forward and administered a sharp slap to the girl's hand. "Do you hear me, Cindie? Are you ill?"

The hand he had smacked went up and passed over the

girl's eyes. "What? . . . What's that? . . . Yes. . . . Yes,
I believe I am ill. My—my head aches."

"Go and lie down, then." Biddow responded instantly to
the wild appeal of her eyes. A wave of compassion swept
away his severity. He made an effort to shield her from the
mocking intruder he detested. "These turns are getting a
little too frequent, of late, Cindie." Glibly he fabricated.
"We shall have to have them seen to. You will excuse her,
Bardia."

"Naturally"—suavely.

Automatically Cindie rose and walked from the room.
Biddow returned to his meal and aloofly took up conversation with his guest. "She works too hard. That's the trouble,
Bardia. Often like this lately. I must send her away for a
trip."

"So? Yes, a trip. Nothing like a change to buck a person up."

Biddow worried himself sick. After getting rid of Bardia,
an easy task once the man's purpose had been achieved, he
seated himself on the front veranda and cogitated agitatedly
on the ramifications of this dreadful revelation. Poor, poor
Cindie! Tough luck. But this time, he determined, there
were no two ways about things. She must go away. Farm
or no farm, she must go. A world trip, that was what she
needed. Damn it all, the whole thing was outrageous. A
mature woman. A kid like Randy. A natural transference
of her—her liking for himself, he supposed. Biddow blushed
in his solitude. His modesty precluded the admission of the
word "love" in such respect.

The afternoon wore on and Biddow mooched about the
homestead miserably. Continually he glanced up at Cindie's
house. Eventually, impelled by sympathy and duty alike, he
climbed the stairs.

"Cindie," he called softly, from the kitchen.

An immediate creaking of her bed was followed by her
appearance in the doorway of her bedroom. "Do you want
me for something, Mr. Biddow?" she asked.

At the sight of her Biddow himself suffered. Like a rock,
he told himself. She's like a rock. The hardness of her, the
determined will to endure that encompassed her like a shell,
was a physical hurt to him.

"I just wanted to know how you were doing," he stammered. The notion he had had of sympathizing, of holding her hand, maybe, seemed now fantastic.

"I'm all right. Don't let's pretend, Mr. Biddow. Pretending gets you all mixed up. I'm all right. This business of Randy and Caro: it would be just the thing, wouldn't it? Just right for the boy."

"Uh—er—well, yes, I suppose so," Biddow faltered. Then with a tremendous effort he brought himself to the point of "common-sense" condolence. "It's the devil, Cindie! It—it couldn't be in any case, Cindie. You can see that? He's—he's only a boy."

"Are you assuming I could ever think otherwise?" Her look and tone were icy.

"No. No. I was only trying to help. Cindie, you must go for a long trip. A long holiday."

"I shall stay exactly where I am. This is my home. Unless you turn me out." She smiled grimly, her eyes never wavering from his.

"Don't be silly. I was only thinking of you." Biddow swallowed.

"I can think for myself, thanks." She turned back into her bedroom. Biddow, with a feeling of defeat and dissatisfaction, slowly returned to the big house.

When Randy returned home that night he was surprised to find his father sitting on the front steps. "Hullo, Dad," he ejaculated, as he rode past. "Not in bed, yet?"

Turning his horse into the paddock, Randy came down to the house and, after standing awkwardly beside the steps for a few moments, accepted his father's invitation to sit down. "Lovely night, Dad," he said loudly.

"Yes. Had a good day, Son?"

"Aw—all right."

Biddow gave him a keen look. "What's wrong, Son?"

"Nothing. There's nothing wrong with me." The tone was defensive.

"No?" In the silence that ensued Randy moved his big body restlessly. Shortly he rose. "Cindie's light's still on, Dad. Think I'll go up for a little while."

"No!" Biddow's tone was forceful. At the boy's astonished

stare he added swiftly: "Son, you take Cindie altogether too much for granted. It's too late to be bothering her. Time for bed."

"That's rot, Dad. I couldn't bother Cindie. I want to talk to her. I've got to talk to her!"

"You can talk to her to-morrow. I mean it, Son. Come on, now. We'll go to bed."

"Aw, all right"—sulkily. But Randy, who since his mother's departure had occupied the sleep-out, waited until he was sure that Biddow had retired and then skipped up the sward that separated the two houses.

Cindie heard his coming. She had heard him ride up the track, had stolen out and watched his light go on in the sleep-out. She had recovered from the most poignant of her suffering. For the last hour or two she had felt numbed. Numbed by her adamantine resolve to crush this astounding and idiotic "sentimentality" into nothingness.

Not that she was overwhelmed by Bardia's tidings in respect of the boy and Caroline.

That, she only half accepted. For Caroline had clung with extraordinary fidelity to her passion for Jeff Grey. Everybody knew it. The girl had been unable in the first place to conceal it and afterwards, with head high, had dared comment. Cindie scarcely took that matter into account in her tragedy of facing up to her own ill luck. How, how had her maternal love for a boy she had partially reared from babyhood converted into a mature passion for a man?

But now she panicked at Randy's coming. Her actions were dictated by instinct rather than by thought. She blew out the kerosene lamp and went out swiftly to meet him. They almost collided as he took the last two steps at a jump.

"Gosh!" Randy exclaimed as he clutched at her. "Nearly knocked you down."

"What are you doing up here at this time of night, Randy?"

"I want to talk to you, Cindie. I must talk to you!"

"Come on to the balcony." Cindie's whole body was tremblingly astir. He had kept his arm about her, had pressed her to him in the affectionate manner he had assumed with her since his return home. He put her into a chair, dropped on to the boards at her feet and leant his head against her knee. The old posture. But Cindie refrained from ruffling his hair and it pierced her heart that he did not seem to notice that. He did not, as usual, seek her hand and place it upon his head. He kept silent. And still.

"What's the matter?" she asked, gravely, at length.

"Cindie, do you reckon—I'm too young—to go after a girl?"

Cindie's pain seemed to float about her in the night, to pulsate in waves on the darkness. She kept her eyes tightly closed. "That depends, Randy. If you want to go after a girl I don't see how you can be too young. If the girl is young, too."

"She's older than I am. A little"—grudgingly. Then came an outburst of wounded feeling. "But she's a fool, really. She's got no sense. She's only a kid. I'm a man."

"Is it Caroline?"

"Why, yes!" He lifted his head and peered up at her. "How did you know?"

"Mr. Bardia was out here to-day. He told us something."

"Aw, that bloke. He's a bum bloke, that."

"Never mind him. What about Caroline?"

"She reckons I'm too young."

"Did she say so?"

"She said she likes mature men. Say, Cindie." He twisted himself round on to his knees and took both her hands. "Is is true, what they say? That she has been mad on Jeff for years?"

"If it is true, Randy, I don't think anything will come of it. Jeff is not a marrying man."

"True? True, Cindie? You know?"

"No, no! I can't really know, Randy!" Cindie's voice rose on the wings of racking jealousy that suddenly tore at her and bade her thrust him back, slap his face, send him sprawling. This was something new! She had never known jealousy like this! "I think so, that's all. He has told me."

She pulled her hands away from his. "Now you must go, Randy. I'm not well. I've been sick to-day."

"Oh!" He sprang up. "I'm sorry, Cindie. You go to bed." He spoke awkwardly and at the tone Cindie's love came swirling back to engulf the jealousy. She threw her arms round him.

"Randy, Randy darling! Don't you worry. You stick to it and she'll come round. I'll be all right to-morrow and then we shall talk again."

He gave her a quick hug and left her.

CHAPTER XXXVII

BUT THEY DID NOT TALK TOGETHER ON THE MORROW. BIDDOW found jobs for Cindie to do in Port Denham which kept her away from the homestead all day. Randy he kept busy till late at night, and the boy, unable for all his absorption in his own affairs to ignore the grim and ill-looking cast of Cindie's face, took his troubles with him to bed. But on the following day Cindie went out into the paddocks to him and asked him to accompany her on a visit to the coffee plantation. She was worried about the coffee plantation, she told him.

True enough. This year should have seen the maximum crop from the coffee trees but for the first time a bug had appeared in the bean and reduced the expected yield by half. As a consequence, coupled with the uncertainty of the labour situation in general, Cindie and Biddow were debating the wisdom of uprooting the trees in favour of sugar cane.

Immediately, in a carefully calculated manner, Cindie began to speak of the subject that lay between them. As she felt, like a shadow. She had been acutely conscious of the boy's sensitive awkwardness in her presence two nights ago; conscious that he felt she had fallen short of his expectations of her sympathy and help. Now, as he walked beside her, he was clearly under restraint.

She began with indomitable cheeriness. "Now, Randy. let's have this matter out. You really like Caro?"

"Gosh, yes, Cindie!" Instantly the restraint was cast aside. He began to swing along beside her, physical movement keeping pace with the eagerness of his mind.

"Not so fast, Randy, not so fast!" Cindie forced a laugh. "I can't run and talk, too."

"Cripes, Cindie, I'm a fool. You know, Cindie, I was thinking that you didn't want to talk—about Caro. You don't mind?"

"Of course not. I should think not. Who else should you want to talk to, I'd like to know. I've been ill, that's all. Now, tell me. Doesn't she like you a lot?"

"She treats me as though I were a kid. Sticks her nose in the air."

"But, Randy, you *are* young, dear. I understand that all young people fall in—in love. Lots of times. What do you expect of Caroline?"

"I won't fall in love lots of times, Cindie." He was dogged, now. "I reckon that in another year's time I'll be old enough to marry."

"Oh! Do you want me to—to *do* anything about it? I don't see what I *can* do."

"I—I thought you might let her know about—about Grey, Cindie. You know what they say, Cindie. That Jeff has always been after you."

"That's old stuff, Randy. Jeff is not after me, now."

"But he would be, Cindie, if you encouraged him." He stopped, swung round to confront her and took her by the shoulders. "You like him, Cindie, don't you? You don't want to be an old maid?" His voice and eyes pleaded.

"Randy, what are you asking me to do?" Cindie's voice was suddenly strident. She fell back, thrust his hands away from her.

His face fell wretchedly. He half turned, drooped his head and stood still. The errant lock of hair fell forward and hung away from his brow.

"Oh, Randy, Randy!" Cindie clasped her hands and gazed upon him with agonized eyes. "Are you asking me to

—to *marry* Jeff? But you can't want the girl that much, Randy! You're too *young*."

"I'm not." His eyes met hers. And for all their mist of tears Cindie saw in them that which made her quake with horror. Steadfastness, maturity, was there, but something else besides. Resentment against herself. They stared at each other. And gradually in Cindie's breast the horror dissolved and a terrible anger gathered in its place. It gathered and swelled till it seemed to occupy her whole cognizance and streamed in fiery shafts from her eyes.

At first the boy stood up to it. The heat of his resentment dried his eyes of mist and he continued to stare back at her. But as her anger swelled and swelled and stabbed at him he began to blink, his lips to quiver. At length he flinched, flung himself away from her and cried out: "I suppose I'm mad! I know I'm mad!"

Cindie drew a long breath. Her nostrils flared. "Mad, you say! Mad and selfish! Selfish as hell! But it's my fault! I've spoilt you! I've spoilt you all! Old Cindie, that's me! Just old Cindie, the burden carrier!" Here jealousy added fuel to the flames of her fury and made her tongue scorching hot, her aspect magnificently shrewish. "Now, it's: 'Cindie, marry Jeff so that Caroline can't have him! So that she will marry me! Cindie, you don't want to be an old maid!' You fool! You stupid fool!"

Randy was now staring at her in shocked astonishment, his mouth agape. And as he stared, inexperienced as he was he could not mistake the mainspring of the passion that convulsed her. His face went white, slowly, horror creased the skin around his eyes. And suddenly he flung up his hands and blotted out the sight of her.

The action, as though it had been a blow, smote the rage out of Cindie. With her hands pressed upon her breast she fought for calm. But she could not achieve it. All she achieved was an infinite anguish of regret that set her trying to pull his hands down from his face, imploring him brokenly for forgiveness. But Randy opposed his physical strength to her efforts. His arms were like iron against her.

At length Cindie desisted. She dropped her hands, stood perfectly still for a few moments, then set off walking, rapidly, in the direction of the coffee plantation. Randy put down his hands, looked after her dazedly and then wandered back to his work.

That scene, shameful in retrospect to the degree that for her very life's sake Cindie had to falsify it, gloss it over, stabilized her future behaviour. Not dreaming that she had betrayed herself to the boy she set herself to the adoption of a straightforward, companionable attitude which, while acknowledging the rupture, yet consigned it to oblivion. To her next meeting with Randy she brought a rueful smile, a squeeze of his arm and a lightly spoken: "Sorry, Kid. But it hurt me terribly to have you want to get rid of me by marrying me off. Maybe I will marry Jeff some day. If he will have me."

But Randy was unable to reciprocate her unreserve. Involuntarily his arm jerked away from her touch. He blushed furiously and averted his head. "That's all right, Cindie," he mumbled. "Sorry."

His subsequent persistent avoidance of being alone with her, though misconstrued by Cindie, made her vastly thankful. The boy took care that she did not see his surreptitious appraisement of her, his stealthy incredulous stares.

But as time passed and Cindie's resolve to assist him strengthened and she began to seek out Caroline and play a part in bringing them together, Randy began to think that his imagination had played him false. The mounting feverishness of his desire for a scoffing Caroline, his wretched loneliness of spirit, gradually enforced a return to at least a semblance of the old comradeship with Cindie. Particularly was this so after Cindie began to go around with Jeff Grey, to chum up with him in Caroline's presence, to hint to the girl of some special bond between her, Cindie, and Jeff.

However, it cannot be said that Cindie was distressed by the girl's hostile reaction to her manœuvres. There were times, indeed, when Cindie's heart sang to the tune of Caroline's displays of jealousy and chagrin. The girl was incapable of restraint where Grey was concerned. She flagrantly competed with Cindie for his attentions. She stood up to her in the face of Grey, of Randy and anybody else, and with her pretty little face embattled tacitly, almost openly, challenged Cindie's assumption of prerogatives.

Even Randy was forced to see that Cindie's assistance was no assistance at all. For Caroline jeered at him about it, forthrightly accused him of engineering it.

"Old Cindie Comstock!" she flung at him one Saturday afternoon when Cindie had taken Jeff off against Caroline's demand that the two make up a full set on the tennis court. "Sticking her nose in where she's not wanted. It's like her cheek to think she can make me take up with you. As though I don't know all the yarns." With the cruelty of crass jealousy she deliberately chose her weapons and launched them at the boy. "I to take her leavings."

Randy looked at her in puzzlement. "Take her leavings," he echoed. "What do you mean?"

"As though you don't know!" The girl's lip curled in scorn. Her eyes beat at him with hate.

Randy grabbed her arm and jerked her towards him. "I don't know!" he shouted. "What do you mean?"

"You leave me alone, Randy Biddow!" she shouted back.

"You tell me what you mean!" He shook her.

She lifted her racket and hit him over the head with it. "That'll learn you, Mr. Smartie! Now you stick to your old woman Cindie and make her leave Jeff alone!"

To her surprise Randy burst out laughing. He laughed and laughed, while Caroline watched him in scornful fury. "Why, you're jealous of old Cindie!" he threw at her, at length. "You're jealous about me, Caro, not about Jeff at all. And you don't know it, that's all. Jeff's not a cradle-snatcher, Caro." He tapped her lightly on the head with his racket. "I've been taking you too seriously, Caro. I you don't look out you'll be left on the shelf, Caro. I'm the only man who seems to want you, Caro. And it's me you want, really."

But when the girl, at that, burst into tears, Randy's pretence of jocularity fizzled out. "Caro," he breathed, pleadingly. "What's the use of chasing after Jeff? You must see he doesn't want you."

"But he's *got* to want me," she moaned. "If you really liked me you'd see that and help me."

Randy ran a hand through his hair and spoke distractedly. "Caro, girls don't talk like that! It's—it's shameful, the way you talk. The way you run after Jeff. Girls should be —be modest."

She looked at him with a sudden hopeful gleam in her red-rimmed eyes. "Do you think Jeff would like me better if I were modest?"

"Oh gosh! How do I know? I like you! I'm mad about you and you're *not modest*. You—you're *terrible*."

Caroline calmed on the instant. She spoke contemptuously as she wiped her eyes. "There, you see. The modesty business is all tommy rot. But I'll get him. You wait. I'll get him."

Jeff Grey did not leave Cindie in any doubt as to his own understanding of her stratagem. That same afternoon he asked her if she really thought it necessary to give up her rest time to catering for Randy's demands.

"It's a kind of vanity, your noble self-sacrifice, Cindie," he told her with a grin. "Your vanity won't allow you to let that young whelp down."

"It's nothing of the sort," Cindie cried hotly. "It's something I've got to do."

"Well, you might as well give it up," he said, comfortably. "You can see plain enough that you're only putting the girl's back up. You're making things worse."

"You mean—you don't want to marry me, now, Jeff"— forlornly.

Grey frowned. He thought for some time before, very gently, replying: "You are the only woman I would ever marry, Cindie. At least, that's how it is with me, now. But you're not for me, Cindie. Don't pretend that you want to marry me."

"Couldn't you—couldn't you take the girl, Jeff? Couldn't you marry Caro? Randy would get over it, then."

"He'll get over it in any case. Look here, Cindie, you take my advice and stop meddling. You let things drift."

"Why?"

"Never mind why. Forget your vainglory and let others carry their own burdens. I haven't been around much but I've learned that it's good policy to let people work out their own problems where love is concerned. Randy's flame is burning too hot to last long."

After that Cindie had to realize the pointlessness of her line of action. Grey's responsibility balm to her conscience, she resolved to leave Randy to paddle his own canoe. She was very friendly with the boy, friendly in a bright superficial way that kept him and his aching desire for renewed confidences at a distance, that frustrated his burning curiosity about the abrupt termination of her recent renewed interest in Grey. Her manner in general was brittle, a manner so foreign to her and artificial that Biddow and Consuelo, her intimates, were embarrassed and constrained by it. It hurt her terribly to note the dimming of Randy's radiance under the consuming fever of his passion for Caroline, but, holding within her her resolve as though it were something that might spill out at the least unbending, she continued to meet his accusatory eyes with hard smiles, the questions that trembled on his lips with anticipatory evasions.

Thus they came to within a few days of Christmas. Then, without one word of warning, Blanche and Irene came clumping up the track in a gig hired from a stable at Port Denham.

CHAPTER XXXVIII

CINDIE, AT THE TIME, WAS GATHERING PAPAWS IN THE ORCHARD. She climbed down from her perch on a ladder that leant against the tree and, taking up her basket, made slowly up to the big house. Blanche and Irene stood beside the front steps, the girl looking about her with eager curiosity and her mother watching the unloading of a pile of luggage that was strapped on to the back of the vehicle.

Cindie came right to them before either of them spoke to her. Irene was the first to put out a hand. "Hullo, Cindie," she said shyly.

Blanche next. As she offered her hand she smiled graciously and said: "Well, Cindie, we're back."

Thoroughly upset, feeling as though a vacuum yawned in her stomach, Cindie confusedly grasped the hand in her own rough paw. And to her profound astonishment found that from its softness a tiny thrill of warmth and pleasure ran up her arm. Involuntarily her face broke into a smile and, as though Blanche's reappearance had bridged the intervening years with tolerance and forgetfulness and resuscitated her original frankness, she blurted out: "Why, Mrs. Biddow, I believe I am glad to see you!"

The statement, the truth of it shining from Cindie's eyes, threw Blanche in her turn into confusion. "Are you?" she gave back, with a rueful smile and shrug. "I hope Randolph can say the same. Where are they?"

"In the paddocks. Far out. The cut's nearly finished. I'll go out and bring them in."

"No, don't. They will be in to lunch, I suppose."

"Oh, yes."

What now? thought Cindie, as she made tea. The shock of their coming having passed, she trembled inwardly with feeling that was a mixture of foreboding, regret, and semi-pleasurable excitement. Blanche had altered. Superficially, at least. The bloom was off her physical beauty. Her hair was perceptibly greying. Her lips tended to droop. There was an air of repose about her that bordered on weariness. But Lord! wasn't she stylish! Her travelling suit was beautifully cut. The ground-length skirt flared from the knees down, the tiny waist of her jacket gave on to padded hips, her sleeves were prodigiously full, with elbow-length cuffs. The lace neck of her muslin blouse was stiffened by supports that reached behind the ears so that the frill around the top formed a delicate frame for her face. Her hat was a straw "sailor" perched sideways on the top of her curls and held in place by a voluminous white chiffon scarf tied beneath her chin in a bow.

Irene, too, was stylish. Her maid's frock of heavy tweed reached almost to the top of her buttoned black kid boots. She wore the same strangling lace neck gear as her mother but in the shape of a fichu. The same straw "sailor" perched on the top of her mass of burnished copper hair. Half of her hair was coiled on the top of her head, the rest hung below her shoulders and was tied by a wide cream ribbon at the base of her neck.

But apart from her hair Irene had little in the way of looks to commend her. Cindie was shocked to find how plain the girl had grown.

"You look well, Irene," she said as the three sat down together to take tea. "Your hair is still lovely."

"And my face is still ugly," laughed the girl. "Randy got all the looks."

"Your face is not ugly, Irene. And anyhow, you don't want to envy people with good looks. They don't get all they want out of life, not by a long chalk."

Blanche gave her old fascinating chuckle, a chuckle that had ever ill accorded with her autocratic bearing and looks. Her eyes met Cindie's, narrowed and cynical.

And while Blanche launched a series of questions at Cindie about the farm and the country-side, the latter, while replying, at the back of her mind pursued a secondary line of cerebration, concerned with the events that had determined Blanche's departure from her home. Time, apparently, had disclosed no ground for the most heart-rending of their fears. Still, it would be comforting to know how Fraser fared. . .

Obviously Blanche had come home "for good". Her line of talk established that. Obviously, too, she was not sure of Biddow's reception of her, for her luggage, she told Cindie, "would do all right in the corridor till Randolph came in". Conning over this aspect of things, Cindie shortly excused herself on the plea of a multiplicity of tasks connected with the Christmas festivities. Slipping up to the horse paddock she sent Kooka off with a message for Biddow and Randy; as a consequence of which the boy came tearing home long before the usual time. Biddow came in, too, but unhurriedly.

Biddow's face, as he came over the paddocks, reflected worry and vacillation, but when Irene came rushing up to meet him he opened his arms to her and melted into a mood of joyous welcome. He held her off and looked her up and down. "Quite the young lady, now, eh?"—judicially.

"I'm seventeen, Daddy. Mother says I may put my hair up at Christmas."

With arms interlocked they made down towards the house.

"And are you—accomplished, love?"

Irene screwed up her nose. "I am. I can recite and play the piano rather well. And that's all to the good, Daddy, with my looks, don't you think?"

"There's nothing wrong with your looks. Are you—is your mother home for good, Irene?"

"Oh yes, Daddy. Of course." She glanced at him with a tinge of surprise. "Aren't you glad, Daddy?"—more soberly.

"Yes, yes, of course I'm glad." Biddow drew a sigh of relief. That had settled things for him, at any rate. The interests of the children must come first.

Randy and Blanche were waiting for him on the front steps, and as he approached them Biddow's eyes dwelt on his wife with tolerant though keen appraisal. A faint smile twitched the corners of his mouth, indeed, as he glimpsed the trepidation behind her prideful attempt at cool assurance. He went up the steps and, taking her outstretched hand, leant forward and pecked at her cheek with his lips. "You should have let us know you were coming, Blanche." He gave her a smile and then let his eyes slide off her and on to Randy. "You look pleased, Son. Now you will have the job of making a farmer out of Irene."

"I knew you'd be busy, Randolph," said Blanche, as they turned to go indoors together. "Oh, my luggage is still in the passage. I thought I had better consult you about the room we shall occupy."

Biddow's brows came down. "We'll have a talk, Blanche. . . . You will excuse your mother and me for a while, Irene."

In his bedroom Biddow took a chair, straddled it and faced Blanche, who sat on the side of his bed, upright and wary, but lacking, he noted, her old air of domineering self-confidence. For some moments they gazed at each other silently, then Biddow said: "You've aged, Blanche."

"Is it necessary to remind me?"

"Why?"

"What do you mean?"

"Why have you aged so much in so short a time?"

She shrugged. "The natural course of events, I suppose."

"How's your health?"

"There's nothing wrong with my health." His dark expression and narrowed eyes warned her. "Oh, you mean the trouble I had before I went away," she added hastily. "That's all right. I told you in my letters that that had been fixed up."

"Yes. You told me." Biddow's eyes fell to the floor. His brow wrinkled.

"Randolph, if you don't want to sleep with me, say so," Blanche said sharply. "I was not particularly anxious to come home. Even though being a grass widow in Brisbane wasn't all fun. It was Irene."

"What about Irene?" He looked up and spoke swiftly. And with the words there came a sudden reach of his heart towards the woman, an almost sickening resurgence of his old love for her.

Blanche put up a hand and ran it down her face. "The atmosphere of Dad Hilliard's house was not good for her. She's a funny girl. She was getting mixed up with these beastly Labour politics that Dad is intent on returning to."

"Is that all?" Biddow's face lit up. He grinned, looked about him and took his pipe from his pocket. "I guessed something like that from her letters. She's got brains, has she?"

"Of course she's got brains"—sharply. "But I want her to use them in a creditable manner. You can't imagine what freaks some of these Labour men are. Dad's a fool. He's going to lose his seat next election. He will fall between two stools."

Biddow rose, lit his pipe and then, stepping closer to his wife, spoke seriously, almost threateningly. "About us, Blanche. I don't altogether know. I've settled down in my ways. I had a pretty bad time for a spell and I don't intend to go through anything like that again. I don't think you got away with much, Blanche. I can see through a glass wall as well as the next man. Oh, it's all right!" She had flinched before him. "I wasn't the man for you at all. But out of it there came the farm and this life. This life suits me. It suits Randy, too. I'm willing to try and make a go of it if you are. You willing to be friends with Cindie, now?" He shot that question at her.

"I'm not worried about Cindie any more. I've had plenty of time to think"—slowly, almost painfully. Then, flashing her brilliant eyes at him she added brightly: "You might not believe it, Randolph, but Cindie was glad to see me. No, not pretence, really glad. I can't make her out."

"No? I think I can. Well, things haven't gone any too good with Cindie, Blanche. I won't have any more burdens piled on her. But come now. I'll bring in your luggage."

For the rest of that day Cindie stayed away from the big house. Back to her solitary meals. Back to the cheerlessness of enforced solitude. Was she glad to be relieved of the boy's constant presence? Of the strain of constant repression? She could not decide. Momentarily, an ignoble jealousy beset her. Jealousy of Blanche and Irene for any comfort the boy might derive from their presence. . . .

The Christmas festivities were ideally suited for the smooth settling in of the two newcomers. They were part of the generally interrupted routine. The hectic social life of the season engulfed them to the extent of easing the readjustment of affairs for Cindie, physically and mentally. Mother and daughter spent the days in a round of visits and entertaining.

Christmas Eve saw Folkhaven once again the scene of a gathering of planters, workers and townsfolk. No individual invitations were sent out. It was simply made known by grape-vine telegraph that Folkhaven was holding open house on Christmas Eve, and from sunset onwards a constant stream of visitors rode, drove and padded by foot up the track. Once again the trees and shrubs and buildings were festooned with gay Chinese lanterns, the lawns and shrubberies rang with laughter. Once again Cindie's balcony shook and shivered with dancing feet to the music of accordion and mouth organ.

But to Cindie, and to a lesser extent to Biddow, a very cogent something was lacking. Though the huts of the Kanakas, the domiciles of the few Aborigines, were strung with polychromatic light as formerly, though provision had been made for Christmas luxuries for the blacks, the heart had gone out of the homogeneous whole that had been plantation life. The dark people now could bring no enchantment of primitive song and dance to this more sophisticated gathering of whites. These new people, the whites newly settled, the mill workers, the townsfolk, Cindie knew would reject with scorn and contumely any attempt on her part to ignore the line of demarcation between black and white that the White Australia policy, given lawful and legal sanction, had drawn between them.

On a day of her first homecoming Irene had shocked Cindie and Biddow by an unmaidenly tirade against fraternization with the blacks and Chinese. Biddow, proud of the girl's "clever" talk anent politics in general, had taken her up very sharply on this issue. Randy had looked at her, speechless with disgust.

"You are all mixed up, my girl," Biddow had told her. "If that's the kind of Labour politics you've been mixed up with, it was certainly time you came home. I can't see things straight myself, yet, but I'm perfectly sure that racial discrimination is not going to advance this country one whit. Until the Labour politicians learn to discriminate between racial hatred and economic theory they are not going to get my wholehearted support."

"That's because you, as a big farmer, want to retain your cheap labour, Dad," Irene cried. "You're a boss yourself."

"Nothing of the sort, my girl. Yours is not a Labour theory at all. How can the setting of one race or nationality against another advance the conditions of the workers of any country? Tell me that! It can only assist the employing class of all countries to keep them down. Labour may be right in general but in this particular they are playing the game of the most conservative of the tory class. Damned inhuman, I call it! Racial discrimination is a policy for scum! The scum of all nations! Don't let me hear anything more from you along that line!"

"I should think not," Randy had added, superfluously. "You make me sick with your White Australia, Miss."

Not that Cindie and Biddow were alone in regretting the passing of the days when a benevolent semi-feudal régime was in general the order of plantation life and cruelty the uneconomic exception. The Montagues, Callaghans, and many other of the earliest settlers in the district were at one with them in this. But since the day of the Kanaka was numbered, the effortlessness of swimming with the rising tide induced in the majority of these readiness enough to respond to its appeal.

The Kanakas themselves could not fail to be affected by the changing psychology and conditions of the whites around them. Always some interested white was to be found who would take time to explain to the blacks the economic factor, the cheap labour issue, in which their fate as indentured labourers was involved. Many of them understood that aspect of things perfectly and made it a constant subject of discussion among their fellows. The more balanced among them took the question of discrimination on racial grounds with scornful equanimity, observing with contemptuous eyes the debauchery, gambling and irresponsibility of many of the whites. Others reacted with actions of petty vengeance, thieving, sabotage; even, here and there, more serious crimes.

The majority of the Kanakas throughout the State, including many who by long years of exile had become Australianized, in face of the upsurge of feeling against them now yearned for the time of their repatriation. Even Tirwana—cut to the quick by Irene's unexpected rebuff when, on the evening of her arrival home, he had come hurrying up, his handsome face aglow with welcome—over Christmas re-opened with Cindie his own future position.

"Miss Cindie," he said lugubriously, "I've been thinking. What's the use of the black man expecting peace in this country? You saw. The little girl I took on my knee, who used to walk with me hand in hand, now hates me. I think I will go back to my own people, after all."

"Indeed, you'll do nothing of the sort. Tirwana, how can you talk of deserting me? And Mr. Biddow. Irene's just up in the air for a while, Tirwana. It isn't because you are black. It's conceit. She's the same with the white workers. Haven't you noticed that?"

Tirwana regarded her gravely. "No. I haven't noticed that. You really think so?"

"Tirwana, I know. She'll come round. Wait till she's been under our influence for a while. It's the town life, Tirwana. It has spoiled her."

"But, Miss Cindie!" Tirwana began to gesticulate. His voice took on authority. "Irene has come back talking Labour. Everybody knows it. Miss Caroline, when she was here one day, she came to me and said: 'She makes me sick, Tirwana, with her Labour politics.' Well, if Irene is Labour woman why does she think she's so good? Miss Caro, she's not Labour and she doesn't think she's better than me."

"Oh, Tirwana!" Cindie was sorry, now, for her lie. For that Irene was not the same with the white workmen she very well knew. "There's something funny about this business of Labour politics, Tirwana. One of these days I'm going to find out about it. Labour should have nothing to do with this White Australia rubbish. They say the blacks and Chinese reduce the standards of living of the white workers. But the bosses, the tories, with the exception of a few big sugar men, support White Australia, too. And are they concerned about giving their workers good conditions and high wages? . . ."

Watching her opportunity, Cindie broached the matter of Tirwana to Irene. "Irene, dear, I never thought that you would find it in your heart to hurt good old Tirwana. Why did you do it, Irene?"

"Because I don't want to have anything to do with blacks, Cindie. Grandmother was shocked when she found that I talked to the blacks the same as to whites."

"Irene, has your grandmother got more brains than Tirwana, do you think?"

"Well—no. Perhaps not. . . . Of course not, Cindie!" From hesitation the girl's native honesty burst forth. "But Tirwana is black, Cindie. In town no one associates with blacks and yellow men. And even here, Cindie, it's the same, really. Underneath. If not, why do we have a separate carriage for the coloured men on our train?"

"Your father doesn't support it."

"But Dad's the only man I know who really treats the blacks as equals."

"What about Barney Callaghan?"

"Oh yes, and Mr. Callaghan. The rest *like* them, Cindie, but only in the way they like horses and dogs."

"Yes, Irene, I'm afraid you are right there. But think, child, think for yourself. Don't let yourself be dragged at the heels of bad ideas, just because the majority hold them. Your father is proud of you, Irene. He is proud that you are taken up with such things as Labour politics. And I, Irene," Cindie stroked the girl's beautiful hair, "I think there might be great things for a girl like you to do in the future, Irene. Things in the political world, I mean. Now that the Federal Government has given all women the vote. . . . Wouldn't you like to do something big, Irene? to stand out among the people like—like a star? Guiding them to higher things."

Irene gazed at her solemnly. "Yes, I think I would," she said slowly. "I want to do big things, Cindie. When I'm in bed at night I think about what went on in Granddad's house. About the politicians who came there. They were not good men, many of them, Cindie. Some of them were always planning for their own ends. And even those who were good were not—not brainy, Cindie. Not compared with Dad, and Tirwana and you. . . ."

Tirwana was overjoyed when Irene came to him, that very evening, and with shy charm asked him to take her out in the fields on the morrow, to show her his plot of land.

So of all the household Randy alone, that Christmas, was dejected in spirit. For Cindie, whatever her altruistic desire, could not but find inspiriting the boy's continued failure to make headway with his suit. Irene, with sisterly frankness, from her first apprehension of Randy's love-lorn condition, made it a subject of open and critical discussion and dispute and Biddow, on the assumption that an airing of affairs might dissipate the boy's misery, did not discourage her in this. Blanche, very much concerned with the resumption of her relations with her husband, more nearly contented than at any time in the whole of her married life, did not take the matter seriously.

"Never mind, Randy," she told him on one occasion, when Irene had brought him almost to tears with her protestations over his "chasing after a girl who talks to him as though he were a dog". "It's a disease that all boys catch at some time or other. You'll get over it."

An attitude that elicited looks of hate from the boy.

CHAPTER XXXIX

THEN, ON NEW YEAR'S DAY, CAME THAT CONFLICT, OF HISTORIC significance in the far north, between whites and Kanakas and out of it came—— But this time I shall not anticipate.

This year the people of Masterman, influenced mainly by Chris Martin, lessee of two hundred acres of Biddow's land, decided to establish a precedent by holding their New Year's Day sports in their own area instead of flocking as usual to Port Denham. A sports committee, which included Cindie and Consuelo, had been elected at a public meeting and given the job of deciding upon a site and organizing events. The site chosen was the main street of the town itself, the triangle of green sward at the top and making excellent provision for a picnic lunch and foot races.

On the afternoon of New Year's Eve, the committee met at a pub in the town to finalize arrangements and here Chris Martin, elected for his general energetic espousal of Masterman interests to the Chair, made an issue of whether or not the coloured people should be permitted to participate in the sporting events.

Cindie immediately moved that the sports be conducted in the time-honoured far-northern way, which signified the inclusion of the blacks and Chinese. Martin, long notorious for his aberrant hatred of "colour" and still nursing his years-old grudge against Cindie for her fraternization with "niggers", vehemently opposed her. But, the chief deciding factors being the physical prowess of the blacks and the desire of the majority of committee members to make the initial sports day in the town of maximum interest, he found himself out-voted.

Martin, however, was unable to accept his defeat with

good grace. That night, when the town, now of considerable size, saw the Old Year out and the New Year in with all the traditional rough-house revelry of frontier life *en fête*, Martin, staggering from bar to bar in his cups, left a trail of pessimistic speculation behind him as to what might occur on the morrow should the man's inflamed prejudices against "niggers and chows" and "the Comstock bitch" not be properly cooled. It did not help any that Martin went home with a black eye administered by Jeff Grey for the smut and bawdry he had entangled with Cindie's name.

When Martin appeared on the sports ground the next morning, the black eye and his glowering visage, coupled with reports, occasioned a few of the leading citizens and planters to approach him with some advice.

"We don't want any trouble here to-day," Louis Montague, their chosen spokesman, told him. "Sure you've got yourself in hand? Maybe you would like the Old Man, or Callaghan or Biddow, to make the awards in your place. The Kanakas are bound to run off with most of the prizes."

"I'm all right," was the surly response. "You do your job as handicapper properly and the niggers won't have a chance."

"I don't need any advice about my job. Anyhow, you've been warned."

All went well until, nearing lunch-time, a Solomon Islander from Glenelg named Dudu came up to Martin, to receive from him, as Chairman of the committee, his third winning prize, which happened to be a cooked ham. Dudu came up the sward between the lines of spectators glowing with pride in the applause. His step was springy, his black skin sparkled with sweat, his tight-fitting singlet and moleskin shorts revealed the play of his lithe body beneath them. As he neared Martin and those members of the committee who supported him, Old Man Montague called to him from the side lines: "Good boy, Dudu! Good boy!"

Dudu stopped, singled out Montague from the crowd and called back: "Thank you, Boss. I do good job for Glenelg."

And Martin, in his mind the fact that Louis Montague was handicapper, with a flare-up of fury shouted: "Hurry up, you myall! Don't keep me standing here all day!"

Dead silence fell upon that section of the crowd who heard the words. Myall! Name for wild Aborigine. Fighting name to a Kanaka.

At that hated word Dudu's head went up. He hesitated for a second, then wheeled and, his body held regally erect, scorning to make through the spectators, marched back the entire length of the running pitch. Murmurings arose among the people. Those who had not heard pushed forward and questioned. Those who had, reacted in divers ways. Some laughed uncomfortably. Others were angered. Most people, even those who shared Martin's prejudices on the question of colour, regretted the incident in that it marred the harmony of the day.

Martin himself was struck with compunction the moment the words were out of his mouth. Not out of decency, but for the foolishness of being left standing with the ham in his hands and after that the possible retrogressive effect upon his mounting political aspirations. Beneath his breath he swore, vilely, then looked about him in half-defiant trepidation.

Louis Montague stepped up to him. "I've half a mind to give you a back-hander for that," he said angrily.

Dropping the ham to the ground, Martin growled: "It slipped out, curse it."

A townsman came hurrying up. "Better get on with the programme. Quick. The Kanakas are pulling out. God damn you, Martin. Some of them have had drink."

The next item was rapidly proceeded with, but the sight of about a hundred and fifty Kanakas withdrawing from the crowd and ganging up along the street was frightening to the women with children and depressed even the menfolk. Cindie conferred with Biddow in respect of the Folkhaven Kanakas.

"I don't see that we can do anything," he concluded, in his moderate way. "I don't think there will be any trouble. They are only signifying their opinion of Martin. Tirwana is moving among them. For their own sakes he will try to keep them quiet."

Shortly, about half the Kanakas, among them all the Folkhaven group with the exception of Tirwana, Sow and

Charity, slowly wandered out of the street and took their way back to their respective plantations. But among those left were included several who by illegal means had procured a measure of whisky and rum and it was with foreboding that the whites watched the scattered small gangs come together at the far end of the street, near the mill.

Cindie, over-confident of her ability to handle any situation involving the prestige of the coloured people, proposed to the committee that several of them accompany her along the street and issue an invitation to the Kanakas to return and engage in the sports. But to begin with, the only support she got was from the Montagues and the Callaghans. Wrong or no wrong, it stuck in the gizzard of most whites to "crawl to the niggers". Eventually, however, it was agreed that she, Biddow, Bert Callaghan and Louis Montague should approach the Islanders.

Tirwana left the group of his fellows and came forward to meet them. "This is bad business," he said at once, his eyes on Biddow. "Some say they will fight Chris Martin. Others want him to apologize to Dudu."

"And so he should," Cindie spoke up crisply. Her companions, however, realized the impossibility of getting Martin to do any such thing. And Biddow alone agreed with Cindie as to its advisability.

"After all," said Louis Montague, "we can only go a certain way to meet them, Miss Comstock. If they start any funny business they will simply have to be taught a lesson."

And taught a lesson they were.

Determined in the group as they never could have been singly, the Kanakas demanded that Martin apologize to Dudu on pain of their refusal to work the fields on the morrow.

"The Japs who work around the mill," declared Dudu, with sullen pride, "they strike for better conditions. We strike, too, for the shame of being insult."

"And what would you use for food, in that case?" Louis Montague asked him.

Dudu smiled. His eyes slid past Louis to linger on the forested range. A tincture of contempt marked his tone as he replied: "White man, Jesus give the bush to the black man, so he won't starve."

Cindie was chagrined to find that handling a group of men united and standing firm on what they considered a justifiable grievance, was something quite different from management under conditions of routine plantation life. But maybe she got no further than her companions with her line of talk because it rang insincere. Sow came forward, stood beside Dudu and looked on her with grave scepticism. Dudu, like every other Kanaka in the district well acquainted with her record, bent his eyes to her in mock deference. One Buka Buka man whose breath stank with whisky, came close to her, then turned his back on her and spat.

"And can you wonder?" Cindie asked fiercely, as the deputation retired. "They know very well that my place is by their side."

The sports day was ruined. Shortly a section of the Kanakas began to organize their own events. Others sat with their backs against veranda posts or fences and looked on. A few wandered away and disappeared. Cindie was dismayed to note that Charity, who had left her children at home in the care of a Verbena too far advanced in pregnancy to risk excursions, in company with several other Kanaka women had abandoned decorum and was shouting and laughing hilariously.

From racing events the Kanakas got to singing. Then a few of the more bellicose, led by the drunken, began to dance. And because of the mixture of tribes, each with its own speciality in that line, the result was wild confusion which, from comradeship in common purpose, led to the gradual working up of inter-tribal jealousies and feuds. Tanna began to trip up Buka Buka, "accidentally", as it were, and laughed as the latter sprawled. Api pushed Vita Luava and was cuffed in return. The competition in song developed into a bedlam of lusty yelling and war cries, interrupted by sudden grapplings and wrestling.

Before this stage was reached, the white women and their children had been bundled off the street by the menfolk. Those who resided near by went home, those from more outlying farms took refuge in the shops and pubs.

The fight was precipitated by the fear and inexperience of a young policeman, the most recent recruit of the three officers stationed in the area. His older and more tried colleagues acted with discretion, enjoining upon the whites, especially the young hotheads, the utmost care to avoid provocation. But the youthful officer, Policeman Peabody, his natural stupidity a recording instrument for his fear, paraded the street hectoringly, his hand ostentatiously upon the holster that contained his revolver.

But for his exhibitionist tactics the trouble might have blown over. The original cause of the discord might have been obliterated, at least for the time being, by the more general inter-tribal fermentation. Having no weapons at their disposal, the Kanakas' grappling, wrestling, bashing and clawing of each other could have resulted in little real injury.

But it happened that Tirwana, despairing at length of his efforts at pacification, prevailing upon Sow to accompany him, came down the street towards the bands of whites with the intention of passing through them on the way out to Folkhaven. And young Peabody, mistaking for threatening intent Sow's wild gestures and scowling countenance, —actually occasioned by an ineffectual rough and tumble with Charity in an effort to induce her to go home with him—rushed forward waving his arms and shouting:

"Get back, you niggers! Back! Back!"

Sow fell back. The whites of his eyes flashed in alarm. But Tirwana stood his ground.

"D'ye hear me!" yelled the constable. "I told you to get back!"

But now the groups of whites were coming together and crowding forward. The elders swore lustily at the crass folly of Peabody but many of the young men, especially those of Chris Martin's ilk whose irresponsibility had been aggravated by drink, yelled with a rising madness for fight. The Kanakas in the mass, stunned for a few moments into immobility by the sight of the whites charging towards them, then abandoned their inter-tribal dissension and with a concerted shriek tore down the street to accept the apparent challenge.

The women watched the fight from the shop windows and pub balconies. Cindie, seeing Tirwana go down beneath a blow from a chain detached from a cart, screamed out his name. But almost immediately Tirwana arose. He rose up from the earth like a giant inflamed for fight, blood streaming from his head and down his face, his torso, crimsoning his white singlet. His stance as he spread his great legs and knotted his fists was heroic. But he had no chance to do anything. For Chris Martin, seeking gratification for the special hate his mean spirit had cossetted for years for this black man, friend of his joint bugbears Cindie and Biddow, came at him from behind and with the handle of his horsewhip inflicted a crushing blow on the back of Tirwana's head.

Randy, who up till then had remained aloof from the struggle, bewildered and nonplussed, at the sight of this attack emitted a yell and shot into the mêlée around Tirwana. He flung himself upon Martin. Cindie screamed approval. "Good, Randy! Give it to him, Randy! Fight him, Randy, fight him!"

Blanche, leaning over the balcony rail near by, turned on her hysterically. "Stop it, you fool! You'll have the boy killed! Oh! Oh!"

But Biddow had heard Cindie's scream. He flew to Randy's side. The boy and Martin were grappling upon the ground. He separated them and then, standing beside Tirwana, breathing hard, told the boy: "Tear a paling off a fence, Son. . . . Quick. . . . Quiet, Tirwana. Quiet. Here, lean on me." He offered the support of his shoulder.

The big Tanna was reeling upon his feet. The heavy hardwood whip handle had landed upon the wound made by the chain. Scarcely conscious, his eyes closed, he was too heavy for Biddow to support. Biddow lowered him to the ground. He was placing his folded tussore silk coat beneath Tirwana's head when Randy returned with a paling. The boy was now fighting mad but Biddow restrained him. "You can't take the part of the Kanakas, Son. And you can't fight them, either. Stay here with me."

The Kanakas fought with stones torn up from the street, with fence palings, with whips snatched from the whites, but the threatening revolvers of the policemen, in addition to weight of numbers, eventually forced them to give up.

Right at the beginning of the fight the older policemen had taken their young colleague's gun from him. Their own, they used chiefly as a means of persuading the townsmen against using theirs. The planters could be depended upon not to seriously injure their Kanakas, for Kanakas cost money and without their labour the field work could not go on. It was not until things began to look really serious that the officers fired a shot and then they took care merely to clip the natives in the leg.

But the cart chains and spanners, chiefly wielded by townsfolk, did damage enough. Men slipped on the bloodied street as they fought. A Kanaka woman from Glenelg had her arm twisted till the bone snapped. The leg of a Kanaka child was trampled and crushed beneath the hoofs of a horse Chris Martin mounted and rode at a gallop among the natives as they scattered and sought refuge once the tide of battle had definitely turned against them.

Leaving a trail of blood behind them, those Kanakas who could make it pelted through houses and pubs, out the back way and into the bush and the cane. A wild scream echoed through a private house when one native mistook his way and plunged into a bedroom in which a young girl crouched in terror.

Whites invaded the house and spotted the Kanaka as he leapt over the back fence and dropped into the cane. His was the only death. A bullet caught him in the back and, though immediate attention might have saved him, fear of worse punishment if apprehended kept him silent, bleeding to death. Eventually, eighteen Kanakas, Tirwana among them, had to be carried from the street and conveyed to the hospital at Port Denham.

The stern regrets of the older settlers, when calm had been restored, was mingled with rage on the part of all the cane growers for the loss of labour in the fields. In addition to the cot cases many other Kanakas, they knew, had been wounded. Besides, there would be runaways, and the effect of the fight upon those labourers who had not taken part, to be reckoned with. The company of Chris Martin was

eschewed by most planters. The only labour he employed
was two remittance men.

Men set out on horseback to scour the country-side, to
round up runaways, to promise them, by grape-vine telegraph, immunity from punishment should they return home.
That night great bonfires raged in the paddocks, fires around
which the general excitement engendered by the fight found
expression in furious agitation and palaver, in wild dancing
and song. Except at Folkhaven, where for reasons yet to be
outlined, the Kanakas were subdued, scarcely an adult slept.
Gun in hand, men patrolled the farms nightlong.

By nightfall the number of police had been augmented
by half a dozen officers from Port Denham. On the following morning these set to work listing those Kanakas who
had participated in the fight. Sow, who was accounted a
ringleader, was brought into the township from Folkhaven,
and, in the absence of a local jail, with three of his fellows
chained to a log beneath some trees at the western end of
the main street. Not so large a log, though, but that the
prisoners were able to tuck it beneath their arms and respond
to beckonings from secluded spots on the part of sorry whites
who felt they were dispensing with their whisky and rum
a measure of compensation for injustice rendered.

When, at sundown, the policemen brought a meal for their
charges, the four of them were dead to the world in drunken
slumber, and thus they remained throughout the night.
The next morning they were removed to the jail at Port
Denham, and the following week, with a dozen other Kanakas,
haled before the Government agent and fined for "disturbing
the peace".

The older planters paid all the fines, but nevertheless the
work in the paddocks suffered considerably for some time.
For the Kanakas were equally as offended and disgusted by
the fines as they had been by the original insult to Dudu.
As Sow put it to Cindie: "Not right, Missie Cindie, to hit
us with sticks and chains and take our money, too. One
fight, one punish. The bloody white man, he want everything
his way."

CHAPTER XL

JEFF GREY'S CHOSEN PART IN THE BATTLE WITH THE KANAKAS to begin with had been the same as Biddow's: one of neutrality based on expediency and ill-defined principle. But unpremeditated action in defence of a Montague youth against a brawny drunken Kanaka got him a clout on the head that reddened his pacifist outlook. Reason retreated before rage, and as a result he emerged from the conflict the most battered-looking warrior in the ranks of the victorious whites. His shorts were his sole remaining garment. One finger was broken and blood from a split cheek streamed down over his bare torso, imparting a piratical appearance. Dazed, and now mortified at the collapse of his benevolent neutrality, he fell on to a wooden bench in front of the pub in which the Folkhaven women had taken refuge and clapped his hands to his head.

To him there, Caroline came running, full of sympathy and offers of loving assistance. And out of the pub came Blanche, Cindie and Irene, to meet Biddow and Randy. All gathered around Jeff. Only Blanche had a word of sympathy for him. Biddow was noncommittal. Cindie scorched him with the fire of her criticism.

Randy, trembling in the reaction from intensest excitement, became physically sick at the sight of Caroline's flagrant disclosure of her passion for Grey. And when his sharpened apprehensions detected the semblance of a response on the man's part, his stomach rebelled against the nervous strain put upon it by this final dissolving of the world of his hopes. He rushed away from the group and vomited into the roadway.

Cindie returned to Folkhaven with her emotions in a state of liquefaction. She, too, had noted the dawning of a new, semi-humorous complaisance on Jeff's part to Caroline's advances. And she knew that Randy's stunned silence, the desolation of spirit he was totally unable to conceal, was born of a parallel realization. Pity for the boy alternated with upsurges of joy she tried vainly to squelch. She kept

away from the big house, giving her time to the excited
Kanakas at their gathering in Sow's hut, encouraging the
more volatile among them to spill out of their systems through
passionate talk the urgency of their will to vengeance, their
fury of frustration arising from their ignominious subjection.

No disrespect was paid to Cindie. The Kanakas either
ignored her or looked her straight in the eye while they made
forceful argument that was one long repetition. And they
kept on and on until, long after their usual bedtime, Cindie lost
patience and attacked them.

She stepped out in front of the group and pointed a finger
at Sow. He, re-inflamed by the turning up, a few minutes
agone, of a sadly-dishevelled and frightened Charity, had
been the last speaker.

"Now it's finished," she said sharply. "No more talk to-
night. I've given you all a good innings, but before I go I've
got something to tell you Kanakas.

"All this trouble was caused by you people objecting to
Dudu's being called myall. Well, now I'm telling you that
the myall Aborigine is as good as you Kanakas any day.
He's as intelligent as you are and he can work as well as
you can. You object to being treated as inferiors by the
whites. But as long as you think yourselves better than the
Aborigines the whites are quite right in despising you. You
understand?" She raised her voice.

Hostile murmuring rose from the blacks. And in the midst
of it Biddow's voice sounded from behind her.

"I don't quite agree with you, there, Cindie." He came
forward and stood beside her. He smiled, first at her and
then at the Kanakas, who were now keenly alert. "I think
Miss Cindie is only half right there, you fellas." He chose
his words carefully. "I think I am right in stating that you
blokes have learned your contempt for the Australian black
from us whites. You know that we look after you people,
in a sort of way. That policy pays us. You work for us.
You cost us much money. But you see us treat the Aborigines
like animals. You see them belted, shot at, driven from pillar
to post. . . ."

Charity interrupted him. "Not you, Boss. Not Miss
Cindie."

"No. But we are exceptions. Tell me! If you Kanakas had come to this country and found us whites treating the Aborigines the same as we treat you, would you have despised them? Would you object to being called myall?"

The black faces turned to each other in astonishment, which in turn became smiling embarrassment. Heads drooped. Sidelong glances were cast at Biddow and Cindie.

"I'm waiting," Biddow added, mildly.

Then Sow spoke up, quickly and shrewdly. "What you say, Boss, in roundabout way, is that we're fools. Inside your words is same meaning Tirwana always tell us. The white man, he all the time on top, if Kanaka he thinks he better than other black man."

Biddow scratched his head. "Well—I think you have probably put the position in a nutshell there, Sow. Yes, boiled down, it amounts to that."

"Huh!"—contemptuous grunt from another Kanaka. "The black Australian, he just like animal."

"I see white Australian like animal, too," thrust Sow. "I see white Australian crawl on knees with drink. I see him lie on road in own spew. . . ."

Possibly Cindie and Biddow learned as much as they taught, that night. When they left the Kanakas they went down to the big house and over supper, with Blanche not bothering to conceal her boredom, Irene vividly and argumentatively interested and Randy sprawled on a couch a silent and miserable listener, they clarified their attitude towards political Labour.

In respect of its White Australia policy based on racial discrimination, nothing separated the Australian Labour Movement from the most reactionary of the big moneyed men represented by the tories. In respect of its economic theories it stood for the uplift and betterment of the people. And since economic theory, concerned as it was with the basic elements of human life, must in the long run triumph over every other consideration, the Labour Movement merited support. Doubtless experience and industrial development would throw up streams of thought and leadership able to purify and widen the present muddied river of progress. . . .

Cindie went up to her home with her mood mellowed
and calmed by the satisfaction derived from problems clarified. How small and petty were one's personal predicaments
when focused by the camera of national issues! She sighed
as she undressed herself and made ready for bed. A sigh of
physical weariness and of fatalistic acceptance of the difficulties created by the mischance of her love. She threw her
calico nightdress over her head, lay down on the hard, thin
mattress she favoured for its comparative coolness and drew
a sheet over the lower portion of her body. In the dark she
would throw off the sheet entirely. Modesty forbade such
looseness of behaviour in the light.

In pursuance of her habit of reading before sleeping, no
matter how tired, she took up a book. She yawned as she
opened its covers. Then suddenly she stiffened. Lifted her
head and held it in a listening attitude. Soft footfalls on
her stairs. No doubt about it. Like a cat she sprang from
her bed and grabbed the loaded gun that customarily stood
beside it. But already she was thinking that no Kanaka
would dare. Not under such conditions.

"Who's there?" she called, and was not really surprised
when Randy answered, his tone susurrant and pleading.

"It's me, Cindie. Randy."

Relinquishing the gun, Cindie darted back into bed and
pulled the sheet up to her chin. "I'm in bed, Randy," she
called. "It's too late to talk now."

For answer he appeared in the doorway, hesitated there a
moment and then came forward and sat down on her bed.
Well back, he sat, then leant over, put his elbows on his
knees and cupped his forehead in the palms of his hands.

Cindie lay perfectly still, distended eyes upon him, thrill-
ingly conscious of the pressure of his buttocks against her legs.
But not for long. Within a few moments the impropriety of
the situation drew from her a forceful protest. "Randy, you
can't stay here. You must go away."

"I had to come!" He flung round and faced her. His
hands clutched at the sheet. "Cindie! She's going to marry
Jeff! I feel it! I—I could kill him!"

"Oh, Randy, my dear!" Everything but love and pity
forgotten, Cindie threw back the sheet and sat up. She

took his head in her hands. She began to stroke his hair. His head fell forward on to her breast, and as she listened to the convulsive weeping that took him her own face contracted with agonized helplessness. "Randy, dear Randy, don't! You'll get over it, Randy. She's not good enough for you, Randy."

And so they remained for some minutes, the boy gradually quietening, Cindie stroking his head with measured movements and murmuring soft nothings.

And the automatic action of her fingers over the silkiness of his hair, gradually cast a spell over Cindie, induced in her a hypnotic condition of supersensuality that arrested thought. Her eyes filmed with dreaminess, her free hand, of its own volition, pressed the boy's head more closely to her breast. Her mood, in this cataclysmic crisis of her maturity, became one of such swooning voluptuousness that she was only half alive.

The bemused actions of the boy, arising involuntarily out of his consuming need for solace, for assuagement of the grief and jealousy and pain that racked him and under the physical contact converted to all-pervasive desire, scarcely penetrated to Cindie's consciousness. All her defences were tumbled and eclipsed by the age-old betrayer, the entanglement of sexuality and pain. . . .

No talk between them at all, throughout that night. Periodically he awoke and groped for her, as naturally as a child would turn to its mother's breast for comfort. And as naturally Cindie responded. She slept, too, but at length a feeling of the coming of the dawn penetrated her dreamless slumber and roused her to commonsensible action. Tenderly she woke him and told him he must leave her. He sat up, ran his hands through his hair, rubbed his eyes and, without a word, slipped off the bed. He began to dress in the dark, still silent. And then it was that Cindie's heart slipped a beat, for he began to leave her without a word. But suddenly he was back, fumbling for her face. He bent down and for the first time kissed her, full on the lips. "Old Cindie," he muttered, and was gone.

Nothing, thought Cindie, in a delirium of realized fulfilment, could ever worry, hurt or pain her again! She buoyed herself up with no dreams that the boy would come back. In his extremity he had sought her and she had bestowed relief. It was over, she accepted, in her innocence, without question. The night had been a bridge over which Randy had passed from unendurable misery to at least partial restoration of emotional balance.

She left her bed, unable to contain without physical action the happiness that possessed her. She built up the fire and made tea, cooked herself bacon and eggs. She ate a tremendous meal and then, in the red-gold of the swift tropic sun-rising, went out into the fields and walked. She watched the white workers set out for the last lap of the cane cut. She went into the quarters of the Kanakas and at their cheery greetings laughed and joked with them.

Then she went up to the big house, into its kitchen. For now that the Christmas and New Year season was over much cleaning up awaited her direction. The round of the routine days must be set in motion.

Now, however, Cindie found shyness creeping over her at the prospect of facing Randy. The family were at breakfast. She could hear Irene and Randy arguing. Some chairs were pushed back and, following upon that, unexpectedly Randy was coming into the kitchen. He was speaking to her, looking at her with eyes that were half-ringed with black, but softly eager. He came close to her and, without any awkwardness at all, said optimistically: "Maybe we made a mistake yesterday, Cindie. About Caro and Jeff. Would you go over to Jeff's to-day, Cindie? See how he is getting on?" His eyes pleaded.

"Of course I will, Randy." Cindie smiled at him lovingly. "I didn't see anything between them at all, really, dear."

She went and, out of constitutional inability to beat about the bush, before she had been long in Jeff's company asked him outright about the matter.

Jeff blushed. Made gestures of embarrassment. "Now look here, Cindie, you've got to tell me. Did I give the girl the impression that I—that I might get to like her?"

"I don't know." Cindie shrugged. "You gave me—and Randy—the impression that you liked the way she was fussing about you. You did, too, didn't you, Jeff?"

"Yes. I did. For the moment. It was—well—one of those things. I was sore. Ashamed, if you like. You were tongue-banging me. But I don't want the girl, Cindie. I don't want any woman, since you won't—can't——"

Cindie sighed. "Well, that's that."

CHAPTER XLI

"then all i've got to do is stick to it, cindie," randy exclaimed hopefully, in response to her report. "She'll come round. You'll see."

That night he went riding over to Glenelg and on his return could scarcely spare the time to unsaddle his horse in his eagerness to get up to Cindie. They sat on the balcony and talked.

"No, she wasn't any different, Cindie," he told her. "But I can wait." The happenings of the preceding night might not have existed for him.

But within a week Cindie was awakened in the night by him. Involuntarily her arms closed around him. . . .

But afterwards there loomed before her starkly the enormity of the problem that was snaking its coils around her. With a rush of premonition and fear she took the boy by the shoulders. "Randy, this has got to stop. You must not come to me again."

"What? . . . Why, Cindie?" He pulled her head down until her cheek rested on his. "You don't mind. You like it."

"Randy, that's not the point."

"Don't pull away from me, Cindie." Randy reached for her. "I've felt good these last days, Cindie. It's been just as though I've had a weight taken off me. I've been full of silk."

A pause, a hanging fire in Cindie's mind, then she laughed. A breathless little cachinnation. "Randy, tell me just exactly how you have felt these last few days."

"Aw. . . . I don't know. Just good. Free, you know."

"How good? How free? In your mind as well as in your body? What about Caroline?"

"Aw, her! I nearly clipped her under the ear to-night. That's what she wants, Cindie, I reckon. I'll give it to her one of these days, too."

Cindie held her breath. That night she slept little. Her mind opened to new and dazzling possibilities, she stared into the dark, supernormally moved, at moments awed, again quietly ecstatic.

Her following days were sucked into a whirlwind of physical energy. She was here, there and everywhere, her brows bent above eyes that glowed with a tense flame of resolution. It was as though the last years had never been, she had dropped them into oblivion and knitted up the tangled skein of 1896 with the possibilities of 1905. She looked youthful beyond those early years. The almost fierce glow that animated her features erased the tiny lines of drudgery and monotonous, unloved virginity. Even the heavy waving masses of her honey-coloured hair seemed to take on new shine and vitality.

Randy's visits to her continued. Cindie set herself to the task of her determined aspirations. Before a fortnight had elapsed the boy had ceased to ride over to Glenelg. A fact that Irene did not fail to note and remark.

"Well, aren't you satisfied?" Randy threw at her, hectoringly. "Can't I do anything right?"

But Blanche, during those days, came first to a startled and then to a stealthy watching of the boy and Cindie when they came together. She saw nothing that she could lay a tongue to. For Randy's growing absorption in Cindie was as natural to him as breathing. He never betrayed, by word or look, that she was anything but the old Cindie, only more so. This, of course, being the outcome of the complete satisfaction of the needs of his ardent temperament.

As for Cindie, if anything tangible, Blanche could only have fastened on to a certain cautiousness, a calculating insincere reserve that now characterized the girl's attitude towards Randy in the company of others.

Nevertheless, instinct-driven, Blanche often found herself colouring up with anger at thoughts and suspicions that would obtrude themselves. To Biddow she remarked on Randy's sudden lapse into physical leanness, on a slight change in the colour of his eyes. Further she did not dare to go, for in her new-found contentment with her own lot, Blanche did not want to rouse Biddow with a seeming recrudescence of her old antagonism towards Cindie.

Again, there were times when Blanche, crushing back the puritanism of the rake reformed and giving rein to her hard common sense, told herself that a certain relationship between those two might not be a bad thing for the boy. For a time. That's if the girl could look after herself. But of course she could not! Blanche would shake herself out of these recurring speculations and fall into angry exasperated animadversions upon a fate that had doomed her to the bane of "that girl".

But somehow, these days, Blanche was unable to recapture the old hate for Cindie. A husband was a husband and a son was a son. And Blanche had never been particularly motherly.

And so the months of the "wet", this year a comparatively dry season, merged into the mellow golden days of early winter. Now came the time of preparation for the repatriation of the majority of the Kanakas from the Masterman area, and Cindie's singleness of purpose had to yield somewhat to a very real sadness and regret for the passing of a people who with their colourful presence and stimulating personalities had infused charm and fascination into the hard and primitive conditions of pioneering plantation life.

The Folkhaven Kanakas, with the exception of Tirwana, Sow and Charity, in company with their fellows from neighbouring farms, were to embark at Port Denham.

Despite the general desire to have done with restrictions and subjection and return to the freedom of their native islands, there was scarcely one of the Folkhaven Kanakas but on the point of departure could find some reason for despondency. The preceding day Biddow declared a holiday. He, Randy and Cindie, their hearts full, spent the day assisting the black men to pack up the considerable belongings they had accumulated. And Biddow talked to them wisely about the spending of the few pounds which were their last half-yearly legal payment and the five pounds apiece he had given them as a present. Usually an orgy of senseless spending took place in the Port before the embarkation of Kanakas. Their few pounds were wheedled out of them by unscrupulous whites. Coloured shoddy and trinkets at a dozen times their real value were foisted upon the backward natives.

Cindie, also, gave each of them a present "to remember her by". A coloured picture, a picture book, a brush and comb, handkerchiefs. Blanche, glad to be rid of them but impelled by her desire to please Biddow, brought out a box of fine lawn handkerchiefs she had brought up from Brisbane and given him as a Christmas present, and asked him if he would mind very much if she distributed them as parting gifts. Biddow was terribly pleased and for the first time since her return home kissed her unreservedly.

Irene, sentimental and sorry for her lapse into racial discrimination, wept openly when at length the nine Kanakas piled into the buckboard and sulkys and set off for the train that would convey them to Port Denham. "I'm glad you're not going, Tirwana," she told that solemn Tanna who, with Cindie, Biddow and Randy, was to accompany the repatriates to the Port.

However, apart from the Kanakas from Folkhaven and a few from Glenelg and Palmer Estate, few failed to reveal unmixed joy and "thanksgiving to the Lord" for their release from virtual slavery. Port Denham seethed with their presence. Every shop was out to catch its share of the considerable sum which the aggregate of a few pounds each represented.

The schooner upon which they were to embark was late in arriving, which gave several hours to be filled in at the Port. Besides the Folkhaven whites, Louis Montague, Barney and Bert Callaghan and some other planters were there, and these, with the assistance of the Government agent, mounted guard in so far as was possible over the spending capacity of the blacks. They did their best to guide this into sensible channels but nevertheless many a Kanaka went aboard the vessel penniless but beaming in proud possession of a gaudy umbrella, brummagem jewellery, a shoddy mouth organ or a gay piece of cloth. Some of the more sensible bought accordions. One nursed a violin. Another spent six pounds on an illuminated Bible worth thirty shillings at the most. One woman tried to get away with a gun which some white had illegally sold her. She took it to pieces, tied the barrel up her leg, and hid the rest of it beneath her loosely hanging blouse. But so extraordinary a sight did she present that the agent, after questioning her and receiving in reply grave statements to the effect that she was "only sick, Boss. Me got the dropsy", threw his hat on the ground and, stooping to pick it up, looked under her frock and spotted the gun barrel.

Eventually, with little to show on their return to their homeland after years of sunrise-to-sunset toil, tired out with excitement, the majority of the Kanakas gathered on the green sward near the jetty and settled down to wait for the time of embarkation. And gradually the sprinkling of serious-minded men among them began to talk among themselves about the reason for their going. Few whites now bothered about them. Cindie and Randy stuck to the Folkhaven group, sitting with them to one side. Biddow had gone with his fellow-planters to a pub.

And after a time, from the midst of the big gathering there rose up one man, a stranger to Cindie, a grave-looking youth of not more than twenty years. He rose up from a squatting posture, took his way to a stand from which he commanded the whole group, and began to address them.

"Who is he?" Cindie asked Tirwana, after she had heard a few words. "He speaks good English."

"He was house-boy on a farm down south and the woman there taught him. Up here he comes from over the river."

"To-day," the youth began, "we go back in the boat to our own people over the water. I have listened and I know that most of you like this. You want to go back. You want to be free. You want to go about on the land as you please. You don't want to be told: do this, do that, and work hard all day for your food and a few articles of wearing apparel." The pretentious expression brought an involuntary snicker from Randy. Cindie hushed him.

"But I do not want to go back to my homeland. Why? Because I was stolen from my people when I was thirteen

years old. I have lived for years in a good home in this
country. Down south. Yes, I have lived in a good home.
What does it mean for me to go back to the bush? My people
were savage. They hunted for heads. They lived in a very
bad way. I go back to be a stranger to my people. How
shall I live in my people's ways?

"But I do not want to stay here, either. For here I have
lived like a white man and yet I am treated like a horse.
Because my skin is black! So what is there for me in this
world? I do not want to stay here and I do not want to go
back to my people. I have no people. I am alone." He
paused, looking not at the gathering before him but far
away, out to sea.

"Oh, Randy," whispered Cindie, "this is terrible."

A murmuring arose from the assembly and swelled into
a babble. And in the midst of it Tirwana got to his feet. All
eyes turned to him. The babble subsided into expectant,
excited quiet.

Tirwana stretched out an arm and pointed a finger at the
youth. "No!" he cried deeply. "You are not alone! There
are a great multitude of men like you and some of them have
white skins. You, boy, are lucky. You can say out loud
what these other fellas here can only think. What they think
when they lie awake in the night. And when they sweat
in the paddocks. These people here, they laugh and joke
and buy nonsense because they can't talk out loud what is
in their hearts. Like you. But your problems are theirs
too.

"You, boy, people like you who can talk out loud what
is in your hearts, you are lucky people. You are *big* people.
You are *leading* people. Whether you are black or white
you are the same people.

"I, too, have lived like the white man. I, too, have had
a good boss. I have learned. I have used my eyes and
brains. And I have seen that the white man, too, often thinks
he is alone in facing up to problems. But it is only because,
like you, he does not look around him and see the—the
waiting in the hearts of the people who can't talk, how they
wait on him who can talk, who can read their hearts and
talk about it to the world.

"You make the big mistake, young fella, if you think the white man, the white man who works, gets anything out of looking down on the black man. In the long run he *only gets out of it the whip on his back*. The Labour man wants to send you away because you work for little money. But why do you work for little money? Is it because you want to? Haven't you got bellies to fill, don't you like good clo's, good houses, like white men? You work for little money because the white labour man, the white workman, he will not take your hand and call you brother! He will not tell the Government: the black man and the yellow man must get the same wages as the white man!

"Yes, I have seen! I have heard the true white men talk. The white worker, he gets the small wage, the bad conditions, not because you are black men who want to work that way, but because he himself sees crooked. If the white workman gets more wages when you are gone, it won't be because you are gone but because he *fights*! I have seen!" Struggling for clarity, conscious that he was hashing up a good case he only partly understood, Tirwana was now prancing about, shouting in wild-eyed excitement.

"The white man who works is a fool when he does not see that beneath the white skin and the black skin and the yellow skin is one heart, one blood, one blood that is red, one will to live good! The white man who works and does not take the hand of the black and yellow man as brother is *one damn bloody fool*." He collapsed in a frenzy and sank down on the ground. Drops of sweat rolled down his face. His eyes rolled. He drew great panting breaths. . . .

CHAPTER XLII

CINDIE'S SENSE OF IRREPARABLE LOSS WHEN, ON HER RETURN home, she gazed upon the silent empty huts of the Kanakas was poignant and sharp. Blanche excepted, all the dwellers at the homestead, indeed, black and white, were cast down in spirit by a silence that seemed to echo against the hills.

Cindie could not settle down to any task. She was impatient, irritated by routine, a condition that extended itself to a relaxation of her regulation cautious dealing with Randy in the presence of others. And the boy himself, stirred as he had been by Tirwana's oratory at the Port to an excitement that under the circumstances could not but flow into a sensual channel, unconsciously made open display of his emotional dependence upon her.

That evening he insisted on Cindie's dining with himself and parents. Irene had not returned from a jaunt to Glenelg. And throughout the meal he maintained a deference towards her that caused Blanche to fall watchfully silent and Biddow, at length, after some keen, frowning glances at the boy, to take on an air of embarrassment and keep his eyes on his plate.

Cindie made the coffee. When she wheeled the tray mobile in from the kitchen Randy jumped up and, towering above her in the pride of his now six-foot-one height and brawny muscular development, took it from her with proprietorial authority. "You sit down, Cindie," he told her. "I'm pouring the coffee to-night."

Cindie gave him an indulgent smile and cuffed him playfully. "Oh, you! You like to play the boss. Quite the man about the house, isn't he, Mrs. Biddow?"

"You bet I am"—from Randy.

Blanche, divided between jealous anger, maternal solicitude and malicious satisfaction in that Biddow's eyes were open at last, snapped out: "You take too much on yourself, my lad. Man, indeed! Such nonsense! If you were living in town you would still be in school."

"Ah ha!" Randy handed his mother her coffee and with his free hand ruffled her curls. "But I'm not in town, you see. I'm a farmer. And a farmer I will be."

After the coffee he followed Cindie from the house, leaving Biddow to glance at his wife with fearful anticipation of her fury.

"Well?" she cried at him, stridently. "Now what about your precious Cindie? I've seen it all along but of course you—you had to be blind till they thrust it under your nose!"

"Thrust what under my nose?" he rejoined, with pretended innocence.

"Their—their carryings on! Don't you dare try to put it over me, Randolph Biddow! Don't you dare to—to connive at their wickedness!" Now, in the clutch of what she could in the world's face claim a legitimate grievance, all Blanche's old-time jealous hates and prejudices were reborn, frothed up and convulsed her. "It's come to this! She couldn't get you! She tried to break up my home! She tied you to her tails with her—her airs and graces, but she couldn't get you for a lover so she went after the boy! Just a child, a boy!"

There, however, she was pulled up short by a burst of hearty laughter from Biddow. Never before had Blanche heard the man laugh so loudly or so long. The picture she had conjured up of Cindie, Cindie with airs and graces, appealed to Biddow as so utterly ludicrous that before he was restored to calm he was wiping the tears from his eyes.

His laughter was an analgesic to Blanche's torrid ravings. Gradually her embattled demeanour was toned down to discomfort. When at length he was sitting up straightly on a couch, wiping his eyes between twinkling glances at her, she snapped out: "That's right! Behave like a lunatic."

"Come over here, Blanche," said Biddow, amiably. "Sit here beside me."

She gave him a swift look of suspicion and doubt, then slowly, her eyes on the floor, came to him. "Well?"

But Biddow was not in any hurry to speak. He clasped his hands between his knees and looked round and up at her face. He was serious enough, now. "If I were you I wouldn't start anything about Cindie and Randy, Blanche." He spoke very slowly. "You know, I have learned a lot from you, Blanche. I've had to ask myself a lot of questions, over you. And at times I've found the going pretty hard. Some of those questions I've had to think over quite a lot before I've found the answer."

She interrupted him. "What's this nonsense? Stop talking in riddles."

"All right. If that's how you want it." Biddow rose and began to pace the floor. "You've taught me, Blanche, that there's no such thing as cut-and-dried answers to questions of morality. White is not always altogether white nor black always altogether black. You've done some damnable things to me, Blanche. . . . No, don't interrupt. . . . I realize your problems. I realize that another type of husband was what you needed. Another man might have satisfied you. And I wouldn't say that you haven't your right to satisfaction.

"But that's not what I'm getting at. Not your right nor my right. I'm talking about what I've learned from your behaviour. In many ways you're a fine woman, Blanche. You've got beauty and brains, a jolly good combination. But you've got some rotten traits. I repeat, you've done some damnable things to me. But fundamentally, Blanche, you're all right. At least——" Here he shot a penetrating glance at her. "So far as I am able to judge from what I know. Probably you're as all right as most other people.

"You've loved me, Blanche. Oh yes, I know." Here his manner took on a curious gentleness. He stopped pacing and faced her. "But it wasn't because you loved me that you went away rather than take risks with me, Blanche. . . . Oh, yes, my girl, I understand all about Fraser. These things creep in on a man. It was your fundamental sense of rectitude that took you away."

"Ranny!" Blanche's head fell forward on to her hands. Tears gushed from her eyes and dribbled through her fingers. "Oh, Ranny!"

Biddow sat down beside her and put an arm around her. "So you see, my girl, there's no sense in your manufacturing moral tirades against Cindie and Randy."

"But, Ranny, you don't understand!" She sniffled. "They are carrying on! Really *carrying on*. I am sure of it."

"Yes, I do understand, now, I do." He fell into introspective thought and gradually lines of humour appeared about his mouth. Old Cindie, by cripes!

Blanche saw them and herself smiled involuntarily. She wiped her tears away. "It's nothing to laugh at," she grumbled. "How you failed to see it long ago I can't imagine. The boy's gone as lean as a scarecrow. And look how his eyes have lightened. Just like yours. Do you remember how your eyes lost colour?"

"One of them, anyhow." He grinned at her. "The dark one, I think."

"Oh, Ranny!" Blanche threw her arms round his neck and kissed him roughly, on the mouth. "What are we to do? Something's got to be *done*."

"It might blow over."

"But when? Ranny, she might—she might have a baby. She's a fool!" Vigorous, contemptuous criticism.

Biddow sighed, but not mournfully, then flashed a glance at her. "I suppose she's too old to marry him"—artfully.

"I should think so, indeed." But Blanche now fell into deep thought, out of which came: "I would hate a scandal around the boy."

"I bet there's scandal enough already," he remarked sensibly. "If we only knew it I'll bet the whole country-side's talking."

At this stage the plod-plod of Irene's horse sounded, going up past the house to the stables. Biddow rose. "There's the girl. . . . Well, maybe I'd better have a talk to the boy. You think it over." He left her.

Blanche sat on. And the sound of his footsteps had scarcely died away before all thought of Randy's affairs faded from her mind before the enormity of Biddow's revelations anent herself. So he had known! These things crept in on a man. . . . But maybe they had not crept in on him. Maybe Cindie had told, after all. But that idea was swiftly discarded.

A feeling of vast relief overcame her. Now nothing stood between them. She got up and looked at herself in the mirror over the sideboard. She smiled. Beauty and brains. Quite right. And some other reason Blanche had for the blithe humming that seized her. Biddow of late had revealed a resurgence of—temperament. Blanche laughed aloud as she fastened on to that word. What was this talk about men and a dangerous age? It wouldn't be dangerous for her, that she would warrant. She had her beauty and perhaps it wasn't too late to develop her brains. She turned to Randy's bookcase. Looked over the titles with distaste. Oh Lord, no! Not that dry stuff. What she could do was return to her music. Yes, music. He loved her music. And even that she had been too selfish to vouchsafe him.

She was murmuring "Poor old Ranny" when Irene came into the room. "Oh, there you are, Mother!" The girl looked stirred, upset. "I say, Mother, I heard something to-night. Caroline told me something about Randy. You'd never guess."

Blanche sat down and looked at her. Funny how things happened, seemed to fit in. "Perhaps I can guess. What have you heard?"

Irene clasped her hands behind her back. "They were talking over at Glenelg about Randy's not going over there much, now, and Caro said—in that rotten snitching way of hers, you know, Mother—'Why should he? Everybody knows that old Cindie Comstock has got him in her pocket. It was only kid stakes, his running after me.' And the others seemed to believe it, Mother. I got mad and told Caro off." Here, the expression on her mother's face roused Irene to alarm. "Mother, it's not true, is it? You don't think it's true?"

"Yes, I'm afraid it is true, Irene. And I don't see what we can do about it, either. Do you?"

"My good gracious! But, Mother! Cindie's old! Cindie was a woman when Randy was a boy. She couldn't *marry* Randy!"

Blanche jumped up. "Oh, stop talking about people being old, Irene! You make me feel Methuselah."

"But, Mother, if Cindie married Randy you'd be her mother-in-law." A nervous giggle. "And if she had a baby you'd be a grandmother."

Blanche released a mortified laugh. "I'm liable to be a grandmother whether she marries Randy or not, I'm thinking. . . . Oh, what am I saying? Irene, mind your own business."

Blanche flounced out of the room.

Irene flopped on to a chair. Her jaw dropped. Her eyes widened. "Whether she marries Randy or not," she repeated, stupidly. "What on earth can she mean by that?"

CHAPTER XLIII

BLANCHE TOOK HERSELF TO RANDY'S SLEEP-OUT AND, SITTING on his bed, tried to direct the current of her thoughts along practical lines in respect of the boy's affairs. But her mind was fluid. A buoyancy of spirit based on Biddow's revelation dissolved serious reflection as each facet of the situation obtruded itself. Shortly she rose and peered through the louvres through the dusk at Cindie's house. Lights went on up there as she gazed. And presently she saw Cindie come out on to the balcony and seat herself there. Where was Randy, Blanche asked herself. Maybe Randolph had taken him off somewhere and was talking to him even now.

Well, after all, she was used to old Cindie. Blanche shrugged with a rueful smile as she realized that for the first time she had used that affectionate phrase. Still smiling, she wandered out of the sleep-out and up the back lawn. There was no clear purpose in her mind as she made up the stairs, through Cindie's kitchen and on to the balcony.

Cindie looked up as Blanche appeared round a corner. She started. Then instantly took on reserve. "This is a surprise, Mrs. Biddow," she said loudly. "Is anything the matter?"

"Nothing's the matter." Blanche was a trifle embarrassed by her swift apprehension of the thought that had leapt to Cindie's mind: only something unpleasant could have brought her to a voluntary visit. "I just thought I would like to come and see you."

"Oh!" Cindie repeated that. "Oh! . . . Will you sit down?"

Blanche gave an abrupt laugh. "Yes, I will." Then with calculated testiness she added: "You need not speak to me as though I were a chance visitor, Cindie."

"No, of course not." Cindie's mind seemed to be wandering. But now she pulled herself together and blurted out: "But you are, you know."

Blanche laughed again. "Maybe I am. . . . It's nice up here, Cindie. Like old times. The view, you know."

"Yes, the view. When you can see it"—dryly.

"Aren't you feeling too good to-night?" Blanche asked straightly.

Again Cindie bent startled eyes on her. She strained through the violet dusk to read the meaning behind this new attitude of concern. "Not too good. I miss the Kanakas."

"You'll get used to being without them."

Cindie did not reply. Into her consciousness there was creeping a queer feeling of expectation, of dread. This visit of Blanche's, her tone, the manner of insincere graciousness she was now assuming and which Cindie felt rather than saw, was portentous. Something of paramount importance to herself was on the wing. And because Cindie by habit could not associate Blanche with other than inimical action in relation to herself, the muscles of her face began to stiffen, the nerves of her stomach to contract. "I will have to get used to it," she cried, stridently.

Silence. Now it was coming, thought Cindie. She braced herself for a resumption of the old sickening struggle. Randy! It could only be connected with Randy. Well, let it come. With a tingling rush of confidence in the puissance of her vantage ground there, she flung herself round in her chair and threw out a hand towards Blanche. But the blunt question on the tip of her tongue: "Just why have you come?" was not uttered. For Blanche forestalled it.

"Cindie, just exactly how old are you?" she asked, suddenly.

"What?" Cindie stilled. "Did you say? . . . I am thirty. You know that. Why?"

"Cindie, anybody can see that you—you and Randy are —are—— Oh, you know what I mean!"

Again a silence. Cindie drew a deep breath and straightened herself up. "I don't know what you mean," she said steadily. "You will have to tell me."

"You—you *like* Randy."

"Yes, I like Randy." Her tone, the very texture of her words were indicative of an indomitable and immeasurable resistance, and whatever might have lurked subconsciously in the back of Blanche's mind as to the girl's amenability to "reason", was dissipated on the spot. Throwing up her hands with a gesture of final acceptance, she cried: "Oh,

all right! We may as well get it over! Cindie, you and
Randy can't go on like you are. You will either have to
get married or you must clear out."

A long time passed before Cindie was able to grope her
way to an answer to that astounding ultimatum. A revolution
had to take place in her mind. To begin with, her whole
being hung fire, shocked into a cataleptic state. Then a
shattering realization rushed into every cell of her. It seemed
to come with an actual noise, like a beating of wings by a
multitude of birds. The shock of it blinded her while yet
her eyes were wide open. "Did you say: get married?"
Her voice in her own ears sounded like an echo of unspoken
thoughts thrown back by the hills through the night. She
did not really expect a reply from Blanche to those ghostly
fugitive tones.

But to Blanche the question, though delayed, sounded
normal enough. "I did," she said strongly. And swiftly, for
now that the die was cast Blanche felt little pricks of panic
at the "silly sentimentality" of this whole absurd procedure.
She, to be extricating *Cindie* from a difficult position! What
fools these strong women were when it came to a matter of
love! "I can't understand you, Cindie," she went on, impatiently. "You might have come to Mr. Biddow and me.
It isn't as though you were a young girl."

At that, Cindie fell into such a welter of confusion that
for reply she could not get beyond a stutter. They *knew*.
She had not been so clever, after all. But that aspect of things
was of little significance beside the bewildering metamorphosis of Blanche. Her—Cindie's—plan of campaign had
been superfluous! Her plan to force the issue by an eventual
accomplished fact, her own "interesting condition". At
length she got out, shakily: "How did you know?"

"My dear girl, the whole country-side knows." With contemptuous indulgence. Blanche could not resist a display
of superior acumen. "Well, what is it to be? Marriage? Or
do you leave Folkhaven?"

"Mrs. Biddow, Randy has never spoken of marriage to
me. I don't think it has ever entered his head."

"What?—well, I must say! . . . But it has entered your
head, hasn't it?"—acidly.

"N-o-o-o," Cindie lied. She was rapidly regaining contr~l~
of herself. She fought to crush back, with the weight of
shrewd stratagem, the immeasurable elation that now fired
her. Randy must not be pushed into anything! It must
not appear that she was over-willing! "No, it hasn't," she
continued, more confidently. "Randy and I are only
friends. I'm too old for Randy." She would not spare
herself.

"You certainly are." Blanche agreed emphatically. She
took on a warning tone. "Now don't start trying to trick
me, Cindie. I'm not a fool. You get married or you
go."

"Mrs. Biddow!" Cindie took the line of exasperation.
"Do you expect me to ask Randy to marry me?"

"Bosh! . . . Oh, there's Randolph and Randy, now. They
must have gone down the track."

Two figures came out of the moonlight and into the faint
glow diffused by the veranda lantern of the big house through
the drapery of climbers. Simultaneously Irene appeared on
the front steps.

"Where's everybody?" she called to the men, discontent-
edly. "Mother's disappeared. What's the matter with you
two? What's going on in this place?"

Blanche stepped over to the balcony rail. "Randolph,
I'm up here with Cindie. Come up here! Bring Randy."

Now Cindie panicked. "Mrs. Biddow, don't you dare!
Don't you dare propose anything to Randy! Leave this to
me, Mrs. Biddow! I won't have you interfering! You'll spoil
everything! That's what you'll do!"

"So you did have something up your sleeve," commented
Blanche, cynically. "But don't worry, Cindie. Mr. Biddow
has probably been talking to Randy."

The steps of the two men could be heard on the stairs.
Irene came running up the lawn. Biddow appeared first,
followed by the tall figure of his son. Irene burst into their
midst and stood, looking from one to the other.

Biddow's face was expressing frowning doubt of the purpose
of his wife's presence there. His eyes shuttled from one to
the other. Cindie's aspect of furious resentment brought him
to ask sharply: "What's been going on here?"

"Mr. Biddow!" Cindie cried it at him. "Take your wife away! Take her away before I get mad and say things I'll be sorry for."

"You are mad now," he said, as sharply. "What have you been doing, Blanche?"

"I've been trying to tell her that I want her for a daughter-in-law but she thinks"—Blanche spoke wilily—"she thinks Randy doesn't want to marry her."

"Oh!" Biddow's face broke into a smile of gratification. "Well, maybe Randy can fix that. Come, Blanche, Irene, we'll clear out."

The three went away, Irene's steps reluctant. She cast mazed and shocked glances behind her.

Cindie was left standing, aghast, feeling the whole world of her future dissolving into wretchedness around her.

For some moments Randy remained standing well back from her. She felt his eyes probing the shadows cast by the balcony roof. Her pride came to her rescue. "It's all right, Randy." With a miraculous effort she achieved a light tone. "It's all nonsense they've been talking. You don't have to worry."

He came forward then, slowly. "But, Cindie." He was puzzled, afraid. "Don't you want to marry me?"

"Randy, Randy, they shouldn't have interfered!" Cindie's hands went up to her face.

"Cindie!" The boy's voice was now anguished. "If you didn't want to marry me you shouldn't have carried on with me!"

Her hands went down like a shot. "You have never mentioned marriage to me, Randy."

"No—it never occurred to me. But now that Dad has mentioned it—it's just as well to get married, don't you think, Cindie, seeing that we are going to be together here all our lives?"

"Oh, Randy! But—but I'm old!" Rapturously, as she collapsed into a chair. With the native art with which she had cajoled the Aborigines by her dancing in the years agone, Cindie sought to prolong the exquisite delight of those moments.

"Old? What's old? By cripes, you might be old, Cindie,

but I reckon you'll do me!" He was reaching for her, now. "You've taught me a thing or two."

"Do you love me true, Randy?" Cindie whispered. "Do you love me like you loved Caroline?"

"Aw, her! She's rats! By gosh, Cindie, this makes up for the loss of the Kanakas." He slipped down upon the floor and thrust his head into her lap. "I'll be living here, Cindie, living here with you."

Her hands fluttered over his head, fell caressingly upon the heavy silken waves of his hair. She smoothed back from his brow the errant lock. . . .

Down at the big house the piano crashed into a boisterous tune. Irene, sitting on the front steps, marvelling, suddenly smacked her hands together and cried into the night: "So that's what she meant! That must be it! Whoever would have thought it of old Cindie!"

THE END

VIRAGO MODERN CLASSICS

The first Virago Modern Classic, *Frost in May* by Antonia White, was published in 1978. It launched a list dedicated to the celebration of women writers and to the rediscovery and reprinting of their works. Its aim was, and is, to demonstrate the existence of a female tradition in fiction which is both enriching and enjoyable. The Leavisite notion of the 'Great Tradition', and the narrow, academic definition of a 'classic', has meant the neglect of a large number of interesting secondary works of fiction. In calling the series 'Modern Classics' we do not necessarily mean 'great' — although this is often the case. Published with new critical and biographical introductions, books are chosen for many reasons: sometimes for their importance in literary history; sometimes because they illuminate particular aspects of womens' lives, both personal and public. They may be classics of comedy or storytelling; their interest can be historical, feminist, political or literary.

Initially the Virago Modern Classics concentrated on English novels and short stories published in the early decades of this century. As the series has grown it has broadened to include works of fiction from different centuries, different countries, cultures and literary traditions. In 1984 the Victorian Classics were launched; there are separate lists of Irish, Scottish, European, American, Australian and other English speaking countries; there are books written by Black women, by Catholic and Jewish women, and a few relevant novels by men. There is, too, a companion series of Non-Fiction Classics constituting biography, autobiography, travel, journalism, essays, poetry, letters and diaries.

By the end of 1986 over 250 titles will have been published in these two series, many of which have been suggested by our readers.

THE LITTLE COMPANY

By Eleanor Dark

New Introduction by Drusilla Modjeska

It is 1941 and the storm clouds of war gather over Australia. In the mountains outside Sydney the Massey family are reunited by their father's death. Gilbert is a successful novelist, struggling with a writer's block in middle age. A socialist and intellectual, he shares his political understanding – and fears – with his sister Marty and Marxist brother Nick. But he is locked in an unhappy marriage with a woman of little imagination and obsessive respectability, and their daughters, Prue and Virginia, are as incompatible as their parents. With the bombing of Pearl Harbour war becomes a reality. As Gilbert and his family are overtaken by the forces of history they must come to terms with their personal and public failures, and watch as the new generation inevitably mirrors the contradictions and turmoil of the old. This is the first British publication of a remarkable novel. Originally published in Australia in 1945, it combines a moving tale of family life with an acute analysis of politics and war in the 1940s.

PAINTED CLAY

Capel Boake

New Introduction by Christine Downer

"Other people might grow old and faded with a monotonous life but not she. In her heart she cherished a dream that the gods held something wonderful in store for her"

Helen Somerset feels stifled by her loveless home with a repressive father who fears that, like her absent mother, she may be only "painted clay". She wants to know life beyond the confines of Packington, a Melbourne suburb overlooking Port Phillip Bay. And when she is sixteen her father dies, releasing Helen to seek the affection and independence she has been denied. With a clerical job and a room in a lodging house Helen launches herself into the excitement of Bohemian life and free love – only to discover that this liberation has a double edge. First published in 1917, spendidly evoking the bustle of city life before the First World War, this is a moving tale of one woman striving to find herself in a restrictive society.

THE SALZBURG TALES

Christina Stead

New Introduction by Lorna Sage

"They insisted that if the Master of their tongues desired any tales in the afternoon, he should first tell one himself ... and when they were once more assembled, under the thick trees of the Mirabell-garten before the sparkling fountain, he began his tale ..."

The old princely city of Salzburg is the setting for the famous Festival where, one August in the 1930s, a group of visitors meet by chance. Amongst them are the Festival Director, small and stout; a Viennese conductor like a tasselled reed; a Scottish doctress, jolly and fresh-complexioned; an Archbishop grey as a gravestone; a Frenchwoman whose conversation dismayed the dull; and an English country gentleman who speaks of foxhounds in unconscious hexameters. These and others pass their free time in telling a rich and varied collection of idealistic and extravagant tales. In its scope, sheer fantasy and range of characters, *The Salzburg Tales*, first published in 1934, is comparable to *The Decameron* and *The Canterbury Tales*.

TOMORROW AND TOMORROW AND TOMORROW

By M. Barnard Eldershaw

New Introduction by Anne Chisholm

Set in Australia of the past and the future, this remarkable work is two novels in one.

It is the twenty-fourth century. Knarf, a writer, lives in a society of technocratic socialism that has abolished war and poverty through "scientific" laws. Knarf has written a novel which begins in November 1924 and tells the story of an Australian working man, Harry Munster, of his hopes, fears and loves, of his family, their friends and lovers. Through their eyes we experience the terrible years of the Depression: years of rising anger that culminate, at the end of the Second World War, in civil disturbance and the threat of a Third World War. When first published in 1947 these stirring passages were seriously cut by the Government censor: now for the first time the full uncensored text is printed as the authors wrote it. The result is both a warm and vivid portrait of one man and his times, and a prophetic vision of what was to follow – the nuclear shadow which is our common inheritance.

Australian Virago Modern Classics